# THE JUNGLE

# THE JUNGLE

By

UPTON SINCLAIR

ISBN: 978-93-5128-403-1(HB)

First Published in 1906
Indian Reprint in 2017

*Published by*

Kalpaz Publications
C-30, Satyawati Nagar,
Delhi – 110052
E-mail: kalpaz@hotmail.com
Website: kalpazpublications.com
Ph.: +91-9212142040

# CONTENTS

# Chapter 1

It was four o'clock when the ceremony was over and the carriages began to arrive. There had been a crowd following all the way, owing to the exuberance of Marija Berczynskas. The occasion rested heavily upon Marija's broad shoulders—it was her task to see that all things went in due form, and after the best home traditions; and, flying wildly hither and thither, bowling every one out of the way, and scolding and exhorting all day with her tremendous voice, Marija was too eager to see that others conformed to the proprieties to consider them herself. She had left the church last of all, and, desiring to arrive first at the hall, had issued orders to the coachman to drive faster. When that personage had developed a will of his own in the matter, Marija had flung up the window of the carriage, and, leaning out, proceeded to tell him her opinion of him, first in Lithuanian, which he did not understand, and then in Polish, which he did. Having the advantage of her in altitude, the driver had stood his ground and even ventured to attempt to speak; and the result had been a furious altercation, which, continuing all the way down Ashland Avenue, had added a new swarm of urchins to the cortege at each side street for half a mile.

This was unfortunate, for already there was a throng before the door. The music had started up, and half a block away you could hear the dull "broom, broom" of a cello, with the squeaking of two fiddles which vied with each other in intricate and altitudinous gymnastics. Seeing the throng, Marija abandoned precipitately the debate concerning the ancestors of her coachman, and, springing from the moving carriage, plunged in and proceeded to clear a way to the hall. Once within, she turned and began to push the other way, roaring, meantime, "Eik! Eik! Uzdaryk-duris!" in tones which made the orchestral uproar sound like fairy music.

"Z. Graiczunas, Pasilinksminimams darzas. Vynas. Sznapsas. Wines and Liquors. Union Headquarters"—that was the way the signs ran. The reader, who perhaps has never held much converse in the language of far-off Lithuania, will be glad of the explanation that the place was the rear room of a saloon in that part of Chicago known as "back of the yards." This information is definite and suited to the matter of fact; but how pitifully inadequate it would have seemed to one who understood that it was also the supreme hour of ecstasy in the life of one of God's gentlest creatures, the scene of the wedding feast and the joy-transfiguration of little Ona Lukoszaite!

She stood in the doorway, shepherded by Cousin Marija, breathless from pushing through the crowd, and in her happiness painful to look upon. There was a light of wonder in her eyes and her lids trembled, and her otherwise wan little face was flushed. She wore a muslin dress, conspicuously white, and a stiff little veil coming to her shoulders. There were five pink paper roses twisted in the veil, and eleven bright green rose leaves. There were new white cotton gloves upon her hands, and as she stood staring about her she twisted them together feverishly. It was almost too much for her—you could see the pain of too great emotion in her face, and all the tremor of her form. She was so young—not quite sixteen—and small for her age, a mere child; and she had just been married—and married to Jurgis,* (*Pronounced Yoorghis) of all men, to Jurgis Rudkus, he with the white flower in the buttonhole of his new black suit, he with the mighty shoulders and the giant hands.

Ona was blue-eyed and fair, while Jurgis had great black eyes with beetling brows, and thick black hair that curled in waves about his ears—in short, they were one of those incongruous and impossible married couples with which Mother Nature so often wills to confound all prophets, before and after. Jurgis could take up a two-hundred-and-fifty-pound quarter of beef and carry it into a car without a stagger, or even a thought; and now he stood in a far corner, frightened as a hunted animal, and obliged to moisten his lips with his tongue each time before he could answer the congratulations of his friends.

Gradually there was effected a separation between the spectators and the guests—a separation at least sufficiently complete for working purposes. There was no time during the festivities which ensued when there were not groups of onlookers in the doorways and the corners; and if any one of these onlookers came sufficiently close, or looked sufficiently hungry, a chair was offered him, and he was invited to the feast. It was one of the laws of the veselija that no one goes hungry; and, while a rule made in the forests of Lithuania is hard to apply in the stockyards district of Chicago, with its quarter of a million inhabitants, still they did their best, and the children who ran in from the street, and even the dogs, went out again happier. A charming informality was one of the characteristics of this celebration. The men wore their hats, or, if they wished, they took them off, and their coats with them; they ate when and where they pleased, and moved as often as they pleased. There were to be speeches and singing, but no one had to listen who did not care to; if he wished, meantime, to speak or sing himself, he was perfectly free. The resulting medley of sound distracted no one, save possibly alone the babies, of which there were present a number equal to the total possessed by all the guests invited. There was no other place for the babies to be, and so part of the preparations for the evening consisted of a collection of cribs and carriages in one corner. In these the babies slept, three or four together, or wakened together, as the case might be. Those who were still older, and could reach the tables, marched about munching contentedly at meat bones and bologna sausages.

The room is about thirty feet square, with whitewashed walls, bare save for a calendar, a picture of a race horse, and a family tree in a gilded frame. To the right there is a door from the saloon, with a few loafers in the doorway, and in the corner beyond it a bar, with a presiding genius clad in soiled white, with waxed black mustaches and a carefully oiled curl plastered against one side of his forehead. In the opposite corner are two tables, filling a third of the room and laden with dishes and cold viands, which a few of the hungrier guests are already munching. At the head, where sits the bride, is a snow-white cake, with an Eiffel tower of constructed decoration, with sugar roses and two angels upon it, and a generous sprinkling of pink and green and yellow candies. Beyond opens a door into the kitchen, where there is a glimpse to be had of a range with much steam ascending from it, and many women, old and young, rushing hither and thither. In the corner to the left are the three musicians, upon a little platform, toiling heroically to make some impression upon the hubbub; also the babies, similarly occupied, and an open window whence the populace imbibes the sights and sounds and odors.

Suddenly some of the steam begins to advance, and, peering through it, you discern Aunt Elizabeth, Ona's stepmother—Teta Elzbieta, as they call her—bearing aloft a great platter of stewed duck. Behind her is Kotrina, making her way cautiously, staggering beneath a similar burden; and half a minute later there appears old Grandmother Majauszkiene, with a big yellow bowl of smoking potatoes, nearly as big as herself. So, bit by bit, the feast takes form—there is a ham and a dish of sauerkraut, boiled rice, macaroni, bologna sausages, great piles of penny buns, bowls of milk, and foaming pitchers of beer. There is also, not six feet from your back, the bar, where you may order all you please and do not have to pay for it. "Eiksz! Graicziau!" screams Marija Berczynskas, and falls to work herself—for there is more upon the stove inside that will be spoiled if it be not eaten.

So, with laughter and shouts and endless badinage and merriment, the guests take their places. The young men, who for the most part have been huddled near the door, summon their resolution and advance; and the shrinking Jurgis is poked and scolded by the old folks until he consents to seat himself at the right hand of the bride. The two bridesmaids, whose insignia of office are paper wreaths, come next, and after them the rest of the guests, old and young, boys and girls. The spirit of the occasion takes hold of the stately bartender, who condescends to a plate of stewed duck; even the fat policeman—whose duty it will be, later in the evening, to break up the fights—draws up a chair to the foot of the table. And the children shout and the babies yell, and every one laughs and sings and chatters—while above all the deafening clamor Cousin Marija shouts orders to the musicians.

The musicians—how shall one begin to describe them? All this time they have been there, playing in a mad frenzy—all of this scene must be read, or said, or sung, to music. It is the music which makes it what it is; it is the music which changes the place from the rear room of a saloon in back of the yards to a fairy place, a wonderland, a little corner of the high mansions of the sky.

The little person who leads this trio is an inspired man. His fiddle is out of tune, and there is no rosin on his bow, but still he is an inspired man—the hands of the muses have been laid upon him. He plays like one possessed by a demon, by a whole horde of demons. You can feel them in the air round about him, capering frenetically; with their invisible feet they set the pace, and the hair of the leader of the orchestra rises on end, and his eyeballs start from their sockets, as he toils to keep up with them.

Tamoszius Kuszleika is his name, and he has taught himself to play the violin by practicing all night, after working all day on the "killing beds." He is in his shirt sleeves, with a vest figured with faded gold horseshoes, and a pink-striped shirt, suggestive of peppermint candy. A pair of military trousers, light blue with a yellow stripe, serve to give that suggestion of authority proper to the leader of a band. He is only about five feet high, but even so these trousers are about eight inches short of the ground. You wonder where he can have gotten them or rather you would wonder, if the excitement of being in his presence left you time to think of such things.

For he is an inspired man. Every inch of him is inspired—you might almost say inspired separately. He stamps with his feet, he tosses his head, he sways and swings to and fro; he has a wizened-up little face, irresistibly comical; and, when he executes a turn or a flourish, his brows knit and his lips work and his eyelids wink—the very ends of his necktie bristle out. And every now and then he turns upon his companions, nodding, signaling, beckoning frantically—with every inch of him appealing, imploring, in behalf of the muses and their call.

For they are hardly worthy of Tamoszius, the other two members of the orchestra. The second violin is a Slovak, a tall, gaunt man with black-rimmed spectacles and the mute and patient look of an overdriven mule; he responds to the whip but feebly, and then always falls back into his old rut. The third man is very fat, with a round, red, sentimental nose, and he plays with his eyes turned up to the sky and a look of infinite yearning. He is playing a bass part upon his cello, and so the excitement is nothing to him; no matter what happens in the treble, it is his task to saw out one long-drawn and lugubrious note after another, from four o'clock in the afternoon until nearly the same hour next morning, for his third of the total income of one dollar per hour.

Before the feast has been five minutes under way, Tamoszius Kuszleika has risen in his excitement; a minute or two more and you see that he is beginning to edge over toward the tables. His nostrils are dilated and his breath comes fast—his demons are driving him. He nods and shakes his head at his companions, jerking at them with his violin, until at last the long form of the second violinist also rises up. In the end all three of them begin advancing, step by step, upon the banqueters, Valentinavyczia, the cellist, bumping along with his instrument between notes. Finally all three are gathered at the foot of the tables, and there Tamoszius mounts upon a stool.

Now he is in his glory, dominating the scene. Some of the people are eating, some are laughing and talking—but you will make a great mistake if you think there is one of them who does not hear him. His notes are never true, and his fiddle buzzes on the low ones and squeaks and scratches on the high;

but these things they heed no more than they heed the dirt and noise and squalor about them—it is out of this material that they have to build their lives, with it that they have to utter their souls. And this is their utterance; merry and boisterous, or mournful and wailing, or passionate and rebellious, this music is their music, music of home. It stretches out its arms to them, they have only to give themselves up. Chicago and its saloons and its slums fade away—there are green meadows and sunlit rivers, mighty forests and snow-clad hills. They behold home landscapes and childhood scenes returning; old loves and friendships begin to waken, old joys and griefs to laugh and weep. Some fall back and close their eyes, some beat upon the table. Now and then one leaps up with a cry and calls for this song or that; and then the fire leaps brighter in Tamoszius' eyes, and he flings up his fiddle and shouts to his companions, and away they go in mad career. The company takes up the choruses, and men and women cry out like all possessed; some leap to their feet and stamp upon the floor, lifting their glasses and pledging each other. Before long it occurs to some one to demand an old wedding song, which celebrates the beauty of the bride and the joys of love. In the excitement of this masterpiece Tamoszius Kuszleika begins to edge in between the tables, making his way toward the head, where sits the bride. There is not a foot of space between the chairs of the guests, and Tamoszius is so short that he pokes them with his bow whenever he reaches over for the low notes; but still he presses in, and insists relentlessly that his companions must follow. During their progress, needless to say, the sounds of the cello are pretty well extinguished; but at last the three are at the head, and Tamoszius takes his station at the right hand of the bride and begins to pour out his soul in melting strains.

Little Ona is too excited to eat. Once in a while she tastes a little something, when Cousin Marija pinches her elbow and reminds her; but, for the most part, she sits gazing with the same fearful eyes of wonder. Teta Elzbieta is all in a flutter, like a hummingbird; her sisters, too, keep running up behind her, whispering, breathless. But Ona seems scarcely to hear them—the music keeps calling, and the far-off look comes back, and she sits with her hands pressed together over her heart. Then the tears begin to come into her eyes; and as she is ashamed to wipe them away, and ashamed to let them run down her cheeks, she turns and shakes her head a little, and then flushes red when she sees that Jurgis is watching her. When in the end Tamoszius Kuszleika has reached her side, and is waving his magic wand above her, Ona's cheeks are scarlet, and she looks as if she would have to get up and run away.

In this crisis, however, she is saved by Marija Berczynskas, whom the muses suddenly visit. Marija is fond of a song, a song of lovers' parting; she wishes to hear it, and, as the musicians do not know it, she has risen, and is proceeding to teach them. Marija is short, but powerful in build. She works in a canning factory, and all day long she handles cans of beef that weigh fourteen pounds. She has a broad Slavic face, with prominent red cheeks. When she opens her mouth, it is tragical, but you cannot help thinking of a horse. She wears a blue flannel shirt-waist, which is now rolled up at the sleeves, disclosing her brawny arms; she has a carving fork in her hand, with which she pounds on the table to mark the time. As she roars her song, in a voice of which it is enough to say that it leaves no portion of the room vacant, the three musicians follow her, laboriously and note by note, but averaging one note behind; thus they toil through stanza after stanza of a lovesick swain's lamentation:—

"Sudiev' kvietkeli, tu brangiausis;
Sudiev' ir laime, man biednam,
Matau—paskyre teip Aukszcziausis,
Jog vargt ant svieto reik vienam!"

When the song is over, it is time for the speech, and old Dede Antanas rises to his feet. Grandfather Anthony, Jurgis' father, is not more than sixty years of age, but you would think that he was eighty. He has been only six months in America, and the change has not done him good. In his manhood he worked in a cotton mill, but then a coughing fell upon him, and he had to leave; out in the country the trouble disappeared, but he has been working in the pickle rooms at Durham's, and the breathing of the cold, damp air all day has brought it back. Now as he rises he is seized with a coughing fit, and holds himself by his chair and turns away his wan and battered face until it passes.

Generally it is the custom for the speech at a veselija to be taken out of one of the books and learned by heart; but in his youthful days Dede Antanas used to be a scholar, and really make up all the love letters of his friends. Now it is understood that he has composed an original speech of congratulation and benediction, and this is one of the events of the day. Even the boys, who are romping about the room, draw near and listen, and some of the women sob and wipe their aprons in their eyes. It is very solemn, for Antanas Rudkus has become possessed of the idea that he has not much longer to stay with his children. His speech leaves them all so tearful that one of the guests, Jokubas Szedvilas, who keeps a delicatessen store on Halsted Street, and is fat and hearty, is moved to rise and say that things may not be as bad as that, and then to go on and make a little speech of his own, in which he showers congratulations and prophecies of happiness upon the bride and groom, proceeding to particulars which greatly delight the young men, but which cause Ona to blush more furiously than ever. Jokubas possesses what his wife complacently describes as "poetiszka vaidintuve"—a poetical imagination.

Now a good many of the guests have finished, and, since there is no pretense of ceremony, the banquet begins to break up. Some of the men gather about the bar; some wander about, laughing and singing; here and there will be a little group, chanting merrily, and in sublime indifference to the others and to the orchestra as well. Everybody is more or less restless—one would guess that something is on their minds. And so it proves. The last tardy diners are scarcely given time to finish, before the tables and the debris are shoved into the corner, and the chairs and the babies piled out of the way, and the real celebration of the evening begins. Then Tamoszius Kuszleika, after replenishing himself with a pot of beer, returns to his platform, and, standing up, reviews the scene; he taps authoritatively upon the side of his violin, then tucks it carefully under his chin, then waves his bow in an elaborate flourish, and finally smites the sounding strings and closes his eyes, and floats away in spirit upon the wings of a dreamy waltz. His companion follows, but with his eyes open, watching where he treads, so to speak; and finally Valentinavyczia, after waiting for a little and beating with his foot to get the time, casts up his eyes to the ceiling and begins to saw—"Broom! broom! broom!"

The company pairs off quickly, and the whole room is soon in motion. Apparently nobody knows how to waltz, but that is nothing of any consequence—there is music, and they dance, each as he pleases, just as before they sang. Most of them prefer the "two-step," especially the young, with whom it is the fashion. The older people have dances from home, strange and complicated steps which they execute with grave solemnity. Some do not dance anything at all, but simply hold each other's hands and allow the undisciplined joy of motion to express itself with their feet. Among these are Jokubas Szedvilas and his wife, Lucija, who together keep the delicatessen store, and consume nearly as much as they sell; they are too fat to dance, but they stand in the middle of the floor, holding each other fast in their arms, rocking slowly from side to side and grinning seraphically, a picture of toothless and perspiring ecstasy.

Of these older people many wear clothing reminiscent in some detail of home—an embroidered waistcoat or stomacher, or a gaily colored handkerchief, or a coat with large cuffs and fancy buttons. All these things are carefully avoided by the young, most of whom have learned to speak English and to affect the latest style of clothing. The girls wear ready-made dresses or shirt waists, and some of them look quite pretty. Some of the young men you would take to be Americans, of the type of clerks, but for the fact that they wear their hats in the room. Each of these younger couples affects a style of its own in dancing. Some hold each other tightly, some at a cautious distance. Some hold their hands out stiffly, some drop them loosely at their sides. Some dance springily, some glide softly, some move with grave dignity. There are boisterous couples, who tear wildly about the room, knocking every one out of their way. There are nervous couples, whom these frighten, and who cry, "Nusfok! Kas yra?" at them as they pass. Each couple is paired for the evening—you will never see them change about. There is Alena Jasaityte, for instance, who has danced unending hours with Juozas Raczius, to whom she is engaged. Alena is the beauty of the evening, and she would be really beautiful if she were not so proud. She wears a white shirtwaist, which represents, perhaps, half a week's labor painting cans. She holds her skirt with her hand as she dances, with stately precision, after the manner of the grandes dames. Juozas is driving one of Durham's wagons, and is making big wages. He affects a "tough" aspect, wearing his hat on one side and keeping a cigarette in his mouth all the evening. Then there is Jadvyga Marcinkus, who is also beautiful, but humble. Jadvyga likewise paints cans, but then she has an invalid mother and three little sisters to support by it, and so she does not spend her wages for shirtwaists. Jadvyga is small and delicate, with jet-black eyes and hair, the latter twisted into a little knot and tied on the top of her head. She wears an old white dress which she has made herself and worn to parties for the past five years; it is high-waisted—almost under her arms, and not very becoming,—but that does not trouble Jadvyga, who is dancing with her Mikolas. She is small, while he is big and powerful; she nestles in his arms as if she would hide herself from view, and leans her head upon his shoulder. He in turn has clasped his arms tightly around her, as if he would carry her away; and so she dances, and will dance the entire evening, and would dance forever, in ecstasy of bliss. You would smile, perhaps, to see them—but you would not smile if you knew all the story. This is the fifth year, now, that Jadvyga has been engaged to Mikolas, and her heart is sick. They would have been married in the beginning, only Mikolas has a father who is drunk all day, and he is the only other man in a large family. Even so they might have managed it (for Mikolas is a skilled man) but for cruel accidents which have almost taken the heart out of them. He is a beef-boner, and that is a dangerous trade, especially when you are on piecework and trying to earn a bride. Your hands are slippery, and your knife is slippery, and you are toiling like mad, when somebody happens to speak to you, or you strike a bone. Then your hand slips up on the blade, and there is a fearful gash. And that would not be so bad, only for the deadly contagion. The cut may heal, but you never can tell. Twice now; within the last three years, Mikolas has been lying at home with blood poisoning—once for three months and once for nearly seven. The last time, too, he lost his job, and that meant six weeks more of standing at the doors of the packing houses, at six o'clock on bitter winter mornings, with a foot of snow on the ground and more in the air. There are learned people who can tell you out of the statistics that beef-boners make forty cents an hour, but, perhaps, these people have never looked into a beef-boner's hands.

When Tamoszius and his companions stop for a rest, as perforce they must, now and then, the dancers halt where they are and wait patiently. They never seem to tire; and there is no place for them to sit down if they did. It is only for a minute, anyway, for the leader starts up again, in spite of all the protests of the other two. This time it is another sort of a dance, a Lithuanian dance. Those who prefer to, go on with the two-step, but the majority go through an intricate series of motions, resembling more fancy skating than a dance. The climax of it is a furious prestissimo, at which the couples seize hands and begin a mad whirling. This is quite irresistible, and every one in the room joins in, until the place becomes a maze of flying skirts and bodies quite dazzling to look upon. But the sight of sights at this moment is Tamoszius Kuszleika. The old fiddle squeaks and shrieks in protest, but Tamoszius has no mercy. The sweat starts out on his forehead, and he bends over like a cyclist on the last lap of a race. His body shakes and throbs like a runaway steam engine, and the ear cannot follow the flying showers of notes—there is a pale blue mist where you look to see his bowing arm. With a most wonderful rush he comes to the end of the tune, and flings up his hands and staggers back exhausted; and with a final shout of delight the dancers fly apart, reeling here and there, bringing up against the walls of the room.

After this there is beer for every one, the musicians included, and the revelers take a long breath and prepare for the great event of the evening, which is the acziavimas. The acziavimas is a ceremony which, once begun, will continue for three or four hours, and it involves one uninterrupted dance. The guests form a great ring, locking hands, and, when the music starts up, begin to move around in a circle. In the center stands the bride, and, one by one, the men step into the enclosure and dance with her. Each dances for several minutes—as long as he pleases; it is a very merry proceeding, with laughter and singing, and when the guest has finished, he finds himself face to face with Teta Elzbieta, who holds the hat. Into it he drops a sum of money—a dollar, or perhaps five dollars, according to his power, and his estimate of the value of the privilege. The guests are expected to pay for this entertainment; if they be proper guests, they will see that there is a neat sum left over for the bride and bridegroom to start life upon.

Most fearful they are to contemplate, the expenses of this entertainment. They will certainly be over two hundred dollars and maybe three hundred; and three hundred dollars is more than the year's income of many a person in this room. There are able-bodied men here who work from early morning until late at night, in ice-cold cellars with a quarter of an inch of water on the floor—men who for six or seven months in the year never see the sunlight from Sunday afternoon till the next Sunday morning—and who cannot earn three hundred dollars in a year. There are little children here, scarce in their teens, who can hardly see the top of the work benches—whose parents have lied to get them their places—and who do not make the half of three hundred dollars a year, and perhaps not even the third of it. And then to spend such a sum, all in a single day of your life, at a wedding feast! (For obviously it is the same thing, whether you spend it at once for your own wedding, or in a long time, at the weddings of all your friends.)

It is very imprudent, it is tragic—but, ah, it is so beautiful! Bit by bit these poor people have given up everything else; but to this they cling with all the power of their souls—they cannot give up the veselija! To do that would mean, not merely to be defeated, but to acknowledge defeat—and the difference between these two things is what keeps the world going. The veselija has come down to them from a far-off time; and the meaning of it was that one might dwell within the cave and gaze upon shadows, provided only that once in his lifetime he could break his chains, and feel his wings, and behold the sun; provided that once in his lifetime he might testify to the fact that life, with all its cares and its terrors, is no such great thing after all, but merely a bubble upon the surface of a river, a thing that one may toss about and play with as a juggler tosses his golden balls, a thing that one may quaff, like a goblet of rare red wine. Thus having known himself for the master of things, a man could go back to his toil and live upon the memory all his days.

Endlessly the dancers swung round and round—when they were dizzy they swung the other way. Hour after hour this had continued—the darkness had fallen and the room was dim from the light of two smoky oil lamps. The musicians had spent all their fine frenzy by now, and played only one tune, wearily, ploddingly. There were twenty bars or so of it, and when they came to the end they began again. Once every ten minutes or so they would fail to begin again, but instead would sink back exhausted; a circumstance which invariably brought on a painful and terrifying scene, that made the fat policeman stir uneasily in his sleeping place behind the door.

It was all Marija Berczynskas. Marija was one of those hungry souls who cling with desperation to the skirts of the retreating muse. All day long she had been in a state of wonderful exaltation; and now it was leaving—and she would not let it go. Her soul cried out in the words of Faust, "Stay, thou art fair!" Whether it was by beer, or by shouting, or by music, or by motion, she meant that it should not go. And she would go back to the chase of it—and no sooner be fairly started than her chariot would be thrown off the track, so to speak, by the stupidity of those thrice accursed musicians. Each time, Marija would emit a howl and fly at them, shaking her fists in their faces, stamping upon the floor, purple and incoherent with rage. In vain the frightened Tamoszius would attempt to speak, to plead the limitations of the flesh; in vain would the puffing and breathless ponas Jokubas insist, in vain would Teta Elzbieta implore. "Szalin!" Marija would scream. "Palauk! isz kelio! What are you paid for, children of hell?" And so, in sheer terror, the orchestra would strike up again, and Marija would return to her place and take up her task.

She bore all the burden of the festivities now. Ona was kept up by her excitement, but all of the women and most of the men were tired—the soul of Marija was alone unconquered. She drove on the dancers—what had once been the ring had now the shape of a pear, with Marija at the stem, pulling one way and pushing the other, shouting, stamping, singing, a very volcano of energy. Now and then some one coming in or out would leave the door open, and the night air was chill; Marija as she passed would stretch out her foot and kick the doorknob, and slam would go the door! Once this procedure was the cause of a calamity of which Sebastijonas Szedvilas was the hapless victim. Little Sebastijonas, aged three, had been wandering about oblivious to all things, holding turned up over his mouth a bottle of liquid known as "pop," pink-colored, ice-cold, and delicious. Passing through the doorway the door smote him full, and the shriek which followed brought the dancing to a halt. Marija, who threatened horrid murder a hundred times a day, and would weep over the injury of a fly, seized little Sebastijonas in her arms and bid fair to smother him with kisses. There was a long rest for the orchestra, and plenty of refreshments, while Marija was making her peace with her victim, seating him upon the bar, and standing beside him and holding to his lips a foaming schooner of beer.

In the meantime there was going on in another corner of the room an anxious conference between Teta Elzbieta and Dede Antanas, and a few of the more intimate friends of the family. A trouble was come upon them. The veselija is a compact, a compact not expressed, but therefore only the more binding upon all. Every one's share was different—and yet every one knew perfectly well what his share was, and strove to give a little more. Now, however, since they had come to the new country, all this was changing; it seemed as if there must be some subtle poison in the air that one breathed here—it was affecting all the young men at once. They would come in crowds and fill themselves with a fine dinner, and then sneak off. One would throw another's hat out of the window, and both would go out to get it, and neither could be seen again. Or now and then half a dozen of them would get together and march out openly, staring at you, and making fun of you to your face. Still others, worse yet, would crowd about the bar, and at the expense of the host drink themselves sodden, paying not the least attention to any one, and leaving it to be thought that either they had danced with the bride already, or meant to later on.

All these things were going on now, and the family was helpless with dismay. So long they had toiled, and such an outlay they had made! Ona stood by, her eyes wide with terror. Those frightful bills—how they had haunted her, each item gnawing at her soul all day and spoiling her rest at night. How often she had named them over one by one and figured on them as she went to work—fifteen dollars for the hall, twenty-two dollars and a quarter for the ducks, twelve dollars for the musicians, five dollars at the church, and a blessing of the Virgin besides—and so on without an end! Worst of all was the frightful bill that was still to come from Graiczunas for the beer and liquor that might be consumed. One could never get in advance more than a guess as to this from a saloon-keeper—and then, when the time came he always came to you scratching his head and saying that he had guessed too low, but that he had done his best—your guests had gotten so very drunk. By him you were sure to be cheated unmercifully, and that even though you thought yourself the dearest of the hundreds of friends he had. He would begin to serve your guests out of a keg that was half full, and finish with one that was half empty, and then you would be charged for two kegs of beer. He would agree to serve a certain quality at a certain price, and when the time came you and your friends would be drinking some horrible poison that could not be described. You might complain, but you would get nothing for your pains but a ruined evening; while, as for going to law about it, you might as well go to heaven at once. The saloon-keeper stood in with all the big politics men in the district; and when you had once found out what it meant to get into trouble with such people, you would know enough to pay what you were told to pay and shut up.

What made all this the more painful was that it was so hard on the few that had really done their best. There was poor old ponas Jokubas, for instance—he had already given five dollars, and did not every one know that Jokubas Szedvilas had just mortgaged his delicatessen store for two hundred dollars to meet several months' overdue rent? And then there was withered old poni Aniele—who was a widow, and had three children, and the rheumatism besides, and did washing for the tradespeople on Halsted Street at prices it would break your heart to hear named. Aniele had given the entire profit of her chickens for several months. Eight of them she owned, and she kept them in a little place fenced around on her backstairs. All day long the children of Aniele were raking in the dump for food for these chickens; and sometimes, when the competition there was too fierce, you might see them on Halsted Street walking close to the gutters, and with their mother following to see that no one robbed them of their finds. Money could not tell the value of these chickens to old Mrs. Jukniene—she valued them differently, for she had a feeling that she was getting something for nothing by means of them—that with them she was getting the better of a world that was getting the better of her in so many other ways. So she watched them every hour of the day, and had learned to see like an owl at night to watch them then. One of them had been stolen long ago, and not a month passed that some one did not try to steal another. As the frustrating of this one attempt involved a score of false alarms, it will be understood what a tribute old Mrs. Jukniene brought, just because Teta Elzbieta had once loaned her some money for a few days and saved her from being turned out of her house.

More and more friends gathered round while the lamentation about these things was going on. Some drew nearer, hoping to overhear the conversation, who were themselves among the guilty—and surely that was a thing to try the patience of a saint. Finally there came Jurgis, urged by some one, and the story was retold to him. Jurgis listened in silence, with his great black eyebrows knitted. Now and then there would come a gleam underneath them and he would glance about the room. Perhaps he would have liked to go at some of those fellows with his big clenched fists; but then, doubtless, he realized how little good it would do him. No bill would be any less for turning out any one at this time; and then there would be the scandal—and Jurgis wanted nothing except to get away with Ona and to let the world go its own way. So his hands relaxed and he merely said quietly: "It is done, and there is no use in weeping, Teta Elzbieta." Then his look turned toward Ona, who stood close to his side, and he saw the wide look of terror in her eyes. "Little one," he said, in a low voice, "do not worry—it will not matter to us. We will pay them all somehow. I will work harder." That was always what Jurgis said. Ona had grown used to it as the solution of all difficulties—"I will work harder!" He had said that in Lithuania when one official had taken his passport from him, and another had arrested him for being without it, and the two had divided a third of his belongings. He had said it again in New York, when the smooth-spoken agent had taken them in hand and made them pay such high prices, and almost prevented their leaving his place, in spite of their paying. Now he said it a third time, and Ona drew a deep breath; it was so wonderful to have a husband, just like a grown woman—and a husband who could solve all problems, and who was so big and strong!

The last sob of little Sebastijonas has been stifled, and the orchestra has once more been reminded of its duty. The ceremony begins again—but there are few now left to dance with, and so very soon the collection is over and promiscuous dances once more begin. It is now after midnight, however, and things are not as they were before. The dancers are dull and heavy—most of them have been drinking hard, and have long ago passed the stage of exhilaration. They dance in monotonous measure, round after round, hour after hour, with eyes fixed upon vacancy, as if they were only half conscious, in a constantly growing stupor. The men grasp the women very tightly, but there will be half an hour together when neither will see the other's face. Some couples do not care to dance, and have retired to the corners, where they sit with their arms enlaced. Others, who have been drinking still more, wander about the room, bumping into everything; some are in groups of two or three, singing, each group its own song. As time goes on there is a variety of drunkenness, among the younger men especially. Some stagger about in each other's arms, whispering maudlin words—others start quarrels upon the slightest pretext, and come to blows and have to be pulled apart. Now the fat policeman wakens definitely, and feels of his club to see that it is ready for business. He has to be prompt—for these two-o'clock-in-the-morning fights, if they once get out of hand, are like a forest fire, and may mean the whole reserves at the station. The thing to do is to crack every fighting head that you see, before there are so many fighting heads that you cannot crack any of them. There is but scant account kept of cracked heads in back of the yards, for men who have to crack the heads of animals all day seem to get into the habit, and to practice on their friends, and even on their families, between times. This makes it a cause for congratulation that by modern methods a very few men can do the painfully necessary work of head-cracking for the whole of the cultured world.

There is no fight that night—perhaps because Jurgis, too, is watchful—even more so than the policeman. Jurgis has drunk a great deal, as any one naturally would on an occasion when it all has to be paid for, whether it is drunk or not; but he is a very steady man, and does not easily lose his temper. Only once there is a tight shave—and that is the fault of Marija Berczynskas. Marija has apparently concluded about two hours ago that if the altar in the corner, with the deity in soiled white, be not the true home of the muses, it is, at any rate, the nearest substitute on earth attainable. And Marija is just fighting drunk when there come to her ears the facts about the villains who have not paid that night. Marija goes on the warpath straight off, without even the preliminary of a good cursing, and when she is pulled off it is with the coat collars of two villains in her hands. Fortunately, the policeman is disposed to be reasonable, and so it is not Marija who is flung out of the place.

All this interrupts the music for not more than a minute or two. Then again the merciless tune begins—the tune that has been played for the last half-hour without one single change. It is an American tune this time, one which they have picked up on the streets; all seem to know the words of it—or, at any rate, the first line of it, which they hum to themselves, over and over again without rest: "In the good old summertime—in the good old summertime! In the good old summertime—in the good old summertime!" There seems to be something hypnotic about this, with its endlessly recurring dominant. It has put a stupor upon every one who hears it, as well as upon the men who are playing it. No one can get away from it, or even think of getting away from it; it is three o'clock in the morning, and they have danced out all their joy, and danced out all their strength, and all the strength that unlimited drink can lend them—and still there is no one among them who has the power to think of stopping. Promptly at seven o'clock this same Monday morning they will every one of them have to be in their places at Durham's or Brown's or Jones's, each in his working clothes. If one of them be a minute late, he will be docked an hour's pay, and if he be many minutes late, he will be apt to find his brass check turned to the wall, which will send him out to join the hungry mob that waits every morning at the gates of the packing houses, from six o'clock until nearly half-past eight. There is no exception to this rule, not even little Ona—who has asked for a holiday the day after her wedding day, a holiday without pay, and been refused. While there are so many who are anxious to work as you wish, there is no occasion for incommoding yourself with those who must work otherwise.

Little Ona is nearly ready to faint—and half in a stupor herself, because of the heavy scent in the room. She has not taken a drop, but every one else there is literally burning alcohol, as the lamps are burning oil; some of the men who are sound asleep in their chairs or on the floor are reeking of it so that you cannot go near them. Now and then Jurgis gazes at her hungrily—he has long since forgotten his shyness; but then the crowd is there, and he still waits and watches the door, where a carriage is supposed to come. It does not, and finally he will wait no longer, but comes up to Ona, who turns white and trembles. He puts her shawl about her and then his own coat. They live only two blocks away, and Jurgis does not care about the carriage.

There is almost no farewell—the dancers do not notice them, and all of the children and many of the old folks have fallen asleep of sheer exhaustion. Dede Antanas is asleep, and so are the Szedvilases, husband and wife, the former snoring in octaves. There is Teta Elzbieta, and Marija, sobbing loudly; and then there is only the silent night, with the stars beginning to pale a little in the east. Jurgis, without a word, lifts Ona in his arms, and strides out with her, and she sinks her head upon his shoulder with a moan. When he reaches home he is not sure whether she has fainted or is asleep, but when he has to hold her with one hand while he unlocks the door, he sees that she has opened her eyes.

"You shall not go to Brown's today, little one," he whispers, as he climbs the stairs; and she catches his arm in terror, gasping: "No! No! I dare not! It will ruin us!"

But he answers her again: "Leave it to me; leave it to me. I will earn more money—I will work harder."

# Chapter 2

Jurgis talked lightly about work, because he was young. They told him stories about the breaking down of men, there in the stockyards of Chicago, and of what had happened to them afterward—stories to make your flesh creep, but Jurgis would only laugh. He had only been there four months, and he was young, and a giant besides. There was too much health in him. He could not even imagine how it would feel to be beaten. "That is well enough for men like you," he would say, "silpnas, puny fellows—but my back is broad."

Jurgis was like a boy, a boy from the country. He was the sort of man the bosses like to get hold of, the sort they make it a grievance they cannot get hold of. When he was told to go to a certain place, he would go there on the run. When he had nothing to do for the moment, he would stand round fidgeting, dancing, with the overflow of energy that was in him. If he were working in a line of men, the line always moved too slowly for him, and you could pick him out by his impatience and restlessness. That was why he had been picked out on one important occasion; for Jurgis had stood outside of Brown and Company's "Central Time Station" not more than half an hour, the second day of his arrival in Chicago, before he had been beckoned by one of the bosses. Of this he was very proud, and it made him more disposed than ever to laugh at the pessimists. In vain would they all tell him that there were men in that crowd from which he had been chosen who had stood there a month—yes, many months—and not been chosen yet. "Yes," he would say, "but what sort of men? Broken-down tramps and good-for-nothings, fellows who have spent all their money drinking, and want to get more for it. Do you want me to believe that with these arms"—and he would clench his fists and hold them up in the air, so that you might see the rolling muscles—"that with these arms people will ever let me starve?"

"It is plain," they would answer to this, "that you have come from the country, and from very far in the country." And this was the fact, for Jurgis had never seen a city, and scarcely even a fair-sized town, until he had set out to make his fortune in the world and earn his right to Ona. His father, and his father's father before him, and as many ancestors back as legend could go, had lived in that part of Lithuania known as Brelovicz, the Imperial Forest. This is a great tract of a hundred thousand acres, which from time immemorial has been a hunting preserve of the nobility. There are a very few peasants settled in it, holding title from ancient times; and one of these was Antanas Rudkus, who had been reared himself, and had reared his children in turn, upon half a dozen acres of cleared land in the midst of a wilderness. There had been one son besides Jurgis, and one sister. The former had been drafted into the army; that had been over ten years ago, but since that day nothing had ever been heard of him. The sister was married, and her husband had bought the place when old Antanas had decided to go with his son.

It was nearly a year and a half ago that Jurgis had met Ona, at a horse fair a hundred miles from home. Jurgis had never expected to get married—he had laughed at it as a foolish trap for a man to walk into; but here, without ever having spoken a word to her, with no more than the exchange of half a dozen smiles, he found himself, purple in the face with embarrassment and terror, asking her parents to sell her to him for his wife—and offering his father's two horses he had been sent to the fair to sell. But Ona's father proved as a rock—the girl was yet a child, and he was a rich man, and his daughter was not to be had in that way. So Jurgis went home with a heavy heart, and that spring and summer toiled and tried hard to forget. In the fall, after the harvest was over, he saw that it would not do, and tramped the full fortnight's journey that lay between him and Ona.

He found an unexpected state of affairs—for the girl's father had died, and his estate was tied up with creditors; Jurgis' heart leaped as he realized that now the prize was within his reach. There was Elzbieta Lukoszaite, Teta, or Aunt, as they called her, Ona's stepmother, and there were her six children, of all ages. There was also her brother Jonas, a dried-up little man who had worked upon the farm. They were people of great consequence, as it seemed to Jurgis, fresh out of the woods; Ona knew how to read, and knew many other things that he did not know, and now the farm had been sold, and the whole family was adrift—all they owned in the world being about seven hundred rubles which is half as many dollars. They would have had three times that, but it had gone to court, and the judge had decided against them, and it had cost the balance to get him to change his decision.

Ona might have married and left them, but she would not, for she loved Teta Elzbieta. It was Jonas who suggested that they all go to America, where a friend of his had gotten rich. He would work, for his part, and the women would work, and some of the children, doubtless—they would live somehow. Jurgis, too, had heard of America. That was a country where, they said, a man might earn three rubles a day; and Jurgis figured what three rubles a day would mean, with prices as they were where he lived, and decided forthwith that he would go to America and marry, and be a rich man in the bargain. In that country, rich or poor, a man was free, it was said; he did not have to go into the army, he did not have to pay out his money to rascally officials—he might do as he pleased, and count himself as good as any other man. So America was a place of which lovers and young people dreamed. If one could only manage to get the price of a passage, he could count his troubles at an end.

It was arranged that they should leave the following spring, and meantime Jurgis sold himself to a contractor for a certain time, and tramped nearly four hundred miles from home with a gang of men to work upon a railroad in

Smolensk. This was a fearful experience, with filth and bad food and cruelty and overwork; but Jurgis stood it and came out in fine trim, and with eighty rubles sewed up in his coat. He did not drink or fight, because he was thinking all the time of Ona; and for the rest, he was a quiet, steady man, who did what he was told to, did not lose his temper often, and when he did lose it made the offender anxious that he should not lose it again. When they paid him off he dodged the company gamblers and dramshops, and so they tried to kill him; but he escaped, and tramped it home, working at odd jobs, and sleeping always with one eye open.

So in the summer time they had all set out for America. At the last moment there joined them Marija Berczynskas, who was a cousin of Ona's. Marija was an orphan, and had worked since childhood for a rich farmer of Vilna, who beat her regularly. It was only at the age of twenty that it had occurred to Marija to try her strength, when she had risen up and nearly murdered the man, and then come away.

There were twelve in all in the party, five adults and six children—and Ona, who was a little of both. They had a hard time on the passage; there was an agent who helped them, but he proved a scoundrel, and got them into a trap with some officials, and cost them a good deal of their precious money, which they clung to with such horrible fear. This happened to them again in New York—for, of course, they knew nothing about the country, and had no one to tell them, and it was easy for a man in a blue uniform to lead them away, and to take them to a hotel and keep them there, and make them pay enormous charges to get away. The law says that the rate card shall be on the door of a hotel, but it does not say that it shall be in Lithuanian.

It was in the stockyards that Jonas' friend had gotten rich, and so to Chicago the party was bound. They knew that one word, Chicago and that was all they needed to know, at least, until they reached the city. Then, tumbled out of the cars without ceremony, they were no better off than before; they stood staring down the vista of Dearborn Street, with its big black buildings towering in the distance, unable to realize that they had arrived, and why, when they said "Chicago," people no longer pointed in some direction, but instead looked perplexed, or laughed, or went on without paying any attention. They were pitiable in their helplessness; above all things they stood in deadly terror of any sort of person in official uniform, and so whenever they saw a policeman they would cross the street and hurry by. For the whole of the first day they wandered about in the midst of deafening confusion, utterly lost; and it was only at night that, cowering in the doorway of a house, they were finally discovered and taken by a policeman to the station. In the morning an interpreter was found, and they were taken and put upon a car, and taught a new word— "stockyards." Their delight at discovering that they were to get out of this adventure without losing another share of their possessions it would not be possible to describe.

They sat and stared out of the window. They were on a street which seemed to run on forever, mile after mile—thirty-four of them, if they had known it—and each side of it one uninterrupted row of wretched little two-story frame buildings. Down every side street they could see, it was the same—never a hill and never a hollow, but always the same endless vista of ugly and dirty little wooden buildings. Here and there would be a bridge crossing a filthy creek, with hard-baked mud shores and dingy sheds and docks along it; here and there would be a railroad crossing, with a tangle of switches, and locomotives puffing, and rattling freight cars filing by; here and there would be a great factory, a dingy building with innumerable windows in it, and immense volumes of smoke pouring from the chimneys, darkening the air above and making filthy the earth beneath. But after each of these interruptions, the desolate procession would begin again—the procession of dreary little buildings.

A full hour before the party reached the city they had begun to note the perplexing changes in the atmosphere. It grew darker all the time, and upon the earth the grass seemed to grow less green. Every minute, as the train sped on, the colors of things became dingier; the fields were grown parched and yellow, the landscape hideous and bare. And along with the thickening smoke they began to notice another circumstance, a strange, pungent odor. They were not sure that it was unpleasant, this odor; some might have called it sickening, but their taste in odors was not developed, and they were only sure that it was curious. Now, sitting in the trolley car, they realized that they were on their way to the home of it—that they had traveled all the way from Lithuania to it. It was now no longer something far off and faint, that you caught in whiffs; you could literally taste it, as well as smell it—you could take hold of it, almost, and examine it at your leisure. They were divided in their opinions about it. It was an elemental odor, raw and crude; it was rich, almost rancid, sensual, and strong. There were some who drank it in as if it were an intoxicant; there were others who put their handkerchiefs to their faces. The new emigrants were still tasting it, lost in wonder, when suddenly the car came to a halt, and the door was flung open, and a voice shouted—"Stockyards!"

They were left standing upon the corner, staring; down a side street there were two rows of brick houses, and between them a vista: half a dozen chimneys, tall as the tallest of buildings, touching the very sky—and leaping from them half a dozen columns of smoke, thick, oily, and black as night. It might have come from the center of the world, this smoke, where the fires of the ages still smolder. It came as if self-impelled, driving all before it, a perpetual explosion. It was inexhaustible; one stared, waiting to see it stop, but still the great streams rolled out. They spread in vast clouds overhead, writhing, curling; then, uniting in one giant river, they streamed away down the sky, stretching a black pall as far as the eye could reach.

Then the party became aware of another strange thing. This, too, like the color, was a thing elemental; it was a sound, a sound made up of ten thousand little sounds. You scarcely noticed it at first—it sunk into your consciousness, a vague disturbance, a trouble. It was like the murmuring of the bees in the spring, the whisperings of the forest; it suggested endless activity, the rumblings of a world in motion. It was only by an effort that one could realize that it was made by animals, that it was the distant lowing of ten thousand cattle, the distant grunting of ten thousand swine.

They would have liked to follow it up, but, alas, they had no time for adventures just then. The policeman on the corner was beginning to watch them; and so, as usual, they started up the street. Scarcely had they gone a block, however, before Jonas was heard to give a cry, and began pointing excitedly across the street. Before they could gather the meaning of his breathless ejaculations he had bounded away, and they saw him enter a shop, over which was a sign: "J. Szedvilas, Delicatessen." When he came out again it was in company with a very stout gentleman in shirt sleeves and an apron, clasping Jonas by both hands and laughing hilariously. Then Teta Elzbieta recollected suddenly that Szedvilas had been the name of the mythical friend who had made his fortune in America. To find that he had been making it in the delicatessen business was an extraordinary piece of good fortune at this juncture; though it was well on in the morning, they had not breakfasted, and the children were beginning to whimper.

Thus was the happy ending to a woeful voyage. The two families literally fell upon each other's necks—for it had been years since Jokubas Szedvilas had met a man from his part of Lithuania. Before half the day they were lifelong friends. Jokubas understood all the pitfalls of this new world, and could explain all of its mysteries; he could tell them the things they ought to have done in the different emergencies—and what was still more to the point, he could tell them what to do now. He would take them to poni Aniele, who kept a boardinghouse the other side of the yards; old Mrs. Jukniene, he explained, had not what one would call choice accommodations, but they might do for the moment. To this Teta Elzbieta hastened to respond that nothing could be too cheap to suit them just then; for they were quite terrified over the sums they had had to expend. A very few days of practical experience in this land of high wages had been sufficient to make clear to them the cruel fact that it was also a land of high prices, and that in it the poor man was almost as poor as in any other corner of the earth; and so there vanished in a night all the wonderful dreams of wealth that had been haunting Jurgis. What had made the discovery all the more painful was that they were spending, at American prices, money which they had earned at home rates of wages—and so were really being cheated by the world! The last two days they had all but starved themselves—it made them quite sick to pay the prices that the railroad people asked them for food.

Yet, when they saw the home of the Widow Jukniene they could not but recoil, even so, in all their journey they had seen nothing so bad as this. Poni Aniele had a four-room flat in one of that wilderness of two-story frame tenements that lie "back of the yards." There were four such flats in each building, and each of the four was a "boardinghouse" for the occupancy of foreigners—Lithuanians, Poles, Slovaks, or Bohemians. Some of these places were kept by private persons, some were cooperative. There would be an average of half a dozen boarders to each room—sometimes there were thirteen or fourteen to one room, fifty or sixty to a flat. Each one of the occupants furnished his own accommodations—that is, a mattress and some bedding. The mattresses would be spread upon the floor in rows—and there would be nothing else in the place except a stove. It was by no means unusual for two men to own the same mattress in common, one working by day and using it by night, and the other working at night and using it in the daytime. Very frequently a lodging house keeper would rent the same beds to double shifts of men.

Mrs. Jukniene was a wizened-up little woman, with a wrinkled face. Her home was unthinkably filthy; you could not enter by the front door at all, owing to the mattresses, and when you tried to go up the backstairs you found that she had walled up most of the porch with old boards to make a place to keep her chickens. It was a standing jest of the boarders that Aniele cleaned house by letting the chickens loose in the rooms. Undoubtedly this did keep down the vermin, but it seemed probable, in view of all the circumstances, that the old lady regarded it rather as feeding the chickens than as cleaning the rooms. The truth was that she had definitely given up the idea of cleaning anything, under pressure of an attack of rheumatism, which had kept her doubled up in one corner of her room for over a week; during which time eleven of her boarders, heavily in her debt, had concluded to try their chances of employment in Kansas City. This was July, and the fields were green. One never saw the fields, nor any green thing whatever, in Packingtown; but one could go out on the road and "hobo it," as the men phrased it, and see the country, and have a long rest, and an easy time riding on the freight cars.

Such was the home to which the new arrivals were welcomed. There was nothing better to be had—they might not do so well by looking further, for Mrs. Jukniene had at least kept one room for herself and her three little children, and now offered to share this with the women and the girls of the party. They could get bedding at a secondhand store, she explained; and they would not need any, while the weather was so hot—doubtless they would all sleep on the sidewalk such nights as this, as did nearly all of her guests. "Tomorrow," Jurgis said, when they were left alone, "tomorrow I will get a job, and perhaps Jonas will get one also; and then we can get a place of our own."

Later that afternoon he and Ona went out to take a walk and look about them, to see more of this district which was to be their home. In back of the yards the dreary two-story frame houses were scattered farther apart, and there were great spaces bare—that seemingly had been overlooked by the great sore of a city as it spread itself over the surface of the prairie. These bare places were grown up with dingy, yellow weeds, hiding innumerable tomato cans; innumerable children played upon them, chasing one another here and there, screaming and fighting. The most uncanny thing about this neighborhood was the number of the children; you thought there must be a school just out, and it was only after long acquaintance that you were able to realize that there was no school, but that these were the children of the neighborhood—that there were so many children to the block in Packingtown that nowhere on its streets could a horse and buggy move faster than a walk!

It could not move faster anyhow, on account of the state of the streets. Those through which Jurgis and Ona were walking resembled streets less than they did a miniature topographical map. The roadway was commonly several feet lower than the level of the houses, which were sometimes joined by high board walks; there were no pavements—there were mountains and valleys and rivers, gullies and ditches, and great hollows full of stinking green water. In these pools the children played, and rolled about in the mud of the streets; here and there one noticed them digging in it, after trophies which they had stumbled on. One wondered about this, as also about the swarms of flies which hung about the scene, literally blackening the air, and the strange, fetid odor which assailed one's nostrils, a ghastly odor, of all the dead things of the universe. It impelled the visitor to questions and then the residents would explain, quietly, that all this was "made" land, and that it had been "made" by using it as a dumping ground for the city garbage. After a few years the unpleasant effect of this would pass away, it was said; but meantime, in hot weather—and especially when it rained—the flies were apt to be annoying. Was it not unhealthful? the stranger would ask, and the residents would answer, "Perhaps; but there is no telling."

A little way farther on, and Jurgis and Ona, staring open-eyed and wondering, came to the place where this "made" ground was in process of making. Here was a great hole, perhaps two city blocks square, and with long files of garbage wagons creeping into it. The place had an odor for which there are no polite words; and it was sprinkled over with children, who raked in it from dawn till dark. Sometimes visitors from the packing houses would wander out to see this "dump," and they would stand by and debate as to whether the children were eating the food they got, or merely collecting it for the chickens at home. Apparently none of them ever went down to find out.

Beyond this dump there stood a great brickyard, with smoking chimneys. First they took out the soil to make bricks, and then they filled it up again with garbage, which seemed to Jurgis and Ona a felicitous arrangement, characteristic of an enterprising country like America. A little way beyond was another great hole, which they had emptied and not yet filled up. This held water, and all summer it stood there, with the near-by soil draining into it, festering and stewing in the sun; and then, when winter came, somebody cut the ice on it, and sold it to the people of the city. This, too, seemed to the newcomers an economical arrangement; for they did not read the newspapers, and their heads were not full of troublesome thoughts about "germs."

They stood there while the sun went down upon this scene, and the sky in the west turned blood-red, and the tops of the houses shone like fire. Jurgis and Ona were not thinking of the sunset, however—their backs were turned to it, and all their thoughts were of Packingtown, which they could see so plainly in the distance. The line of the buildings stood clear-cut and black against the sky; here and there out of the mass rose the great chimneys, with the river of smoke streaming away to the end of the world. It was a study in colors now, this smoke; in the sunset light it was black and brown and gray and purple. All the sordid suggestions of the place were gone—in the twilight it was a vision of power. To the two who stood watching while the darkness swallowed it up, it seemed a dream of wonder, with its talc of human energy, of things being done, of employment for thousands upon thousands of men, of opportunity and freedom, of life and love and joy. When they came away, arm in arm, Jurgis was saying, "Tomorrow I shall go there and get a job!"

# Chapter 3

In his capacity as delicatessen vender, Jokubas Szedvilas had many acquaintances. Among these was one of the special policemen employed by Durham, whose duty it frequently was to pick out men for employment. Jokubas had never tried it, but he expressed a certainty that he could get some of his friends a job through this man. It was agreed, after consultation, that he should make the effort with old Antanas and with Jonas. Jurgis was confident of his ability to get work for himself, unassisted by any one. As we have said before, he was not mistaken in this. He had gone to Brown's and stood there not more than half an hour before one of the bosses noticed his form towering above the rest, and signaled to him. The colloquy which followed was brief and to the point:

"Speak English?"

"No; Lit-uanian." (Jurgis had studied this word carefully.)

"Job?"

"Je." (A nod.)

"Worked here before?"

"No 'stand."

(Signals and gesticulations on the part of the boss. Vigorous shakes of the head by Jurgis.)

"Shovel guts?"

"No 'stand." (More shakes of the head.)

"Zarnos. Pagaiksztis. Szluofa!" (Imitative motions.)

"Je."

"See door. Durys?" (Pointing.)

"Je."

"To-morrow, seven o'clock. Understand? Rytoj! Prieszpietys! Septyni!"

"Dekui, tamistai!" (Thank you, sir.) And that was all. Jurgis turned away, and then in a sudden rush the full realization of his triumph swept over him, and he gave a yell and a jump, and started off on a run. He had a job! He had a job! And he went all the way home as if upon wings, and burst into the house like a cyclone, to the rage of the numerous lodgers who had just turned in for their daily sleep.

Meantime Jokubas had been to see his friend the policeman, and received encouragement, so it was a happy party. There being no more to be done that day, the shop was left under the care of Lucija, and her husband sallied forth to show his friends the sights of Packingtown. Jokubas did this with the air of a country gentleman escorting a party of visitors over his estate; he was an old-time resident, and all these wonders had grown up under his eyes, and he had a personal pride in them. The packers might own the land, but he claimed the landscape, and there was no one to say nay to this.

They passed down the busy street that led to the yards. It was still early morning, and everything was at its high tide of activity. A steady stream of employees was pouring through the gate—employees of the higher sort, at this hour, clerks and stenographers and such. For the women there were waiting big two-horse wagons, which set off at a gallop as fast as they were filled. In the distance there was heard again the lowing of the cattle, a sound as of a far-off ocean calling. They followed it, this time, as eager as children in sight of a circus menagerie—which, indeed, the scene a good deal resembled. They crossed the railroad tracks, and then on each side of the street were the pens full of cattle; they would have stopped to look, but Jokubas hurried them on, to where there was a stairway and a raised gallery, from which everything could be seen. Here they stood, staring, breathless with wonder.

There is over a square mile of space in the yards, and more than half of it is occupied by cattle pens; north and south as far as the eye can reach there stretches a sea of pens. And they were all filled—so many cattle no one had ever dreamed existed in the world. Red cattle, black, white, and yellow cattle; old cattle and young cattle; great bellowing bulls and little calves not an hour born; meek-eyed milch cows and fierce, long-horned Texas steers. The sound of them here was as of all the barnyards of the universe; and as for counting them—it would have taken all day simply to count the pens. Here and there ran long alleys, blocked at intervals by gates; and Jokubas told them that the number of these gates was twenty-five thousand. Jokubas had recently been reading a newspaper article which was full of statistics such as that, and he was very proud as he repeated them and made his guests cry out with wonder. Jurgis too had a little of this sense of pride. Had he not just gotten a job, and become a sharer in all this activity, a cog in this marvelous machine? Here and there about the alleys galloped men upon horseback, booted, and carrying long whips; they were very busy, calling to each other, and to those who were driving the cattle. They were drovers and stock raisers, who had come from far states, and brokers and commission merchants, and buyers for all the big packing houses.

Here and there they would stop to inspect a bunch of cattle, and there would be a parley, brief and businesslike. The buyer would nod or drop his whip, and that would mean a bargain; and he would note it in his little book, along with hundreds of others he had made that morning. Then Jokubas pointed out the place where the cattle were driven to be weighed, upon a great scale that would weigh a hundred thousand pounds at once and record it automatically. It was near to the east entrance that they stood, and all along this east side of the yards ran the railroad tracks, into which the cars were run, loaded with cattle. All night long this had been going on, and now the pens were full; by tonight they would all be empty, and the same thing would be done again.

"And what will become of all these creatures?" cried Teta Elzbieta.

"By tonight," Jokubas answered, "they will all be killed and cut up; and over there on the other side of the packing houses are more railroad tracks, where the cars come to take them away."

There were two hundred and fifty miles of track within the yards, their guide went on to tell them. They brought about ten thousand head of cattle every day, and as many hogs, and half as many sheep—which meant some eight or ten million live creatures turned into food every year. One stood and watched, and little by little caught the drift of the tide, as it set in the direction of the packing houses. There were groups of cattle being driven to the chutes, which were roadways about fifteen feet wide, raised high above the pens. In these chutes the stream of animals was continuous; it was quite uncanny to watch them, pressing on to their fate, all unsuspicious a very river of death. Our friends were not poetical, and the sight suggested to them no metaphors of human destiny; they thought only of the wonderful efficiency of it all. The chutes into which the hogs went climbed high up—to the very top of the distant buildings; and Jokubas explained that the hogs went up by the power of their own legs, and then their weight carried them back through all the processes necessary to make them into pork.

"They don't waste anything here," said the guide, and then he laughed and added a witticism, which he was pleased that his unsophisticated friends should take to be his own: "They use everything about the hog except the squeal." In front of Brown's General Office building there grows a tiny plot of grass, and this, you may learn, is the only bit of green thing in Packingtown; likewise this jest about the hog and his squeal, the stock in trade of all the guides, is the one gleam of humor that you will find there.

After they had seen enough of the pens, the party went up the street, to the mass of buildings which occupy the center of the yards. These buildings, made of brick and stained with innumerable layers of Packingtown smoke, were painted all over with advertising signs, from which the visitor realized suddenly that he had come to the home of many of the torments of his life. It was here that they made those products with the wonders of which they pestered him so—by placards that defaced the landscape when he traveled, and by staring advertisements in the newspapers and magazines—by silly little jingles that he could not get out of his mind, and gaudy pictures that lurked for him around every street corner. Here was where they made Brown's Imperial Hams and Bacon, Brown's Dressed Beef, Brown's Excelsior Sausages! Here was the headquarters of Durham's Pure Leaf Lard, of Durham's Breakfast Bacon, Durham's Canned Beef, Potted Ham, Deviled Chicken, Peerless Fertilizer!

Entering one of the Durham buildings, they found a number of other visitors waiting; and before long there came a guide, to escort them through the place. They make a great feature of showing strangers through the packing plants, for it is a good advertisement. But Ponas Jokubas whispered maliciously that the visitors did not see any more than the packers wanted them to. They climbed a long series of stairways outside of the building, to the top of its five or six stories. Here was the chute, with its river of hogs, all patiently toiling upward; there was a place for them to rest to cool off, and then through another passageway they went into a room from which there is no returning for hogs.

It was a long, narrow room, with a gallery along it for visitors. At the head there was a great iron wheel, about twenty feet in circumference, with rings here and there along its edge. Upon both sides of this wheel there was a narrow space, into which came the hogs at the end of their journey; in the midst of them stood a great burly Negro, bare-armed and bare-chested. He was resting for the moment, for the wheel had stopped while men were cleaning up. In a minute or two, however, it began slowly to revolve, and then the men upon each side of it sprang to work. They had chains which they fastened about the leg of the nearest hog, and the other end of the chain they hooked into one of the rings upon the wheel. So, as the wheel turned, a hog was suddenly jerked off his feet and borne aloft.

At the same instant the car was assailed by a most terrifying shriek; the visitors started in alarm, the women turned pale and shrank back. The shriek was followed by another, louder and yet more agonizing—for once started upon that journey, the hog never came back; at the top of the wheel he was shunted off upon a trolley, and went sailing down the room. And meantime another was swung up, and then another, and another, until there was a double line of them, each dangling by a foot and kicking in frenzy—and squealing. The uproar was appalling, perilous to the eardrums; one feared there was too much sound for the room to hold—that the walls must give way or the ceiling crack. There were high squeals and low squeals, grunts, and wails of agony; there would come a momentary lull, and then a fresh outburst, louder than ever, surging up to a deafening climax. It was too much for some of the visitors—the men would look at each other, laughing nervously, and the women would stand with hands clenched, and the blood rushing to their faces, and the tears starting in their eyes.

Meantime, heedless of all these things, the men upon the floor were going about their work. Neither squeals of hogs nor tears of visitors made any difference to them; one by one they hooked up the hogs, and one by one with a swift stroke they slit their throats. There was a long line of hogs, with squeals and lifeblood ebbing away together; until at last each started again, and vanished with a splash into a huge vat of boiling water.

It was all so very businesslike that one watched it fascinated. It was porkmaking by machinery, porkmaking by applied mathematics. And yet somehow the most matter-of-fact person could not help thinking of the hogs; they were so innocent, they came so very trustingly; and they were so very human in their protests—and so perfectly within their rights! They had done nothing to deserve it; and it was adding insult to injury, as the thing was done here, swinging them up in this cold-blooded, impersonal way, without a pretense of apology, without the homage of a tear. Now and then a visitor wept, to be sure; but this slaughtering machine ran on, visitors or no visitors. It was like some horrible crime committed in a dungeon, all unseen and unheeded, buried out of sight and of memory.

One could not stand and watch very long without becoming philosophical, without beginning to deal in symbols and similes, and to hear the hog squeal of the universe. Was it permitted to believe that there was nowhere upon the earth, or above the earth, a heaven for hogs, where they were requited for all this suffering? Each one of these hogs was a separate creature. Some were white hogs, some were black; some were brown, some were spotted; some were old, some young; some were long and lean, some were monstrous. And each of them had an individuality of his own, a will of his own, a hope and a heart's desire; each was full of self-confidence, of self-importance, and a sense of dignity. And trusting and strong in faith he had gone about his business, the while a black shadow hung over him and a horrid Fate waited in his pathway. Now suddenly it had swooped upon him, and had seized him by the leg. Relentless, remorseless, it was; all his protests, his screams, were nothing to it—it did its cruel will with him, as if his wishes, his feelings, had simply no existence at all; it cut his throat and watched him gasp out his life. And now was one to believe that there was nowhere a god of hogs, to whom this hog personality was precious, to whom these hog squeals and agonies had a meaning? Who would take this hog into his arms and comfort him, reward him for his work well done, and show him the meaning of his sacrifice? Perhaps some glimpse of all this was in the thoughts of our humble-minded Jurgis, as he turned to go on with the rest of the party, and muttered: "Dieve—but I'm glad I'm not a hog!"

The carcass hog was scooped out of the vat by machinery, and then it fell to the second floor, passing on the way through a wonderful machine with numerous scrapers, which adjusted themselves to the size and shape of the animal, and sent it out at the other end with nearly all of its bristles removed. It was then again strung up by machinery, and sent upon another trolley ride; this time passing between two lines of men, who sat upon a raised platform, each doing a certain single thing to the carcass as it came to him. One scraped the outside of a leg; another scraped the inside of the same leg. One with a swift stroke cut the throat; another with two swift strokes severed the head, which fell to the floor and vanished through a hole. Another made a slit down the body; a second opened the body wider; a third with a saw cut the breastbone; a fourth loosened the entrails; a fifth pulled them out—and they also slid through a hole in the floor. There were men to scrape each side and men to scrape the back; there were men to clean the carcass inside, to trim it and wash it. Looking down this room, one saw, creeping slowly, a line of dangling hogs a hundred yards in length; and for every yard there was a man, working as if a demon were after him. At the end of this hog's progress every inch of the carcass had been gone over several times; and then it was rolled into the chilling room, where it stayed for twenty-four hours, and where a stranger might lose himself in a forest of freezing hogs.

Before the carcass was admitted here, however, it had to pass a government inspector, who sat in the doorway and felt of the glands in the neck for tuberculosis. This government inspector did not have the manner of a man who was worked to death; he was apparently not haunted by a fear that the hog might get by him before he had finished his testing. If you were a sociable person, he was quite willing to enter into conversation with you, and to explain to you the deadly nature of the ptomaines which are found in tubercular pork; and while he was talking with you you could hardly be so ungrateful as to notice that a dozen carcasses were passing him untouched. This inspector wore a blue uniform, with brass buttons, and he gave an atmosphere of authority to the scene, and, as it were, put the stamp of official approval upon the things which were done in Durham's.

Jurgis went down the line with the rest of the visitors, staring open-mouthed, lost in wonder. He had dressed hogs himself in the forest of Lithuania; but he had never expected to live to see one hog dressed by several hundred men. It was like a wonderful poem to him, and he took it all in guilelessly—even to the conspicuous signs demanding immaculate cleanliness of the employees. Jurgis was vexed when the cynical Jokubas translated these signs with sarcastic comments, offering to take them to the secret rooms where the spoiled meats went to be doctored.

The party descended to the next floor, where the various waste materials were treated. Here came the entrails, to be scraped and washed clean for sausage casings; men and women worked here in the midst of a sickening stench, which caused the visitors to hasten by, gasping. To another room came all the scraps to be "tanked," which meant boiling and pumping off the grease to make soap and lard; below they took out the refuse, and this, too, was a region in which the visitors did not linger. In still other places men were engaged in cutting up the carcasses that had been through the chilling rooms. First there were the "splitters," the most expert workmen in the plant, who earned as high as fifty cents an hour, and did not a thing all day except chop hogs down the middle. Then there were "cleaver men," great giants with muscles of iron; each had two men to attend him—to slide the half carcass in front of him on the table, and hold it while he chopped it, and then turn each piece so that he might chop it once more. His cleaver had a blade about two feet long, and he never made but one cut; he made it so neatly, too, that his implement did not smite through and dull itself—there was just enough force for a perfect cut, and no more. So through various yawning holes there slipped to the floor below—to one room hams, to another forequarters, to another sides of pork. One might go down to this floor and see the pickling rooms, where the hams were put into vats, and the great smoke rooms, with their airtight iron doors. In other rooms they prepared salt pork—there were whole cellars full of it, built up in great towers to the ceiling. In yet other rooms they were putting up meats in boxes and barrels, and wrapping hams and bacon in oiled paper, sealing and labeling and sewing them. From the doors of these rooms went men with loaded trucks, to the platform where freight cars were waiting to be filled; and one went out there and realized with a start that he had come at last to the ground floor of this enormous building.

Then the party went across the street to where they did the killing of beef—where every hour they turned four or five hundred cattle into meat. Unlike the place they had left, all this work was done on one floor; and instead of there being one line of carcasses which moved to the workmen, there were fifteen or twenty lines, and the men moved from one to another of these. This made a scene of intense activity, a picture of human power wonderful to watch. It was all in one great room, like a circus amphitheater, with a gallery for visitors running over the center.

Along one side of the room ran a narrow gallery, a few feet from the floor; into which gallery the cattle were driven by men with goads which gave them electric shocks. Once crowded in here, the creatures were prisoned, each in a separate pen, by gates that shut, leaving them no room to turn around; and while they stood bellowing and plunging, over the top of the pen there leaned one of the "knockers," armed with a sledge hammer, and watching for a chance to deal a blow. The room echoed with the thuds in quick succession, and the stamping and kicking of the steers. The instant the animal had fallen, the "knocker" passed on to another; while a second man raised a lever, and the side of the pen was raised, and the animal, still kicking and struggling, slid out to the "killing bed." Here a man put shackles about one leg, and pressed another lever, and the body was jerked up into the air. There were fifteen or twenty such pens, and it was a matter of only a couple of minutes to knock fifteen or twenty cattle and roll them out. Then once more the gates were opened, and another lot rushed in; and so out of each pen there rolled a steady stream of carcasses, which the men upon the killing beds had to get out of the way.

The manner in which they did this was something to be seen and never forgotten. They worked with furious intensity, literally upon the run—at a pace with which there is nothing to be compared except a football game. It was all highly specialized labor, each man having his task to do; generally this would consist of only two or three specific cuts, and he would pass down the line of fifteen or twenty carcasses, making these cuts upon each. First there came the "butcher," to bleed them; this meant one swift stroke, so swift that you could not see it—only the flash of the knife; and before you could realize it, the man had darted on to the next line, and a stream of bright red was pouring out upon the floor. This floor was half an inch deep with blood, in spite of the best efforts of men who kept shoveling it through holes; it must have made the floor slippery, but no one could have guessed this by watching the men at work.

The carcass hung for a few minutes to bleed; there was no time lost, however, for there were several hanging in each line, and one was always ready. It was let down to the ground, and there came the "headsman," whose task it was to sever the head, with two or three swift strokes. Then came the "floorsman," to make the first cut in the skin; and then another to finish ripping the skin down the center; and then half a dozen more in swift succession, to finish the skinning. After they were through, the carcass was again swung up; and while a man with a stick examined the skin, to make sure that it had not been cut, and another rolled it up and tumbled it through one of the inevitable holes in the floor, the beef proceeded on its journey. There were men to cut it, and men to split it, and men to gut it and scrape it clean inside. There were some with hose which threw jets of boiling water upon it, and others who removed the feet and added the final touches. In the end, as with the hogs, the finished beef was run into the chilling room, to hang its appointed time.

The visitors were taken there and shown them, all neatly hung in rows, labeled conspicuously with the tags of the government inspectors—and some, which had been killed by a special process, marked with the sign of the kosher rabbi, certifying that it was fit for sale to the orthodox. And then the visitors were taken to the other parts of the building, to see what became of each particle of the waste material that had vanished through the floor; and to the pickling rooms, and the salting rooms, the canning rooms, and the packing rooms, where choice meat was prepared for shipping in refrigerator cars, destined to be eaten in all the four corners of civilization. Afterward they went outside, wandering about among the mazes of buildings in which was done the work auxiliary to this great industry. There was scarcely a thing needed in the business that Durham and Company did not make for themselves. There was a great steam power plant and an electricity plant. There was a barrel factory, and a boiler-repair shop. There was a building to which the grease was piped, and made into soap and lard; and then there was a factory for making lard cans, and another for making soap boxes. There was a building in which the bristles were cleaned and dried, for the making of hair cushions and such things; there was a building where the skins were dried and tanned, there was another where heads and feet were made into glue, and another where bones were made into fertilizer. No tiniest particle of organic matter was wasted in Durham's. Out of the horns of the cattle they made combs, buttons, hairpins, and imitation ivory; out of the shinbones and other big bones they cut knife and toothbrush handles, and mouthpieces for pipes; out of the hoofs they cut hairpins and buttons, before they made the rest into glue. From such things as feet, knuckles, hide clippings, and sinews came such strange and unlikely products as gelatin, isinglass, and phosphorus, bone black, shoe blacking, and bone oil. They had curled-hair works for the cattle tails, and a "wool pullery" for the sheepskins; they made pepsin from the stomachs of the pigs, and albumen from the blood, and violin strings from the ill-smelling entrails. When there was nothing else to be done with a thing, they first put it into a tank and got out of it all the tallow and grease, and then they made it into fertilizer. All these industries were gathered into buildings near by, connected by galleries and railroads with the main establishment; and it was estimated that they had handled nearly a quarter of a billion of animals since the founding of the plant by the elder Durham a generation and more ago. If you counted with it the other big plants—

and they were now really all one—it was, so Jokubas informed them, the greatest aggregation of labor and capital ever gathered in one place. It employed thirty thousand men; it supported directly two hundred and fifty thousand people in its neighborhood, and indirectly it supported half a million. It sent its products to every country in the civilized world, and it furnished the food for no less than thirty million people!

To all of these things our friends would listen open-mouthed—it seemed to them impossible of belief that anything so stupendous could have been devised by mortal man. That was why to Jurgis it seemed almost profanity to speak about the place as did Jokubas, skeptically; it was a thing as tremendous as the universe—the laws and ways of its working no more than the universe to be questioned or understood. All that a mere man could do, it seemed to Jurgis, was to take a thing like this as he found it, and do as he was told; to be given a place in it and a share in its wonderful activities was a blessing to be grateful for, as one was grateful for the sunshine and the rain. Jurgis was even glad that he had not seen the place before meeting with his triumph, for he felt that the size of it would have overwhelmed him. But now he had been admitted—he was a part of it all! He had the feeling that this whole huge establishment had taken him under its protection, and had become responsible for his welfare. So guileless was he, and ignorant of the nature of business, that he did not even realize that he had become an employee of Brown's, and that Brown and Durham were supposed by all the world to be deadly rivals—were even required to be deadly rivals by the law of the land, and ordered to try to ruin each other under penalty of fine and imprisonment!

# Chapter 4

Promptly at seven the next morning Jurgis reported for work. He came to the door that had been pointed out to him, and there he waited for nearly two hours. The boss had meant for him to enter, but had not said this, and so it was only when on his way out to hire another man that he came upon Jurgis. He gave him a good cursing, but as Jurgis did not understand a word of it he did not object. He followed the boss, who showed him where to put his street clothes, and waited while he donned the working clothes he had bought in a secondhand shop and brought with him in a bundle; then he led him to the "killing beds." The work which Jurgis was to do here was very simple, and it took him but a few minutes to learn it. He was provided with a stiff besom, such as is used by street sweepers, and it was his place to follow down the line the man who drew out the smoking entrails from the carcass of the steer; this mass was to be swept into a trap, which was then closed, so that no one might slip into it. As Jurgis came in, the first cattle of the morning were just making their appearance; and so, with scarcely time to look about him, and none to speak to any one, he fell to work. It was a sweltering day in July, and the place ran with steaming hot blood—one waded in it on the floor. The stench was almost overpowering, but to Jurgis it was nothing. His whole soul was dancing with joy—he was at work at last! He was at work and earning money! All day long he was figuring to himself. He was paid the fabulous sum of seventeen and a half cents an hour; and as it proved a rush day and he worked until nearly seven o'clock in the evening, he went home to the family with the tidings that he had earned more than a dollar and a half in a single day!

At home, also, there was more good news; so much of it at once that there was quite a celebration in Aniele's hall bedroom. Jonas had been to have an interview with the special policeman to whom Szedvilas had introduced him, and had been taken to see several of the bosses, with the result that one had promised him a job the beginning of the next week. And then there was Marija Berczynskas, who, fired with jealousy by the success of Jurgis, had set out upon her own responsibility to get a place. Marija had nothing to take with her save her two brawny arms and the word "job," laboriously learned; but with these she had marched about Packingtown all day, entering every door where there were signs of activity. Out of some she had been ordered with curses; but Marija was not afraid of man or devil, and asked every one she saw—visitors and strangers, or work-people like herself, and once or twice even high and lofty office personages, who stared at her as if they thought she was crazy. In the end, however, she had reaped her reward. In one of the smaller plants she had stumbled upon a room where scores of women and girls were sitting at long tables preparing smoked beef in cans; and wandering through room after room, Marija came at last to the place where the sealed cans were being painted and labeled, and here she had the good fortune to encounter the "forelady." Marija did not understand then, as she was destined to understand later, what there was attractive to a "forelady" about the combination of a face full of boundless good nature and the muscles of a dray horse; but the woman had told her to come the next day and she would perhaps give her a chance to learn the trade of painting cans. The painting of cans being skilled piecework, and paying as much as two dollars a day, Marija burst in upon the family with the yell of a Comanche Indian, and fell to capering about the room so as to frighten the baby almost into convulsions.

Better luck than all this could hardly have been hoped for; there was only one of them left to seek a place. Jurgis was determined that Teta Elzbieta should stay at home to keep house, and that Ona should help her. He would not have Ona working—he was not that sort of a man, he said, and she was not that sort of a woman. It would be a strange thing if a man like him could not support the family, with the help of the board of Jonas and Marija. He would not even hear of letting the children go to work—there were schools here in America for children, Jurgis had heard, to which they could go for nothing. That the priest would object to these schools was something of which he had as yet no idea, and for the present his mind was made up that the children of Teta Elzbieta should have as fair a chance as any other children. The oldest of them, little Stanislovas, was but thirteen, and small for his age at that; and while the oldest son of Szedvilas was only twelve, and had worked for over a year at Jones's, Jurgis would have it that Stanislovas should learn to speak English, and grow up to be a skilled man.

So there was only old Dede Antanas; Jurgis would have had him rest too, but he was forced to acknowledge that this was not possible, and, besides, the old man would not hear it spoken of—it was his whim to insist that he was as lively as any boy. He had come to America as full of hope as the best of them; and now he was the chief problem that worried his son. For every one that Jurgis spoke to assured him that it was a waste of time to seek employment for the old man in Packingtown. Szedvilas told him that the packers did not even keep the men who had grown old in their own service—to say nothing of taking on new ones. And not only was it the rule here, it was the rule everywhere in America, so far as he knew. To satisfy Jurgis he had asked the policeman, and brought back the message that the thing was not to be thought of. They had not told this to old Anthony, who had consequently spent the two days wandering about from one part of the yards to another, and had now come home to hear about the triumph of the others, smiling bravely and saying that it would be his turn another day.

Their good luck, they felt, had given them the right to think about a home; and sitting out on the doorstep that summer evening, they held consultation about it, and Jurgis took occasion to broach a weighty subject. Passing down the avenue to work that morning he had seen two boys leaving an advertisement from house to house; and seeing that there were pictures upon it, Jurgis had asked for one, and had rolled it up and tucked it into his shirt. At noontime a man with whom he had been talking had read it to him and told him a little about it, with the result that Jurgis had conceived a wild idea.

He brought out the placard, which was quite a work of art. It was nearly two feet long, printed on calendered paper, with a selection of colors so bright that they shone even in the moonlight. The center of the placard was occupied by a house, brilliantly painted, new, and dazzling. The roof of it was of a purple hue, and trimmed with gold; the house itself was silvery, and the doors and windows red. It was a two-story building, with a porch in front, and a very fancy scrollwork around the edges; it was complete in every tiniest detail, even the doorknob, and there was a hammock on the porch and white lace curtains in the windows. Underneath this, in one corner, was a picture of a husband and wife in loving embrace; in the opposite corner was a cradle, with fluffy curtains drawn over it, and a smiling cherub hovering upon silver-colored wings. For fear that the significance of all this should be lost, there was a label, in Polish, Lithuanian, and German—"Dom. Namai. Heim." "Why pay rent?" the linguistic circular went on to demand. "Why not own your own home? Do you know that you can buy one for less than your rent? We have built thousands of homes which are now occupied by happy families."—So it became eloquent, picturing the blissfulness of married life in a house with nothing to pay. It even quoted "Home, Sweet Home," and made bold to translate it into Polish—though for some reason it omitted the Lithuanian of this. Perhaps the translator found it a difficult matter to be sentimental in a language in which a sob is known as a gukcziojimas and a smile as a nusiszypsojimas.

Over this document the family pored long, while Ona spelled out its contents. It appeared that this house contained four rooms, besides a basement, and that it might be bought for fifteen hundred dollars, the lot and all. Of this, only three hundred dollars had to be paid down, the balance being paid at the rate of twelve dollars a month. These were frightful sums, but then they were in America, where people talked about such without fear. They had learned that they would have to pay a rent of nine dollars a month for a flat, and there was no way of doing better, unless the family of twelve was to exist in one or two rooms, as at present. If they paid rent, of course, they might pay forever, and be no better off; whereas, if they could only meet the extra expense in the beginning, there would at last come a time when they would not have any rent to pay for the rest of their lives.

They figured it up. There was a little left of the money belonging to Teta Elzbieta, and there was a little left to Jurgis. Marija had about fifty dollars pinned up somewhere in her stockings, and Grandfather Anthony had part of the money he had gotten for his farm. If they all combined, they would have enough to make the first payment; and if they had employment, so that they could be sure of the future, it might really prove the best plan. It was, of course, not a thing even to be talked of lightly; it was a thing they would have to sift to the bottom. And yet, on the other hand, if they were going to make the venture, the sooner they did it the better, for were they not paying rent all the time, and living in a most horrible way besides? Jurgis was used to dirt—there was nothing could scare a man who had been with a railroad gang, where one could gather up the fleas off the floor of the sleeping room by the handful. But that sort of thing would not do for Ona. They must have a better place of some sort soon—Jurgis said it with all the assurance of a man who had just made a dollar and fifty-seven cents in a single day. Jurgis was at a loss to understand why, with wages as they were, so many of the people of this district should live the way they did.

The next day Marija went to see her "forelady," and was told to report the first of the week, and learn the business of can-painter. Marija went home, singing out loud all the way, and was just in time to join Ona and her stepmother as they were setting out to go and make inquiry concerning the house. That evening the three made their report to the men—the thing was altogether as represented in the circular, or at any rate so the agent had said. The houses lay to the south, about a mile and a half from the yards; they were wonderful bargains, the gentleman had assured them—personally, and for their own good. He could do this, so he explained to them, for the reason that he had himself no interest in their sale—he was merely the agent for a company that had built them. These were the last, and the company was going out of business, so if any one wished to take advantage of this wonderful no-rent plan, he would have to be very quick. As a matter of fact there was just a little uncertainty as to whether there was a single house left; for the agent had taken so many people to see them, and for all he knew the company might have parted with the last. Seeing Teta Elzbieta's evident grief at this news, he added, after some hesitation, that if they really intended to make a purchase, he would send a telephone message at his own expense, and have one of the houses kept. So it had finally been arranged—and they were to go and make an inspection the following Sunday morning.

That was Thursday; and all the rest of the week the killing gang at Brown's worked at full pressure, and Jurgis cleared a dollar seventy-five every day. That was at the rate of ten and one-half dollars a week, or forty-five a month. Jurgis was not able to figure, except it was a very simple sum, but Ona was like lightning at such things, and she worked out the problem for the family. Marija and Jonas were each to pay sixteen dollars a month board, and the old man insisted that he could do the same as soon as he got a place—which might be any day now. That would make ninety-three dollars. Then Marija and Jonas were between them to take a third share in the house, which would leave only eight dollars a month for Jurgis to contribute to the payment. So they would have eighty-five dollars a month—or, supposing that Dede Antanas did not get work at once, seventy dollars a month—which ought surely to be sufficient for the support of a family of twelve.

An hour before the time on Sunday morning the entire party set out. They had the address written on a piece of paper, which they showed to some one now and then. It proved to be a long mile and a half, but they walked it, and half an hour or so later the agent put in an appearance. He was a smooth and florid personage, elegantly dressed, and he spoke their language freely, which gave him a great advantage in dealing with them. He escorted them to the house, which was one of a long row of the typical frame dwellings of the neighborhood, where architecture is a luxury that is dispensed with. Ona's heart sank, for the house was not as it was shown in the picture; the color scheme was different, for one thing, and then it did not seem quite so big. Still, it was freshly painted, and made a considerable show. It was all brand-new, so the agent told them, but he talked so incessantly that they were quite confused, and did not have time to ask many questions. There were all sorts of things they had made up their minds to inquire about, but when the time came, they either forgot them or lacked the courage. The other houses in the row did not seem to be new, and few of them seemed to be occupied. When they ventured to hint at this, the agent's reply was that the purchasers would be moving in shortly. To press the matter would have seemed to be doubting his word, and never in their lives had any one of them ever spoken to a person of the class called "gentleman" except with deference and humility.

The house had a basement, about two feet below the street line, and a single story, about six feet above it, reached by a flight of steps. In addition there was an attic, made by the peak of the roof, and having one small window in each end. The street in front of the house was unpaved and unlighted, and the view from it consisted of a few exactly similar houses, scattered here and there upon lots grown up with dingy brown weeds. The house inside contained four rooms, plastered white; the basement was but a frame, the walls being unplastered and the floor not laid. The agent explained that the houses were built that way, as the purchasers generally preferred to finish the basements to suit their own taste. The attic was also unfinished—the family had been figuring that in case of an emergency they could rent this attic, but they found that there was not even a floor, nothing but joists, and beneath them the lath and plaster of the ceiling below. All of this, however, did not chill their ardor as much as might have been expected, because of the volubility of the agent. There was no end to the advantages of the house, as he set them forth, and he was not silent for an instant; he showed them everything, down to the locks on the doors and the catches on the windows, and how to work them. He showed them the sink in the kitchen, with running water and a faucet, something which Teta Elzbieta had never in her wildest dreams hoped to possess. After a discovery such as that it would have seemed ungrateful to find any fault, and so they tried to shut their eyes to other defects.

Still, they were peasant people, and they hung on to their money by instinct; it was quite in vain that the agent hinted at promptness—they would see, they would see, they told him, they could not decide until they had had more time. And so they went home again, and all day and evening there was figuring and debating. It was an agony to them to have to make up their minds in a matter such as this. They never could agree all together; there were so many arguments upon each side, and one would be obstinate, and no sooner would the rest have convinced him than it would transpire that his arguments had caused another to waver. Once, in the evening, when they were all in harmony, and the house was as good as bought, Szedvilas came in and upset them again. Szedvilas had no use for property owning. He told them cruel stories of people who had been done to death in this "buying a home" swindle. They would be almost sure to get into a tight place and lose all their money; and there was no end of expense that one could never foresee; and the house might be good-for-nothing from top to bottom—how was a poor man to know? Then, too, they would swindle you with the contract—and how was a poor man to understand anything about a contract? It was all nothing but robbery, and there was no safety but in keeping out of it. And pay rent? asked Jurgis. Ah, yes, to be sure, the other answered, that too was robbery. It was all robbery, for a poor man. After half an hour of such depressing conversation, they had their minds quite made up that they had been saved at the brink of a precipice; but then Szedvilas went away, and Jonas, who was a sharp little man, reminded them that the delicatessen business was a failure, according to its proprietor, and that this might account for his pessimistic views. Which, of course, reopened the subject!

The controlling factor was that they could not stay where they were—they had to go somewhere. And when they gave up the house plan and decided to rent, the prospect of paying out nine dollars a month forever they found just as hard to face. All day and all night for nearly a whole week they wrestled with the problem, and then in the end Jurgis took the responsibility. Brother Jonas had gotten his job, and was pushing a truck in Durham's; and the killing gang at Brown's continued to work early and late, so that Jurgis grew more confident every hour, more certain of his mastership. It was the kind of thing the man of the family had to decide and carry through, he told himself. Others might have failed at it, but he was not the failing kind—he would show them how to do it. He would work all day, and all night, too, if need be; he would never rest until the house was paid for and his people had a home. So he told them, and so in the end the decision was made.

They had talked about looking at more houses before they made the purchase; but then they did not know where any more were, and they did not know any way of finding out. The one they had seen held the sway in their thoughts; whenever they thought of themselves in a house, it was this house that they thought of. And so they went and told the agent that they were ready to make the agreement. They knew, as an abstract proposition, that in matters of business all men are to be accounted liars; but they could not but have been influenced by all they had heard from the eloquent agent, and were quite persuaded that the house was something they had run a risk of losing by their delay. They drew a deep breath when he told them that they were still in time.

They were to come on the morrow, and he would have the papers all drawn up. This matter of papers was one in which Jurgis understood to the full the need of caution; yet he could not go himself—every one told him that he could not get a holiday, and that he might lose his job by asking. So there was nothing to be done but to trust it to the women, with Szedvilas, who promised to go with them. Jurgis spent a whole evening impressing upon them the seriousness of the occasion—and then finally, out of innumerable hiding places about their persons and in their baggage, came forth the precious wads of money, to be done up tightly in a little bag and sewed fast in the lining of Teta Elzbieta's dress.

Early in the morning they sallied forth. Jurgis had given them so many instructions and warned them against so many perils, that the women were quite pale with fright, and even the imperturbable delicatessen vender, who prided himself upon being a businessman, was ill at ease. The agent had the deed all ready, and invited them to sit down and read it; this Szedvilas proceeded to do—a painful and laborious process, during which the agent drummed upon the desk. Teta Elzbieta was so embarrassed that the perspiration came out upon her forehead in beads; for was not this reading as much as to say plainly to the gentleman's face that they doubted his honesty? Yet Jokubas Szedvilas read on and on; and presently there developed that he had good reason for doing so. For a horrible suspicion had begun dawning in his mind; he knitted his brows more and more as he read. This was not a deed of sale at all, so far as he could see—it provided only for the renting of the property! It was hard to tell, with all this strange legal jargon, words he had never heard before; but was not this plain—"the party of the first part hereby covenants and agrees to rent to the said party of the second part!" And then again—"a monthly rental of twelve dollars, for a period of eight years and four months!" Then Szedvilas took off his spectacles, and looked at the agent, and stammered a question.

The agent was most polite, and explained that that was the usual formula; that it was always arranged that the property should be merely rented. He kept trying to show them something in the next paragraph; but Szedvilas could not get by the word "rental"—and when he translated it to Teta Elzbieta, she too was thrown into a fright. They would not own the home at all, then, for nearly nine years! The agent, with infinite patience, began to explain again; but no explanation would do now. Elzbieta had firmly fixed in her mind the last solemn warning of Jurgis: "If there is anything wrong, do not give him the money, but go out and get a lawyer." It was an agonizing moment, but she sat in the chair, her hands clenched like death, and made a fearful effort, summoning all her powers, and gasped out her purpose.

Jokubas translated her words. She expected the agent to fly into a passion, but he was, to her bewilderment, as ever imperturbable; he even offered to go and get a lawyer for her, but she declined this. They went a long way, on purpose to find a man who would not be a confederate. Then let any one imagine their dismay, when, after half an hour, they came in with a lawyer, and heard him greet the agent by his first name! They felt that all was lost; they sat like prisoners summoned to hear the reading of their death warrant. There was nothing more that they could do—they were trapped! The lawyer read over the deed, and when he had read it he informed Szedvilas that it was all perfectly regular, that the deed was a blank deed such as was often used in these sales. And was the price as agreed? the old man asked—three hundred dollars down, and the balance at twelve dollars a month, till the total of fifteen hundred dollars had been paid? Yes, that was correct. And it was for the sale of such and such a house—the house and lot and everything? Yes,—and the lawyer showed him where that was all written. And it was all perfectly regular—there were no tricks about it of any sort? They were poor people, and this was all they had in the world, and if there was anything wrong they would be ruined. And so Szedvilas went on, asking one trembling question after another, while the eyes of the women folks were fixed upon him in mute agony. They could not understand what he was saying, but they knew that upon it their fate depended. And when at last he had questioned until there was no more questioning to be done, and the time came for them to make up their minds, and either close the bargain or reject it, it was all that poor Teta Elzbieta could do to keep from bursting into tears. Jokubas had asked her if she wished to sign; he had asked her twice—and what could she say? How did she know if this lawyer were telling the truth—that he was not in the conspiracy? And yet, how could she say so—what excuse could she give? The eyes of every one in the room were upon her, awaiting her decision; and at last, half blind with her tears, she began fumbling in her jacket, where she had pinned the precious money. And she brought it out and unwrapped it before the men. All of this Ona sat watching, from a corner of the room, twisting her hands together, meantime, in a fever of fright. Ona longed to cry out and tell her stepmother to stop, that it was all a trap; but there seemed to be something clutching her by the throat, and she could not make a sound. And so Teta Elzbieta laid the money on the table, and the agent picked it up and counted it, and then wrote them a receipt for it and passed them the deed. Then he gave a sigh of satisfaction, and rose and shook hands with them all, still as smooth and polite as at the beginning. Ona had a dim recollection of the lawyer telling Szedvilas that his charge was a dollar, which occasioned some debate, and more agony; and then, after they had paid that, too, they went out into the street, her stepmother clutching the deed in her hand. They were so weak from fright that they could not walk, but had to sit down on the way.

So they went home, with a deadly terror gnawing at their souls; and that evening Jurgis came home and heard their story, and that was the end. Jurgis was sure that they had been swindled, and were ruined; and he tore his hair and cursed like a madman, swearing that he would kill the agent that very night. In the end he seized the paper and rushed out of the house, and all the way across the yards to Halsted Street. He dragged Szedvilas out from his supper, and together they rushed to consult another lawyer. When they entered his office the lawyer sprang up, for Jurgis looked like a crazy person, with flying hair and bloodshot eyes. His companion explained the situation, and the lawyer took the paper and began to read it, while Jurgis stood clutching the desk with knotted hands, trembling in every nerve.

Once or twice the lawyer looked up and asked a question of Szedvilas; the other did not know a word that he was saying, but his eyes were fixed upon the lawyer's face, striving in an agony of dread to read his mind. He saw the lawyer look up and laugh, and he gave a gasp; the man said something to Szedvilas, and Jurgis turned upon his friend, his heart almost stopping.

"Well?" he panted.

"He says it is all right," said Szedvilas.

"All right!"

"Yes, he says it is just as it should be." And Jurgis, in his relief, sank down into a chair.

"Are you sure of it?" he gasped, and made Szedvilas translate question after question. He could not hear it often enough; he could not ask with enough variations. Yes, they had bought the house, they had really bought it. It belonged to them, they had only to pay the money and it would be all right. Then Jurgis covered his face with his hands, for there were tears in his eyes, and he felt like a fool. But he had had such a horrible fright; strong man as he was, it left him almost too weak to stand up.

The lawyer explained that the rental was a form—the property was said to be merely rented until the last payment had been made, the purpose being to make it easier to turn the party out if he did not make the payments. So long as they paid, however, they had nothing to fear, the house was all theirs.

Jurgis was so grateful that he paid the half dollar the lawyer asked without winking an eyelash, and then rushed home to tell the news to the family. He found Ona in a faint and the babies screaming, and the whole house in an uproar—for it had been believed by all that he had gone to murder the agent. It was hours before the excitement could be calmed; and all through that cruel night Jurgis would wake up now and then and hear Ona and her stepmother in the next room, sobbing softly to themselves.

# Chapter 5

They had bought their home. It was hard for them to realize that the wonderful house was theirs to move into whenever they chose. They spent all their time thinking about it, and what they were going to put into it. As their week with Aniele was up in three days, they lost no time in getting ready. They had to make some shift to furnish it, and every instant of their leisure was given to discussing this.

A person who had such a task before him would not need to look very far in Packingtown—he had only to walk up the avenue and read the signs, or get into a streetcar, to obtain full information as to pretty much everything a human creature could need. It was quite touching, the zeal of people to see that his health and happiness were provided for. Did the person wish to smoke? There was a little discourse about cigars, showing him exactly why the Thomas Jefferson Five-cent Perfecto was the only cigar worthy of the name. Had he, on the other hand, smoked too much? Here was a remedy for the smoking habit, twenty-five doses for a quarter, and a cure absolutely guaranteed in ten doses. In innumerable ways such as this, the traveler found that somebody had been busied to make smooth his paths through the world, and to let him know what had been done for him. In Packingtown the advertisements had a style all of their own, adapted to the peculiar population. One would be tenderly solicitous. "Is your wife pale?" it would inquire. "Is she discouraged, does she drag herself about the house and find fault with everything? Why do you not tell her to try Dr. Lanahan's Life Preservers?" Another would be jocular in tone, slapping you on the back, so to speak. "Don't be a chump!" it would exclaim. "Go and get the Goliath Bunion Cure." "Get a move on you!" would chime in another. "It's easy, if you wear the Eureka Two-fifty Shoe."

Among these importunate signs was one that had caught the attention of the family by its pictures. It showed two very pretty little birds building themselves a home; and Marija had asked an acquaintance to read it to her, and told them that it related to the furnishing of a house. "Feather your nest," it ran—and went on to say that it could furnish all the necessary feathers for a four-room nest for the ludicrously small sum of seventy-five dollars. The particularly important thing about this offer was that only a small part of the money need be had at once—the rest one might pay a few dollars every month. Our friends had to have some furniture, there was no getting away from that; but their little fund of money had sunk so low that they could hardly get to sleep at night, and so they fled to this as their deliverance. There was more agony and another paper for Elzbieta to sign, and then one night when Jurgis came home, he was told the breathless tidings that the furniture had arrived and was safely stowed in the house: a parlor set of four pieces, a bedroom set of three pieces, a dining room table and four chairs, a toilet set with beautiful pink roses painted all over it, an assortment of crockery, also with pink roses—and so on. One of the plates in the set had been found broken when they unpacked it, and Ona was going to the store the first thing in the morning to make them change it; also they had promised three saucepans, and there had only two come, and did Jurgis think that they were trying to cheat them?

The next day they went to the house; and when the men came from work they ate a few hurried mouthfuls at Aniele's, and then set to work at the task of carrying their belongings to their new home. The distance was in reality over two miles, but Jurgis made two trips that night, each time with a huge pile of mattresses and bedding on his head, with bundles of clothing and bags and things tied up inside. Anywhere else in Chicago he would have stood a good chance of being arrested; but the policemen in Packingtown were apparently used to these informal movings, and contented themselves with a cursory examination now and then. It was quite wonderful to see how fine the house looked, with all the things in it, even by the dim light of a lamp: it was really home, and almost as exciting as the placard had described it. Ona was fairly dancing, and she and Cousin Marija took Jurgis by the arm and escorted him from room to room, sitting in each chair by turns, and then insisting that he should do the same. One chair squeaked with his great weight, and they screamed with fright, and woke the baby and brought everybody running. Altogether it was a great day; and tired as they were, Jurgis and Ona sat up late, contented simply to hold each other and gaze in rapture about the room. They were going to be married as soon as they could get everything settled, and a little spare money put by; and this was to be their home—that little room yonder would be theirs!

It was in truth a never-ending delight, the fixing up of this house. They had no money to spend for the pleasure of spending, but there were a few absolutely necessary things, and the buying of these was a perpetual adventure for Ona. It must always be done at night, so that Jurgis could go along; and even if it were only a pepper cruet, or half a dozen glasses for ten cents, that was enough for an expedition. On Saturday night they came home with a great basketful of things, and spread them out on the table, while every one stood round, and the children climbed up on the chairs, or howled to be lifted up to see. There were sugar and salt and tea and crackers, and a can of lard and a milk pail, and a scrubbing brush, and a pair of shoes for the second oldest boy, and a can of oil, and a tack hammer, and a pound of nails. These last were to be driven into the walls of the kitchen and the bedrooms, to hang things on; and there was a family discussion as to the place where each one was to be driven. Then Jurgis would try to hammer, and hit his fingers because the hammer was too small, and get mad because Ona had refused to let him pay fifteen cents more and get a bigger hammer; and Ona would be invited to try it herself, and hurt her thumb, and cry out, which necessitated the thumb's being kissed by Jurgis. Finally, after every one had had a try, the nails would be driven, and something hung up. Jurgis had come home with a big packing box on his head, and he sent Jonas to get another that he had bought. He meant to take one side out of these tomorrow, and put shelves in them, and make them into bureaus and places to keep things for the bedrooms. The nest which had been advertised had not included feathers for quite so many birds as there were in this family.

They had, of course, put their dining table in the kitchen, and the dining room was used as the bedroom of Teta Elzbieta and five of her children. She and the two youngest slept in the only bed, and the other three had a mattress on the floor. Ona and her cousin dragged a mattress into the parlor and slept at night, and the three men and the oldest boy slept in the other room, having nothing but the very level floor to rest on for the present. Even so, however, they slept soundly—it was necessary for Teta Elzbieta to pound more than once on the door at a quarter past five every morning. She would have ready a great pot full of steaming black coffee, and oatmeal and bread and smoked sausages; and then she would fix them their dinner pails with more thick slices of bread with lard between them—they could not afford butter—and some onions and a piece of cheese, and so they would tramp away to work.

This was the first time in his life that he had ever really worked, it seemed to Jurgis; it was the first time that he had ever had anything to do which took all he had in him. Jurgis had stood with the rest up in the gallery and watched the men on the killing beds, marveling at their speed and power as if they had been wonderful machines; it somehow never occurred to one to think of the flesh-and-blood side of it—that is, not until he actually got down into the pit and took off his coat. Then he saw things in a different light, he got at the inside of them. The pace they set here, it was one that called for every faculty of a man—from the instant the first steer fell till the sounding of the noon whistle, and again from half-past twelve till heaven only knew what hour in the late afternoon or evening, there was never one instant's rest for a man, for his hand or his eye or his brain. Jurgis saw how they managed it; there were portions of the work which determined the pace of the rest, and for these they had picked men whom they paid high wages, and whom they changed frequently. You might easily pick out these pacemakers, for they worked under the eye of the bosses, and they worked like men possessed. This was called "speeding up the gang," and if any man could not keep up with the pace, there were hundreds outside begging to try.

Yet Jurgis did not mind it; he rather enjoyed it. It saved him the necessity of flinging his arms about and fidgeting as he did in most work. He would laugh to himself as he ran down the line, darting a glance now and then at the man ahead of him. It was not the pleasantest work one could think of, but it was necessary work; and what more had a man the right to ask than a chance to do something useful, and to get good pay for doing it?

So Jurgis thought, and so he spoke, in his bold, free way; very much to his surprise, he found that it had a tendency to get him into trouble. For most of the men here took a fearfully different view of the thing. He was quite dismayed when he first began to find it out—that most of the men hated their work. It seemed strange, it was even terrible, when you came to find out the universality of the sentiment; but it was certainly the fact—they hated their work. They hated the bosses and they hated the owners; they hated the whole place, the whole neighborhood—even the whole city, with an all-inclusive hatred, bitter and fierce. Women and little children would fall to cursing about it; it was rotten, rotten as hell—everything was rotten. When Jurgis would ask them what they meant, they would begin to get suspicious, and content themselves with saying, "Never mind, you stay here and see for yourself."

One of the first problems that Jurgis ran upon was that of the unions. He had had no experience with unions, and he had to have it explained to him that the men were banded together for the purpose of fighting for their rights. Jurgis asked them what they meant by their rights, a question in which he was quite sincere, for he had not any idea of any rights that he had, except the right to hunt for a job, and do as he was told when he got it. Generally, however, this harmless question would only make his fellow workingmen lose their tempers and call him a fool. There was a delegate of the butcher-helpers' union who came to see Jurgis to enroll him; and when Jurgis found that this meant that he would have to part with some of his money, he froze up directly, and the delegate, who was an Irishman and only knew a few words of Lithuanian, lost his temper and began to threaten him. In the end Jurgis got into a fine rage, and made it sufficiently plain that it would take more than one Irishman to scare him into a union. Little by little he gathered that the main thing the men wanted was to put a stop to the habit of "speeding-up"; they were trying their best to force a lessening of the pace, for there were some, they said, who could not keep up with it, whom it was killing. But Jurgis had no sympathy with such ideas as this—he could do the work himself, and so could the rest of them, he declared, if they were good for anything. If they couldn't do it, let them go somewhere else. Jurgis had not studied the books, and he would not have known how to pronounce "laissez faire"; but he had been round the world enough to know that a man has to shift for himself in it, and that if he gets the worst of it, there is nobody to listen to him holler.

Yet there have been known to be philosophers and plain men who swore by Malthus in the books, and would, nevertheless, subscribe to a relief fund in time of a famine. It was the same with Jurgis, who consigned the unfit to destruction, while going about all day sick at heart because of his poor old father, who was wandering somewhere in the yards begging for a chance to earn his bread. Old Antanas had been a worker ever since he was a child; he had run away from home when he was twelve, because his father beat him for trying to learn to read. And he was a faithful man, too; he was a man you might leave alone for a month, if only you had made him understand what you wanted him to do in the meantime. And now here he was, worn out in soul and body, and with no more place in the world than a sick dog. He had his home, as it happened, and some one who would care for him if he never got a job; but his son could not help thinking, suppose this had not been the case. Antanas Rudkus had been into every building in Packingtown by this time, and into nearly every room; he had stood mornings among the crowd of applicants till the very policemen had come to know his face and to tell him to go home and give it up. He had been likewise to all the stores and saloons for a mile about, begging for some little thing to do; and everywhere they had ordered him out, sometimes with curses, and not once even stopping to ask him a question.

So, after all, there was a crack in the fine structure of Jurgis' faith in things as they are. The crack was wide while Dede Antanas was hunting a job—and it was yet wider when he finally got it. For one evening the old man came home in a great state of excitement, with the tale that he had been approached by a man in one of the corridors of the pickle rooms of Durham's, and asked what he would pay to get a job. He had not known what to make of this at first; but the man had gone on with matter-of-fact frankness to say that he could get him a job, provided that he were willing to pay one-third of his wages for it. Was he a boss? Antanas had asked; to which the man had replied that that was nobody's business, but that he could do what he said.

Jurgis had made some friends by this time, and he sought one of them and asked what this meant. The friend, who was named Tamoszius Kuszleika, was a sharp little man who folded hides on the killing beds, and he listened to what Jurgis had to say without seeming at all surprised. They were common enough, he said, such cases of petty graft. It was simply some boss who proposed to add a little to his income. After Jurgis had been there awhile he would know that the plants were simply honeycombed with rottenness of that sort—the bosses grafted off the men, and they grafted off each other; and some day the superintendent would find out about the boss, and then he would graft off the boss. Warming to the subject, Tamoszius went on to explain the situation. Here was Durham's, for instance, owned by a man who was trying to make as much money out of it as he could, and did not care in the least how he did it; and underneath him, ranged in ranks and grades like an army, were managers and superintendents and foremen, each one driving the man next below him and trying to squeeze out of him as much work as possible. And all the men of the same rank were pitted against each other; the accounts of each were kept separately, and every man lived in terror of losing his job, if another made a better record than he. So from top to bottom the place was simply a seething caldron of jealousies and hatreds; there was no loyalty or decency anywhere about it, there was no place in it where a man counted for anything against a dollar. And worse than there being no decency, there was not even any honesty. The reason for that? Who could say? It must have been old Durham in the beginning; it was a heritage which the self-made merchant had left to his son, along with his millions.

Jurgis would find out these things for himself, if he stayed there long enough; it was the men who had to do all the dirty jobs, and so there was no deceiving them; and they caught the spirit of the place, and did like all the rest. Jurgis had come there, and thought he was going to make himself useful, and rise and become a skilled man; but he would soon find out his error—for nobody rose in Packingtown by doing good work. You could lay that down for a rule—if you met a man who was rising in Packingtown, you met a knave. That man who had been sent to Jurgis' father by the boss, he would rise; the man who told tales and spied upon his fellows would rise; but the man who minded his own business and did his work—why, they would "speed him up" till they had worn him out, and then they would throw him into the gutter.

Jurgis went home with his head buzzing. Yet he could not bring himself to believe such things—no, it could not be so. Tamoszius was simply another of the grumblers. He was a man who spent all his time fiddling; and he would go to parties at night and not get home till sunrise, and so of course he did not feel like work. Then, too, he was a puny little chap; and so he had been left behind in the race, and that was why he was sore. And yet so many strange things kept coming to Jurgis' notice every day!

He tried to persuade his father to have nothing to do with the offer. But old Antanas had begged until he was worn out, and all his courage was gone; he wanted a job, any sort of a job. So the next day he went and found the man who had spoken to him, and promised to bring him a third of all he earned; and that same day he was put to work in Durham's cellars. It was a "pickle room," where there was never a dry spot to stand upon, and so he had to take nearly the whole of his first week's earnings to buy him a pair of heavy-soled boots. He was a "squeedgie" man; his job was to go about all day with a long-handled mop, swabbing up the floor. Except that it was damp and dark, it was not an unpleasant job, in summer.

Now Antanas Rudkus was the meekest man that God ever put on earth; and so Jurgis found it a striking confirmation of what the men all said, that his father had been at work only two days before he came home as bitter as any of them, and cursing Durham's with all the power of his soul. For they had set him to cleaning out the traps; and the family sat round and listened in wonder while he told them what that meant. It seemed that he was working in the room where the men prepared the beef for canning, and the beef had lain in vats full of chemicals, and men with great forks speared it out and dumped it into trucks, to be taken to the cooking room. When they had speared out all they could reach, they emptied the vat on the floor, and then with shovels scraped up the balance and dumped it into the truck. This floor was filthy, yet they set Antanas with his mop slopping the "pickle" into a hole that connected with a sink, where it was caught and used over again forever; and if that were not enough, there was a trap in the pipe, where all the scraps of meat and odds and ends of refuse were caught, and every few days it was the old man's task to clean these out, and shovel their contents into one of the trucks with the rest of the meat!

This was the experience of Antanas; and then there came also Jonas and Marija with tales to tell. Marija was working for one of the independent packers, and was quite beside herself and outrageous with triumph over the sums of money she was making as a painter of cans. But one day she walked home with a pale-faced little woman who worked opposite to her, Jadvyga Marcinkus by name, and Jadvyga told her how she, Marija, had chanced to get her job. She had taken the place of an Irishwoman who had been working in that factory ever since any one could remember. For over fifteen years, so she declared. Mary Dennis was her name, and a long time ago she had been seduced, and had a little boy; he was a cripple, and an epileptic, but still he was all that she had in the world to love, and they had lived in a little room alone somewhere back of Halsted Street, where the Irish were. Mary had had consumption, and all day long you might hear her coughing as she worked; of late she had been going all to pieces, and when Marija came, the "forelady" had suddenly decided to turn her off. The forelady had to come up to a certain standard herself, and could not stop for sick people, Jadvyga explained. The fact that Mary had been there so long had not made any difference to her—it was doubtful if she even knew that, for both the forelady and the superintendent were new people, having only been there two or three years themselves. Jadvyga did not know what had become of the poor creature; she would have gone to see her, but had been sick herself. She had pains in her back all the time, Jadvyga explained, and feared that she had womb trouble. It was not fit work for a woman, handling fourteen-pound cans all day.

It was a striking circumstance that Jonas, too, had gotten his job by the misfortune of some other person. Jonas pushed a truck loaded with hams from the smoke rooms on to an elevator, and thence to the packing rooms. The trucks were all of iron, and heavy, and they put about threescore hams on each of them, a load of more than a quarter of a ton. On the uneven floor it was a task for a man to start one of these trucks, unless he was a giant; and when it was once started he naturally tried his best to keep it going. There was always the boss prowling about, and if there was a second's delay he would fall to cursing; Lithuanians and Slovaks and such, who could not understand what was said to them, the bosses were wont to kick about the place like so many dogs. Therefore these trucks went for the most part on the run; and the predecessor of Jonas had been jammed against the wall by one and crushed in a horrible and nameless manner.

All of these were sinister incidents; but they were trifles compared to what Jurgis saw with his own eyes before long. One curious thing he had noticed, the very first day, in his profession of shoveler of guts; which was the sharp trick of the floor bosses whenever there chanced to come a "slunk" calf. Any man who knows anything about butchering knows that the flesh of a cow that is about to calve, or has just calved, is not fit for food. A good many of these came every day to the packing houses—and, of course, if they had chosen, it would have been an easy matter for the packers to keep them till they were fit for food. But for the saving of time and fodder, it was the law that cows of that sort came along with the others, and whoever noticed it would tell the boss, and the boss would start up a conversation with the government inspector, and the two would stroll away. So in a trice the carcass of the cow would be cleaned out, and entrails would have vanished; it was Jurgis' task to slide them into the trap, calves and all, and on the floor below they took out these "slunk" calves, and butchered them for meat, and used even the skins of them.

One day a man slipped and hurt his leg; and that afternoon, when the last of the cattle had been disposed of, and the men were leaving, Jurgis was ordered to remain and do some special work which this injured man had usually done. It was late, almost dark, and the government inspectors had all gone, and there were only a dozen or two of men on the floor. That day they had killed about four thousand cattle, and these cattle had come in freight trains from far states, and some of them had got hurt. There were some with broken legs, and some with gored sides; there were some that had died, from what cause no one could say; and they were all to be disposed of, here in darkness and silence. "Downers," the men called them; and the packing house had a special elevator upon which they were raised to the killing beds, where the gang proceeded to handle them, with an air of businesslike nonchalance which said plainer than any words that it was a matter of everyday routine. It took a couple of hours to get them out of the way, and in the end Jurgis saw them go into the chilling rooms with the rest of the meat, being carefully scattered here and there so that they could not be identified. When he came home that night he was in a very somber mood, having begun to see at last how those might be right who had laughed at him for his faith in America.

# Chapter 6

Jurgis and Ona were very much in love; they had waited a long time—it was now well into the second year, and Jurgis judged everything by the criterion of its helping or hindering their union. All his thoughts were there; he accepted the family because it was a part of Ona. And he was interested in the house because it was to be Ona's home. Even the tricks and cruelties he saw at Durham's had little meaning for him just then, save as they might happen to affect his future with Ona.

The marriage would have been at once, if they had had their way; but this would mean that they would have to do without any wedding feast, and when they suggested this they came into conflict with the old people. To Teta Elzbieta especially the very suggestion was an affliction. What! she would cry. To be married on the roadside like a parcel of beggars! No! No!—Elzbieta had some traditions behind her; she had been a person of importance in her girlhood—had lived on a big estate and had servants, and might have married well and been a lady, but for the fact that there had been nine daughters and no sons in the family. Even so, however, she knew what was decent, and clung to her traditions with desperation. They were not going to lose all caste, even if they had come to be unskilled laborers in Packingtown; and that Ona had even talked of omitting a *veselija* was enough to keep her stepmother lying awake all night. It was in vain for them to say that they had so few friends; they were bound to have friends in time, and then the friends would talk about it. They must not give up what was right for a little money—if they did, the money would never do them any good, they could depend upon that. And Elzbieta would call upon Dede Antanas to support her; there was a fear in the souls of these two, lest this journey to a new country might somehow undermine the old home virtues of their children. The very first Sunday they had all been taken to mass; and poor as they were, Elzbieta had felt it advisable to invest a little of her resources in a representation of the babe of Bethlehem, made in plaster, and painted in brilliant colors. Though it was only a foot high, there was a shrine with four snow-white steeples, and the Virgin standing with her child in her arms, and the kings and shepherds and wise men bowing down before him. It had cost fifty cents; but Elzbieta had a feeling that money spent for such things was not to be counted too closely, it would come back in hidden ways. The piece was beautiful on the parlor mantel, and one could not have a home without some sort of ornament.

The cost of the wedding feast would, of course, be returned to them; but the problem was to raise it even temporarily. They had been in the neighborhood so short a time that they could not get much credit, and there was no one except Szedvilas from whom they could borrow even a little. Evening after evening Jurgis and Ona would sit and figure the expenses, calculating the term of their separation. They could not possibly manage it decently for less than two hundred dollars, and even though they were welcome to count in the whole of the earnings of Marija and Jonas, as a loan, they could not hope to raise this sum in less than four or five months. So Ona began thinking of seeking employment herself, saying that if she had even ordinarily good luck, she might be able to take two months off the time. They were just beginning to adjust themselves to this necessity, when out of the clear sky there fell a thunderbolt upon them—a calamity that scattered all their hopes to the four winds.

About a block away from them there lived another Lithuanian family, consisting of an elderly widow and one grown son; their name was Majauszkis, and our friends struck up an acquaintance with them before long. One evening they came over for a visit, and naturally the first subject upon which the conversation turned was the neighborhood and its history; and then Grandmother Majauszkiene, as the old lady was called, proceeded to recite to them a string of horrors that fairly froze their blood. She was a wrinkled-up and wizened personage—she must have been eighty—and as she mumbled the grim story through her toothless gums, she seemed a very old witch to them. Grandmother Majauszkiene had lived in the midst of misfortune so long that it had come to be her element, and she talked about starvation, sickness, and death as other people might about weddings and holidays.

The thing came gradually. In the first place as to the house they had bought, it was not new at all, as they had supposed; it was about fifteen years old, and there was nothing new upon it but the paint, which was so bad that it needed to be put on new every year or two. The house was one of a whole row that was built by a company which existed to make money by swindling poor people. The family had paid fifteen hundred dollars for it, and it had not cost the builders five hundred, when it was new. Grandmother Majauszkiene knew that because her son belonged to a political organization with a contractor who put up exactly such houses. They used the very flimsiest and cheapest material; they built the houses a dozen at a time, and they cared about nothing at all except the outside shine. The family could take her word as to the trouble they would have, for she had been through it all—she and her son had bought their house in exactly the same way. They had fooled the company, however, for her son was a skilled man, who made as high as a hundred dollars a month, and as he had had sense enough not to marry, they had been able to pay for the house.

Grandmother Majauszkiene saw that her friends were puzzled at this remark; they did not quite see how paying for the house was "fooling the company." Evidently they were very inexperienced. Cheap as the houses were, they were sold with the idea that the people who bought them would not be able to pay for them. When they failed—if it were only by a single month—they would lose the house and all that they had paid on it, and then the company would sell it over again. And did they often get a chance to do that? Dieve! (Grandmother Majauszkiene raised her hands.) They did it—how often no one could say, but certainly more than half of the time. They might ask any one who knew anything at all about Packingtown as to that; she had been living here ever since this house was built, and she could tell them all about it. And had it ever been sold before? Susimilkie! Why, since it had been built, no less than four families that their informant could name had tried to buy it and failed. She would tell them a little about it.

The first family had been Germans. The families had all been of different nationalities—there had been a representative of several races that had displaced each other in the stockyards. Grandmother Majauszkiene had come to America with her son at a time when so far as she knew there was only one other Lithuanian family in the district; the workers had all been Germans then—skilled cattle butchers that the packers had brought from abroad to start the business. Afterward, as cheaper labor had come, these Germans had moved away. The next were the Irish—there had been six or eight years when Packingtown had been a regular Irish city. There were a few colonies of them still here, enough to run all the unions and the police force and get all the graft; but most of those who were working in the packing houses had gone away at the next drop in wages—after the big strike. The Bohemians had come then, and after them the Poles. People said that old man Durham himself was responsible for these immigrations; he had sworn that he would fix the people of Packingtown so that they would never again call a strike on him, and so he had sent his agents into every city and village in Europe to spread the tale of the chances of work and high wages at the stockyards. The people had come in hordes; and old Durham had squeezed them tighter and tighter, speeding them up and grinding them to pieces and sending for new ones. The Poles, who had come by tens of thousands, had been driven to the wall by the Lithuanians, and now the Lithuanians were giving way to the Slovaks. Who there was poorer and more miserable than the Slovaks, Grandmother Majauszkiene had no idea, but the packers would find them, never fear. It was easy to bring them, for wages were really much higher, and it was only when it was too late that the poor people found out that everything else was higher too. They were like rats in a trap, that was the truth; and more of them were piling in every day. By and by they would have their revenge, though, for the thing was getting beyond human endurance, and the people would rise and murder the packers. Grandmother Majauszkiene was a socialist, or some such strange thing; another son of hers was working in the mines of Siberia, and the old lady herself had made speeches in her time—which made her seem all the more terrible to her present auditors.

They called her back to the story of the house. The German family had been a good sort. To be sure there had been a great many of them, which was a common failing in Packingtown; but they had worked hard, and the father had been a steady man, and they had a good deal more than half paid for the house. But he had been killed in an elevator accident in Durham's.

Then there had come the Irish, and there had been lots of them, too; the husband drank and beat the children—the neighbors could hear them shrieking any night. They were behind with their rent all the time, but the company was good to them; there was some politics back of that, Grandmother Majauszkiene could not say just what, but the Laffertys had belonged to the "War Whoop League," which was a sort of political club of all the thugs and rowdies in the district; and if you belonged to that, you could never be arrested for anything. Once upon a time old Lafferty had been caught with a gang that had stolen cows from several of the poor people of the neighborhood and butchered them in an old shanty back of the yards and sold them. He had been in jail only three days for it, and had come out laughing, and had not even lost his place in the packing house. He had gone all to ruin with the drink, however, and lost his power; one of his sons, who was a good man, had kept him and the family up for a year or two, but then he had got sick with consumption.

That was another thing, Grandmother Majauszkiene interrupted herself—this house was unlucky. Every family that lived in it, some one was sure to get consumption. Nobody could tell why that was; there must be something about the house, or the way it was built—some folks said it was because the building had been begun in the dark of the moon. There were dozens of houses that way in Packingtown. Sometimes there would be a particular room that you could point out—if anybody slept in that room he was just as good as dead. With this house it had been the Irish first; and then a Bohemian family had lost a child of it—though, to be sure, that was uncertain, since it was hard to tell what was the matter with children who worked in the yards. In those days there had been no law about the age of children—the packers had worked all but the babies. At this remark the family looked puzzled, and Grandmother Majauszkiene again had to make an explanation—that it was against the law for children to work before they were sixteen. What was the sense of that? they asked. They had been thinking of letting little Stanislovas go to work. Well, there was no need to worry, Grandmother Majauszkiene said—the law made no difference except that it forced people to lie about the ages of their children. One would like to know what the lawmakers expected them to do; there were families that had no possible means of support except the children, and the law provided them no other way of getting a living. Very often a man could get no work in Packingtown for months, while a child could go and get a place easily; there was always some new machine, by which the packers could get as much work out of a child as they had been able to get out of a man, and for a third of the pay.

To come back to the house again, it was the woman of the next family that had died. That was after they had been there nearly four years, and this woman had had twins regularly every year—and there had been more than you could count when they moved in. After she died the man would go to work all day and leave them to shift for themselves—the neighbors would help them now and then, for they would almost freeze to death. At the end there were three days that they were alone, before it was found out that the father was dead. He was a "floorsman" at Jones's, and a wounded steer had broken loose and mashed him against a pillar. Then the children had been taken away, and the company had sold the house that very same week to a party of emigrants.

So this grim old women went on with her tale of horrors. How much of it was exaggeration—who could tell? It was only too plausible. There was that about consumption, for instance. They knew nothing about consumption whatever, except that it made people cough; and for two weeks they had been worrying about a coughing-spell of Antanas. It seemed to shake him all over, and it never stopped; you could see a red stain wherever he had spit upon the floor.

And yet all these things were as nothing to what came a little later. They had begun to question the old lady as to why one family had been unable to pay, trying to show her by figures that it ought to have been possible; and Grandmother Majauszkiene had disputed their figures—"You say twelve dollars a month; but that does not include the interest."

Then they stared at her. "Interest!" they cried.

"Interest on the money you still owe," she answered.

"But we don't have to pay any interest! they exclaimed, three or four at once.

"We only have to pay twelve dollars each month."

And for this she laughed at them. "You are like all the rest," she said; "they trick you and eat you alive. They never sell the houses without interest. Get your deed, and see."

Then, with a horrible sinking of the heart, Teta Elzbieta unlocked her bureau and brought out the paper that had already caused them so many agonies. Now they sat round, scarcely breathing, while the old lady, who could read English, ran over it. "Yes," she said, finally, "here it is, of course: 'With interest thereon monthly, at the rate of seven per cent per annum.'"

And there followed a dead silence. "What does that mean?" asked Jurgis finally, almost in a whisper.

"That means," replied the other, "that you have to pay them seven dollars next month, as well as the twelve dollars."

Then again there was not a sound. It was sickening, like a nightmare, in which suddenly something gives way beneath you, and you feel yourself sinking, sinking, down into bottomless abysses. As if in a flash of lightning they saw themselves—victims of a relentless fate, cornered, trapped, in the grip of destruction. All the fair structure of their hopes came crashing about their ears.—And all the time the old woman was going on talking. They wished that she would be still; her voice sounded like the croaking of some dismal raven. Jurgis sat with his hands clenched and beads of perspiration on his forehead, and there was a great lump in Ona's throat, choking her. Then suddenly Teta Elzbieta broke the silence with a wail, and Marija began to wring her hands and sob,

"Ai! Ai! Beda man!"

All their outcry did them no good, of course. There sat Grandmother Majauszkiene, unrelenting, typifying fate. No, of course it was not fair, but then fairness had nothing to do with it. And of course they had not known it. They had not been intended to know it. But it was in the deed, and that was all that was necessary, as they would find when the time came.

Somehow or other they got rid of their guest, and then they passed a night of lamentation. The children woke up and found out that something was wrong, and they wailed and would not be comforted. In the morning, of course, most of them had to go to work, the packing houses would not stop for their sorrows; but by seven o'clock Ona and her stepmother were standing at the door of the office of the agent. Yes, he told them, when he came, it was quite true that they would have to pay interest. And then Teta Elzbieta broke forth into protestations and reproaches, so that the people outside stopped and peered in at the window. The agent was as bland as ever. He was deeply pained, he said. He had not told them, simply because he had supposed they would understand that they had to pay interest upon their debt, as a matter of course.

So they came away, and Ona went down to the yards, and at noontime saw Jurgis and told him. Jurgis took it stolidly—he had made up his mind to it by this time. It was part of fate; they would manage it somehow—he made his usual answer, "I will work harder." It would upset their plans for a time; and it would perhaps be necessary for Ona to get work after all. Then Ona added that Teta Elzbieta had decided that little Stanislovas would have to work too. It was not fair to let Jurgis and her support the family—the family would have to help as it could. Previously Jurgis had scouted this idea, but now knit his brows and nodded his head slowly—yes, perhaps it would be best; they would all have to make some sacrifices now.

So Ona set out that day to hunt for work; and at night Marija came home saying that she had met a girl named Jasaityte who had a friend that worked in one of the wrapping rooms in Brown's, and might get a place for Ona there; only the forelady was the kind that takes presents—it was no use for any one to ask her for a place unless at the same time they slipped a ten-dollar bill into her hand. Jurgis was not in the least surprised at this now—he merely asked what the wages of the place would be. So negotiations were opened, and after an interview Ona came home and reported that the forelady seemed to like her, and had said that, while she was not sure, she thought she might be able to put her at work sewing covers on hams, a job at which she would earn as much as eight or ten dollars a week. That was a bid, so Marija reported, after consulting her friend; and then there was an anxious conference at home. The work was done in one of the cellars, and Jurgis did not want Ona to work in such a place; but then it was easy work, and one could not have everything. So in the end Ona, with a ten-dollar bill burning a hole in her palm, had another interview with the forelady.

Meantime Teta Elzbieta had taken Stanislovas to the priest and gotten a certificate to the effect that he was two years older than he was; and with it the little boy now sallied forth to make his fortune in the world. It chanced that Durham had just put in a wonderful new lard machine, and when the special policeman in front of the time station saw Stanislovas and his document, he smiled to himself and told him to go—"Czia! Czia!" pointing. And so Stanislovas went down a long stone corridor, and up a flight of stairs, which took him into a room lighted by electricity, with the new machines for filling lard cans at work in it. The lard was finished on the floor above, and it came in little jets, like beautiful, wriggling, snow-white snakes of unpleasant odor. There were several kinds and sizes of jets, and after a certain precise quantity had come out, each stopped automatically, and the wonderful machine made a turn, and took the can under another jet, and so on, until it was filled neatly to the brim, and pressed tightly, and smoothed off. To attend to all this and fill several hundred cans of lard per hour, there were necessary two human creatures, one of whom knew how to place an empty lard can on a certain spot every few seconds, and the other of whom knew how to take a full lard can off a certain spot every few seconds and set it upon a tray.

And so, after little Stanislovas had stood gazing timidly about him for a few minutes, a man approached him, and asked what he wanted, to which Stanislovas said, "Job." Then the man said "How old?" and Stanislovas answered, "Sixtin." Once or twice every year a state inspector would come wandering through the packing plants, asking a child here and there how old he was; and so the packers were very careful to comply with the law, which cost them as much trouble as was now involved in the boss's taking the document from the little boy, and glancing at it, and then sending it to the office to be filed away. Then he set some one else at a different job, and showed the lad how to place a lard can every time the empty arm of the remorseless machine came to him; and so was decided the place in the universe of little Stanislovas, and his destiny till the end of his days. Hour after hour, day after day, year after year, it was fated that he should stand upon a certain square foot of floor from seven in the morning until noon, and again from half-past twelve till half-past five, making never a motion and thinking never a thought, save for the setting of lard cans. In summer the stench of the warm lard would be nauseating, and in winter the cans would all but freeze to his naked little fingers in the unheated cellar. Half the year it would be dark as night when he went in to work, and dark as night again when he came out, and so he would never know what the sun looked like on weekdays. And for this, at the end of the week, he would carry home three dollars to his family, being his pay at the rate of five cents per hour—just about his proper share of the total earnings of the million and three-quarters of children who are now engaged in earning their livings in the United States.

And meantime, because they were young, and hope is not to be stifled before its time, Jurgis and Ona were again calculating; for they had discovered that the wages of Stanislovas would a little more than pay the interest, which left them just about as they had been before! It would be but fair to them to say that the little boy was delighted with his work, and at the idea of earning a lot of money; and also that the two were very much in love with each other.

# Chapter 7

All summer long the family toiled, and in the fall they had money enough for Jurgis and Ona to be married according to home traditions of decency. In the latter part of November they hired a hall, and invited all their new acquaintances, who came and left them over a hundred dollars in debt.

It was a bitter and cruel experience, and it plunged them into an agony of despair. Such a time, of all times, for them to have it, when their hearts were made tender! Such a pitiful beginning it was for their married life; they loved each other so, and they could not have the briefest respite! It was a time when everything cried out to them that they ought to be happy; when wonder burned in their hearts, and leaped into flame at the slightest breath. They were shaken to the depths of them, with the awe of love realized—and was it so very weak of them that they cried out for a little peace? They had opened their hearts, like flowers to the springtime, and the merciless winter had fallen upon them. They wondered if ever any love that had blossomed in the world had been so crushed and trampled!

Over them, relentless and savage, there cracked the lash of want; the morning after the wedding it sought them as they slept, and drove them out before daybreak to work. Ona was scarcely able to stand with exhaustion; but if she were to lose her place they would be ruined, and she would surely lose it if she were not on time that day. They all had to go, even little Stanislovas, who was ill from overindulgence in sausages and sarsaparilla. All that day he stood at his lard machine, rocking unsteadily, his eyes closing in spite of him; and he all but lost his place even so, for the foreman booted him twice to waken him.

It was fully a week before they were all normal again, and meantime, with whining children and cross adults, the house was not a pleasant place to live in. Jurgis lost his temper very little, however, all things considered. It was because of Ona; the least glance at her was always enough to make him control himself. She was so sensitive—she was not fitted for such a life as this; and a hundred times a day, when he thought of her, he would clench his hands and fling himself again at the task before him. She was too good for him, he told himself, and he was afraid, because she was his. So long he had hungered to possess her, but now that the time had come he knew that he had not earned the right; that she trusted him so was all her own simple goodness, and no virtue of his. But he was resolved that she should never find this out, and so was always on the watch to see that he did not betray any of his ugly self; he would take care even in little matters, such as his manners, and his habit of swearing when things went wrong. The tears came so easily into Ona's eyes, and she would look at him so appealingly—it kept Jurgis quite busy making resolutions, in addition to all the other things he had on his mind. It was true that more things were going on at this time in the mind of Jurgis than ever had in all his life before.

He had to protect her, to do battle for her against the horror he saw about them. He was all that she had to look to, and if he failed she would be lost; he would wrap his arms about her, and try to hide her from the world. He had learned the ways of things about him now. It was a war of each against all, and the devil take the hindmost. You did not give feasts to other people, you waited for them to give feasts to you. You went about with your soul full of suspicion and hatred; you understood that you were environed by hostile powers that were trying to get your money, and who used all the virtues to bait their traps with. The store-keepers plastered up their windows with all sorts of lies to entice you; the very fences by the wayside, the lampposts and telegraph poles, were pasted over with lies. The great corporation which employed you lied to you, and lied to the whole country—from top to bottom it was nothing but one gigantic lie.

So Jurgis said that he understood it; and yet it was really pitiful, for the struggle was so unfair—some had so much the advantage! Here he was, for instance, vowing upon his knees that he would save Ona from harm, and only a week later she was suffering atrociously, and from the blow of an enemy that he could not possibly have thwarted. There came a day when the rain fell in torrents; and it being December, to be wet with it and have to sit all day long in one of the cold cellars of Brown's was no laughing matter. Ona was a working girl, and did not own waterproofs and such things, and so Jurgis took her and put her on the streetcar. Now it chanced that this car line was owned by gentlemen who were trying to make money. And the city having passed an ordinance requiring them to give transfers, they had fallen into a rage; and first they had made a rule that transfers could be had only when the fare was paid; and later, growing still uglier, they had made another—that the passenger must ask for the transfer, the conductor was not allowed to offer it. Now Ona had been told that she was to get a transfer; but it was not her way to speak up, and so she merely waited, following the conductor about with her eyes, wondering when he would think of her. When at last the time came for her to get out, she asked for the transfer, and was refused. Not knowing what to make of this, she began to argue with the conductor, in a language of which he did not understand a word. After warning her several times, he pulled the bell and the car went on—at which Ona burst into tears. At the next corner she got out, of course; and as she had no more money, she had to walk the rest of the way to the yards in the pouring rain. And so all day long she sat shivering, and came home at night with her teeth chattering and pains in her head and back. For two weeks afterward she suffered cruelly—and yet every day she had to drag herself to her work. The forewoman was especially severe with Ona, because she believed that she was obstinate on account of having been refused a holiday the day after her wedding. Ona had an idea that her "forelady" did not like to have her girls marry—perhaps because she was old and ugly and unmarried herself.

There were many such dangers, in which the odds were all against them. Their children were not as well as they had been at home; but how could they know that there was no sewer to their house, and that the drainage of fifteen years was in a cesspool under it? How could they know that the pale-blue milk that they bought around the corner was watered, and doctored with formaldehyde besides? When the children were not well at home, Teta Elzbieta would gather herbs and cure them; now she was obliged to go to the drugstore and buy extracts—and how was she to know that they were all adulterated? How could they find out that their tea and coffee, their sugar and flour, had been doctored; that their canned peas had been colored with copper salts, and their fruit jams with aniline dyes? And even if they had known it, what good would it have done them, since there was no place within miles of them where any other sort was to be had? The bitter winter was coming, and they had to save money to get more clothing and bedding; but it would not matter in the least how much they saved, they could not get anything to keep them warm. All the clothing that was to be had in the stores was made of cotton and shoddy, which is made by tearing old clothes to pieces and weaving the fiber again. If they paid higher prices, they might get frills and fanciness, or be cheated; but genuine quality they could not obtain for love nor money. A young friend of Szedvilas', recently come from abroad, had become a clerk in a store on Ashland Avenue, and he narrated with glee a trick that had been played upon an unsuspecting countryman by his boss. The customer had desired to purchase an alarm clock, and the boss had shown him two exactly similar, telling him that the price of one was a dollar and of the other a dollar seventy-five. Upon being asked what the difference was, the man had wound up the first halfway and the second all the way, and showed the customer how the latter made twice as much noise; upon which the customer remarked that he was a sound sleeper, and had better take the more expensive clock!

There is a poet who sings that

> "Deeper their heart grows and nobler their bearing,
> Whose youth in the fires of anguish hath died."

But it was not likely that he had reference to the kind of anguish that comes with destitution, that is so endlessly bitter and cruel, and yet so sordid and petty, so ugly, so humiliating—unredeemed by the slightest touch of dignity or even of pathos. It is a kind of anguish that poets have not commonly dealt with; its very words are not admitted into the vocabulary of poets—the details of it cannot be told in polite society at all. How, for instance, could any one expect to excite sympathy among lovers of good literature by telling how a family found their home alive with vermin, and of all the suffering and inconvenience and humiliation they were put to, and the hard-earned money they spent, in efforts to get rid of them? After long hesitation and uncertainty they paid twenty-five cents for a big package of insect powder—a patent preparation which chanced to be ninety-five per cent gypsum, a harmless earth which had cost about two cents to prepare. Of course it had not the least effect, except upon a few roaches which had the misfortune to drink water after eating it, and so got their inwards set in a coating of plaster of Paris. The family, having no idea of this, and no more money to throw away, had nothing to do but give up and submit to one more misery for the rest of their days.

Then there was old Antanas. The winter came, and the place where he worked was a dark, unheated cellar, where you could see your breath all day, and where your fingers sometimes tried to freeze. So the old man's cough grew every day worse, until there came a time when it hardly ever stopped, and he had become a nuisance about the place. Then, too, a still more dreadful thing happened to him; he worked in a place where his feet were soaked in chemicals, and it was not long before they had eaten through his new boots. Then sores began to break out on his feet, and grow worse and worse. Whether it was that his blood was bad, or there had been a cut, he could not say; but he asked the men about it, and learned that it was a regular thing—it was the saltpeter. Every one felt it, sooner or later, and then it was all up with him, at least for that sort of work. The sores would never heal—in the end his toes would drop off, if he did not quit. Yet old Antanas would not quit; he saw the suffering of his family, and he remembered what it had cost him to get a job. So he tied up his feet, and went on limping about and coughing, until at last he fell to pieces, all at once and in a heap, like the One-Horse Shay. They carried him to a dry place and laid him on the floor, and that night two of the men helped him home. The poor old man was put to bed, and though he tried it every morning until the end, he never could get up again. He would lie there and cough and cough, day and night, wasting away to a mere skeleton. There came a time when there was so little flesh on him that the bones began to poke through—which was a horrible thing to see or even to think of. And one night he had a choking fit, and a little river of blood came out of his mouth. The family, wild with terror, sent for a doctor, and paid half a dollar to be told that there was nothing to be done. Mercifully the doctor did not say this so that the old man could hear, for he was still clinging to the faith that tomorrow or next day he would be better, and could go back to his job. The company had sent word to him that they would keep it for him—or rather Jurgis had bribed one of the men to come one Sunday afternoon and say they had. Dede Antanas continued to believe it, while three more hemorrhages came; and then at last one morning they found him stiff and cold. Things were not going well with them then, and though it nearly broke Teta Elzbieta's heart, they were forced to dispense with nearly all the decencies of a funeral; they had only a hearse, and one hack for the women and children; and Jurgis, who was learning things fast, spent all Sunday making a bargain for these, and he made it in the presence of witnesses, so that when the man tried to charge him for all sorts of incidentals, he did not have to pay. For twenty-five years old Antanas Rudkus and his son had dwelt in the forest together, and it was hard to part in this way; perhaps it was just as well that Jurgis had to give all his attention to the task of having a funeral without being bankrupted, and so had no time to indulge in memories and grief.

Now the dreadful winter was come upon them. In the forests, all summer long, the branches of the trees do battle for light, and some of them lose and die; and then come the raging blasts, and the storms of snow and hail, and strew the ground with these weaker branches. Just so it was in Packingtown; the whole district braced itself for the struggle that was an agony, and those whose time was come died off in hordes. All the year round they had been serving as cogs in the great packing machine; and now was the time for the renovating of it, and the replacing of damaged parts. There came pneumonia and grippe, stalking among them, seeking for weakened constitutions; there was the annual harvest of those whom tuberculosis had been dragging down. There came cruel, cold, and biting winds, and blizzards of snow, all testing relentlessly for failing muscles and impoverished blood. Sooner or later came the day when the unfit one did not report for work; and then, with no time lost in waiting, and no inquiries or regrets, there was a chance for a new hand.

The new hands were here by the thousands. All day long the gates of the packing houses were besieged by starving and penniless men; they came, literally, by the thousands every single morning, fighting with each other for a chance for life. Blizzards and cold made no difference to them, they were always on hand; they were on hand two hours before the sun rose, an hour before the work began. Sometimes their faces froze, sometimes their feet and their hands; sometimes they froze all together—but still they came, for they had no other place to go. One day Durham advertised in the paper for two hundred men to cut ice; and all that day the homeless and starving of the city came trudging through the snow from all over its two hundred square miles. That night forty score of them crowded into the station house of the stockyards district—they filled the rooms, sleeping in each other's laps, toboggan fashion, and they piled on top of each other in the corridors, till the police shut the doors and left some to freeze outside. On the morrow, before daybreak, there were three thousand at Durham's, and the police reserves had to be sent for to quell the riot. Then Durham's bosses picked out twenty of the biggest; the "two hundred" proved to have been a printer's error.

Four or five miles to the eastward lay the lake, and over this the bitter winds came raging. Sometimes the thermometer would fall to ten or twenty degrees below zero at night, and in the morning the streets would be piled with snowdrifts up to the first-floor windows. The streets through which our friends had to go to their work were all unpaved and full of deep holes and gullies; in summer, when it rained hard, a man might have to wade to his waist to get to his house; and now in winter it was no joke getting through these places, before light in the morning and after dark at night. They would wrap up in all they owned, but they could not wrap up against exhaustion; and many a man gave out in these battles with the snowdrifts, and lay down and fell asleep.

And if it was bad for the men, one may imagine how the women and children fared. Some would ride in the cars, if the cars were running; but when you are making only five cents an hour, as was little Stanislovas, you do not like to spend that much to ride two miles. The children would come to the yards with great shawls about their ears, and so tied up that you could hardly find them—and still there would be accidents. One bitter morning in February the little boy who worked at the lard machine with Stanislovas came about an hour late, and screaming with pain. They unwrapped him, and a man began vigorously rubbing his ears; and as they were frozen stiff, it took only two or three rubs to break them short off. As a result of this, little Stanislovas conceived a terror of the cold that was almost a mania. Every morning, when it came time to start for the yards, he would begin to cry and protest. Nobody knew quite how to manage him, for threats did no good—it seemed to be something that he could not control, and they feared sometimes that he would go into convulsions. In the end it had to be arranged that he always went with Jurgis, and came home with him again; and often, when the snow was deep, the man would carry him the whole way on his shoulders. Sometimes Jurgis would be working until late at night, and then it was pitiful, for there was no place for the little fellow to wait, save in the doorways or in a corner of the killing beds, and he would all but fall asleep there, and freeze to death.

There was no heat upon the killing beds; the men might exactly as well have worked out of doors all winter. For that matter, there was very little heat anywhere in the building, except in the cooking rooms and such places—and it was the men who worked in these who ran the most risk of all, because whenever they had to pass to another room they had to go through ice-cold corridors, and sometimes with nothing on above the waist except a sleeveless undershirt. On the killing beds you were apt to be covered with blood, and it would freeze solid; if you leaned against a pillar, you would freeze to that, and if you put your hand upon the blade of your knife, you would run a chance of leaving your skin on it. The men would tie up their feet in newspapers and old sacks, and these would be soaked in blood and frozen, and then soaked again, and so on, until by nighttime a man would be walking on great lumps the size of the feet of an elephant. Now and then, when the bosses were not looking, you would see them plunging their feet and ankles into the steaming hot carcass of the steer, or darting across the room to the hot-water jets. The cruelest thing of all was that nearly all of them—all of those who used knives—were unable to wear gloves, and their arms would be white with frost and their hands would grow numb, and then of course there would be accidents. Also the air would be full of steam, from the hot water and the hot blood, so that you could not see five feet before you; and then, with men rushing about at the speed they kept up on the killing beds, and all with butcher knives, like razors, in their hands—well, it was to be counted as a wonder that there were not more men slaughtered than cattle.

And yet all this inconvenience they might have put up with, if only it had not been for one thing—if only there had been some place where they might eat. Jurgis had either to eat his dinner amid the stench in which he had worked, or else to rush, as did all his companions, to any one of the hundreds of liquor stores which stretched out their arms to him. To the west of the yards ran Ashland Avenue, and here was an unbroken line of saloons—"Whiskey Row," they called it; to the north was Forty-seventh Street, where there were half a dozen to the block, and at the angle of the two was "Whiskey Point," a space of fifteen or twenty acres, and containing one glue factory and about two hundred saloons.

One might walk among these and take his choice: "Hot pea-soup and boiled cabbage today." "Sauerkraut and hot frankfurters. Walk in." "Bean soup and stewed lamb. Welcome." All of these things were printed in many languages, as were also the names of the resorts, which were infinite in their variety and appeal. There was the "Home Circle" and the "Cosey Corner"; there were "Firesides" and "Hearthstones" and "Pleasure Palaces" and "Wonderlands" and "Dream Castles" and "Love's Delights." Whatever else they were called, they were sure to be called "Union Headquarters," and to hold out a welcome to workingmen; and there was always a warm stove, and a chair near it, and some friends to laugh and talk with. There was only one condition attached,—you must drink. If you went in not intending to drink, you would be put out in no time, and if you were slow about going, like as not you would get your head split open with a beer bottle in the bargain. But all of the men understood the convention and drank; they believed that by it they were getting something for nothing—for they did not need to take more than one drink, and upon the strength of it they might fill themselves up with a good hot dinner. This did not always work out in practice, however, for there was pretty sure to be a friend who would treat you, and then you would have to treat him. Then some one else would come in—and, anyhow, a few drinks were good for a man who worked hard. As he went back he did not shiver so, he had more courage for his task; the deadly brutalizing monotony of it did not afflict him so,—he had ideas while he worked, and took a more cheerful view of his circumstances. On the way home, however, the shivering was apt to come on him again; and so he would have to stop once or twice to warm up against the cruel cold. As there were hot things to eat in this saloon too, he might get home late to his supper, or he might not get home at all. And then his wife might set out to look for him, and she too would feel the cold; and perhaps she would have some of the children with her—and so a whole family would drift into drinking, as the current of a river drifts downstream. As if to complete the chain, the packers all paid their men in checks, refusing all requests to pay in coin; and where in Packingtown could a man go to have his check cashed but to a saloon, where he could pay for the favor by spending a part of the money?

From all of these things Jurgis was saved because of Ona. He never would take but the one drink at noontime; and so he got the reputation of being a surly fellow, and was not quite welcome at the saloons, and had to drift about from one to another. Then at night he would go straight home, helping Ona and Stanislovas, or often putting the former on a car. And when he got home perhaps he would have to trudge several blocks, and come staggering back through the snowdrifts with a bag of coal upon his shoulder. Home was not a very attractive place—at least not this winter. They had only been able to buy one stove, and this was a small one, and proved not big enough to warm even the kitchen in the bitterest weather. This made it hard for Teta Elzbieta all day, and for the children when they could not get to school. At night they would sit huddled round this stove, while they ate their supper off their laps; and then Jurgis and Jonas would smoke a pipe, after which they would all crawl into their beds to get warm, after putting out the fire to save the coal. Then they would have some frightful experiences with the cold. They would sleep with all their clothes on, including their overcoats, and put over them all the bedding and spare clothing they owned; the children would sleep all crowded into one bed, and yet even so they could not keep warm. The outside ones would be shivering and sobbing, crawling over the others and trying to get down into the center, and causing a fight. This old house with the leaky weatherboards was a very different thing from their cabins at home, with great thick walls plastered inside and outside with mud; and the cold which came upon them was a living thing, a demon-presence in the room. They would waken in the midnight hours, when everything was black; perhaps they would hear it yelling outside, or perhaps there would be deathlike stillness—and that would be worse yet. They could feel the cold as it crept in through the cracks, reaching out for them with its icy, death-dealing fingers; and they would crouch and cower, and try to hide from it, all in vain. It would come, and it would come; a grisly thing, a specter born in the black caverns of terror; a power primeval, cosmic, shadowing the tortures of the lost souls flung out to chaos and destruction. It was cruel iron-hard; and hour after hour they would cringe in its grasp, alone, alone. There would be no one to hear them if they cried out; there would be no help, no mercy. And so on until morning—when they would go out to another day of toil, a little weaker, a little nearer to the time when it would be their turn to be shaken from the tree.

# Chapter 8

Yet even by this deadly winter the germ of hope was not to be kept from sprouting in their hearts. It was just at this time that the great adventure befell Marija.

The victim was Tamoszius Kuszleika, who played the violin. Everybody laughed at them, for Tamoszius was petite and frail, and Marija could have picked him up and carried him off under one arm. But perhaps that was why she fascinated him; the sheer volume of Marija's energy was overwhelming. That first night at the wedding Tamoszius had hardly taken his eyes off her; and later on, when he came to find that she had really the heart of a baby, her voice and her violence ceased to terrify him, and he got the habit of coming to pay her visits on Sunday afternoons. There was no place to entertain company except in the kitchen, in the midst of the family, and Tamoszius would sit there with his hat between his knees, never saying more than half a dozen words at a time, and turning red in the face before he managed to say those; until finally Jurgis would clap him upon the back, in his hearty way, crying, "Come now, brother, give us a tune." And then Tamoszius' face would light up and he would get out his fiddle, tuck it under his chin, and play. And forthwith the soul of him would flame up and become eloquent—it was almost an impropriety, for all the while his gaze would be fixed upon Marija's face, until she would begin to turn red and lower her eyes. There was no resisting the music of Tamoszius, however; even the children would sit awed and wondering, and the tears would run down Teta Elzbieta's cheeks. A wonderful privilege it was to be thus admitted into the soul of a man of genius, to be allowed to share the ecstasies and the agonies of his inmost life.

Then there were other benefits accruing to Marija from this friendship—benefits of a more substantial nature. People paid Tamoszius big money to come and make music on state occasions; and also they would invite him to parties and festivals, knowing well that he was too good-natured to come without his fiddle, and that having brought it, he could be made to play while others danced. Once he made bold to ask Marija to accompany him to such a party, and Marija accepted, to his great delight—after which he never went anywhere without her, while if the celebration were given by friends of his, he would invite the rest of the family also. In any case Marija would bring back a huge pocketful of cakes and sandwiches for the children, and stories of all the good things she herself had managed to consume. She was compelled, at these parties, to spend most of her time at the refreshment table, for she could not dance with anybody except other women and very old men; Tamoszius was of an excitable temperament, and afflicted with a frantic jealousy, and any unmarried man who ventured to put his arm about the ample waist of Marija would be certain to throw the orchestra out of tune.

It was a great help to a person who had to toil all the week to be able to look forward to some such relaxation as this on Saturday nights. The family was too poor and too hardworked to make many acquaintances; in Packingtown, as a rule, people know only their near neighbors and shopmates, and so the place is like a myriad of little country villages. But now there was a member of the family who was permitted to travel and widen her horizon; and so each week there would be new personalities to talk about,—how so-and-so was dressed, and where she worked, and what she got, and whom she was in love with; and how this man had jilted his girl, and how she had quarreled with the other girl, and what had passed between them; and how another man beat his wife, and spent all her earnings upon drink, and pawned her very clothes. Some people would have scorned this talk as gossip; but then one has to talk about what one knows.

It was one Saturday night, as they were coming home from a wedding, that Tamoszius found courage, and set down his violin case in the street and spoke his heart; and then Marija clasped him in her arms. She told them all about it the next day, and fairly cried with happiness, for she said that Tamoszius was a lovely man. After that he no longer made love to her with his fiddle, but they would sit for hours in the kitchen, blissfully happy in each other's arms; it was the tacit convention of the family to know nothing of what was going on in that corner.

They were planning to be married in the spring, and have the garret of the house fixed up, and live there. Tamoszius made good wages; and little by little the family were paying back their debt to Marija, so she ought soon to have enough to start life upon—only, with her preposterous softheartedness, she would insist upon spending a good part of her money every week for things which she saw they needed. Marija was really the capitalist of the party, for she had become an expert can painter by this time—she was getting fourteen cents for every hundred and ten cans, and she could paint more than two cans every minute. Marija felt, so to speak, that she had her hand on the throttle, and the neighborhood was vocal with her rejoicings.

Yet her friends would shake their heads and tell her to go slow; one could not count upon such good fortune forever—there were accidents that always happened. But Marija was not to be prevailed upon, and went on planning and dreaming of all the treasures she was going to have for her home; and so, when the crash did come, her grief was painful to see.

For her canning factory shut down! Marija would about as soon have expected to see the sun shut down—the huge establishment had been to her a thing akin to the planets and the seasons. But now it was shut! And they had not given her any explanation, they had not even given her a day's warning; they had simply posted a notice one Saturday that all hands would be paid off that afternoon, and would not resume work for at least a month! And that was all that there was to it—her job was gone!

It was the holiday rush that was over, the girls said in answer to Marija's inquiries; after that there was always a slack. Sometimes the factory would start up on half time after a while, but there was no telling—it had been known to stay closed until way into the summer. The prospects were bad at present, for truckmen who worked in the storerooms said that these were piled up to the ceilings, so that the firm could not have found room for another week's output of cans. And they had turned off three-quarters of these men, which was a still worse sign, since it meant that there were no orders to be filled. It was all a swindle, can-painting, said the girls—you were crazy with delight because you were making twelve or fourteen dollars a week, and saving half of it; but you had to spend it all keeping alive while you were out, and so your pay was really only half what you thought.

Marija came home, and because she was a person who could not rest without danger of explosion, they first had a great house cleaning, and then she set out to search Packingtown for a job to fill up the gap. As nearly all the canning establishments were shut down, and all the girls hunting work, it will be readily understood that Marija did not find any. Then she took to trying the stores and saloons, and when this failed she even traveled over into the far-distant regions near the lake front, where lived the rich people in great palaces, and begged there for some sort of work that could be done by a person who did not know English.

The men upon the killing beds felt also the effects of the slump which had turned Marija out; but they felt it in a different way, and a way which made Jurgis understand at last all their bitterness. The big packers did not turn their hands off and close down, like the canning factories; but they began to run for shorter and shorter hours. They had always required the men to be on the killing beds and ready for work at seven o'clock, although there was almost never any work to be done till the buyers out in the yards had gotten to work, and some cattle had come over the chutes. That would often be ten or eleven o'clock, which was bad enough, in all conscience; but now, in the slack season, they would perhaps not have a thing for their men to do till late in the afternoon. And so they would have to loaf around, in a place where the thermometer might be twenty degrees below zero! At first one would see them running about, or skylarking with each other, trying to keep warm; but before the day was over they would become quite chilled through and exhausted, and, when the cattle finally came, so near frozen that to move was an agony. And then suddenly the place would spring into activity, and the merciless "speeding-up" would begin!

There were weeks at a time when Jurgis went home after such a day as this with not more than two hours' work to his credit—which meant about thirty-five cents. There were many days when the total was less than half an hour, and others when there was none at all. The general average was six hours a day, which meant for Jurgis about six dollars a week; and this six hours of work would be done after standing on the killing bed till one o'clock, or perhaps even three or four o'clock, in the afternoon. Like as not there would come a rush of cattle at the very end of the day, which the men would have to dispose of before they went home, often working by electric light till nine or ten, or even twelve or one o'clock, and without a single instant for a bite of supper. The men were at the mercy of the cattle. Perhaps the buyers would be holding off for better prices—if they could scare the shippers into thinking that they meant to buy nothing that day, they could get their own terms. For some reason the cost of fodder for cattle in the yards was much above the market price—and you were not allowed to bring your own fodder! Then, too, a number of cars were apt to arrive late in the day, now that the roads were blocked with snow, and the packers would buy their cattle that night, to get them cheaper, and then would come into play their ironclad rule, that all cattle must be killed the same day they were bought. There was no use kicking about this—there had been one delegation after another to see the packers about it, only to be told that it was the rule, and that there was not the slightest chance of its ever being altered. And so on Christmas Eve Jurgis worked till nearly one o'clock in the morning, and on Christmas Day he was on the killing bed at seven o'clock.

All this was bad; and yet it was not the worst. For after all the hard work a man did, he was paid for only part of it. Jurgis had once been among those who scoffed at the idea of these huge concerns cheating; and so now he could appreciate the bitter irony of the fact that it was precisely their size which enabled them to do it with impunity. One of the rules on the killing beds was that a man who was one minute late was docked an hour; and this was economical, for he was made to work the balance of the hour—he was not allowed to stand round and wait. And on the other hand if he came ahead of time he got no pay for that—though often the bosses would start up the gang ten or fifteen minutes before the whistle. And this same custom they carried over to the end of the day; they did not pay for any fraction of an hour—for "broken time." A man might work full fifty minutes, but if there was no work to fill out the hour, there was no pay for him. Thus the end of every day was a sort of lottery—a struggle, all but breaking into open war between the bosses and the men, the former trying to rush a job through and the latter trying to stretch it out. Jurgis blamed the bosses for this, though the truth to be told it was not always their fault; for the packers kept them frightened for their lives—and when one was in danger of falling behind the standard, what was easier than to catch up by making the gang work awhile "for the church"? This was a savage witticism the men had, which Jurgis had to have explained to him. Old man Jones was great on missions and such things, and so whenever they were doing some particularly disreputable job, the men would wink at each other and say, "Now we're working for the church!"

One of the consequences of all these things was that Jurgis was no longer perplexed when he heard men talk of fighting for their rights. He felt like fighting now himself; and when the Irish delegate of the butcher-helpers' union came to him a second time, he received him in a far different spirit. A wonderful idea it now seemed to Jurgis, this of the men—that by combining they might be able to make a stand and conquer the packers! Jurgis wondered who had first thought of it; and when he was told that it was a common thing for men to do in America, he got the first inkling of a meaning in the phrase "a free country." The delegate explained to him how it depended upon their being able to get every man to join and stand by the organization, and so Jurgis signified that he was willing to do his share. Before another month was by, all the working members of his family had union cards, and wore their union buttons conspicuously and with pride. For fully a week they were quite blissfully happy, thinking that belonging to a union meant an end to all their troubles.

But only ten days after she had joined, Marija's canning factory closed down, and that blow quite staggered them. They could not understand why the union had not prevented it, and the very first time she attended a meeting Marija got up and made a speech about it. It was a business meeting, and was transacted in English, but that made no difference to Marija; she said what was in her, and all the pounding of the chairman's gavel and all the uproar and confusion in the room could not prevail. Quite apart from her own troubles she was boiling over with a general sense of the injustice of it, and she told what she thought of the packers, and what she thought of a world where such things were allowed to happen; and then, while the echoes of the hall rang with the shock of her terrible voice, she sat down again and fanned herself, and the meeting gathered itself together and proceeded to discuss the election of a recording secretary.

Jurgis too had an adventure the first time he attended a union meeting, but it was not of his own seeking. Jurgis had gone with the desire to get into an inconspicuous corner and see what was done; but this attitude of silent and open-eyed attention had marked him out for a victim. Tommy Finnegan was a little Irishman, with big staring eyes and a wild aspect, a "hoister" by trade, and badly cracked. Somewhere back in the far-distant past Tommy Finnegan had had a strange experience, and the burden of it rested upon him. All the balance of his life he had done nothing but try to make it understood. When he talked he caught his victim by the buttonhole, and his face kept coming closer and closer—which was trying, because his teeth were so bad. Jurgis did not mind that, only he was frightened. The method of operation of the higher intelligences was Tom Finnegan's theme, and he desired to find out if Jurgis had ever considered that the representation of things in their present similarity might be altogether unintelligible upon a more elevated plane. There were assuredly wonderful mysteries about the developing of these things; and then, becoming confidential, Mr. Finnegan proceeded to tell of some discoveries of his own. "If ye have iver had onything to do wid shperrits," said he, and looked inquiringly at Jurgis, who kept shaking his head. "Niver mind, niver mind," continued the other, "but their influences may be operatin' upon ye; it's shure as I'm tellin' ye, it's them that has the reference to the immejit surroundin's that has the most of power. It was vouchsafed to me in me youthful days to be acquainted with shperrits" and so Tommy Finnegan went on, expounding a system of philosophy, while the perspiration came out on Jurgis' forehead, so great was his agitation and embarrassment. In the end one of the men, seeing his plight, came over and rescued him; but it was some time before he was able to find any one to explain things to him, and meanwhile his fear lest the strange little Irishman should get him cornered again was enough to keep him dodging about the room the whole evening.

He never missed a meeting, however. He had picked up a few words of English by this time, and friends would help him to understand. They were often very turbulent meetings, with half a dozen men declaiming at once, in as many dialects of English; but the speakers were all desperately in earnest, and Jurgis was in earnest too, for he understood that a fight was on, and that it was his fight. Since the time of his disillusionment, Jurgis had sworn to trust no man, except in his own family; but here he discovered that he had brothers in affliction, and allies. Their one chance for life was in union, and so the struggle became a kind of crusade. Jurgis had always been a member of the church, because it was the right thing to be, but the church had never touched him, he left all that for the women. Here, however, was a new religion—one that did touch him, that took hold of every fiber of him; and with all the zeal and fury of a convert he went out as a missionary. There were many nonunion men among the Lithuanians, and with these he would labor and wrestle in prayer, trying to show them the right. Sometimes they would be obstinate and refuse to see it, and Jurgis, alas, was not always patient! He forgot how he himself had been blind, a short time ago—after the fashion of all crusaders since the original ones, who set out to spread the gospel of Brotherhood by force of arms.

# Chapter 9

One of the first consequences of the discovery of the union was that Jurgis became desirous of learning English. He wanted to know what was going on at the meetings, and to be able to take part in them, and so he began to look about him, and to try to pick up words. The children, who were at school, and learning fast, would teach him a few; and a friend loaned him a little book that had some in it, and Ona would read them to him. Then Jurgis became sorry that he could not read himself; and later on in the winter, when some one told him that there was a night school that was free, he went and enrolled. After that, every evening that he got home from the yards in time, he would go to the school; he would go even if he were in time for only half an hour. They were teaching him both to read and to speak English—and they would have taught him other things, if only he had had a little time.

Also the union made another great difference with him—it made him begin to pay attention to the country. It was the beginning of democracy with him. It was a little state, the union, a miniature republic; its affairs were every man's affairs, and every man had a real say about them. In other words, in the union Jurgis learned to talk politics. In the place where he had come from there had not been any politics—in Russia one thought of the government as an affliction like the lightning and the hail. "Duck, little brother, duck," the wise old peasants would whisper; "everything passes away." And when Jurgis had first come to America he had supposed that it was the same. He had heard people say that it was a free country—but what did that mean? He found that here, precisely as in Russia, there were rich men who owned everything; and if one could not find any work, was not the hunger he began to feel the same sort of hunger?

When Jurgis had been working about three weeks at Brown's, there had come to him one noontime a man who was employed as a night watchman, and who asked him if he would not like to take out naturalization papers and become a citizen. Jurgis did not know what that meant, but the man explained the advantages. In the first place, it would not cost him anything, and it would get him half a day off, with his pay just the same; and then when election time came he would be able to vote—and there was something in that. Jurgis was naturally glad to accept, and so the night watchman said a few words to the boss, and he was excused for the rest of the day. When, later on, he wanted a holiday to get married he could not get it; and as for a holiday with pay just the same—what power had wrought that miracle heaven only knew! However, he went with the man, who picked up several other newly landed immigrants, Poles, Lithuanians, and Slovaks, and took them all outside, where stood a great four-horse tallyho coach, with fifteen or twenty men already in it. It was a fine chance to see the sights of the city, and the party had a merry time, with plenty of beer handed up from inside. So they drove downtown and stopped before an imposing granite building, in which they interviewed an official, who had the papers all ready, with only the names to be filled in. So each man in turn took an oath of which he did not understand a word, and then was presented with a handsome ornamented document with a big red seal and the shield of the United States upon it, and was told that he had become a citizen of the Republic and the equal of the President himself.

A month or two later Jurgis had another interview with this same man, who told him where to go to "register." And then finally, when election day came, the packing houses posted a notice that men who desired to vote might remain away until nine that morning, and the same night watchman took Jurgis and the rest of his flock into the back room of a saloon, and showed each of them where and how to mark a ballot, and then gave each two dollars, and took them to the polling place, where there was a policeman on duty especially to see that they got through all right. Jurgis felt quite proud of this good luck till he got home and met Jonas, who had taken the leader aside and whispered to him, offering to vote three times for four dollars, which offer had been accepted.

And now in the union Jurgis met men who explained all this mystery to him; and he learned that America differed from Russia in that its government existed under the form of a democracy. The officials who ruled it, and got all the graft, had to be elected first; and so there were two rival sets of grafters, known as political parties, and the one got the office which bought the most votes. Now and then, the election was very close, and that was the time the poor man came in. In the stockyards this was only in national and state elections, for in local elections the Democratic Party always carried everything. The ruler of the district was therefore the Democratic boss, a little Irishman named Mike Scully. Scully held an important party office in the state, and bossed even the mayor of the city, it was said; it was his boast that he carried the stockyards in his pocket. He was an enormously rich man—he had a hand in all the big graft in the neighborhood. It was Scully, for instance, who owned that dump which Jurgis and Ona had seen the first day of their arrival. Not only did he own the dump, but he owned the brick factory as well, and first he took out the clay and made it into bricks, and then he had the city bring garbage to fill up the hole, so that he could build houses to sell to the people. Then, too, he sold the bricks to the city, at his own price, and the city came and got them in its own wagons. And also he owned the other hole near by, where the stagnant water was; and it was he who cut the ice and sold it; and what was more, if the men told truth, he had not had to pay any taxes for the water, and he had built the ice-house out of city lumber, and had not had to pay anything for that. The newspapers had got hold of that story, and there had been a scandal; but Scully had hired somebody to confess and take all the blame, and then skip the country. It was said, too, that he had built his brick-kiln in the same way, and that the workmen were on the city payroll while they did it; however, one had to press closely to get these things out of the men, for it was not their business, and Mike Scully was a good man to stand in with. A note signed by him was equal to a job any time at the packing houses; and also he employed a good many men himself, and worked them only eight hours a day, and paid them the highest wages. This gave him many friends—all of whom he had gotten together into the "War Whoop League," whose clubhouse you might see just outside of the yards. It was the biggest clubhouse, and the biggest club, in all Chicago; and they had prizefights every now and then, and cockfights and even dogfights. The policemen in the district all belonged to the league, and instead of suppressing the fights, they sold tickets for them. The man that had taken Jurgis to be naturalized was one of these "Indians," as they were called; and on election day there would be hundreds of them out, and all with big wads of money in their pockets and free drinks at every saloon in the district. That was another thing, the men said—all the saloon-keepers had to be "Indians," and to put up on demand, otherwise they could not do business on Sundays, nor have any gambling at all. In the same way Scully had all the jobs in the fire department at his disposal, and all the rest of the city graft in the stockyards district; he was building a block of flats somewhere up on Ashland Avenue, and the man who was overseeing it for him was drawing pay as a city inspector of sewers. The city inspector of water pipes had been dead and buried for over a year, but somebody was still drawing his pay. The city inspector of sidewalks was a barkeeper at the War Whoop Cafe—and maybe he could make it uncomfortable for any tradesman who did not stand in with Scully!

Even the packers were in awe of him, so the men said. It gave them pleasure to believe this, for Scully stood as the people's man, and boasted of it boldly when election day came. The packers had wanted a bridge at Ashland Avenue, but they had not been able to get it till they had seen Scully; and it was the same with "Bubbly Creek," which the city had threatened to make the packers cover over, till Scully had come to their aid. "Bubbly Creek" is an arm of the Chicago River, and forms the southern boundary of the yards: all the drainage of the square mile of packing houses empties into it, so that it is really a great open sewer a hundred or two feet wide. One long arm of it is blind, and the filth stays there forever and a day. The grease and chemicals that are poured into it undergo all sorts of strange transformations, which are the cause of its name; it is constantly in motion, as if huge fish were feeding in it, or great leviathans disporting themselves in its depths. Bubbles of carbonic acid gas will rise to the surface and burst, and make rings two or three feet wide. Here and there the grease and filth have caked solid, and the creek looks like a bed of lava; chickens walk about on it, feeding, and many times an unwary stranger has started to stroll across, and vanished temporarily. The packers used to leave the creek that way, till every now and then the surface would catch on fire and burn furiously, and the fire department would have to come and put it out. Once, however, an ingenious stranger came and started to gather this filth in scows, to make lard out of; then the packers took the cue, and got out an injunction to stop him, and afterward gathered it themselves. The banks of "Bubbly Creek" are plastered thick with hairs, and this also the packers gather and clean.

And there were things even stranger than this, according to the gossip of the men. The packers had secret mains, through which they stole billions of gallons of the city's water. The newspapers had been full of this scandal—once there had even been an investigation, and an actual uncovering of the pipes; but nobody had been punished, and the thing went right on. And then there was the condemned meat industry, with its endless horrors. The people of Chicago saw the government inspectors in Packingtown, and they all took that to mean that they were protected from diseased meat; they did not understand that these hundred and sixty-three inspectors had been appointed at the request of the packers, and that they were paid by the United States government to certify that all the diseased meat was kept in the state. They had no authority beyond that; for the inspection of meat to be sold in the city and state the whole force in Packingtown consisted of three henchmen of the local political machine!*

(*Rules and Regulations for the Inspection of Livestock and Their Products. United States Department of Agriculture, Bureau of Animal Industries, Order No. 125:—

Section 1. Proprietors of slaughterhouses, canning, salting, packing, or rendering establishments engaged in the slaughtering of cattle, sheep, or swine, or the packing of any of their products, the carcasses or products of which are to become subjects of interstate or foreign commerce, shall make application to the Secretary of Agriculture for inspection of said animals and their products....

Section 15. Such rejected or condemned animals shall at once be removed by the owners from the pens containing animals which have been inspected and found to be free from disease and fit for human food, and shall be disposed of in accordance with the laws, ordinances, and regulations of the state and municipality in which said rejected or condemned animals are located....

Section 25. A microscopic examination for trichinae shall be made of all swine products exported to countries requiring such examination. No microscopic examination will be made of hogs slaughtered for interstate trade, but this examination shall be confined to those intended for the export trade.)

And shortly afterward one of these, a physician, made the discovery that the carcasses of steers which had been condemned as tubercular by the government inspectors, and which therefore contained ptomaines, which are deadly poisons, were left upon an open platform and carted away to be sold in the city; and so he insisted that these carcasses be treated with an injection of kerosene—and was ordered to resign the same week! So indignant were the packers that they went farther, and compelled the mayor to abolish the whole bureau of inspection; so that since then there has not been even a pretense of any interference with the graft. There was said to be two thousand dollars a week hush money from the tubercular steers alone; and as much again from the hogs which had died of cholera on the trains, and which you might see any day being loaded into boxcars and hauled away to a place called Globe, in Indiana, where they made a fancy grade of lard.

Jurgis heard of these things little by little, in the gossip of those who were obliged to perpetrate them. It seemed as if every time you met a person from a new department, you heard of new swindles and new crimes. There was, for instance, a Lithuanian who was a cattle butcher for the plant where Marija had worked, which killed meat for canning only; and to hear this man describe the animals which came to his place would have been worthwhile for a Dante or a Zola. It seemed that they must have agencies all over the country, to hunt out old and crippled and diseased cattle to be canned. There were cattle which had been fed on "whisky-malt," the refuse of the breweries, and had become what the men called "steerly"—which means covered with boils. It was a nasty job killing these, for when you plunged your knife into them they would burst and splash foul-smelling stuff into your face; and when a man's sleeves were smeared with blood, and his hands steeped in it, how was he ever to wipe his face, or to clear his eyes so that he could see? It was stuff such as this that made the "embalmed beef" that had killed several times as many United States soldiers as all the bullets of the Spaniards; only the army beef, besides, was not fresh canned, it was old stuff that had been lying for years in the cellars.

Then one Sunday evening, Jurgis sat puffing his pipe by the kitchen stove, and talking with an old fellow whom Jonas had introduced, and who worked in the canning rooms at Durham's; and so Jurgis learned a few things about the great and only Durham canned goods, which had become a national institution. They were regular alchemists at Durham's; they advertised a mushroom-catsup, and the men who made it did not know what a mushroom looked like. They advertised "potted chicken,"—and it was like the boardinghouse soup of the comic papers, through which a chicken had walked with rubbers on. Perhaps they had a secret process for making chickens chemically—who knows? said Jurgis' friend; the things that went into the mixture were tripe, and the fat of pork, and beef suet, and hearts of beef, and finally the waste ends of veal, when they had any. They put these up in several grades, and sold them at several prices; but the contents of the cans all came out of the same hopper. And then there was "potted game" and "potted grouse," "potted ham," and "deviled ham"—de-vyled, as the men called it. "De-vyled" ham was made out of the waste ends of smoked beef that were too small to be sliced by the machines; and also tripe, dyed with chemicals so that it would not show white; and trimmings of hams and corned beef; and potatoes, skins and all; and finally the hard cartilaginous gullets of beef, after the tongues had been cut out. All this ingenious mixture was ground up and flavored with spices to make it taste like something. Anybody who could invent a new imitation had been sure of a fortune from old Durham, said Jurgis' informant; but it was hard to think of anything new in a place where so many sharp wits had been at work for so long; where men welcomed tuberculosis in the cattle they were feeding, because it made them fatten more quickly; and where they bought up all the old rancid butter left over in the grocery stores of a continent, and "oxidized" it by a forced-air process, to take away the odor, rechurned it with skim milk, and sold it in bricks in the cities! Up to a year or two ago it had been the custom to kill horses in the yards—ostensibly for fertilizer; but after long agitation the newspapers had been able to make the public realize that the horses were being canned. Now it was against the law to kill horses in Packingtown, and the law was really complied with—for the present, at any rate. Any day, however, one might see sharp-horned and shaggy-haired creatures running with the sheep and yet what a job you would have to get the public to believe that a good part of what it buys for lamb and mutton is really goat's flesh!

There was another interesting set of statistics that a person might have gathered in Packingtown—those of the various afflictions of the workers. When Jurgis had first inspected the packing plants with Szedvilas, he had marveled while he listened to the tale of all the things that were made out of the carcasses of animals, and of all the lesser industries that were maintained there; now he found that each one of these lesser industries was a separate little inferno, in its way as horrible as the killing beds, the source and fountain of them all. The workers in each of them had their own peculiar diseases. And the wandering visitor might be skeptical about all the swindles, but he could not be skeptical about these, for the worker bore the evidence of them about on his own person—generally he had only to hold out his hand.

There were the men in the pickle rooms, for instance, where old Antanas had gotten his death; scarce a one of these that had not some spot of horror on his person. Let a man so much as scrape his finger pushing a truck in the pickle rooms, and he might have a sore that would put him out of the world; all the joints in his fingers might be eaten by the acid, one by one. Of the butchers and floorsmen, the beef-boners and trimmers, and all those who used knives, you could scarcely find a person who had the use of his thumb; time and time again the base of it had been slashed, till it was a mere lump of flesh against which the man pressed the knife to hold it. The hands of these men would be criss-crossed with cuts, until you could no longer pretend to count them or to trace them. They would have no nails,—they had worn them off pulling hides; their knuckles were swollen so that their fingers spread out like a fan. There were men who worked in the cooking rooms, in the midst of steam and sickening odors, by artificial light; in these rooms the germs of tuberculosis might live for two years, but the supply was renewed every hour. There were the beef-luggers, who carried two-hundred-pound quarters into the refrigerator-cars; a fearful kind of work, that began at four o'clock in the morning, and that wore out the most powerful men in a few years. There were those who worked in the chilling rooms, and whose special disease was rheumatism; the time limit that a man could work in the chilling rooms was said to be five years. There were the wool-pluckers, whose hands went to pieces even sooner than the hands of the pickle men; for the pelts of the sheep had to be painted with acid to loosen the wool, and then the pluckers had to pull out this wool with their bare hands, till the acid had eaten their fingers off. There were those who made the tins for the canned meat; and their hands, too, were a maze of cuts, and each cut represented a chance for blood poisoning. Some worked at the stamping machines, and it was very seldom that one could work long there at the pace that was set, and not give out and forget himself and have a part of his hand chopped off. There were the "hoisters," as they were called, whose task it was to press the lever which lifted the dead cattle off the floor. They ran along upon a rafter, peering down through the damp and the steam; and as old Durham's architects had not built the killing room for the convenience of the hoisters, at every few feet they would have to stoop under a beam, say four feet above the one they ran on; which got them into the habit of stooping, so that in a few years they would be walking like chimpanzees. Worst of any, however, were the fertilizer men, and those who served in the cooking rooms. These people could not be shown to the visitor,—for the odor of a fertilizer man would scare any ordinary visitor at a hundred yards, and as for the other men, who worked in tank rooms full of steam, and in some of which there were open vats near the level of the floor, their peculiar trouble was that they fell into the vats; and when they were fished out, there was never enough of them left to be worth exhibiting,—sometimes they would be overlooked for days, till all but the bones of them had gone out to the world as Durham's Pure Leaf Lard!

# Chapter 10

During the early part of the winter the family had had money enough to live and a little over to pay their debts with; but when the earnings of Jurgis fell from nine or ten dollars a week to five or six, there was no longer anything to spare. The winter went, and the spring came, and found them still living thus from hand to mouth, hanging on day by day, with literally not a month's wages between them and starvation. Marija was in despair, for there was still no word about the reopening of the canning factory, and her savings were almost entirely gone. She had had to give up all idea of marrying then; the family could not get along without her—though for that matter she was likely soon to become a burden even upon them, for when her money was all gone, they would have to pay back what they owed her in board. So Jurgis and Ona and Teta Elzbieta would hold anxious conferences until late at night, trying to figure how they could manage this too without starving.

Such were the cruel terms upon which their life was possible, that they might never have nor expect a single instant's respite from worry, a single instant in which they were not haunted by the thought of money. They would no sooner escape, as by a miracle, from one difficulty, than a new one would come into view. In addition to all their physical hardships, there was thus a constant strain upon their minds; they were harried all day and nearly all night by worry and fear. This was in truth not living; it was scarcely even existing, and they felt that it was too little for the price they paid. They were willing to work all the time; and when people did their best, ought they not to be able to keep alive?

There seemed never to be an end to the things they had to buy and to the unforeseen contingencies. Once their water pipes froze and burst; and when, in their ignorance, they thawed them out, they had a terrifying flood in their house. It happened while the men were away, and poor Elzbieta rushed out into the street screaming for help, for she did not even know whether the flood could be stopped, or whether they were ruined for life. It was nearly as bad as the latter, they found in the end, for the plumber charged them seventy-five cents an hour, and seventy-five cents for another man who had stood and watched him, and included all the time the two had been going and coming, and also a charge for all sorts of material and extras. And then again, when they went to pay their January's installment on the house, the agent terrified them by asking them if they had had the insurance attended to yet. In answer to their inquiry he showed them a clause in the deed which provided that they were to keep the house insured for one thousand dollars, as soon as the present policy ran out, which would happen in a few days. Poor Elzbieta, upon whom again fell the blow, demanded how much it would cost them. Seven dollars, the man said; and that night came Jurgis, grim and determined, requesting that the agent would be good enough to inform him, once for all, as to all the expenses they were liable for. The deed was signed now, he said, with sarcasm proper to the new way of life he had learned—the deed was signed, and so the agent had no longer anything to gain by keeping quiet. And Jurgis looked the fellow squarely in the eye, and so the fellow wasted no time in conventional protests, but read him the deed. They would have to renew the insurance every year; they would have to pay the taxes, about ten dollars a year; they would have to pay the water tax, about six dollars a year—(Jurgis silently resolved to shut off the hydrant). This, besides the interest and the monthly installments, would be all—unless by chance the city should happen to decide to put in a sewer or to lay a sidewalk. Yes, said the agent, they would have to have these, whether they wanted them or not, if the city said so. The sewer would cost them about twenty-two dollars, and the sidewalk fifteen if it were wood, twenty-five if it were cement.

So Jurgis went home again; it was a relief to know the worst, at any rate, so that he could no more be surprised by fresh demands. He saw now how they had been plundered; but they were in for it, there was no turning back. They could only go on and make the fight and win—for defeat was a thing that could not even be thought of.

When the springtime came, they were delivered from the dreadful cold, and that was a great deal; but in addition they had counted on the money they would not have to pay for coal—and it was just at this time that Marija's board began to fail. Then, too, the warm weather brought trials of its own; each season had its trials, as they found. In the spring there were cold rains, that turned the streets into canals and bogs; the mud would be so deep that wagons would sink up to the hubs, so that half a dozen horses could not move them. Then, of course, it was impossible for any one to get to work with dry feet; and this was bad for men that were poorly clad and shod, and still worse for women and children. Later came midsummer, with the stifling heat, when the dingy killing beds of Durham's became a very purgatory; one time, in a single day, three men fell dead from sunstroke. All day long the rivers of hot blood poured forth, until, with the sun beating down, and the air motionless, the stench was enough to knock a man over; all the old smells of a generation would be drawn out by this heat—for there was never any washing of the walls and rafters and pillars, and they were caked with the filth of a lifetime. The men who worked on the killing beds would come to reek with foulness, so that you could smell one of them fifty feet away; there was simply no such thing as keeping decent, the most careful man gave it up in the end, and wallowed in uncleanness. There was not even a place where a man could wash his hands, and the men ate as much raw blood as food at dinnertime. When they were at work they could not even wipe off their faces—they were as helpless as newly born babes in that respect; and it may seem like a small matter, but when the sweat began to run down their necks and tickle them, or a fly to bother them, it was a torture like being burned alive. Whether it was the slaughterhouses or the dumps that were responsible, one could not say, but with the hot weather there descended upon Packingtown a veritable Egyptian plague of flies; there could be no describing this—the houses would be black with them. There was no escaping; you might provide all your doors and windows with screens, but their buzzing outside would be like the swarming of bees, and whenever you opened the door they would rush in as if a storm of wind were driving them.

Perhaps the summertime suggests to you thoughts of the country, visions of green fields and mountains and sparkling lakes. It had no such suggestion for the people in the yards. The great packing machine ground on remorselessly, without thinking of green fields; and the men and women and children who were part of it never saw any green thing, not even a flower. Four or five miles to the east of them lay the blue waters of Lake Michigan; but for all the good it did them it might have been as far away as the Pacific Ocean. They had only Sundays, and then they were too tired to walk. They were tied to the great packing machine, and tied to it for life. The managers and superintendents and clerks of Packingtown were all recruited from another class, and never from the workers; they scorned the workers, the very meanest of them. A poor devil of a bookkeeper who had been working in Durham's for twenty years at a salary of six dollars a week, and might work there for twenty more and do no better, would yet consider himself a gentleman, as far removed as the poles from the most skilled worker on the killing beds; he would dress differently, and live in another part of the town, and come to work at a different hour of the day, and in every way make sure that he never rubbed elbows with a laboring man. Perhaps this was due to the repulsiveness of the work; at any rate, the people who worked with their hands were a class apart, and were made to feel it.

In the late spring the canning factory started up again, and so once more Marija was heard to sing, and the love-music of Tamoszius took on a less melancholy tone. It was not for long, however; for a month or two later a dreadful calamity fell upon Marija. Just one year and three days after she had begun work as a can-painter, she lost her job.

It was a long story. Marija insisted that it was because of her activity in the union. The packers, of course, had spies in all the unions, and in addition they made a practice of buying up a certain number of the union officials, as many as they thought they needed. So every week they received reports as to what was going on, and often they knew things before the members of the union knew them. Any one who was considered to be dangerous by them would find that he was not a favorite with his boss; and Marija had been a great hand for going after the foreign people and preaching to them. However that might be, the known facts were that a few weeks before the factory closed, Marija had been cheated out of her pay for three hundred cans. The girls worked at a long table, and behind them walked a woman with pencil and notebook, keeping count of the number they finished. This woman was, of course, only human, and sometimes made mistakes; when this happened, there was no redress—if on Saturday you got less money than you had earned, you had to make the best of it. But Marija did not understand this, and made a disturbance. Marija's disturbances did not mean anything, and while she had known only Lithuanian and Polish, they had done no harm, for people only laughed at her and made her cry. But now Marija was able to call names in English, and so she got the woman who made the mistake to disliking her. Probably, as Marija claimed, she made mistakes on purpose after that; at any rate, she made them, and the third time it happened Marija went on the warpath and took the matter first to the forelady, and when she got no satisfaction there, to the superintendent. This was unheard-of presumption, but the superintendent said he would see about it, which Marija took to mean that she was going to get her money; after waiting three days, she went to see the superintendent again. This time the man frowned, and said that he had not had time to attend to it; and when Marija, against the advice and warning of every one, tried it once more, he ordered her back to her work in a passion. Just how things happened after that Marija was not sure, but that afternoon the forelady told her that her services would not be any longer required. Poor Marija could not have been more dumfounded had the woman knocked her over the head; at first she could not believe what she heard, and then she grew furious and swore that she would come anyway, that her place belonged to her. In the end she sat down in the middle of the floor and wept and wailed.

It was a cruel lesson; but then Marija was headstrong—she should have listened to those who had had experience. The next time she would know her place, as the forelady expressed it; and so Marija went out, and the family faced the problem of an existence again.

It was especially hard this time, for Ona was to be confined before long, and Jurgis was trying hard to save up money for this. He had heard dreadful stories of the midwives, who grow as thick as fleas in Packingtown; and he had made up his mind that Ona must have a man-doctor. Jurgis could be very obstinate when he wanted to, and he was in this case, much to the dismay of the women, who felt that a man-doctor was an impropriety, and that the matter really belonged to them. The cheapest doctor they could find would charge them fifteen dollars, and perhaps more when the bill came in; and here was Jurgis, declaring that he would pay it, even if he had to stop eating in the meantime!

Marija had only about twenty-five dollars left. Day after day she wandered about the yards begging a job, but this time without hope of finding it. Marija could do the work of an able-bodied man, when she was cheerful, but discouragement wore her out easily, and she would come home at night a pitiable object. She learned her lesson this time, poor creature; she learned it ten times over. All the family learned it along with her—that when you have once got a job in Packingtown, you hang on to it, come what will.

Four weeks Marija hunted, and half of a fifth week. Of course she stopped paying her dues to the union. She lost all interest in the union, and cursed herself for a fool that she had ever been dragged into one. She had about made up her mind that she was a lost soul, when somebody told her of an opening, and she went and got a place as a "beef-trimmer." She got this because the boss saw that she had the muscles of a man, and so he discharged a man and put Marija to do his work, paying her a little more than half what he had been paying before.

When she first came to Packingtown, Marija would have scorned such work as this. She was in another canning factory, and her work was to trim the meat of those diseased cattle that Jurgis had been told about not long before. She was shut up in one of the rooms where the people seldom saw the daylight; beneath her were the chilling rooms, where the meat was frozen, and above her were the cooking rooms; and so she stood on an ice-cold floor, while her head was often so hot that she could scarcely breathe. Trimming beef off the bones by the hundred-weight, while standing up from early morning till late at night, with heavy boots on and the floor always damp and full of puddles, liable to be thrown out of work indefinitely because of a slackening in the trade, liable again to be kept overtime in rush seasons, and be worked till she trembled in every nerve and lost her grip on her slimy knife, and gave herself a poisoned wound—that was the new life that unfolded itself before Marija. But because Marija was a human horse she merely laughed and went at it; it would enable her to pay her board again, and keep the family going. And as for Tamoszius—well, they had waited a long time, and they could wait a little longer. They could not possibly get along upon his wages alone, and the family could not live without hers. He could come and visit her, and sit in the kitchen and hold her hand, and he must manage to be content with that. But day by day the music of Tamoszius' violin became more passionate and heartbreaking; and Marija would sit with her hands clasped and her cheeks wet and all her body a-tremble, hearing in the wailing melodies the voices of the unborn generations which cried out in her for life.

Marija's lesson came just in time to save Ona from a similar fate. Ona, too, was dissatisfied with her place, and had far more reason than Marija. She did not tell half of her story at home, because she saw it was a torment to Jurgis, and she was afraid of what he might do. For a long time Ona had seen that Miss Henderson, the forelady in her department, did not like her. At first she thought it was the old-time mistake she had made in asking for a holiday to get married. Then she concluded it must be because she did not give the forelady a present occasionally—she was the kind that took presents from the girls, Ona learned, and made all sorts of discriminations in favor of those who gave them. In the end, however, Ona discovered that it was even worse than that. Miss Henderson was a newcomer, and it was some time before rumor made her out; but finally it transpired that she was a kept woman, the former mistress of the superintendent of a department in the same building. He had put her there to keep her quiet, it seemed—and that not altogether with success, for once or twice they had been heard quarreling. She had the temper of a hyena, and soon the place she ran was a witch's caldron. There were some of the girls who were of her own sort, who were willing to toady to her and flatter her; and these would carry tales about the rest, and so the furies were unchained in the place. Worse than this, the woman lived in a bawdy-house downtown, with a coarse, red-faced Irishman named Connor, who was the boss of the loading-gang outside, and would make free with the girls as they went to and from their work. In the slack seasons some of them would go with Miss Henderson to this house downtown—in fact, it would not be too much to say that she managed her department at Brown's in conjunction with it. Sometimes women from the house would be given places alongside of decent girls, and after other decent girls had been turned off to make room for them. When you worked in this woman's department the house downtown was never out of your thoughts all day—there were always whiffs of it to be caught, like the odor of the Packingtown rendering plants at night, when the wind shifted suddenly. There would be stories about it going the rounds; the girls opposite you would be telling them and winking at you. In such a place Ona would not have stayed a day, but for starvation; and, as it was, she was never sure that she could stay the next day. She understood now that the real reason that Miss Henderson hated her was that she was a decent married girl; and she knew that the talebearers and the toadies hated her for the same reason, and were doing their best to make her life miserable.

But there was no place a girl could go in Packingtown, if she was particular about things of this sort; there was no place in it where a prostitute could not get along better than a decent girl. Here was a population, low-class and mostly foreign, hanging always on the verge of starvation, and dependent for its opportunities of life upon the whim of men every bit as brutal and unscrupulous as the old-time slave drivers; under such circumstances immorality was exactly as inevitable, and as prevalent, as it was under the system of chattel slavery. Things that were quite unspeakable went on there in the packing houses all the time, and were taken for granted by everybody; only they did not show, as in the old slavery times, because there was no difference in color between master and slave.

One morning Ona stayed home, and Jurgis had the man-doctor, according to his whim, and she was safely delivered of a fine baby. It was an enormous big boy, and Ona was such a tiny creature herself, that it seemed quite incredible. Jurgis would stand and gaze at the stranger by the hour, unable to believe that it had really happened.

The coming of this boy was a decisive event with Jurgis. It made him irrevocably a family man; it killed the last lingering impulse that he might have had to go out in the evenings and sit and talk with the men in the saloons. There was nothing he cared for now so much as to sit and look at the baby. This was very curious, for Jurgis had never been interested in babies before. But then, this was a very unusual sort of a baby. He had the brightest little black eyes, and little black ringlets all over his head; he was the living image of his father, everybody said—and Jurgis found this a fascinating circumstance. It was sufficiently perplexing that this tiny mite of life should have come into the world at all in the manner that it had; that it should have come with a comical imitation of its father's nose was simply uncanny.

Perhaps, Jurgis thought, this was intended to signify that it was his baby; that it was his and Ona's, to care for all its life. Jurgis had never possessed anything nearly so interesting—a baby was, when you came to think about it, assuredly a marvelous possession. It would grow up to be a man, a human soul, with a personality all its own, a will of its own! Such thoughts would keep haunting Jurgis, filling him with all sorts of strange and almost painful excitements. He was wonderfully proud of little Antanas; he was curious about all the details of him—the washing and the dressing and the eating and the sleeping of him, and asked all sorts of absurd questions. It took him quite a while to get over his alarm at the incredible shortness of the little creature's legs.

Jurgis had, alas, very little time to see his baby; he never felt the chains about him more than just then. When he came home at night, the baby would be asleep, and it would be the merest chance if he awoke before Jurgis had to go to sleep himself. Then in the morning there was no time to look at him, so really the only chance the father had was on Sundays. This was more cruel yet for Ona, who ought to have stayed home and nursed him, the doctor said, for her own health as well as the baby's; but Ona had to go to work, and leave him for Teta Elzbieta to feed upon the pale blue poison that was called milk at the corner grocery. Ona's confinement lost her only a week's wages—she would go to the factory the second Monday, and the best that Jurgis could persuade her was to ride in the car, and let him run along behind and help her to Brown's when she alighted. After that it would be all right, said Ona, it was no strain sitting still sewing hams all day; and if she waited longer she might find that her dreadful forelady had put some one else in her place. That would be a greater calamity than ever now, Ona continued, on account of the baby. They would all have to work harder now on his account. It was such a responsibility—they must not have the baby grow up to suffer as they had. And this indeed had been the first thing that Jurgis had thought of himself—he had clenched his hands and braced himself anew for the struggle, for the sake of that tiny mite of human possibility.

And so Ona went back to Brown's and saved her place and a week's wages; and so she gave herself some one of the thousand ailments that women group under the title of "womb trouble," and was never again a well person as long as she lived. It is difficult to convey in words all that this meant to Ona; it seemed such a slight offense, and the punishment was so out of all proportion, that neither she nor any one else ever connected the two. "Womb trouble" to Ona did not mean a specialist's diagnosis, and a course of treatment, and perhaps an operation or two; it meant simply headaches and pains in the back, and depression and heartsickness, and neuralgia when she had to go to work in the rain. The great majority of the women who worked in Packingtown suffered in the same way, and from the same cause, so it was not deemed a thing to see the doctor about; instead Ona would try patent medicines, one after another, as her friends told her about them. As these all contained alcohol, or some other stimulant, she found that they all did her good while she took them; and so she was always chasing the phantom of good health, and losing it because she was too poor to continue.

# Chapter 11

During the summer the packing houses were in full activity again, and Jurgis made more money. He did not make so much, however, as he had the previous summer, for the packers took on more hands. There were new men every week, it seemed—it was a regular system; and this number they would keep over to the next slack season, so that every one would have less than ever. Sooner or later, by this plan, they would have all the floating labor of Chicago trained to do their work. And how very cunning a trick was that! The men were to teach new hands, who would some day come and break their strike; and meantime they were kept so poor that they could not prepare for the trial!

But let no one suppose that this superfluity of employees meant easier work for any one! On the contrary, the speeding-up seemed to be growing more savage all the time; they were continually inventing new devices to crowd the work on—it was for all the world like the thumbscrew of the medieval torture chamber. They would get new pacemakers and pay them more; they would drive the men on with new machinery—it was said that in the hog-killing rooms the speed at which the hogs moved was determined by clockwork, and that it was increased a little every day. In piecework they would reduce the time, requiring the same work in a shorter time, and paying the same wages; and then, after the workers had accustomed themselves to this new speed, they would reduce the rate of payment to correspond with the reduction in time! They had done this so often in the canning establishments that the girls were fairly desperate; their wages had gone down by a full third in the past two years, and a storm of discontent was brewing that was likely to break any day. Only a month after Marija had become a beef-trimmer the canning factory that she had left posted a cut that would divide the girls' earnings almost squarely in half; and so great was the indignation at this that they marched out without even a parley, and organized in the street outside. One of the girls had read somewhere that a red flag was the proper symbol for oppressed workers, and so they mounted one, and paraded all about the yards, yelling with rage. A new union was the result of this outburst, but the impromptu strike went to pieces in three days, owing to the rush of new labor. At the end of it the girl who had carried the red flag went downtown and got a position in a great department store, at a salary of two dollars and a half a week.

Jurgis and Ona heard these stories with dismay, for there was no telling when their own time might come. Once or twice there had been rumors that one of the big houses was going to cut its unskilled men to fifteen cents an hour, and Jurgis knew that if this was done, his turn would come soon. He had learned by this time that Packingtown was really not a number of firms at all, but one great firm, the Beef Trust. And every week the managers of it got together and compared notes, and there was one scale for all the workers in the yards and one standard of efficiency. Jurgis was told that they also fixed the price they would pay for beef on the hoof and the price of all dressed meat in the country; but that was something he did not understand or care about.

The only one who was not afraid of a cut was Marija, who congratulated herself, somewhat naively, that there had been one in her place only a short time before she came. Marija was getting to be a skilled beef-trimmer, and was mounting to the heights again. During the summer and fall Jurgis and Ona managed to pay her back the last penny they owed her, and so she began to have a bank account. Tamoszius had a bank account also, and they ran a race, and began to figure upon household expenses once more.

The possession of vast wealth entails cares and responsibilities, however, as poor Marija found out. She had taken the advice of a friend and invested her savings in a bank on Ashland Avenue. Of course she knew nothing about it, except that it was big and imposing—what possible chance has a poor foreign working girl to understand the banking business, as it is conducted in this land of frenzied finance? So Marija lived in a continual dread lest something should happen to her bank, and would go out of her way mornings to make sure that it was still there. Her principal thought was of fire, for she had deposited her money in bills, and was afraid that if they were burned up the bank would not give her any others. Jurgis made fun of her for this, for he was a man and was proud of his superior knowledge, telling her that the bank had fireproof vaults, and all its millions of dollars hidden safely away in them.

However, one morning Marija took her usual detour, and, to her horror and dismay, saw a crowd of people in front of the bank, filling the avenue solid for half a block. All the blood went out of her face for terror. She broke into a run, shouting to the people to ask what was the matter, but not stopping to hear what they answered, till she had come to where the throng was so dense that she could no longer advance. There was a "run on the bank," they told her then, but she did not know what that was, and turned from one person to another, trying in an agony of fear to make out what they meant. Had something gone wrong with the bank? Nobody was sure, but they thought so. Couldn't she get her money? There was no telling; the people were afraid not, and they were all trying to get it. It was too early yet to tell anything—the bank would not open for nearly three hours. So in a frenzy of despair Marija began to claw her way toward the doors of this building, through a throng of men, women, and children, all as excited as herself. It was a scene of wild confusion, women shrieking and wringing their hands and fainting, and men fighting and trampling down everything in their way. In the midst of the melee Marija recollected that she did not have her bankbook, and could not get her money anyway, so she fought her way out and started on a run for home. This was fortunate for her, for a few minutes later the police reserves arrived.

In half an hour Marija was back, Teta Elzbieta with her, both of them breathless with running and sick with fear. The crowd was now formed in a line, extending for several blocks, with half a hundred policemen keeping guard, and so there was nothing for them to do but to take their places at the end of it. At nine o'clock the bank opened and began to pay the waiting throng; but then, what good did that do Marija, who saw three thousand people before her—enough to take out the last penny of a dozen banks?

To make matters worse a drizzling rain came up, and soaked them to the skin; yet all the morning they stood there, creeping slowly toward the goal—all the afternoon they stood there, heartsick, seeing that the hour of closing was coming, and that they were going to be left out. Marija made up her mind that, come what might, she would stay there and keep her place; but as nearly all did the same, all through the long, cold night, she got very little closer to the bank for that. Toward evening Jurgis came; he had heard the story from the children, and he brought some food and dry wraps, which made it a little easier.

The next morning, before daybreak, came a bigger crowd than ever, and more policemen from downtown. Marija held on like grim death, and toward afternoon she got into the bank and got her money—all in big silver dollars, a handkerchief full. When she had once got her hands on them her fear vanished, and she wanted to put them back again; but the man at the window was savage, and said that the bank would receive no more deposits from those who had taken part in the run. So Marija was forced to take her dollars home with her, watching to right and left, expecting every instant that some one would try to rob her; and when she got home she was not much better off. Until she could find another bank there was nothing to do but sew them up in her clothes, and so Marija went about for a week or more, loaded down with bullion, and afraid to cross the street in front of the house, because Jurgis told her she would sink out of sight in the mud. Weighted this way she made her way to the yards, again in fear, this time to see if she had lost her place; but fortunately about ten per cent of the working people of Packingtown had been depositors in that bank, and it was not convenient to discharge that many at once. The cause of the panic had been the attempt of a policeman to arrest a drunken man in a saloon next door, which had drawn a crowd at the hour the people were on their way to work, and so started the "run."

About this time Jurgis and Ona also began a bank account. Besides having paid Jonas and Marija, they had almost paid for their furniture, and could have that little sum to count on. So long as each of them could bring home nine or ten dollars a week, they were able to get along finely. Also election day came round again, and Jurgis made half a week's wages out of that, all net profit. It was a very close election that year, and the echoes of the battle reached even to Packingtown. The two rival sets of grafters hired halls and set off fireworks and made speeches, to try to get the people interested in the matter. Although Jurgis did not understand it all, he knew enough by this time to realize that it was not supposed to be right to sell your vote. However, as every one did it, and his refusal to join would not have made the slightest difference in the results, the idea of refusing would have seemed absurd, had it ever come into his head.

Now chill winds and shortening days began to warn them that the winter was coming again. It seemed as if the respite had been too short—they had not had time enough to get ready for it; but still it came, inexorably, and the hunted look began to come back into the eyes of little Stanislovas. The prospect struck fear to the heart of Jurgis also, for he knew that Ona was not fit to face the cold and the snowdrifts this year. And suppose that some day when a blizzard struck them and the cars were not running, Ona should have to give up, and should come the next day to find that her place had been given to some one who lived nearer and could be depended on?

It was the week before Christmas that the first storm came, and then the soul of Jurgis rose up within him like a sleeping lion. There were four days that the Ashland Avenue cars were stalled, and in those days, for the first time in his life, Jurgis knew what it was to be really opposed. He had faced difficulties before, but they had been child's play; now there was a death struggle, and all the furies were unchained within him. The first morning they set out two hours before dawn, Ona wrapped all in blankets and tossed upon his shoulder like a sack of meal, and the little boy, bundled nearly out of sight, hanging by his coat-tails. There was a raging blast beating in his face, and the thermometer stood below zero; the snow was never short of his knees, and in some of the drifts it was nearly up to his armpits. It would catch his feet and try to trip him; it would build itself into a wall before him to beat him back; and he would fling himself into it, plunging like a wounded buffalo, puffing and snorting in rage. So foot by foot he drove his way, and when at last he came to Durham's he was staggering and almost blind, and leaned against a pillar, gasping, and thanking God that the cattle came late to the killing beds that day. In the evening the same thing had to be done again; and because Jurgis could not tell what hour of the night he would get off, he got a saloon-keeper to let Ona sit and wait for him in a corner. Once it was eleven o'clock at night, and black as the pit, but still they got home.

That blizzard knocked many a man out, for the crowd outside begging for work was never greater, and the packers would not wait long for any one. When it was over, the soul of Jurgis was a song, for he had met the enemy and conquered, and felt himself the master of his fate.—So it might be with some monarch of the forest that has vanquished his foes in fair fight, and then falls into some cowardly trap in the night-time.

A time of peril on the killing beds was when a steer broke loose. Sometimes, in the haste of speeding-up, they would dump one of the animals out on the floor before it was fully stunned, and it would get upon its feet and run amuck. Then there would be a yell of warning—the men would drop everything and dash for the nearest pillar, slipping here and there on the floor, and tumbling over each other. This was bad enough in the summer, when a man could see; in wintertime it was enough to make your hair stand up, for the room would be so full of steam that you could not make anything out five feet in front of you. To be sure, the steer was generally blind and frantic, and not especially bent on hurting any one; but think of the chances of running upon a knife, while nearly every man had one in his hand! And then, to cap the climax, the floor boss would come rushing up with a rifle and begin blazing away!

It was in one of these melees that Jurgis fell into his trap. That is the only word to describe it; it was so cruel, and so utterly not to be foreseen. At first he hardly noticed it, it was such a slight accident—simply that in leaping out of the way he turned his ankle. There was a twinge of pain, but Jurgis was used to pain, and did not coddle himself. When he came to walk home, however, he realized that it was hurting him a great deal; and in the morning his ankle was swollen out nearly double its size, and he could not get his foot into his shoe. Still, even then, he did nothing more than swear a little, and wrapped his foot in old rags, and hobbled out to take the car. It chanced to be a rush day at Durham's, and all the long morning he limped about with his aching foot; by noontime the pain was so great that it made him faint, and after a couple of hours in the afternoon he was fairly beaten, and had to tell the boss. They sent for the company doctor, and he examined the foot and told Jurgis to go home to bed, adding that he had probably laid himself up for months by his folly. The injury was not one that Durham and Company could be held responsible for, and so that was all there was to it, so far as the doctor was concerned.

Jurgis got home somehow, scarcely able to see for the pain, and with an awful terror in his soul, Elzbieta helped him into bed and bandaged his injured foot with cold water and tried hard not to let him see her dismay; when the rest came home at night she met them outside and told them, and they, too, put on a cheerful face, saying it would only be for a week or two, and that they would pull him through.

When they had gotten him to sleep, however, they sat by the kitchen fire and talked it over in frightened whispers. They were in for a siege, that was plainly to be seen. Jurgis had only about sixty dollars in the bank, and the slack season was upon them. Both Jonas and Marija might soon be earning no more than enough to pay their board, and besides that there were only the wages of Ona and the pittance of the little boy. There was the rent to pay, and still some on the furniture; there was the insurance just due, and every month there was sack after sack of coal. It was January, midwinter, an awful time to have to face privation. Deep snows would come again, and who would carry Ona to her work now? She might lose her place—she was almost certain to lose it. And then little Stanislovas began to whimper—who would take care of him?

It was dreadful that an accident of this sort, that no man can help, should have meant such suffering. The bitterness of it was the daily food and drink of Jurgis. It was of no use for them to try to deceive him; he knew as much about the situation as they did, and he knew that the family might literally starve to death. The worry of it fairly ate him up—he began to look haggard the first two or three days of it. In truth, it was almost maddening for a strong man like him, a fighter, to have to lie there helpless on his back. It was for all the world the old story of Prometheus bound. As Jurgis lay on his bed, hour after hour there came to him emotions that he had never known before. Before this he had met life with a welcome—it had its trials, but none that a man could not face. But now, in the nighttime, when he lay tossing about, there would come stalking into his chamber a grisly phantom, the sight of which made his flesh curl and his hair to bristle up. It was like seeing the world fall away from underneath his feet; like plunging down into a bottomless abyss into yawning caverns of despair. It might be true, then, after all, what others had told him about life, that the best powers of a man might not be equal to it! It might be true that, strive as he would, toil as he would, he might fail, and go down and be destroyed! The thought of this was like an icy hand at his heart; the thought that here, in this ghastly home of all horror, he and all those who were dear to him might lie and perish of starvation and cold, and there would be no ear to hear their cry, no hand to help them! It was true, it was true,—that here in this huge city, with its stores of heaped-up wealth, human creatures might be hunted down and destroyed by the wild-beast powers of nature, just as truly as ever they were in the days of the cave men!

Ona was now making about thirty dollars a month, and Stanislovas about thirteen. To add to this there was the board of Jonas and Marija, about forty-five dollars. Deducting from this the rent, interest, and installments on the furniture, they had left sixty dollars, and deducting the coal, they had fifty. They did without everything that human beings could do without; they went in old and ragged clothing, that left them at the mercy of the cold, and when the children's shoes wore out, they tied them up with string. Half invalid as she was, Ona would do herself harm by walking in the rain and cold when she ought to have ridden; they bought literally nothing but food—and still they could not keep alive on fifty dollars a month. They might have done it, if only they could have gotten pure food, and at fair prices; or if only they had known what to get—if they had not been so pitifully ignorant! But they had come to a new country, where everything was different, including the food. They had always been accustomed to eat a great deal of smoked sausage, and how could they know that what they bought in America was not the same—that its color was made by chemicals, and its smoky flavor by more chemicals, and that it was full of "potato flour" besides? Potato flour is the waste of potato after the starch and alcohol have been extracted; it has no more food value than so much wood, and as its use as a food adulterant is a penal offense in Europe, thousands of tons of it are shipped to America every year. It was amazing what quantities of food such as this were needed every day, by eleven hungry persons. A dollar sixty-five a day was simply not enough to feed them, and there was no use trying; and so each week they made an inroad upon the pitiful little bank account that Ona had begun. Because the account was in her name, it was possible for her to keep this a secret from her husband, and to keep the heartsickness of it for her own.

It would have been better if Jurgis had been really ill; if he had not been able to think. For he had no resources such as most invalids have; all he could do was to lie there and toss about from side to side. Now and then he would break into cursing, regardless of everything; and now and then his impatience would get the better of him, and he would try to get up, and poor Teta Elzbieta would have to plead with him in a frenzy. Elzbieta was all alone with him the greater part of the time. She would sit and smooth his forehead by the hour, and talk to him and try to make him forget. Sometimes it would be too cold for the children to go to school, and they would have to play in the kitchen, where Jurgis was, because it was the only room that was half warm. These were dreadful times, for Jurgis would get as cross as any bear; he was scarcely to be blamed, for he had enough to worry him, and it was hard when he was trying to take a nap to be kept awake by noisy and peevish children.

Elzbieta's only resource in those times was little Antanas; indeed, it would be hard to say how they could have gotten along at all if it had not been for little Antanas. It was the one consolation of Jurgis' long imprisonment that now he had time to look at his baby. Teta Elzbieta would put the clothes-basket in which the baby slept alongside of his mattress, and Jurgis would lie upon one elbow and watch him by the hour, imagining things. Then little Antanas would open his eyes—he was beginning to take notice of things now; and he would smile—how he would smile! So Jurgis would begin to forget and be happy because he was in a world where there was a thing so beautiful as the smile of little Antanas, and because such a world could not but be good at the heart of it. He looked more like his father every hour, Elzbieta would say, and said it many times a day, because she saw that it pleased Jurgis; the poor little terror-stricken woman was planning all day and all night to soothe the prisoned giant who was intrusted to her care. Jurgis, who knew nothing about the age-long and everlasting hypocrisy of woman, would take the bait and grin with delight; and then he would hold his finger in front of little Antanas' eyes, and move it this way and that, and laugh with glee to see the baby follow it. There is no pet quite so fascinating as a baby; he would look into Jurgis' face with such uncanny seriousness, and Jurgis would start and cry: "Palauk! Look, Muma, he knows his papa! He does, he does! Tu mano szirdele, the little rascal!"

# Chapter 12

For three weeks after his injury Jurgis never got up from bed. It was a very obstinate sprain; the swelling would not go down, and the pain still continued. At the end of that time, however, he could contain himself no longer, and began trying to walk a little every day, laboring to persuade himself that he was better. No arguments could stop him, and three or four days later he declared that he was going back to work. He limped to the cars and got to Brown's, where he found that the boss had kept his place—that is, was willing to turn out into the snow the poor devil he had hired in the meantime. Every now and then the pain would force Jurgis to stop work, but he stuck it out till nearly an hour before closing. Then he was forced to acknowledge that he could not go on without fainting; it almost broke his heart to do it, and he stood leaning against a pillar and weeping like a child. Two of the men had to help him to the car, and when he got out he had to sit down and wait in the snow till some one came along.

So they put him to bed again, and sent for the doctor, as they ought to have done in the beginning. It transpired that he had twisted a tendon out of place, and could never have gotten well without attention. Then he gripped the sides of the bed, and shut his teeth together, and turned white with agony, while the doctor pulled and wrenched away at his swollen ankle. When finally the doctor left, he told him that he would have to lie quiet for two months, and that if he went to work before that time he might lame himself for life.

Three days later there came another heavy snowstorm, and Jonas and Marija and Ona and little Stanislovas all set out together, an hour before daybreak, to try to get to the yards. About noon the last two came back, the boy screaming with pain. His fingers were all frosted, it seemed. They had had to give up trying to get to the yards, and had nearly perished in a drift. All that they knew how to do was to hold the frozen fingers near the fire, and so little Stanislovas spent most of the day dancing about in horrible agony, till Jurgis flew into a passion of nervous rage and swore like a madman, declaring that he would kill him if he did not stop. All that day and night the family was half-crazed with fear that Ona and the boy had lost their places; and in the morning they set out earlier than ever, after the little fellow had been beaten with a stick by Jurgis. There could be no trifling in a case like this, it was a matter of life and death; little Stanislovas could not be expected to realize that he might a great deal better freeze in the snowdrift than lose his job at the lard machine. Ona was quite certain that she would find her place gone, and was all unnerved when she finally got to Brown's, and found that the forelady herself had failed to come, and was therefore compelled to be lenient.

One of the consequences of this episode was that the first joints of three of the little boy's fingers were permanently disabled, and another that thereafter he always had to be beaten before he set out to work, whenever there was fresh snow on the ground. Jurgis was called upon to do the beating, and as it hurt his foot he did it with a vengeance; but it did not tend to add to the sweetness of his temper. They say that the best dog will turn cross if he be kept chained all the time, and it was the same with the man; he had not a thing to do all day but lie and curse his fate, and the time came when he wanted to curse everything.

This was never for very long, however, for when Ona began to cry, Jurgis could not stay angry. The poor fellow looked like a homeless ghost, with his cheeks sunken in and his long black hair straggling into his eyes; he was too discouraged to cut it, or to think about his appearance. His muscles were wasting away, and what were left were soft and flabby. He had no appetite, and they could not afford to tempt him with delicacies. It was better, he said, that he should not eat, it was a saving. About the end of March he had got hold of Ona's bankbook, and learned that there was only three dollars left to them in the world.

But perhaps the worst of the consequences of this long siege was that they lost another member of their family; Brother Jonas disappeared. One Saturday night he did not come home, and thereafter all their efforts to get trace of him were futile. It was said by the boss at Durham's that he had gotten his week's money and left there. That might not be true, of course, for sometimes they would say that when a man had been killed; it was the easiest way out of it for all concerned. When, for instance, a man had fallen into one of the rendering tanks and had been made into pure leaf lard and peerless fertilizer, there was no use letting the fact out and making his family unhappy. More probable, however, was the theory that Jonas had deserted them, and gone on the road, seeking happiness. He had been discontented for a long time, and not without some cause. He paid good board, and was yet obliged to live in a family where nobody had enough to eat. And Marija would keep giving them all her money, and of course he could not but feel that he was called upon to do the same. Then there were crying brats, and all sorts of misery; a man would have had to be a good deal of a hero to stand it all without grumbling, and Jonas was not in the least a hero—he was simply a weatherbeaten old fellow who liked to have a good supper and sit in the corner by the fire and smoke his pipe in peace before he went to bed. Here there was not room by the fire, and through the winter the kitchen had seldom been warm enough for comfort. So, with the springtime, what was more likely than that the wild idea of escaping had come to him? Two years he had been yoked like a horse to a half-ton truck in Durham's dark cellars, with never a rest, save on Sundays and four holidays in the year, and with never a word of thanks—only kicks and blows and curses, such as no decent dog would have stood. And now the winter was over, and the spring winds were blowing—and with a day's walk a man might put the smoke of Packingtown behind him forever, and be where the grass was green and the flowers all the colors of the rainbow!

But now the income of the family was cut down more than one-third, and the food demand was cut only one-eleventh, so that they were worse off than ever. Also they were borrowing money from Marija, and eating up her bank account, and spoiling once again her hopes of marriage and happiness. And they were even going into debt to Tamoszius Kuszleika and letting him impoverish himself. Poor Tamoszius was a man without any relatives, and with a wonderful talent besides, and he ought to have made money and prospered; but he had fallen in love, and so given hostages to fortune, and was doomed to be dragged down too.

So it was finally decided that two more of the children would have to leave school. Next to Stanislovas, who was now fifteen, there was a girl, little Kotrina, who was two years younger, and then two boys, Vilimas, who was eleven, and Nikalojus, who was ten. Both of these last were bright boys, and there was no reason why their family should starve when tens of thousands of children no older were earning their own livings. So one morning they were given a quarter apiece and a roll with a sausage in it, and, with their minds top-heavy with good advice, were sent out to make their way to the city and learn to sell newspapers. They came back late at night in tears, having walked for the five or six miles to report that a man had offered to take them to a place where they sold newspapers, and had taken their money and gone into a store to get them, and nevermore been seen. So they both received a whipping, and the next morning set out again. This time they found the newspaper place, and procured their stock; and after wandering about till nearly noontime, saying "Paper?" to every one they saw, they had all their stock taken away and received a thrashing besides from a big newsman upon whose territory they had trespassed. Fortunately, however, they had already sold some papers, and came back with nearly as much as they started with.

After a week of mishaps such as these, the two little fellows began to learn the ways of the trade—the names of the different papers, and how many of each to get, and what sort of people to offer them to, and where to go and where to stay away from. After this, leaving home at four o'clock in the morning, and running about the streets, first with morning papers and then with evening, they might come home late at night with twenty or thirty cents apiece—possibly as much as forty cents. From this they had to deduct their carfare, since the distance was so great; but after a while they made friends, and learned still more, and then they would save their carfare. They would get on a car when the conductor was not looking, and hide in the crowd; and three times out of four he would not ask for their fares, either not seeing them, or thinking they had already paid; or if he did ask, they would hunt through their pockets, and then begin to cry, and either have their fares paid by some kind old lady, or else try the trick again on a new car. All this was fair play, they felt. Whose fault was it that at the hours when workingmen were going to their work and back, the cars were so crowded that the conductors could not collect all the fares? And besides, the companies were thieves, people said—had stolen all their franchises with the help of scoundrelly politicians!

Now that the winter was by, and there was no more danger of snow, and no more coal to buy, and another room warm enough to put the children into when they cried, and enough money to get along from week to week with, Jurgis was less terrible than he had been. A man can get used to anything in the course of time, and Jurgis had gotten used to lying about the house. Ona saw this, and was very careful not to destroy his peace of mind, by letting him know how very much pain she was suffering. It was now the time of the spring rains, and Ona had often to ride to her work, in spite of the expense; she was getting paler every day, and sometimes, in spite of her good resolutions, it pained her that Jurgis did not notice it. She wondered if he cared for her as much as ever, if all this misery was not wearing out his love. She had to be away from him all the time, and bear her own troubles while he was bearing his; and then, when she came home, she was so worn out; and whenever they talked they had only their worries to talk of—truly it was hard, in such a life, to keep any sentiment alive. The woe of this would flame up in Ona sometimes—at night she would suddenly clasp her big husband in her arms and break into passionate weeping, demanding to know if he really loved her. Poor Jurgis, who had in truth grown more matter-of-fact, under the endless pressure of penury, would not know what to make of these things, and could only try to recollect when he had last been cross; and so Ona would have to forgive him and sob herself to sleep.

The latter part of April Jurgis went to see the doctor, and was given a bandage to lace about his ankle, and told that he might go back to work. It needed more than the permission of the doctor, however, for when he showed up on the killing floor of Brown's, he was told by the foreman that it had not been possible to keep his job for him. Jurgis knew that this meant simply that the foreman had found some one else to do the work as well and did not want to bother to make a change. He stood in the doorway, looking mournfully on, seeing his friends and companions at work, and feeling like an outcast. Then he went out and took his place with the mob of the unemployed.

This time, however, Jurgis did not have the same fine confidence, nor the same reason for it. He was no longer the finest-looking man in the throng, and the bosses no longer made for him; he was thin and haggard, and his clothes were seedy, and he looked miserable. And there were hundreds who looked and felt just like him, and who had been wandering about Packingtown for months begging for work. This was a critical time in Jurgis' life, and if he had been a weaker man he would have gone the way the rest did. Those out-of-work wretches would stand about the packing houses every morning till the police drove them away, and then they would scatter among the saloons. Very few of them had the nerve to face the rebuffs that they would encounter by trying to get into the buildings to interview the bosses; if they did not get a chance in the morning, there would be nothing to do but hang about the saloons the rest of the day and night. Jurgis was saved from all this—partly, to be sure, because it was pleasant weather, and there was no need to be indoors; but mainly because he carried with him always the pitiful little face of his wife. He must get work, he told himself, fighting the battle with despair every hour of the day. He must get work! He must have a place again and some money saved up, before the next winter came.

But there was no work for him. He sought out all the members of his union—Jurgis had stuck to the union through all this—and begged them to speak a word for him. He went to every one he knew, asking for a chance, there or anywhere. He wandered all day through the buildings; and in a week or two, when he had been all over the yards, and into every room to which he had access, and learned that there was not a job anywhere, he persuaded himself that there might have been a change in the places he had first visited, and began the round all over; till finally the watchmen and the "spotters" of the companies came to know him by sight and to order him out with threats. Then there was nothing more for him to do but go with the crowd in the morning, and keep in the front row and look eager, and when he failed, go back home, and play with little Kotrina and the baby.

The peculiar bitterness of all this was that Jurgis saw so plainly the meaning of it. In the beginning he had been fresh and strong, and he had gotten a job the first day; but now he was second-hand, a damaged article, so to speak, and they did not want him. They had got the best of him—they had worn him out, with their speeding-up and their carelessness, and now they had thrown him away! And Jurgis would make the acquaintance of others of these unemployed men and find that they had all had the same experience. There were some, of course, who had wandered in from other places, who had been ground up in other mills; there were others who were out from their own fault—some, for instance, who had not been able to stand the awful grind without drink. The vast majority, however, were simply the worn-out parts of the great merciless packing machine; they had toiled there, and kept up with the pace, some of them for ten or twenty years, until finally the time had come when they could not keep up with it any more. Some had been frankly told that they were too old, that a sprier man was needed; others had given occasion, by some act of carelessness or incompetence; with most, however, the occasion had been the same as with Jurgis. They had been overworked and underfed so long, and finally some disease had laid them on their backs, or they had cut themselves, and had blood poisoning, or met with some other accident. When a man came back after that, he would get his place back only by the courtesy of the boss. To this there was no exception, save when the accident was one for which the firm was liable; in that case they would send a slippery lawyer to see him, first to try to get him to sign away his claims, but if he was too smart for that, to promise him that he and his should always be provided with work. This promise they would keep, strictly and to the letter—for two years. Two years was the "statute of limitations," and after that the victim could not sue.

What happened to a man after any of these things, all depended upon the circumstances. If he were of the highly skilled workers, he would probably have enough saved up to tide him over. The best paid men, the "splitters," made fifty cents an hour, which would be five or six dollars a day in the rush seasons, and one or two in the dullest. A man could live and save on that; but then there were only half a dozen splitters in each place, and one of them that Jurgis knew had a family of twenty-two children, all hoping to grow up to be splitters like their father. For an unskilled man, who made ten dollars a week in the rush seasons and five in the dull, it all depended upon his age and the number he had dependent upon him. An unmarried man could save, if he did not drink, and if he was absolutely selfish—that is, if he paid no heed to the demands of his old parents, or of his little brothers and sisters, or of any other relatives he might have, as well as of the members of his union, and his chums, and the people who might be starving to death next door.

# Chapter 13

During this time that Jurgis was looking for work occurred the death of little Kristoforas, one of the children of Teta Elzbieta. Both Kristoforas and his brother, Juozapas, were cripples, the latter having lost one leg by having it run over, and Kristoforas having congenital dislocation of the hip, which made it impossible for him ever to walk. He was the last of Teta Elzbieta's children, and perhaps he had been intended by nature to let her know that she had had enough. At any rate he was wretchedly sick and undersized; he had the rickets, and though he was over three years old, he was no bigger than an ordinary child of one. All day long he would crawl around the floor in a filthy little dress, whining and fretting; because the floor was full of drafts he was always catching cold, and snuffling because his nose ran. This made him a nuisance, and a source of endless trouble in the family. For his mother, with unnatural perversity, loved him best of all her children, and made a perpetual fuss over him—would let him do anything undisturbed, and would burst into tears when his fretting drove Jurgis wild.

And now he died. Perhaps it was the smoked sausage he had eaten that morning—which may have been made out of some of the tubercular pork that was condemned as unfit for export. At any rate, an hour after eating it, the child had begun to cry with pain, and in another hour he was rolling about on the floor in convulsions. Little Kotrina, who was all alone with him, ran out screaming for help, and after a while a doctor came, but not until Kristoforas had howled his last howl. No one was really sorry about this except poor Elzbieta, who was inconsolable. Jurgis announced that so far as he was concerned the child would have to be buried by the city, since they had no money for a funeral; and at this the poor woman almost went out of her senses, wringing her hands and screaming with grief and despair. Her child to be buried in a pauper's grave! And her stepdaughter to stand by and hear it said without protesting! It was enough to make Ona's father rise up out of his grave to rebuke her! If it had come to this, they might as well give up at once, and be buried all of them together! . . . In the end Marija said that she would help with ten dollars; and Jurgis being still obdurate, Elzbieta went in tears and begged the money from the neighbors, and so little Kristoforas had a mass and a hearse with white plumes on it, and a tiny plot in a graveyard with a wooden cross to mark the place. The poor mother was not the same for months after that; the mere sight of the floor where little Kristoforas had crawled about would make her weep. He had never had a fair chance, poor little fellow, she would say. He had been handicapped from his birth. If only she had heard about it in time, so that she might have had that great doctor to cure him of his lameness! . . . Some time ago, Elzbieta was told, a Chicago billionaire had paid a fortune to bring a great European surgeon over to cure his little daughter of the same disease from which Kristoforas had suffered. And because this surgeon had to have bodies to demonstrate upon, he announced that he would treat the children of the poor, a piece of magnanimity over which the papers became quite eloquent. Elzbieta, alas, did not read the papers, and no one had told her; but perhaps it was as well, for just then they would not have had the carfare to spare to go every day to wait upon the surgeon, nor for that matter anybody with the time to take the child.

All this while that he was seeking for work, there was a dark shadow hanging over Jurgis; as if a savage beast were lurking somewhere in the pathway of his life, and he knew it, and yet could not help approaching the place. There are all stages of being out of work in Packingtown, and he faced in dread the prospect of reaching the lowest. There is a place that waits for the lowest man—the fertilizer plant!

The men would talk about it in awe-stricken whispers. Not more than one in ten had ever really tried it; the other nine had contented themselves with hearsay evidence and a peep through the door. There were some things worse than even starving to death. They would ask Jurgis if he had worked there yet, and if he meant to; and Jurgis would debate the matter with himself. As poor as they were, and making all the sacrifices that they were, would he dare to refuse any sort of work that was offered to him, be it as horrible as ever it could? Would he dare to go home and eat bread that had been earned by Ona, weak and complaining as she was, knowing that he had been given a chance, and had not had the nerve to take it?—And yet he might argue that way with himself all day, and one glimpse into the fertilizer works would send him away again shuddering. He was a man, and he would do his duty; he went and made application—but surely he was not also required to hope for success!

The fertilizer works of Durham's lay away from the rest of the plant. Few visitors ever saw them, and the few who did would come out looking like Dante, of whom the peasants declared that he had been into hell. To this part of the yards came all the "tankage" and the waste products of all sorts; here they dried out the bones,—and in suffocating cellars where the daylight never came you might see men and women and children bending over whirling machines and sawing bits of bone into all sorts of shapes, breathing their lungs full of the fine dust, and doomed to die, every one of them, within a certain definite time. Here they made the blood into albumen, and made other foul-smelling things into things still more foul-smelling. In the corridors and caverns where it was done you might lose yourself as in the great caves of Kentucky. In the dust and the steam the electric lights would shine like far-off twinkling stars—red and blue-green and purple stars, according to the color of the mist and the brew from which it came. For the odors of these ghastly charnel houses there may be words in Lithuanian, but there are none in English. The person entering would have to summon his courage as for a cold-water plunge. He would go in like a man swimming under water; he would put his handkerchief over his face, and begin to cough and choke; and then, if he were still obstinate, he would find his head beginning to ring, and the veins in his forehead to throb, until finally he would be assailed by an overpowering blast of ammonia fumes, and would turn and run for his life, and come out half-dazed.

On top of this were the rooms where they dried the "tankage," the mass of brown stringy stuff that was left after the waste portions of the carcasses had had the lard and tallow dried out of them. This dried material they would then grind to a fine powder, and after they had mixed it up well with a mysterious but inoffensive brown rock which they brought in and ground up by the hundreds of carloads for that purpose, the substance was ready to be put into bags and sent out to the world as any one of a hundred different brands of standard bone phosphate. And then the farmer in Maine or California or Texas would buy this, at say twenty-five dollars a ton, and plant it with his corn; and for several days after the operation the fields would have a strong odor, and the farmer and his wagon and the very horses that had hauled it would all have it too. In Packingtown the fertilizer is pure, instead of being a flavoring, and instead of a ton or so spread out on several acres under the open sky, there are hundreds and thousands of tons of it in one building, heaped here and there in haystack piles, covering the floor several inches deep, and filling the air with a choking dust that becomes a blinding sandstorm when the wind stirs.

It was to this building that Jurgis came daily, as if dragged by an unseen hand. The month of May was an exceptionally cool one, and his secret prayers were granted; but early in June there came a record-breaking hot spell, and after that there were men wanted in the fertilizer mill.

The boss of the grinding room had come to know Jurgis by this time, and had marked him for a likely man; and so when he came to the door about two o'clock this breathless hot day, he felt a sudden spasm of pain shoot through him—the boss beckoned to him! In ten minutes more Jurgis had pulled off his coat and overshirt, and set his teeth together and gone to work. Here was one more difficulty for him to meet and conquer!

His labor took him about one minute to learn. Before him was one of the vents of the mill in which the fertilizer was being ground—rushing forth in a great brown river, with a spray of the finest dust flung forth in clouds. Jurgis was given a shovel, and along with half a dozen others it was his task to shovel this fertilizer into carts. That others were at work he knew by the sound, and by the fact that he sometimes collided with them; otherwise they might as well not have been there, for in the blinding dust storm a man could not see six feet in front of his face. When he had filled one cart he had to grope around him until another came, and if there was none on hand he continued to grope till one arrived. In five minutes he was, of course, a mass of fertilizer from head to feet; they gave him a sponge to tie over his mouth, so that he could breathe, but the sponge did not prevent his lips and eyelids from caking up with it and his ears from filling solid. He looked like a brown ghost at twilight—from hair to shoes he became the color of the building and of everything in it, and for that matter a hundred yards outside it. The building had to be left open, and when the wind blew Durham and Company lost a great deal of fertilizer.

Working in his shirt sleeves, and with the thermometer at over a hundred, the phosphates soaked in through every pore of Jurgis' skin, and in five minutes he had a headache, and in fifteen was almost dazed. The blood was pounding in his brain like an engine's throbbing; there was a frightful pain in the top of his skull, and he could hardly control his hands. Still, with the memory of his four months' siege behind him, he fought on, in a frenzy of determination; and half an hour later he began to vomit—he vomited until it seemed as if his inwards must be torn into shreds. A man could get used to the fertilizer mill, the boss had said, if he would make up his mind to it; but Jurgis now began to see that it was a question of making up his stomach.

At the end of that day of horror, he could scarcely stand. He had to catch himself now and then, and lean against a building and get his bearings. Most of the men, when they came out, made straight for a saloon—they seemed to place fertilizer and rattlesnake poison in one class. But Jurgis was too ill to think of drinking—he could only make his way to the street and stagger on to a car. He had a sense of humor, and later on, when he became an old hand, he used to think it fun to board a streetcar and see what happened. Now, however, he was too ill to notice it—how the people in the car began to gasp and sputter, to put their handkerchiefs to their noses, and transfix him with furious glances. Jurgis only knew that a man in front of him immediately got up and gave him a seat; and that half a minute later the two people on each side of him got up; and that in a full minute the crowded car was nearly empty—those passengers who could not get room on the platform having gotten out to walk.

Of course Jurgis had made his home a miniature fertilizer mill a minute after entering. The stuff was half an inch deep in his skin—his whole system was full of it, and it would have taken a week not merely of scrubbing, but of vigorous exercise, to get it out of him. As it was, he could be compared with nothing known to men, save that newest discovery of the savants, a substance which emits energy for an unlimited time, without being itself in the least diminished in power. He smelled so that he made all the food at the table taste, and set the whole family to vomiting; for himself it was three days before he could keep anything upon his stomach—he might wash his hands, and use a knife and fork, but were not his mouth and throat filled with the poison?

And still Jurgis stuck it out! In spite of splitting headaches he would stagger down to the plant and take up his stand once more, and begin to shovel in the blinding clouds of dust. And so at the end of the week he was a fertilizer man for life—he was able to eat again, and though his head never stopped aching, it ceased to be so bad that he could not work.

So there passed another summer. It was a summer of prosperity, all over the country, and the country ate generously of packing house products, and there was plenty of work for all the family, in spite of the packers' efforts to keep a superfluity of labor. They were again able to pay their debts and to begin to save a little sum; but there were one or two sacrifices they considered too heavy to be made for long—it was too bad that the boys should have to sell papers at their age. It was utterly useless to caution them and plead with them; quite without knowing it, they were taking on the tone of their new environment. They were learning to swear in voluble English; they were learning to pick up cigar stumps and smoke them, to pass hours of their time gambling with pennies and dice and cigarette cards; they were learning the location of all the houses of prostitution on the "Levee," and the names of the "madames" who kept them, and the days when they gave their state banquets, which the police captains and the big politicians all attended. If a visiting "country customer" were to ask them, they could show him which was "Hinkydink's" famous saloon, and could even point out to him by name the different gamblers and thugs and "hold-up men" who made the place their headquarters. And worse yet, the boys were getting out of the habit of coming home at night. What was the use, they would ask, of wasting time and energy and a possible carfare riding out to the stockyards every night when the weather was pleasant and they could crawl under a truck or into an empty doorway and sleep exactly as well? So long as they brought home a half dollar for each day, what mattered it when they brought it? But Jurgis declared that from this to ceasing to come at all would not be a very long step, and so it was decided that Vilimas and Nikalojus should return to school in the fall, and that instead Elzbieta should go out and get some work, her place at home being taken by her younger daughter.

Little Kotrina was like most children of the poor, prematurely made old; she had to take care of her little brother, who was a cripple, and also of the baby; she had to cook the meals and wash the dishes and clean house, and have supper ready when the workers came home in the evening. She was only thirteen, and small for her age, but she did all this without a murmur; and her mother went out, and after trudging a couple of days about the yards, settled down as a servant of a "sausage machine."

Elzbieta was used to working, but she found this change a hard one, for the reason that she had to stand motionless upon her feet from seven o'clock in the morning till half-past twelve, and again from one till half-past five. For the first few days it seemed to her that she could not stand it—she suffered almost as much as Jurgis had from the fertilizer, and would come out at sundown with her head fairly reeling. Besides this, she was working in one of the dark holes, by electric light, and the dampness, too, was deadly—there were always puddles of water on the floor, and a sickening odor of moist flesh in the room. The people who worked here followed the ancient custom of nature, whereby the ptarmigan is the color of dead leaves in the fall and of snow in the winter, and the chameleon, who is black when he lies upon a stump and turns green when he moves to a leaf. The men and women who worked in this department were precisely the color of the "fresh country sausage" they made.

The sausage-room was an interesting place to visit, for two or three minutes, and provided that you did not look at the people; the machines were perhaps the most wonderful things in the entire plant. Presumably sausages were once chopped and stuffed by hand, and if so it would be interesting to know how many workers had been displaced by these inventions. On one side of the room were the hoppers, into which men shoveled loads of meat and wheelbarrows full of spices; in these great bowls were whirling knives that made two thousand revolutions a minute, and when the meat was ground fine and adulterated with potato flour, and well mixed with water, it was forced to the stuffing machines on the other side of the room. The latter were tended by women; there was a sort of spout, like the nozzle of a hose, and one of the women would take a long string of "casing" and put the end over the nozzle and then work the whole thing on, as one works on the finger of a tight glove. This string would be twenty or thirty feet long, but the woman would have it all on in a jiffy; and when she had several on, she would press a lever, and a stream of sausage meat would be shot out, taking the casing with it as it came. Thus one might stand and see appear, miraculously born from the machine, a wriggling snake of sausage of incredible length. In front was a big pan which caught these creatures, and two more women who seized them as fast as they appeared and twisted them into links. This was for the uninitiated the most perplexing work of all; for all that the woman had to give was a single turn of the wrist; and in some way she contrived to give it so that instead of an endless chain of sausages, one after another, there grew under her hands a bunch of strings, all dangling from a single center. It was quite like the feat of a prestidigitator—for the woman worked so fast that the eye could literally not follow her, and there was only a mist of motion, and tangle after tangle of sausages appearing. In the midst of the mist, however, the visitor would suddenly notice the tense set face, with the two wrinkles graven in the forehead, and the ghastly pallor of the cheeks; and then he would suddenly recollect that it was time he was going on. The woman did not go on; she stayed right there—hour after hour, day after day, year after year, twisting sausage links and racing with death. It was piecework, and she was apt to have a family to keep alive; and stern and ruthless economic laws had arranged it that she could only do this by working just as she did, with all her soul upon her work, and with never an instant for a glance at the well-dressed ladies and gentlemen who came to stare at her, as at some wild beast in a menagerie.

# Chapter 14

With one member trimming beef in a cannery, and another working in a sausage factory, the family had a first-hand knowledge of the great majority of Packingtown swindles. For it was the custom, as they found, whenever meat was so spoiled that it could not be used for anything else, either to can it or else to chop it up into sausage. With what had been told them by Jonas, who had worked in the pickle rooms, they could now study the whole of the spoiled-meat industry on the inside, and read a new and grim meaning into that old Packingtown jest—that they use everything of the pig except the squeal.

Jonas had told them how the meat that was taken out of pickle would often be found sour, and how they would rub it up with soda to take away the smell, and sell it to be eaten on free-lunch counters; also of all the miracles of chemistry which they performed, giving to any sort of meat, fresh or salted, whole or chopped, any color and any flavor and any odor they chose. In the pickling of hams they had an ingenious apparatus, by which they saved time and increased the capacity of the plant—a machine consisting of a hollow needle attached to a pump; by plunging this needle into the meat and working with his foot, a man could fill a ham with pickle in a few seconds. And yet, in spite of this, there would be hams found spoiled, some of them with an odor so bad that a man could hardly bear to be in the room with them. To pump into these the packers had a second and much stronger pickle which destroyed the odor—a process known to the workers as "giving them thirty per cent." Also, after the hams had been smoked, there would be found some that had gone to the bad. Formerly these had been sold as "Number Three Grade," but later on some ingenious person had hit upon a new device, and now they would extract the bone, about which the bad part generally lay, and insert in the hole a white-hot iron. After this invention there was no longer Number One, Two, and Three Grade—there was only Number One Grade. The packers were always originating such schemes—they had what they called "boneless hams," which were all the odds and ends of pork stuffed into casings; and "California hams," which were the shoulders, with big knuckle joints, and nearly all the meat cut out; and fancy "skinned hams," which were made of the oldest hogs, whose skins were so heavy and coarse that no one would buy them—that is, until they had been cooked and chopped fine and labeled "head cheese!"

It was only when the whole ham was spoiled that it came into the department of Elzbieta. Cut up by the two-thousand-revolutions-a-minute flyers, and mixed with half a ton of other meat, no odor that ever was in a ham could make any difference. There was never the least attention paid to what was cut up for sausage; there would come all the way back from Europe old sausage that had been rejected, and that was moldy and white—it would be dosed with borax and glycerine, and dumped into the hoppers, and made over again for home consumption. There would be meat that had tumbled out on the floor, in the dirt and sawdust, where the workers had tramped and spit uncounted billions of consumption germs. There would be meat stored in great piles in rooms; and the water from leaky roofs would drip over it, and thousands of rats would race about on it. It was too dark in these storage places to see well, but a man could run his hand over these piles of meat and sweep off handfuls of the dried dung of rats. These rats were nuisances, and the packers would put poisoned bread out for them; they would die, and then rats, bread, and meat would go into the hoppers together. This is no fairy story and no joke; the meat would be shoveled into carts, and the man who did the shoveling would not trouble to lift out a rat even when he saw one—there were things that went into the sausage in comparison with which a poisoned rat was a tidbit. There was no place for the men to wash their hands before they ate their dinner, and so they made a practice of washing them in the water that was to be ladled into the sausage. There were the butt-ends of smoked meat, and the scraps of corned beef, and all the odds and ends of the waste of the plants, that would be dumped into old barrels in the cellar and left there. Under the system of rigid economy which the packers enforced, there were some jobs that it only paid to do once in a long time, and among these was the cleaning out of the waste barrels. Every spring they did it; and in the barrels would be dirt and rust and old nails and stale water—and cartload after cartload of it would be taken up and dumped into the hoppers with fresh meat, and sent out to the public's breakfast. Some of it they would make into "smoked" sausage—but as the smoking took time, and was therefore expensive, they would call upon their chemistry department, and preserve it with borax and color it with gelatine to make it brown. All of their sausage came out of the same bowl, but when they came to wrap it they would stamp some of it "special," and for this they would charge two cents more a pound.

Such were the new surroundings in which Elzbieta was placed, and such was the work she was compelled to do. It was stupefying, brutalizing work; it left her no time to think, no strength for anything. She was part of the machine she tended, and every faculty that was not needed for the machine was doomed to be crushed out of existence. There was only one mercy about the cruel grind—that it gave her the gift of insensibility. Little by little she sank into a torpor—she fell silent. She would meet Jurgis and Ona in the evening, and the three would walk home together, often without saying a word. Ona, too, was falling into a habit of silence—Ona, who had once gone about singing like a bird. She was sick and miserable, and often she would barely have strength enough to drag herself home. And there they would eat what they had to eat, and afterward, because there was only their misery to talk of, they would crawl into bed and fall into a stupor and never stir until it was time to get up again, and dress by candlelight, and go back to the machines. They were so numbed that they did not even suffer much from hunger, now; only the children continued to fret when the food ran short.

Yet the soul of Ona was not dead—the souls of none of them were dead, but only sleeping; and now and then they would waken, and these were cruel times. The gates of memory would roll open—old joys would stretch out their arms to them, old hopes and dreams would call to them, and they would stir beneath the burden that lay upon them, and feel its forever immeasurable weight. They could not even cry out beneath it; but anguish would seize them, more dreadful than the agony of death. It was a thing scarcely to be spoken—a thing never spoken by all the world, that will not know its own defeat.

They were beaten; they had lost the game, they were swept aside. It was not less tragic because it was so sordid, because it had to do with wages and grocery bills and rents. They had dreamed of freedom; of a chance to look about them and learn something; to be decent and clean, to see their child grow up to be strong. And now it was all gone—it would never be! They had played the game and they had lost. Six years more of toil they had to face before they could expect the least respite, the cessation of the payments upon the house; and how cruelly certain it was that they could never stand six years of such a life as they were living! They were lost, they were going down—and there was no deliverance for them, no hope; for all the help it gave them the vast city in which they lived might have been an ocean waste, a wilderness, a desert, a tomb. So often this mood would come to Ona, in the nighttime, when something wakened her; she would lie, afraid of the beating of her own heart, fronting the blood-red eyes of the old primeval terror of life. Once she cried aloud, and woke Jurgis, who was tired and cross. After that she learned to weep silently—their moods so seldom came together now! It was as if their hopes were buried in separate graves.

Jurgis, being a man, had troubles of his own. There was another specter following him. He had never spoken of it, nor would he allow any one else to speak of it—he had never acknowledged its existence to himself. Yet the battle with it took all the manhood that he had—and once or twice, alas, a little more. Jurgis had discovered drink.

He was working in the steaming pit of hell; day after day, week after week—until now, there was not an organ of his body that did its work without pain, until the sound of ocean breakers echoed in his head day and night, and the buildings swayed and danced before him as he went down the street. And from all the unending horror of this there was a respite, a deliverance—he could drink! He could forget the pain, he could slip off the burden; he would see clearly again, he would be master of his brain, of his thoughts, of his will. His dead self would stir in him, and he would find himself laughing and cracking jokes with his companions—he would be a man again, and master of his life.

It was not an easy thing for Jurgis to take more than two or three drinks. With the first drink he could eat a meal, and he could persuade himself that

that was economy; with the second he could eat another meal—but there would come a time when he could eat no more, and then to pay for a drink was an unthinkable extravagance, a defiance of the age-long instincts of his hunger-haunted class. One day, however, he took the plunge, and drank up all that he had in his pockets, and went home half "piped," as the men phrase it. He was happier than he had been in a year; and yet, because he knew that the happiness would not last, he was savage, too with those who would wreck it, and with the world, and with his life; and then again, beneath this, he was sick with the shame of himself. Afterward, when he saw the despair of his family, and reckoned up the money he had spent, the tears came into his eyes, and he began the long battle with the specter.

It was a battle that had no end, that never could have one. But Jurgis did not realize that very clearly; he was not given much time for reflection. He simply knew that he was always fighting. Steeped in misery and despair as he was, merely to walk down the street was to be put upon the rack. There was surely a saloon on the corner—perhaps on all four corners, and some in the middle of the block as well; and each one stretched out a hand to him each one had a personality of its own, allurements unlike any other. Going and coming—before sunrise and after dark—there was warmth and a glow of light, and the steam of hot food, and perhaps music, or a friendly face, and a word of good cheer. Jurgis developed a fondness for having Ona on his arm whenever he went out on the street, and he would hold her tightly, and walk fast. It was pitiful to have Ona know of this—it drove him wild to think of it; the thing was not fair, for Ona had never tasted drink, and so could not understand. Sometimes, in desperate hours, he would find himself wishing that she might learn what it was, so that he need not be ashamed in her presence. They might drink together, and escape from the horror—escape for a while, come what would.

So there came a time when nearly all the conscious life of Jurgis consisted of a struggle with the craving for liquor. He would have ugly moods, when he hated Ona and the whole family, because they stood in his way. He was a fool to have married; he had tied himself down, had made himself a slave. It was all because he was a married man that he was compelled to stay in the yards; if it had not been for that he might have gone off like Jonas, and to hell with the packers. There were few single men in the fertilizer mill—and those few were working only for a chance to escape. Meantime, too, they had something to think about while they worked,—they had the memory of the last time they had been drunk, and the hope of the time when they would be drunk again. As for Jurgis, he was expected to bring home every penny; he could not even go with the men at noontime—he was supposed to sit down and eat his dinner on a pile of fertilizer dust.

This was not always his mood, of course; he still loved his family. But just now was a time of trial. Poor little Antanas, for instance—who had never failed to win him with a smile—little Antanas was not smiling just now, being a mass of fiery red pimples. He had had all the diseases that babies are heir to, in quick succession, scarlet fever, mumps, and whooping cough in the first year, and now he was down with the measles. There was no one to attend him but Kotrina; there was no doctor to help him, because they were too poor, and children did not die of the measles—at least not often. Now and then Kotrina would find time to sob over his woes, but for the greater part of the time he had to be left alone, barricaded upon the bed. The floor was full of drafts, and if he caught cold he would die. At night he was tied down, lest he should kick the covers off him, while the family lay in their stupor of exhaustion. He would lie and scream for hours, almost in convulsions; and then, when he was worn out, he would lie whimpering and wailing in his torment. He was burning up with fever, and his eyes were running sores; in the daytime he was a thing uncanny and impish to behold, a plaster of pimples and sweat, a great purple lump of misery.

Yet all this was not really as cruel as it sounds, for, sick as he was, little Antanas was the least unfortunate member of that family. He was quite able to bear his sufferings—it was as if he had all these complaints to show what a prodigy of health he was. He was the child of his parents' youth and joy; he grew up like the conjurer's rosebush, and all the world was his oyster. In general, he toddled around the kitchen all day with a lean and hungry look—the portion of the family's allowance that fell to him was not enough, and he was unrestrainable in his demand for more. Antanas was but little over a year old, and already no one but his father could manage him.

It seemed as if he had taken all of his mother's strength—had left nothing for those that might come after him. Ona was with child again now, and it was a dreadful thing to contemplate; even Jurgis, dumb and despairing as he was, could not but understand that yet other agonies were on the way, and shudder at the thought of them.

For Ona was visibly going to pieces. In the first place she was developing a cough, like the one that had killed old Dede Antanas. She had had a trace of it ever since that fatal morning when the greedy streetcar corporation had turned her out into the rain; but now it was beginning to grow serious, and to wake her up at night. Even worse than that was the fearful nervousness from which she suffered; she would have frightful headaches and fits of aimless weeping; and sometimes she would come home at night shuddering and moaning, and would fling herself down upon the bed and burst into tears. Several times she was quite beside herself and hysterical; and then Jurgis would go half-mad with fright. Elzbieta would explain to him that it could not be helped, that a woman was subject to such things when she was pregnant; but he was hardly to be persuaded, and would beg and plead to know what had happened. She had never been like this before, he would argue—it was monstrous and unthinkable. It was the life she had to live, the accursed work she had to do, that was killing her by inches. She was not fitted for it—no woman was fitted for it, no woman ought to be allowed to do such work; if the world could not keep them alive any other way it ought to kill them at once and be done with it. They ought not to marry, to have children; no workingman ought to marry—if he, Jurgis, had known what a woman was like, he would have had his eyes torn out first. So he would carry on, becoming half hysterical himself, which was an unbearable thing to see in a big man; Ona would pull herself together and fling herself into his arms, begging him to stop, to be still, that she would be better, it would be all right. So she would lie and sob out her grief upon his shoulder, while he gazed at her, as helpless as a wounded animal, the target of unseen enemies.

# Chapter 15

The beginning of these perplexing things was in the summer; and each time Ona would promise him with terror in her voice that it would not happen again—but in vain. Each crisis would leave Jurgis more and more frightened, more disposed to distrust Elzbieta's consolations, and to believe that there was some terrible thing about all this that he was not allowed to know. Once or twice in these outbreaks he caught Ona's eye, and it seemed to him like the eye of a hunted animal; there were broken phrases of anguish and despair now and then, amid her frantic weeping. It was only because he was so numb and beaten himself that Jurgis did not worry more about this. But he never thought of it, except when he was dragged to it—he lived like a dumb beast of burden, knowing only the moment in which he was.

The winter was coming on again, more menacing and cruel than ever. It was October, and the holiday rush had begun. It was necessary for the packing machines to grind till late at night to provide food that would be eaten at Christmas breakfasts; and Marija and Elzbieta and Ona, as part of the machine, began working fifteen or sixteen hours a day. There was no choice about this—whatever work there was to be done they had to do, if they wished to keep their places; besides that, it added another pittance to their incomes. So they staggered on with the awful load. They would start work every morning at seven, and eat their dinners at noon, and then work until ten or eleven at night without another mouthful of food. Jurgis wanted to wait for them, to help them home at night, but they would not think of this; the fertilizer mill was not running overtime, and there was no place for him to wait save in a saloon. Each would stagger out into the darkness, and make her way to the corner, where they met; or if the others had already gone, would get into a car, and begin a painful struggle to keep awake. When they got home they were always too tired either to eat or to undress; they would crawl into bed with their shoes on, and lie like logs. If they should fail, they would certainly be lost; if they held out, they might have enough coal for the winter.

A day or two before Thanksgiving Day there came a snowstorm. It began in the afternoon, and by evening two inches had fallen. Jurgis tried to wait for the women, but went into a saloon to get warm, and took two drinks, and came out and ran home to escape from the demon; there he lay down to wait for them, and instantly fell asleep. When he opened his eyes again he was in the midst of a nightmare, and found Elzbieta shaking him and crying out. At first he could not realize what she was saying—Ona had not come home. What time was it, he asked. It was morning—time to be up. Ona had not been home that night! And it was bitter cold, and a foot of snow on the ground.

Jurgis sat up with a start. Marija was crying with fright and the children were wailing in sympathy—little Stanislovas in addition, because the terror of the snow was upon him. Jurgis had nothing to put on but his shoes and his coat, and in half a minute he was out of the door. Then, however, he realized that there was no need of haste, that he had no idea where to go. It was still dark as midnight, and the thick snowflakes were sifting down—everything was so silent that he could hear the rustle of them as they fell. In the few seconds that he stood there hesitating he was covered white.

He set off at a run for the yards, stopping by the way to inquire in the saloons that were open. Ona might have been overcome on the way; or else she might have met with an accident in the machines. When he got to the place where she worked he inquired of one of the watchmen—there had not been any accident, so far as the man had heard. At the time office, which he found already open, the clerk told him that Ona's check had been turned in the night before, showing that she had left her work.

After that there was nothing for him to do but wait, pacing back and forth in the snow, meantime, to keep from freezing. Already the yards were full of activity; cattle were being unloaded from the cars in the distance, and across the way the "beef-luggers" were toiling in the darkness, carrying two-hundred-pound quarters of bullocks into the refrigerator cars. Before the first streaks of daylight there came the crowding throngs of workingmen, shivering, and swinging their dinner pails as they hurried by. Jurgis took up his stand by the time-office window, where alone there was light enough for him to see; the snow fell so quick that it was only by peering closely that he could make sure that Ona did not pass him.

Seven o'clock came, the hour when the great packing machine began to move. Jurgis ought to have been at his place in the fertilizer mill; but instead he was waiting, in an agony of fear, for Ona. It was fifteen minutes after the hour when he saw a form emerge from the snow mist, and sprang toward it with a cry. It was she, running swiftly; as she saw him, she staggered forward, and half fell into his outstretched arms.

"What has been the matter?" he cried, anxiously. "Where have you been?"

It was several seconds before she could get breath to answer him. "I couldn't get home," she exclaimed. "The snow—the cars had stopped."

"But where were you then?" he demanded.

"I had to go home with a friend," she panted—"with Jadvyga."

Jurgis drew a deep breath; but then he noticed that she was sobbing and trembling—as if in one of those nervous crises that he dreaded so. "But what's the matter?" he cried. "What has happened?"

"Oh, Jurgis, I was so frightened!" she said, clinging to him wildly. "I have been so worried!"

They were near the time station window, and people were staring at them. Jurgis led her away. "How do you mean?" he asked, in perplexity.

"I was afraid—I was just afraid!" sobbed Ona. "I knew you wouldn't know where I was, and I didn't know what you might do. I tried to get home, but I was so tired. Oh, Jurgis, Jurgis!"

He was so glad to get her back that he could not think clearly about anything else. It did not seem strange to him that she should be so very much upset; all her fright and incoherent protestations did not matter since he had her back. He let her cry away her tears; and then, because it was nearly eight o'clock, and they would lose another hour if they delayed, he left her at the packing house door, with her ghastly white face and her haunted eyes of terror.

There was another brief interval. Christmas was almost come; and because the snow still held, and the searching cold, morning after morning Jurgis half carried his wife to her post, staggering with her through the darkness; until at last, one night, came the end.

It lacked but three days of the holidays. About midnight Marija and Elzbieta came home, exclaiming in alarm when they found that Ona had not come. The two had agreed to meet her; and, after waiting, had gone to the room where she worked; only to find that the ham-wrapping girls had quit work an hour before, and left. There was no snow that night, nor was it especially cold; and still Ona had not come! Something more serious must be wrong this time.

They aroused Jurgis, and he sat up and listened crossly to the story. She must have gone home again with Jadvyga, he said; Jadvyga lived only two blocks from the yards, and perhaps she had been tired. Nothing could have happened to her—and even if there had, there was nothing could be done about it until morning. Jurgis turned over in his bed, and was snoring again before the two had closed the door.

In the morning, however, he was up and out nearly an hour before the usual time. Jadvyga Marcinkus lived on the other side of the yards, beyond Halsted Street, with her mother and sisters, in a single basement room—for Mikolas had recently lost one hand from blood poisoning, and their marriage had been put off forever. The door of the room was in the rear, reached by a narrow court, and Jurgis saw a light in the window and heard something frying as he passed; he knocked, half expecting that Ona would answer.

Instead there was one of Jadvyga's little sisters, who gazed at him through a crack in the door. "Where's Ona?" he demanded; and the child looked at him in perplexity. "Ona?" she said.

"Yes," said Jurgis, "isn't she here?"

"No," said the child, and Jurgis gave a start. A moment later came Jadvyga, peering over the child's head. When she saw who it was, she slid around out of sight, for she was not quite dressed. Jurgis must excuse her, she began, her mother was very ill—

"Ona isn't here?" Jurgis demanded, too alarmed to wait for her to finish.

"Why, no," said Jadvyga. "What made you think she would be here? Had she said she was coming?"

"No," he answered. "But she hasn't come home—and I thought she would be here the same as before."

"As before?" echoed Jadvyga, in perplexity.

"The time she spent the night here," said Jurgis.

"There must be some mistake," she answered, quickly. "Ona has never spent the night here."

He was only half able to realize the words. "Why—why—" he exclaimed. "Two weeks ago. Jadvyga! She told me so the night it snowed, and she could not get home."

"There must be some mistake," declared the girl, again; "she didn't come here."

He steadied himself by the door-sill; and Jadvyga in her anxiety—for she was fond of Ona—opened the door wide, holding her jacket across her throat. "Are you sure you didn't misunderstand her?" she cried. "She must have meant somewhere else. She—"

"She said here," insisted Jurgis. "She told me all about you, and how you were, and what you said. Are you sure? You haven't forgotten? You weren't away?"

"No, no!" she exclaimed—and then came a peevish voice—"Jadvyga, you are giving the baby a cold. Shut the door!" Jurgis stood for half a minute more, stammering his perplexity through an eighth of an inch of crack; and then, as there was really nothing more to be said, he excused himself and went away.

He walked on half dazed, without knowing where he went. Ona had deceived him! She had lied to him! And what could it mean—where had she been? Where was she now? He could hardly grasp the thing—much less try to solve it; but a hundred wild surmises came to him, a sense of impending calamity overwhelmed him.

Because there was nothing else to do, he went back to the time office to watch again. He waited until nearly an hour after seven, and then went to the room where Ona worked to make inquiries of Ona's "forelady." The "forelady," he found, had not yet come; all the lines of cars that came from downtown were stalled—there had been an accident in the powerhouse, and no cars had been running since last night. Meantime, however, the ham-wrappers were working away, with some one else in charge of them. The girl who answered Jurgis was busy, and as she talked she looked to see if she were being watched. Then a man came up, wheeling a truck; he knew Jurgis for Ona's husband, and was curious about the mystery.

"Maybe the cars had something to do with it," he suggested—"maybe she had gone down-town."

"No," said Jurgis, "she never went down-town."

“Perhaps not,” said the man. Jurgis thought he saw him exchange a swift glance with the girl as he spoke, and he demanded quickly. “What do you know about it?”

But the man had seen that the boss was watching him; he started on again, pushing his truck. “I don’t know anything about it,” he said, over his shoulder. “How should I know where your wife goes?”

Then Jurgis went out again and paced up and down before the building. All the morning he stayed there, with no thought of his work. About noon he went to the police station to make inquiries, and then came back again for another anxious vigil. Finally, toward the middle of the afternoon, he set out for home once more.

He was walking out Ashland Avenue. The streetcars had begun running again, and several passed him, packed to the steps with people. The sight of them set Jurgis to thinking again of the man’s sarcastic remark; and half involuntarily he found himself watching the cars—with the result that he gave a sudden startled exclamation, and stopped short in his tracks.

Then he broke into a run. For a whole block he tore after the car, only a little ways behind. That rusty black hat with the drooping red flower, it might not be Ona’s, but there was very little likelihood of it. He would know for certain very soon, for she would get out two blocks ahead. He slowed down, and let the car go on.

She got out: and as soon as she was out of sight on the side street Jurgis broke into a run. Suspicion was rife in him now, and he was not ashamed to shadow her: he saw her turn the corner near their home, and then he ran again, and saw her as she went up the porch steps of the house. After that he turned back, and for five minutes paced up and down, his hands clenched tightly and his lips set, his mind in a turmoil. Then he went home and entered.

As he opened the door, he saw Elzbieta, who had also been looking for Ona, and had come home again. She was now on tiptoe, and had a finger on her lips. Jurgis waited until she was close to him.

“Don’t make any noise,” she whispered, hurriedly.

“What’s the matter’?” he asked. “Ona is asleep,” she panted. “She’s been very ill. I’m afraid her mind’s been wandering, Jurgis. She was lost on the street all night, and I’ve only just succeeded in getting her quiet.”

“When did she come in?” he asked.

“Soon after you left this morning,” said Elzbieta.

“And has she been out since?”

“No, of course not. She’s so weak, Jurgis, she—”

And he set his teeth hard together. “You are lying to me,” he said.

Elzbieta started, and turned pale. “Why!” she gasped. “What do you mean?”

But Jurgis did not answer. He pushed her aside, and strode to the bedroom door and opened it.

Ona was sitting on the bed. She turned a startled look upon him as he entered. He closed the door in Elzbieta's face, and went toward his wife. "Where have you been?" he demanded.

She had her hands clasped tightly in her lap, and he saw that her face was as white as paper, and drawn with pain. She gasped once or twice as she tried to answer him, and then began, speaking low, and swiftly. "Jurgis, I—I think I have been out of my mind. I started to come last night, and I could not find the way. I walked—I walked all night, I think, and—and I only got home—this morning."

"You needed a rest," he said, in a hard tone. "Why did you go out again?"

He was looking her fairly in the face, and he could read the sudden fear and wild uncertainty that leaped into her eyes. "I—I had to go to—to the store," she gasped, almost in a whisper, "I had to go—"

"You are lying to me," said Jurgis. Then he clenched his hands and took a step toward her. "Why do you lie to me?" he cried, fiercely. "What are you doing that you have to lie to me?"

"Jurgis!" she exclaimed, starting up in fright. "Oh, Jurgis, how can you?"

"You have lied to me, I say!" he cried. "You told me you had been to Jadvyga's house that other night, and you hadn't. You had been where you were last night—somewheres downtown, for I saw you get off the car. Where were you?"

It was as if he had struck a knife into her. She seemed to go all to pieces. For half a second she stood, reeling and swaying, staring at him with horror in her eyes; then, with a cry of anguish, she tottered forward, stretching out her arms to him. But he stepped aside, deliberately, and let her fall. She caught herself at the side of the bed, and then sank down, burying her face in her hands and bursting into frantic weeping.

There came one of those hysterical crises that had so often dismayed him. Ona sobbed and wept, her fear and anguish building themselves up into long climaxes. Furious gusts of emotion would come sweeping over her, shaking her as the tempest shakes the trees upon the hills; all her frame would quiver and throb with them—it was as if some dreadful thing rose up within her and took possession of her, torturing her, tearing her. This thing had been wont to set Jurgis quite beside himself; but now he stood with his lips set tightly and his hands clenched—she might weep till she killed herself, but she should not move him this time—not an inch, not an inch. Because the sounds she made set his blood to running cold and his lips to quivering in spite of himself, he was glad of the diversion when Teta Elzbieta, pale with fright, opened the door and rushed in; yet he turned upon her with an oath. "Go out!" he cried, "go out!" And then, as she stood hesitating, about to speak, he seized her by the arm, and half flung her from the room, slamming the door and barring it with a table. Then he turned again and faced Ona, crying—"Now, answer me!"

Yet she did not hear him—she was still in the grip of the fiend. Jurgis could see her outstretched hands, shaking and twitching, roaming here and there over the bed at will, like living things; he could see convulsive shudderings start in her body and run through her limbs. She was sobbing and choking—it was as if there were too many sounds for one throat, they came chasing each other, like waves upon the sea. Then her voice would begin to rise into screams, louder and louder until it broke in wild, horrible peals of laughter. Jurgis bore it until he could bear it no longer, and then he sprang at her, seizing her by the shoulders and shaking her, shouting into her ear: "Stop it, I say! Stop it!"

She looked up at him, out of her agony; then she fell forward at his feet. She caught them in her hands, in spite of his efforts to step aside, and with her face upon the floor lay writhing. It made a choking in Jurgis' throat to hear her, and he cried again, more savagely than before: "Stop it, I say!"

This time she heeded him, and caught her breath and lay silent, save for the gasping sobs that wrenched all her frame. For a long minute she lay there, perfectly motionless, until a cold fear seized her husband, thinking that she was dying. Suddenly, however, he heard her voice, faintly: "Jurgis! Jurgis!"

"What is it?" he said.

He had to bend down to her, she was so weak. She was pleading with him, in broken phrases, painfully uttered: "Have faith in me! Believe me!"

"Believe what?" he cried.

"Believe that I—that I know best—that I love you! And do not ask me—what you did. Oh, Jurgis, please, please! It is for the best—it is—"

He started to speak again, but she rushed on frantically, heading him off. "If you will only do it! If you will only—only believe me! It wasn't my fault—I couldn't help it—it will be all right—it is nothing—it is no harm. Oh, Jurgis—please, please!"

She had hold of him, and was trying to raise herself to look at him; he could feel the palsied shaking of her hands and the heaving of the bosom she pressed against him. She managed to catch one of his hands and gripped it convulsively, drawing it to her face, and bathing it in her tears. "Oh, believe me, believe me!" she wailed again; and he shouted in fury, "I will not!"

But still she clung to him, wailing aloud in her despair: "Oh, Jurgis, think what you are doing! It will ruin us—it will ruin us! Oh, no, you must not do it! No, don't, don't do it. You must not do it! It will drive me mad—it will kill me—no, no, Jurgis, I am crazy—it is nothing. You do not really need to know. We can be happy—we can love each other just the same. Oh, please, please, believe me!"

Her words fairly drove him wild. He tore his hands loose, and flung her off. "Answer me," he cried. "God damn it, I say—answer me!"

She sank down upon the floor, beginning to cry again. It was like listening to the moan of a damned soul, and Jurgis could not stand it. He smote his fist upon the table by his side, and shouted again at her, "Answer me!"

She began to scream aloud, her voice like the voice of some wild beast: "Ah! Ah! I can't! I can't do it!"

"Why can't you do it?" he shouted.

"I don't know how!"

He sprang and caught her by the arm, lifting her up, and glaring into her face. "Tell me where you were last night!" he panted. "Quick, out with it!"

Then she began to whisper, one word at a time: "I—was in—a house—downtown—"

"What house? What do you mean?"

She tried to hide her eyes away, but he held her. "Miss Henderson's house," she gasped. He did not understand at first. "Miss Henderson's house," he echoed. And then suddenly, as in an explosion, the horrible truth burst over him, and he reeled and staggered back with a scream. He caught himself against the wall, and put his hand to his forehead, staring about him, and whispering, "Jesus! Jesus!"

An instant later he leaped at her, as she lay groveling at his feet. He seized her by the throat. "Tell me!" he gasped, hoarsely. "Quick! Who took you to that place?"

She tried to get away, making him furious; he thought it was fear, of the pain of his clutch—he did not understand that it was the agony of her shame. Still she answered him, "Connor."

"Connor," he gasped. "Who is Connor?"

"The boss," she answered. "The man—"

He tightened his grip, in his frenzy, and only when he saw her eyes closing did he realize that he was choking her. Then he relaxed his fingers, and crouched, waiting, until she opened her lids again. His breath beat hot into her face.

"Tell me," he whispered, at last, "tell me about it."

She lay perfectly motionless, and he had to hold his breath to catch her words. "I did not want—to do it," she said; "I tried—I tried not to do it. I only did it—to save us. It was our only chance."

Again, for a space, there was no sound but his panting. Ona's eyes closed and when she spoke again she did not open them. "He told me—he would have me turned off. He told me he would—we would all of us lose our places. We could never get anything to do—here—again. He—he meant it—he would have ruined us."

Jurgis' arms were shaking so that he could scarcely hold himself up, and lurched forward now and then as he listened. "When—when did this begin?" he gasped.

"At the very first," she said. She spoke as if in a trance. "It was all—it was their plot—Miss Henderson's plot. She hated me. And he—he wanted me. He used to speak to me—out on the platform. Then he began to—to make love to me. He offered me money. He begged me—he said he loved me. Then he threatened me. He knew all about us, he knew we would starve. He knew your boss—he knew Marija's. He would hound us to death, he said—then he said if

I would—if I—we would all of us be sure of work—always. Then one day he caught hold of me—he would not let go—he—he—"

"Where was this?"

"In the hallway—at night—after every one had gone. I could not help it. I thought of you—of the baby—of mother and the children. I was afraid of him—afraid to cry out."

A moment ago her face had been ashen gray, now it was scarlet. She was beginning to breathe hard again. Jurgis made not a sound.

"That was two months ago. Then he wanted me to come—to that house. He wanted me to stay there. He said all of us—that we would not have to work. He made me come there—in the evenings. I told you—you thought I was at the factory. Then—one night it snowed, and I couldn't get back. And last night—the cars were stopped. It was such a little thing—to ruin us all. I tried to walk, but I couldn't. I didn't want you to know. It would have—it would have been all right. We could have gone on—just the same—you need never have known about it. He was getting tired of me—he would have let me alone soon. I am going to have a baby—I am getting ugly. He told me that—twice, he told me, last night. He kicked me—last night—too. And now you will kill him—you—you will kill him—and we shall die."

All this she had said without a quiver; she lay still as death, not an eyelid moving. And Jurgis, too, said not a word. He lifted himself by the bed, and stood up. He did not stop for another glance at her, but went to the door and opened it. He did not see Elzbieta, crouching terrified in the corner. He went out, hatless, leaving the street door open behind him. The instant his feet were on the sidewalk he broke into a run.

He ran like one possessed, blindly, furiously, looking neither to the right nor left. He was on Ashland Avenue before exhaustion compelled him to slow down, and then, noticing a car, he made a dart for it and drew himself aboard. His eyes were wild and his hair flying, and he was breathing hoarsely, like a wounded bull; but the people on the car did not notice this particularly—perhaps it seemed natural to them that a man who smelled as Jurgis smelled should exhibit an aspect to correspond. They began to give way before him as usual. The conductor took his nickel gingerly, with the tips of his fingers, and then left him with the platform to himself. Jurgis did not even notice it—his thoughts were far away. Within his soul it was like a roaring furnace; he stood waiting, waiting, crouching as if for a spring.

He had some of his breath back when the car came to the entrance of the yards, and so he leaped off and started again, racing at full speed. People turned and stared at him, but he saw no one—there was the factory, and he bounded through the doorway and down the corridor. He knew the room where Ona worked, and he knew Connor, the boss of the loading-gang outside. He looked for the man as he sprang into the room.

The truckmen were hard at work, loading the freshly packed boxes and barrels upon the cars. Jurgis shot one swift glance up and down the platform—

the man was not on it. But then suddenly he heard a voice in the corridor, and started for it with a bound. In an instant more he fronted the boss.

He was a big, red-faced Irishman, coarse-featured, and smelling of liquor. He saw Jurgis as he crossed the threshold, and turned white. He hesitated one second, as if meaning to run; and in the next his assailant was upon him. He put up his hands to protect his face, but Jurgis, lunging with all the power of his arm and body, struck him fairly between the eyes and knocked him backward. The next moment he was on top of him, burying his fingers in his throat.

To Jurgis this man's whole presence reeked of the crime he had committed; the touch of his body was madness to him—it set every nerve of him a-tremble, it aroused all the demon in his soul. It had worked its will upon Ona, this great beast—and now he had it, he had it! It was his turn now! Things swam blood before him, and he screamed aloud in his fury, lifting his victim and smashing his head upon the floor.

The place, of course, was in an uproar; women fainting and shrieking, and men rushing in. Jurgis was so bent upon his task that he knew nothing of this, and scarcely realized that people were trying to interfere with him; it was only when half a dozen men had seized him by the legs and shoulders and were pulling at him, that he understood that he was losing his prey. In a flash he had bent down and sunk his teeth into the man's cheek; and when they tore him away he was dripping with blood, and little ribbons of skin were hanging in his mouth.

They got him down upon the floor, clinging to him by his arms and legs, and still they could hardly hold him. He fought like a tiger, writhing and twisting, half flinging them off, and starting toward his unconscious enemy. But yet others rushed in, until there was a little mountain of twisted limbs and bodies, heaving and tossing, and working its way about the room. In the end, by their sheer weight, they choked the breath out of him, and then they carried him to the company police station, where he lay still until they had summoned a patrol wagon to take him away.

# Chapter 16

When Jurgis got up again he went quietly enough. He was exhausted and half-dazed, and besides he saw the blue uniforms of the policemen. He drove in a patrol wagon with half a dozen of them watching him; keeping as far away as possible, however, on account of the fertilizer. Then he stood before the sergeant's desk and gave his name and address, and saw a charge of assault and battery entered against him. On his way to his cell a burly policeman cursed him because he started down the wrong corridor, and then added a kick when he was not quick enough; nevertheless, Jurgis did not even lift his eyes—he had lived two years and a half in Packingtown, and he knew what the police were. It was as much as a man's very life was worth to anger them, here in their inmost lair; like as not a dozen would pile on to him at once, and pound his face into a pulp. It would be nothing unusual if he got his skull cracked in the melee—in which case they would report that he had been drunk and had fallen down, and there would be no one to know the difference or to care.

So a barred door clanged upon Jurgis and he sat down upon a bench and buried his face in his hands. He was alone; he had the afternoon and all of the night to himself.

At first he was like a wild beast that has glutted itself; he was in a dull stupor of satisfaction. He had done up the scoundrel pretty well—not as well as he would have if they had given him a minute more, but pretty well, all the same; the ends of his fingers were still tingling from their contact with the fellow's throat. But then, little by little, as his strength came back and his senses cleared, he began to see beyond his momentary gratification; that he had nearly killed the boss would not help Ona—not the horrors that she had borne, nor the memory that would haunt her all her days. It would not help to feed her and her child; she would certainly lose her place, while he—what was to happen to him God only knew.

Half the night he paced the floor, wrestling with this nightmare; and when he was exhausted he lay down, trying to sleep, but finding instead, for the first time in his life, that his brain was too much for him. In the cell next to him was a drunken wife-beater and in the one beyond a yelling maniac. At midnight they opened the station house to the homeless wanderers who were crowded about the door, shivering in the winter blast, and they thronged into the corridor outside of the cells. Some of them stretched themselves out on the bare stone floor and fell to snoring, others sat up, laughing and talking, cursing and quarreling. The air was fetid with their breath, yet in spite of this some of them smelled Jurgis and called down the torments of hell upon him, while he lay in a far corner of his cell, counting the throbbings of the blood in his forehead.

They had brought him his supper, which was "duffers and dope"—being hunks of dry bread on a tin plate, and coffee, called "dope" because it was drugged to keep the prisoners quiet. Jurgis had not known this, or he would have swallowed the stuff in desperation; as it was, every nerve of him was a-quiver with shame and rage. Toward morning the place fell silent, and he got up and began to pace his cell; and then within the soul of him there rose up a fiend, red-eyed and cruel, and tore out the strings of his heart.

It was not for himself that he suffered—what did a man who worked in Durham's fertilizer mill care about anything that the world might do to him! What was any tyranny of prison compared with the tyranny of the past, of the thing that had happened and could not be recalled, of the memory that could never be effaced! The horror of it drove him mad; he stretched out his arms to heaven, crying out for deliverance from it—and there was no deliverance, there was no power even in heaven that could undo the past. It was a ghost that would not drown; it followed him, it seized upon him and beat him to the ground. Ah, if only he could have foreseen it—but then, he would have foreseen it, if he had not been a fool! He smote his hands upon his forehead, cursing himself because he had ever allowed Ona to work where she had, because he had not stood between her and a fate which every one knew to be so common. He should have taken her away, even if it were to lie down and die of starvation in the gutters of Chicago's streets! And now—oh, it could not be true; it was too monstrous, too horrible.

It was a thing that could not be faced; a new shuddering seized him every time he tried to think of it. No, there was no bearing the load of it, there was no living under it. There would be none for her—he knew that he might pardon her, might plead with her on his knees, but she would never look him in the face again, she would never be his wife again. The shame of it would kill her—there could be no other deliverance, and it was best that she should die.

This was simple and clear, and yet, with cruel inconsistency, whenever he escaped from this nightmare it was to suffer and cry out at the vision of Ona starving. They had put him in jail, and they would keep him here a long time, years maybe. And Ona would surely not go to work again, broken and crushed as she was. And Elzbieta and Marija, too, might lose their places—if that hell fiend Connor chose to set to work to ruin them, they would all be turned out. And even if he did not, they could not live—even if the boys left school again, they could surely not pay all the bills without him and Ona. They had only a few dollars now—they had just paid the rent of the house a week ago, and that after it was two weeks overdue. So it would be due again in a week! They would have no money to pay it then—and they would lose the house, after all their long, heartbreaking struggle. Three times now the agent had warned him that he would not tolerate another delay. Perhaps it was very base of Jurgis to be thinking about the house when he had the other unspeakable thing to fill his mind; yet, how much he had suffered for this house, how much they had all of them suffered! It was their one hope of respite, as long as they lived; they had put all their money into it—and they were working people, poor people, whose money was their strength, the very substance of them, body and soul, the thing by which they lived and for lack of which they died.

And they would lose it all; they would be turned out into the streets, and have to hide in some icy garret, and live or die as best they could! Jurgis had all the night—and all of many more nights—to think about this, and he saw the thing in its details; he lived it all, as if he were there. They would sell their furniture, and then run into debt at the stores, and then be refused credit; they would borrow a little from the Szedvilases, whose delicatessen store was tottering on the brink of ruin; the neighbors would come and help them a little—poor, sick Jadvyga would bring a few spare pennies, as she always did when people were starving, and Tamoszius Kuszleika would bring them the proceeds of a night's fiddling. So they would struggle to hang on until he got out of jail—or would they know that he was in jail, would they be able to find out anything about him? Would they be allowed to see him—or was it to be part of his punishment to be kept in ignorance about their fate?

His mind would hang upon the worst possibilities; he saw Ona ill and tortured, Marija out of her place, little Stanislovas unable to get to work for the snow, the whole family turned out on the street. God Almighty! would they actually let them lie down in the street and die? Would there be no help even then—would they wander about in the snow till they froze? Jurgis had never seen any dead bodies in the streets, but he had seen people evicted and disappear, no one knew where; and though the city had a relief bureau, though there was a charity organization society in the stockyards district, in all his life there he had never heard of either of them. They did not advertise their activities, having more calls than they could attend to without that.

—So on until morning. Then he had another ride in the patrol wagon, along with the drunken wife-beater and the maniac, several "plain drunks" and "saloon fighters," a burglar, and two men who had been arrested for stealing meat from the packing houses. Along with them he was driven into a large, white-walled room, stale-smelling and crowded. In front, upon a raised platform behind a rail, sat a stout, florid-faced personage, with a nose broken out in purple blotches.

Our friend realized vaguely that he was about to be tried. He wondered what for—whether or not his victim might be dead, and if so, what they would do with him. Hang him, perhaps, or beat him to death—nothing would have surprised Jurgis, who knew little of the laws. Yet he had picked up gossip enough to have it occur to him that the loud-voiced man upon the bench might be the notorious Justice Callahan, about whom the people of Packingtown spoke with bated breath.

"Pat" Callahan—"Growler" Pat, as he had been known before he ascended the bench—had begun life as a butcher boy and a bruiser of local reputation;

he had gone into politics almost as soon as he had learned to talk, and had held two offices at once before he was old enough to vote. If Scully was the thumb, Pat Callahan was the first finger of the unseen hand whereby the packers held down the people of the district. No politician in Chicago ranked higher in their confidence; he had been at it a long time—had been the business agent in the city council of old Durham, the self-made merchant, way back in the early days, when the whole city of Chicago had been up at auction. "Growler" Pat had given up holding city offices very early in his career—caring only for party power, and giving the rest of his time to superintending his dives and brothels. Of late years, however, since his children were growing up, he had begun to value respectability, and had had himself made a magistrate; a position for which he was admirably fitted, because of his strong conservatism and his contempt for "foreigners."

Jurgis sat gazing about the room for an hour or two; he was in hopes that some one of the family would come, but in this he was disappointed. Finally, he was led before the bar, and a lawyer for the company appeared against him. Connor was under the doctor's care, the lawyer explained briefly, and if his Honor would hold the prisoner for a week—"Three hundred dollars," said his Honor, promptly.

Jurgis was staring from the judge to the lawyer in perplexity. "Have you any one to go on your bond?" demanded the judge, and then a clerk who stood at Jurgis' elbow explained to him what this meant. The latter shook his head, and before he realized what had happened the policemen were leading him away again. They took him to a room where other prisoners were waiting and here he stayed until court adjourned, when he had another long and bitterly cold ride in a patrol wagon to the county jail, which is on the north side of the city, and nine or ten miles from the stockyards.

Here they searched Jurgis, leaving him only his money, which consisted of fifteen cents. Then they led him to a room and told him to strip for a bath; after which he had to walk down a long gallery, past the grated cell doors of the inmates of the jail. This was a great event to the latter—the daily review of the new arrivals, all stark naked, and many and diverting were the comments. Jurgis was required to stay in the bath longer than any one, in the vain hope of getting out of him a few of his phosphates and acids. The prisoners roomed two in a cell, but that day there was one left over, and he was the one.

The cells were in tiers, opening upon galleries. His cell was about five feet by seven in size, with a stone floor and a heavy wooden bench built into it. There was no window—the only light came from windows near the roof at one end of the court outside. There were two bunks, one above the other, each with a straw mattress and a pair of gray blankets—the latter stiff as boards with filth, and alive with fleas, bedbugs, and lice. When Jurgis lifted up the mattress he discovered beneath it a layer of scurrying roaches, almost as badly frightened as himself.

Here they brought him more "duffers and dope," with the addition of a bowl of soup. Many of the prisoners had their meals brought in from a restaurant, but Jurgis had no money for that. Some had books to read and cards to play, with candles to burn by night, but Jurgis was all alone in darkness and silence. He could not sleep again; there was the same maddening procession of thoughts that lashed him like whips upon his naked back. When night fell he was pacing up and down his cell like a wild beast that breaks its teeth upon the bars of its cage. Now and then in his frenzy he would fling himself against the walls of the place, beating his hands upon them. They cut him and bruised him—they were cold and merciless as the men who had built them.

In the distance there was a church-tower bell that tolled the hours one by one. When it came to midnight Jurgis was lying upon the floor with his head in his arms, listening. Instead of falling silent at the end, the bell broke into a sudden clangor. Jurgis raised his head; what could that mean—a fire? God! Suppose there were to be a fire in this jail! But then he made out a melody in the ringing; there were chimes. And they seemed to waken the city—all around, far and near, there were bells, ringing wild music; for fully a minute Jurgis lay lost in wonder, before, all at once, the meaning of it broke over him—that this was Christmas Eve!

Christmas Eve—he had forgotten it entirely! There was a breaking of floodgates, a whirl of new memories and new griefs rushing into his mind. In far Lithuania they had celebrated Christmas; and it came to him as if it had been yesterday—himself a little child, with his lost brother and his dead father in the cabin—in the deep black forest, where the snow fell all day and all night and buried them from the world. It was too far off for Santa Claus in Lithuania, but it was not too far for peace and good will to men, for the wonder-bearing vision of the Christ Child. And even in Packingtown they had not forgotten it—some gleam of it had never failed to break their darkness. Last Christmas Eve and all Christmas Day Jurgis had toiled on the killing beds, and Ona at wrapping hams, and still they had found strength enough to take the children for a walk upon the avenue, to see the store windows all decorated with Christmas trees and ablaze with electric lights. In one window there would be live geese, in another marvels in sugar—pink and white canes big enough for ogres, and cakes with cherubs upon them; in a third there would be rows of fat yellow turkeys, decorated with rosettes, and rabbits and squirrels hanging; in a fourth would be a fairyland of toys—lovely dolls with pink dresses, and woolly sheep and drums and soldier hats. Nor did they have to go without their share of all this, either. The last time they had had a big basket with them and all their Christmas marketing to do—a roast of pork and a cabbage and some rye bread, and a pair of mittens for Ona, and a rubber doll that squeaked, and a little green cornucopia full of candy to be hung from the gas jet and gazed at by half a dozen pairs of longing eyes.

Even half a year of the sausage machines and the fertilizer mill had not been able to kill the thought of Christmas in them; there was a choking in

Jurgis' throat as he recalled that the very night Ona had not come home Teta Elzbieta had taken him aside and shown him an old valentine that she had picked up in a paper store for three cents—dingy and shopworn, but with bright colors, and figures of angels and doves. She had wiped all the specks off this, and was going to set it on the mantel, where the children could see it. Great sobs shook Jurgis at this memory—they would spend their Christmas in misery and despair, with him in prison and Ona ill and their home in desolation. Ah, it was too cruel! Why at least had they not left him alone—why, after they had shut him in jail, must they be ringing Christmas chimes in his ears!

But no, their bells were not ringing for him—their Christmas was not meant for him, they were simply not counting him at all. He was of no consequence—he was flung aside, like a bit of trash, the carcass of some animal. It was horrible, horrible! His wife might be dying, his baby might be starving, his whole family might be perishing in the cold—and all the while they were ringing their Christmas chimes! And the bitter mockery of it—all this was punishment for him! They put him in a place where the snow could not beat in, where the cold could not eat through his bones; they brought him food and drink—why, in the name of heaven, if they must punish him, did they not put his family in jail and leave him outside—why could they find no better way to punish him than to leave three weak women and six helpless children to starve and freeze? That was their law, that was their justice!

Jurgis stood upright; trembling with passion, his hands clenched and his arms upraised, his whole soul ablaze with hatred and defiance. Ten thousand curses upon them and their law! Their justice—it was a lie, it was a lie, a hideous, brutal lie, a thing too black and hateful for any world but a world of nightmares. It was a sham and a loathsome mockery. There was no justice, there was no right, anywhere in it—it was only force, it was tyranny, the will and the power, reckless and unrestrained! They had ground him beneath their heel, they had devoured all his substance; they had murdered his old father, they had broken and wrecked his wife, they had crushed and cowed his whole family; and now they were through with him, they had no further use for him—and because he had interfered with them, had gotten in their way, this was what they had done to him! They had put him behind bars, as if he had been a wild beast, a thing without sense or reason, without rights, without affections, without feelings. Nay, they would not even have treated a beast as they had treated him! Would any man in his senses have trapped a wild thing in its lair, and left its young behind to die?

These midnight hours were fateful ones to Jurgis; in them was the beginning of his rebellion, of his outlawry and his unbelief. He had no wit to trace back the social crime to its far sources—he could not say that it was the thing men have called "the system" that was crushing him to the earth; that it was the packers, his masters, who had bought up the law of the land, and had dealt out their brutal will to him from the seat of justice. He only knew that he was wronged, and that the world had wronged him; that the law, that society, with all its powers, had declared itself his foe. And every hour his soul grew blacker, every hour he dreamed new dreams of vengeance, of defiance, of raging, frenzied hate.

The vilest deeds, like poison weeds,
Bloom well in prison air;
It is only what is good in Man
That wastes and withers there;
Pale Anguish keeps the heavy gate,
And the Warder is Despair.

So wrote a poet, to whom the world had dealt its justice—

I know not whether Laws be right,
Or whether Laws be wrong;
All that we know who lie in gaol
Is that the wall is strong.
And they do well to hide their hell,
For in it things are done
That Son of God nor son of Man
Ever should look upon!

# Chapter 17

At seven o'clock the next morning Jurgis was let out to get water to wash his cell—a duty which he performed faithfully, but which most of the prisoners were accustomed to shirk, until their cells became so filthy that the guards interposed. Then he had more "duffers and dope," and afterward was allowed three hours for exercise, in a long, cement-walked court roofed with glass. Here were all the inmates of the jail crowded together. At one side of the court was a place for visitors, cut off by two heavy wire screens, a foot apart, so that nothing could be passed in to the prisoners; here Jurgis watched anxiously, but there came no one to see him.

Soon after he went back to his cell, a keeper opened the door to let in another prisoner. He was a dapper young fellow, with a light brown mustache and blue eyes, and a graceful figure. He nodded to Jurgis, and then, as the keeper closed the door upon him, began gazing critically about him.

"Well, pal," he said, as his glance encountered Jurgis agai"good morning."

"Good morning," said Jurgis.

"A rum go for Christmas, eh?" added the other.

Jurgis nodded.

The newcomer went to the bunks and inspected the blankets; he lifted up the mattress, and then dropped it with an exclamation. "My God!" he said, "that's the worst yet."

He glanced at Jurgis again. "Looks as if it hadn't been slept in last night. Couldn't stand it, eh?"

"I didn't want to sleep last night," said Jurgis.

"When did you come in?"

"Yesterday."

The other had another look around, and then wrinkled up his nose. "There's the devil of a stink in here," he said, suddenly. "What is it?"

"It's me," said Jurgis.

"You?"

"Yes, me."

"Didn't they make you wash?"

"Yes, but this don't wash."

"What is it?"

"Fertilizer."

"Fertilizer! The deuce! What are you?"

"I work in the stockyards—at least I did until the other day. It's in my clothes."

"That's a new one on me," said the newcomer. "I thought I'd been up against 'em all. What are you in for?"

"I hit my boss."

"Oh—that's it. What did he do?"

"He—he treated me mean."

"I see. You're what's called an honest workingman!"

"What are you?" Jurgis asked.

"I?" The other laughed. "They say I'm a cracksman," he said.

"What's that?" asked Jurgis.

"Safes, and such things," answered the other.

"Oh," said Jurgis, wonderingly, and stared at the speaker in awe. "You mean you break into them—you—you—"

"Yes," laughed the other, "that's what they say."

He did not look to be over twenty-two or three, though, as Jurgis found afterward, he was thirty. He spoke like a man of education, like what the world calls a "gentleman."

"Is that what you're here for?" Jurgis inquired.

"No," was the answer. "I'm here for disorderly conduct. They were mad because they couldn't get any evidence.

"What's your name?" the young fellow continued after a pause. "My name's Duane—Jack Duane. I've more than a dozen, but that's my company one." He seated himself on the floor with his back to the wall and his legs crossed, and went on talking easily; he soon put Jurgis on a friendly footing—he was evidently a man of the world, used to getting on, and not too proud to hold conversation with a mere laboring man. He drew Jurgis out, and heard all about his life all but the one unmentionable thing; and then he told stories about his own life. He was a great one for stories, not always of the choicest. Being sent to jail had apparently not disturbed his cheerfulness; he had "done time" twice before, it seemed, and he took it all with a frolic welcome. What with women and wine and the excitement of his vocation, a man could afford to rest now and then.

Naturally, the aspect of prison life was changed for Jurgis by the arrival of a cell mate. He could not turn his face to the wall and sulk, he had to speak when he was spoken to; nor could he help being interested in the conversation of Duane—the first educated man with whom he had ever talked. How could he help listening with wonder while the other told of midnight ventures and perilous escapes, of feastings and orgies, of fortunes squandered in a night? The young fellow had an amused contempt for Jurgis, as a sort of working mule; he, too, had felt the world's injustice, but instead of bearing it patiently, he had struck back, and struck hard. He was striking all the time—there was war between him and society. He was a genial freebooter, living off the enemy, without fear or shame. He was not always victorious, but then defeat did not mean annihilation, and need not break his spirit.

Withal he was a goodhearted fellow—too much so, it appeared. His story came out, not in the first day, nor the second, but in the long hours that dragged by, in which they had nothing to do but talk and nothing to talk of but themselves. Jack Duane was from the East; he was a college-bred man—had been studying electrical engineering. Then his father had met with misfortune in business and killed himself; and there had been his mother and a younger brother and sister. Also, there was an invention of Duane's; Jurgis could not understand it clearly, but it had to do with telegraphing, and it was a very important thing—there were fortunes in it, millions upon millions of dollars. And Duane had been robbed of it by a great company, and got tangled up in lawsuits and lost all his money. Then somebody had given him a tip on a horse race, and he had tried to retrieve his fortune with another person's money, and had to run away, and all the rest had come from that. The other asked him what had led him to safe-breaking—to Jurgis a wild and appalling occupation to think about. A man he had met, his cell mate had replied—one thing leads to another. Didn't he ever wonder about his family, Jurgis asked. Sometimes, the other answered, but not often—he didn't allow it. Thinking about it would make it no better. This wasn't a world in which a man had any business with a family; sooner or later Jurgis would find that out also, and give up the fight and shift for himself.

Jurgis was so transparently what he pretended to be that his cell mate was as open with him as a child; it was pleasant to tell him adventures, he was so full of wonder and admiration, he was so new to the ways of the country. Duane did not even bother to keep back names and places—he told all his triumphs and his failures, his loves and his griefs. Also he introduced Jurgis to many of the other prisoners, nearly half of whom he knew by name. The crowd had already given Jurgis a name—they called him "the stinker." This was cruel, but they meant no harm by it, and he took it with a good-natured grin.

Our friend had caught now and then a whiff from the sewers over which he lived, but this was the first time that he had ever been splashed by their filth. This jail was a Noah's ark of the city's crime—there were murderers, "hold-up men" and burglars, embezzlers, counterfeiters and forgers, bigamists, "shoplifters," "confidence men," petty thieves and pickpockets, gamblers and procurers, brawlers, beggars, tramps and drunkards; they were black and white, old and young, Americans and natives of every nation under the sun. There were hardened criminals and innocent men too poor to give bail; old men, and boys literally not yet in their teens. They were the drainage of the great festering ulcer of society; they were hideous to look upon, sickening to talk to. All life had turned to rottenness and stench in them—love was a beastliness, joy was a snare, and God was an imprecation. They strolled here and there about the courtyard, and Jurgis listened to them. He was ignorant and they were wise;

they had been everywhere and tried everything. They could tell the whole hateful story of it, set forth the inner soul of a city in which justice and honor, women's bodies and men's souls, were for sale in the marketplace, and human beings writhed and fought and fell upon each other like wolves in a pit; in which lusts were raging fires, and men were fuel, and humanity was festering and stewing and wallowing in its own corruption. Into this wild-beast tangle these men had been born without their consent, they had taken part in it because they could not help it; that they were in jail was no disgrace to them, for the game had never been fair, the dice were loaded. They were swindlers and thieves of pennies and dimes, and they had been trapped and put out of the way by the swindlers and thieves of millions of dollars.

To most of this Jurgis tried not to listen. They frightened him with their savage mockery; and all the while his heart was far away, where his loved ones were calling. Now and then in the midst of it his thoughts would take flight; and then the tears would come into his eyes—and he would be called back by the jeering laughter of his companions.

He spent a week in this company, and during all that time he had no word from his home. He paid one of his fifteen cents for a postal card, and his companion wrote a note to the family, telling them where he was and when he would be tried. There came no answer to it, however, and at last, the day before New Year's, Jurgis bade good-by to Jack Duane. The latter gave him his address, or rather the address of his mistress, and made Jurgis promise to look him up. "Maybe I could help you out of a hole some day," he said, and added that he was sorry to have him go. Jurgis rode in the patrol wagon back to Justice Callahan's court for trial.

One of the first things he made out as he entered the room was Teta Elzbieta and little Kotrina, looking pale and frightened, seated far in the rear. His heart began to pound, but he did not dare to try to signal to them, and neither did Elzbieta. He took his seat in the prisoners' pen and sat gazing at them in helpless agony. He saw that Ona was not with them, and was full of foreboding as to what that might mean. He spent half an hour brooding over this—and then suddenly he straightened up and the blood rushed into his face. A man had come in—Jurgis could not see his features for the bandages that swathed him, but he knew the burly figure. It was Connor! A trembling seized him, and his limbs bent as if for a spring. Then suddenly he felt a hand on his collar, and heard a voice behind him: "Sit down, you son of a—!"

He subsided, but he never took his eyes off his enemy. The fellow was still alive, which was a disappointment, in one way; and yet it was pleasant to see him, all in penitential plasters. He and the company lawyer, who was with him, came and took seats within the judge's railing; and a minute later the clerk called Jurgis' name, and the policeman jerked him to his feet and led him before the bar, gripping him tightly by the arm, lest he should spring upon the boss.

Jurgis listened while the man entered the witness chair, took the oath, and told his story. The wife of the prisoner had been employed in a department near him, and had been discharged for impudence to him. Half an hour later he had been violently attacked, knocked down, and almost choked to death. He had brought witnesses—

"They will probably not be necessary," observed the judge and he turned to Jurgis. "You admit attacking the plaintiff?" he asked.

"Him?" inquired Jurgis, pointing at the boss.

"Yes," said the judge. "I hit him, sir," said Jurgis.

"Say 'your Honor,'" said the officer, pinching his arm hard.

"Your Honor," said Jurgis, obediently.

"You tried to choke him?"

"Yes, sir, your Honor."

"Ever been arrested before?"

"No, sir, your Honor."

"What have you to say for yourself?"

Jurgis hesitated. What had he to say? In two years and a half he had learned to speak English for practical purposes, but these had never included the statement that some one had intimidated and seduced his wife. He tried once or twice, stammering and balking, to the annoyance of the judge, who was gasping from the odor of fertilizer. Finally, the prisoner made it understood that his vocabulary was inadequate, and there stepped up a dapper young man with waxed mustaches, bidding him speak in any language he knew.

Jurgis began; supposing that he would be given time, he explained how the boss had taken advantage of his wife's position to make advances to her and had threatened her with the loss of her place. When the interpreter had translated this, the judge, whose calendar was crowded, and whose automobile was ordered for a certain hour, interrupted with the remark: "Oh, I see. Well, if he made love to your wife, why didn't she complain to the superintendent or leave the place?"

Jurgis hesitated, somewhat taken aback; he began to explain that they were very poor—that work was hard to get—

"I see," said Justice Callahan; "so instead you thought you would knock him down." He turned to the plaintiff, inquiring, "Is there any truth in this story, Mr. Connor?"

"Not a particle, your Honor," said the boss. "It is very unpleasant—they tell some such tale every time you have to discharge a woman—"

"Yes, I know," said the judge. "I hear it often enough. The fellow seems to have handled you pretty roughly. Thirty days and costs. Next case."

Jurgis had been listening in perplexity. It was only when the policeman who had him by the arm turned and started to lead him away that he realized that sentence had been passed. He gazed round him wildly. "Thirty days!" he panted and then he whirled upon the judge. "What will my family do?" he cried frantically. "I have a wife and baby, sir, and they have no money—my God, they will starve to death!"

"You would have done well to think about them before you committed the assault," said the judge dryly, as he turned to look at the next prisoner.

Jurgis would have spoken again, but the policeman had seized him by the collar and was twisting it, and a second policeman was making for him with evidently hostile intentions. So he let them lead him away. Far down the room he saw Elzbieta and Kotrina, risen from their seats, staring in fright; he made one effort to go to them, and then, brought back by another twist at his throat, he bowed his head and gave up the struggle. They thrust him into a cell room, where other prisoners were waiting; and as soon as court had adjourned they led him down with them into the "Black Maria," and drove him away.

This time Jurgis was bound for the "Bridewell," a petty jail where Cook County prisoners serve their time. It was even filthier and more crowded than the county jail; all the smaller fry out of the latter had been sifted into it—the petty thieves and swindlers, the brawlers and vagrants. For his cell mate Jurgis had an Italian fruit seller who had refused to pay his graft to the policeman, and been arrested for carrying a large pocketknife; as he did not understand a word of English our friend was glad when he left. He gave place to a Norwegian sailor, who had lost half an ear in a drunken brawl, and who proved to be quarrelsome, cursing Jurgis because he moved in his bunk and caused the roaches to drop upon the lower one. It would have been quite intolerable, staying in a cell with this wild beast, but for the fact that all day long the prisoners were put at work breaking stone.

Ten days of his thirty Jurgis spent thus, without hearing a word from his family; then one day a keeper came and informed him that there was a visitor to see him. Jurgis turned white, and so weak at the knees that he could hardly leave his cell.

The man led him down the corridor and a flight of steps to the visitors' room, which was barred like a cell. Through the grating Jurgis could see some one sitting in a chair; and as he came into the room the person started up, and he saw that it was little Stanislovas. At the sight of some one from home the big fellow nearly went to pieces—he had to steady himself by a chair, and he put his other hand to his forehead, as if to clear away a mist. "Well?" he said, weakly.

Little Stanislovas was also trembling, and all but too frightened to speak. "They—they sent me to tell you—" he said, with a gulp.

"Well?" Jurgis repeated. He followed the boy's glance to where the keeper was standing watching them. "Never mind that," Jurgis cried, wildly. "How are they?"

"Ona is very sick," Stanislovas said; "and we are almost starving. We can't get along; we thought you might be able to help us."

Jurgis gripped the chair tighter; there were beads of perspiration on his forehead, and his hand shook. "I—can't help you," he said.

"Ona lies in her room all day," the boy went on, breathlessly. "She won't eat anything, and she cries all the time. She won't tell what is the matter and she won't go to work at all. Then a long time ago the man came for the rent. He was very cross. He came again last week. He said he would turn us out of the house. And then Marija—"

A sob choked Stanislovas, and he stopped. "What's the matter with Marija?" cried Jurgis.

"She's cut her hand!" said the boy. "She's cut it bad, this time, worse than before. She can't work and it's all turning green, and the company doctor says she may—she may have to have it cut off. And Marija cries all the time—her money is nearly all gone, too, and we can't pay the rent and the interest on the house; and we have no coal and nothing more to eat, and the man at the store, he says—"

The little fellow stopped again, beginning to whimper. "Go on!" the other panted in frenzy—"Go on!"

"I—I will," sobbed Stanislovas. "It's so—so cold all the time. And last Sunday it snowed again—a deep, deep snow—and I couldn't—couldn't get to work."

"God!" Jurgis half shouted, and he took a step toward the child. There was an old hatred between them because of the snow—ever since that dreadful morning when the boy had had his fingers frozen and Jurgis had had to beat him to send him to work. Now he clenched his hands, looking as if he would try to break through the grating. "You little villain," he cried, "you didn't try!"

"I did—I did!" wailed Stanislovas, shrinking from him in terror. "I tried all day—two days. Elzbieta was with me, and she couldn't either. We couldn't walk at all, it was so deep. And we had nothing to eat, and oh, it was so cold! I tried, and then the third day Ona went with me—"

"Ona!"

"Yes. She tried to get to work, too. She had to. We were all starving. But she had lost her place—"

Jurgis reeled, and gave a gasp. "She went back to that place?" he screamed. "She tried to," said Stanislovas, gazing at him in perplexity. "Why not, Jurgis?"

The man breathed hard, three or four times. "Go—on," he panted, finally.

"I went with her," said Stanislovas, "but Miss Henderson wouldn't take her back. And Connor saw her and cursed her. He was still bandaged up—why did you hit him, Jurgis?" (There was some fascinating mystery about this, the little fellow knew; but he could get no satisfaction.)

Jurgis could not speak; he could only stare, his eyes starting out. "She has been trying to get other work," the boy went on; "but she's so weak she can't keep up. And my boss would not take me back, either—Ona says he knows

Connor, and that's the reason; they've all got a grudge against us now. So I've got to go downtown and sell papers with the rest of the boys and Kotrina—"

"Kotrina!"

"Yes, she's been selling papers, too. She does best, because she's a girl. Only the cold is so bad—it's terrible coming home at night, Jurgis. Sometimes they can't come home at all—I'm going to try to find them tonight and sleep where they do, it's so late and it's such a long ways home. I've had to walk, and I didn't know where it was—I don't know how to get back, either. Only mother said I must come, because you would want to know, and maybe somebody would help your family when they had put you in jail so you couldn't work. And I walked all day to get here—and I only had a piece of bread for breakfast, Jurgis. Mother hasn't any work either, because the sausage department is shut down; and she goes and begs at houses with a basket, and people give her food. Only she didn't get much yesterday; it was too cold for her fingers, and today she was crying—"

So little Stanislovas went on, sobbing as he talked; and Jurgis stood, gripping the table tightly, saying not a word, but feeling that his head would burst; it was like having weights piled upon him, one after another, crushing the life out of him. He struggled and fought within himself—as if in some terrible nightmare, in which a man suffers an agony, and cannot lift his hand, nor cry out, but feels that he is going mad, that his brain is on fire—

Just when it seemed to him that another turn of the screw would kill him, little Stanislovas stopped. "You cannot help us?" he said weakly.

Jurgis shook his head.

"They won't give you anything here?"

He shook it again.

"When are you coming out?"

"Three weeks yet," Jurgis answered.

And the boy gazed around him uncertainly. "Then I might as well go, " he said.

Jurgis nodded. Then, suddenly recollecting, he put his hand into his pocket and drew it out, shaking. "Here," he said, holding out the fourteen cents. "Take this to them."

And Stanislovas took it, and after a little more hesitation, started for the door. "Good-by, Jurgis," he said, and the other noticed that he walked unsteadily as he passed out of sight.

For a minute or so Jurgis stood clinging to his chair, reeling and swaying; then the keeper touched him on the arm, and he turned and went back to breaking stone.

# Chapter 18

Jurgis did not get out of the Bridewell quite as soon as he had expected. To his sentence there were added "court costs" of a dollar and a half—he was supposed to pay for the trouble of putting him in jail, and not having the money, was obliged to work it off by three days more of toil. Nobody had taken the trouble to tell him this—only after counting the days and looking forward to the end in an agony of impatience, when the hour came that he expected to be free he found himself still set at the stone heap, and laughed at when he ventured to protest. Then he concluded he must have counted wrong; but as another day passed, he gave up all hope—and was sunk in the depths of despair, when one morning after breakfast a keeper came to him with the word that his time was up at last. So he doffed his prison garb, and put on his old fertilizer clothing, and heard the door of the prison clang behind him.

He stood upon the steps, bewildered; he could hardly believe that it was true,—that the sky was above him again and the open street before him; that he was a free man. But then the cold began to strike through his clothes, and he started quickly away.

There had been a heavy snow, and now a thaw had set in; fine sleety rain was falling, driven by a wind that pierced Jurgis to the bone. He had not stopped for his-overcoat when he set out to "do up" Connor, and so his rides in the patrol wagons had been cruel experiences; his clothing was old and worn thin, and it never had been very warm. Now as he trudged on the rain soon wet it through; there were six inches of watery slush on the sidewalks, so that his feet would soon have been soaked, even had there been no holes in his shoes.

Jurgis had had enough to eat in the jail, and the work had been the least trying of any that he had done since he came to Chicago; but even so, he had not grown strong—the fear and grief that had preyed upon his mind had worn him thin. Now he shivered and shrunk from the rain, hiding his hands in his pockets and hunching his shoulders together. The Bridewell grounds were on the outskirts of the city and the country around them was unsettled and wild—on one side was the big drainage canal, and on the other a maze of railroad tracks, and so the wind had full sweep.

After walking a ways, Jurgis met a little ragamuffin whom he hailed: "Hey, sonny!" The boy cocked one eye at him—he knew that Jurgis was a "jailbird" by his shaven head. "Wot yer want?" he queried.

"How do you go to the stockyards?" Jurgis demanded.

"I don't go," replied the boy.

Jurgis hesitated a moment, nonplussed. Then he said, "I mean which is the way?"

"Why don't yer say so then?" was the response, and the boy pointed to the northwest, across the tracks. "That way."

"How far is it?" Jurgis asked. "I dunno," said the other. "Mebbe twenty miles or so."

"Twenty miles!" Jurgis echoed, and his face fell. He had to walk every foot of it, for they had turned him out of jail without a penny in his pockets.

Yet, when he once got started, and his blood had warmed with walking, he forgot everything in the fever of his thoughts. All the dreadful imaginations that had haunted him in his cell now rushed into his mind at once. The agony was almost over—he was going to find out; and he clenched his hands in his pockets as he strode, following his flying desire, almost at a run. Ona—the baby—the family—the house—he would know the truth about them all! And he was coming to the rescue—he was free again! His hands were his own, and he could help them, he could do battle for them against the world.

For an hour or so he walked thus, and then he began to look about him. He seemed to be leaving the city altogether. The street was turning into a country road, leading out to the westward; there were snow-covered fields on either side of him. Soon he met a farmer driving a two-horse wagon loaded with straw, and he stopped him.

"Is this the way to the stockyards?" he asked.

The farmer scratched his head. "I dunno jest where they be," he said. "But they're in the city somewhere, and you're going dead away from it now."

Jurgis looked dazed. "I was told this was the way," he said.

"Who told you?"

"A boy."

"Well, mebbe he was playing a joke on ye. The best thing ye kin do is to go back, and when ye git into town ask a policeman. I'd take ye in, only I've come a long ways an' I'm loaded heavy. Git up!"

So Jurgis turned and followed, and toward the end of the morning he began to see Chicago again. Past endless blocks of two-story shanties he walked, along wooden sidewalks and unpaved pathways treacherous with deep slush holes. Every few blocks there would be a railroad crossing on the level with the sidewalk, a deathtrap for the unwary; long freight trains would be passing, the cars clanking and crashing together, and Jurgis would pace about waiting, burning up with a fever of impatience. Occasionally the cars would stop for some minutes, and wagons and streetcars would crowd together waiting, the drivers swearing at each other, or hiding beneath umbrellas out of the rain; at such times Jurgis would dodge under the gates and run across the tracks and between the cars, taking his life into his hands.

He crossed a long bridge over a river frozen solid and covered with slush. Not even on the river bank was the snow white—the rain which fell was a diluted solution of smoke, and Jurgis' hands and face were streaked with black. Then he came into the business part of the city, where the streets were sewers of inky blackness, with horses sleeping and plunging, and women and children flying across in panic-stricken droves. These streets were huge canyons formed by towering black buildings, echoing with the clang of car gongs and the shouts of drivers; the people who swarmed in them were as busy as ants—all hurrying breathlessly, never stopping to look at anything nor at each other. The solitary trampish-looking foreigner, with water-soaked clothing and haggard face and anxious eyes, was as much alone as he hurried past them, as much unheeded and as lost, as if he had been a thousand miles deep in a wilderness.

A policeman gave him his direction and told him that he had five miles to go. He came again to the slum districts, to avenues of saloons and cheap stores, with long dingy red factory buildings, and coal-yards and railroad tracks; and then Jurgis lifted up his head and began to sniff the air like a startled animal—scenting the far-off odor of home. It was late afternoon then, and he was hungry, but the dinner invitations hung out of the saloons were not for him.

So he came at last to the stockyards, to the black volcanoes of smoke and the lowing cattle and the stench. Then, seeing a crowded car, his impatience got the better of him and he jumped aboard, hiding behind another man, unnoticed by the conductor. In ten minutes more he had reached his street, and home.

He was half running as he came round the corner. There was the house, at any rate—and then suddenly he stopped and stared. What was the matter with the house?

Jurgis looked twice, bewildered; then he glanced at the house next door and at the one beyond—then at the saloon on the corner. Yes, it was the right place, quite certainly—he had not made any mistake. But the house—the house was a different color!

He came a couple of steps nearer. Yes; it had been gray and now it was yellow! The trimmings around the windows had been red, and now they were green! It was all newly painted! How strange it made it seem!

Jurgis went closer yet, but keeping on the other side of the street. A sudden and horrible spasm of fear had come over him. His knees were shaking beneath him, and his mind was in a whirl. New paint on the house, and new weatherboards, where the old had begun to rot off, and the agent had got after them! New shingles over the hole in the roof, too, the hole that had for six months been the bane of his soul—he having no money to have it fixed and no time to fix it himself, and the rain leaking in, and overflowing the pots and pans he put to catch it, and flooding the attic and loosening the plaster. And now it was fixed! And the broken windowpane replaced! And curtains in the windows! New, white curtains, stiff and shiny!

Then suddenly the front door opened. Jurgis stood, his chest heaving as he struggled to catch his breath. A boy had come out, a stranger to him; a big, fat, rosy-cheeked youngster, such as had never been seen in his home before.

Jurgis stared at the boy, fascinated. He came down the steps whistling, kicking off the snow. He stopped at the foot, and picked up some, and then leaned against the railing, making a snowball. A moment later he looked around and saw Jurgis, and their eyes met; it was a hostile glance, the boy evidently thinking that the other had suspicions of the snowball. When Jurgis started slowly across the street toward him, he gave a quick glance about, meditating retreat, but then he concluded to stand his ground.

Jurgis took hold of the railing of the steps, for he was a little unsteady. "What—what are you doing here?" he managed to gasp.

"Go on!" said the boy.

"You—" Jurgis tried again. "What do you want here?"

"Me?" answered the boy, angrily. "I live here."

"You live here!" Jurgis panted. He turned white and clung more tightly to the railing. "You live here! Then where's my family?"

The boy looked surprised. "Your family!" he echoed.

And Jurgis started toward him. "I—this is my house!" he cried.

"Come off!" said the boy; then suddenly the door upstairs opened, and he called: "Hey, ma! Here's a fellow says he owns this house."

A stout Irishwoman came to the top of the steps. "What's that?" she demanded.

Jurgis turned toward her. "Where is my family?" he cried, wildly. "I left them here! This is my home! What are you doing in my home?"

The woman stared at him in frightened wonder, she must have thought she was dealing with a maniac—Jurgis looked like one. "Your home!" she echoed.

"My home!" he half shrieked. "I lived here, I tell you."

"You must be mistaken," she answered him. "No one ever lived here. This is a new house. They told us so. They—"

"What have they done with my family?" shouted Jurgis, frantically.

A light had begun to break upon the woman; perhaps she had had doubts of what "they" had told her. "I don't know where your family is," she said. "I bought the house only three days ago, and there was nobody here, and they told me it was all new. Do you really mean you had ever rented it?"

"Rented it!" panted Jurgis. "I bought it! I paid for it! I own it! And they—my God, can't you tell me where my people went?"

She made him understand at last that she knew nothing. Jurgis' brain was so confused that he could not grasp the situation. It was as if his family had been wiped out of existence; as if they were proving to be dream people, who never had existed at all. He was quite lost—but then suddenly he thought of Grandmother Majauszkiene, who lived in the next block. She would know! He turned and started at a run.

Grandmother Majauszkiene came to the door herself. She cried out when she saw Jurgis, wild-eyed and shaking. Yes, yes, she could tell him. The family had moved; they had not been able to pay the rent and they had been turned out into the snow, and the house had been repainted and sold again the next week. No, she had not heard how they were, but she could tell him that they had gone back to Aniele Jukniene, with whom they had stayed when they first came to the yards. Wouldn't Jurgis come in and rest? It was certainly too bad—if only he had not got into jail—

And so Jurgis turned and staggered away. He did not go very far round the corner he gave out completely, and sat down on the steps of a saloon, and hid his face in his hands, and shook all over with dry, racking sobs.

Their home! Their home! They had lost it! Grief, despair, rage, overwhelmed him—what was any imagination of the thing to this heartbreaking, crushing reality of it—to the sight of strange people living in his house, hanging their curtains to his windows, staring at him with hostile eyes! It was monstrous, it was unthinkable—they could not do it—it could not be true! Only think what he had suffered for that house—what miseries they had all suffered for it—the price they had paid for it!

The whole long agony came back to him. Their sacrifices in the beginning, their three hundred dollars that they had scraped together, all they owned in the world, all that stood between them and starvation! And then their toil, month by month, to get together the twelve dollars, and the interest as well, and now and then the taxes, and the other charges, and the repairs, and what not! Why, they had put their very souls into their payments on that house, they had paid for it with their sweat and tears—yes, more, with their very lifeblood. Dede Antanas had died of the struggle to earn that money—he would have been alive and strong today if he had not had to work in Durham's dark cellars to earn his share. And Ona, too, had given her health and strength to pay for it—she was wrecked and ruined because of it; and so was he, who had been a big, strong man three years ago, and now sat here shivering, broken, cowed, weeping like a hysterical child. Ah! they had cast their all into the fight; and they had lost, they had lost! All that they had paid was gone—every cent of it. And their house was gone—they were back where they had started from, flung out into the cold to starve and freeze!

Jurgis could see all the truth now—could see himself, through the whole long course of events, the victim of ravenous vultures that had torn into his vitals and devoured him; of fiends that had racked and tortured him, mocking him, meantime, jeering in his face. Ah, God, the horror of it, the monstrous, hideous, demoniacal wickedness of it! He and his family, helpless women and children, struggling to live, ignorant and defenseless and forlorn as they were—and the enemies that had been lurking for them, crouching upon their trail and thirsting for their blood! That first lying circular, that smooth-tongued slippery agent! That trap of the extra payments, the interest, and all the other charges that they had not the means to pay, and would never have attempted to pay! And then all the tricks of the packers, their masters, the tyrants who ruled them—the shutdowns and the scarcity of work, the irregular hours and the cruel speeding-up, the lowering of wages, the raising of prices! The mercilessness of nature about them, of heat and cold, rain and snow; the mercilessness of the city, of the country in which they lived, of its laws and customs that they did not understand! All of these things had worked together for the company that had marked them for its prey and was waiting for its chance. And now, with this last hideous injustice, its time had come, and it had turned them out bag and baggage, and taken their house and sold it again! And they could do nothing, they were tied hand and foot—the law was against them, the whole machinery of society was at their oppressors' command! If Jurgis so much as raised a hand against them, back he would go into that wild-beast pen from which he had just escaped!

To get up and go away was to give up, to acknowledge defeat, to leave the strange family in possession; and Jurgis might have sat shivering in the rain for hours before he could do that, had it not been for the thought of his family. It might be that he had worse things yet to learn—and so he got to his feet and started away, walking on, wearily, half-dazed.

To Aniele's house, in back of the yards, was a good two miles; the distance had never seemed longer to Jurgis, and when he saw the familiar dingy-gray shanty his heart was beating fast. He ran up the steps and began to hammer upon the door.

The old woman herself came to open it. She had shrunk all up with her rheumatism since Jurgis had seen her last, and her yellow parchment face stared up at him from a little above the level of the doorknob. She gave a start when she saw him. "Is Ona here?" he cried, breathlessly.

"Yes," was the answer, "she's here."

"How—" Jurgis began, and then stopped short, clutching convulsively at the side of the door. From somewhere within the house had come a sudden cry, a wild, horrible scream of anguish. And the voice was Ona's. For a moment Jurgis stood half-paralyzed with fright; then he bounded past the old woman and into the room.

It was Aniele's kitchen, and huddled round the stove were half a dozen women, pale and frightened. One of them started to her feet as Jurgis entered; she was haggard and frightfully thin, with one arm tied up in bandages—he hardly realized that it was Marija. He looked first for Ona; then, not seeing her, he stared at the women, expecting them to speak. But they sat dumb, gazing back at him, panic-stricken; and a second later came another piercing scream.

It was from the rear of the house, and upstairs. Jurgis bounded to a door of the room and flung it open; there was a ladder leading through a trap door to the garret, and he was at the foot of it when suddenly he heard a voice behind him, and saw Marija at his heels. She seized him by the sleeve with her good hand, panting wildly, "No, no, Jurgis! Stop!"

"What do you mean?" he gasped.

"You mustn't go up," she cried.

Jurgis was half-crazed with bewilderment and fright. "What's the matter?" he shouted. "What is it?"

Marija clung to him tightly; he could hear Ona sobbing and moaning above, and he fought to get away and climb up, without waiting for her reply. "No, no," she rushed on. "Jurgis! You mustn't go up! It's—it's the child!"

"The child?" he echoed in perplexity. "Antanas?"

Marija answered him, in a whisper: "The new one!"

And then Jurgis went limp, and caught himself on the ladder. He stared at her as if she were a ghost. "The new one!" he gasped. "But it isn't time," he added, wildly.

Marija nodded. "I know," she said; "but it's come."

And then again came Ona's scream, smiting him like a blow in the face, making him wince and turn white. Her voice died away into a wail—then he heard her sobbing again, "My God—let me die, let me die!" And Marija hung her arms about him, crying: "Come out! Come away!"

She dragged him back into the kitchen, half carrying him, for he had gone all to pieces. It was as if the pillars of his soul had fallen in—he was blasted with horror. In the room he sank into a chair, trembling like a leaf, Marija still holding him, and the women staring at him in dumb, helpless fright.

And then again Ona cried out; he could hear it nearly as plainly here, and he staggered to his feet. "How long has this been going on?" he panted.

"Not very long," Marija answered, and then, at a signal from Aniele, she rushed on: "You go away, Jurgis you can't help—go away and come back later. It's all right—it's—"

"Who's with her?" Jurgis demanded; and then, seeing Marija hesitating, he cried again, "Who's with her?"

"She's—she's all right," she answered. "Elzbieta's with her."

"But the doctor!" he panted. "Some one who knows!"

He seized Marija by the arm; she trembled, and her voice sank beneath a whisper as she replied, "We—we have no money." Then, frightened at the look on his face, she exclaimed: "It's all right, Jurgis! You don't understand—go away—go away! Ah, if you only had waited!"

Above her protests Jurgis heard Ona again; he was almost out of his mind. It was all new to him, raw and horrible—it had fallen upon him like a lightning stroke. When little Antanas was born he had been at work, and had known nothing about it until it was over; and now he was not to be controlled. The frightened women were at their wits' end; one after another they tried to reason with him, to make him understand that this was the lot of woman. In the end they half drove him out into the rain, where he began to pace up and down, bareheaded and frantic. Because he could hear Ona from the street, he would first go away to escape the sounds, and then come back because he could not help it. At the end of a quarter of an hour he rushed up the steps again, and for fear that he would break in the door they had to open it and let him in.

There was no arguing with him. They could not tell him that all was going well—how could they know, he cried—why, she was dying, she was being torn to pieces! Listen to her—listen! Why, it was monstrous—it could not be allowed—there must be some help for it! Had they tried to get a doctor? They might pay him afterward—they could promise—

"We couldn't promise, Jurgis," protested Marija. "We had no money—we have scarcely been able to keep alive."

"But I can work," Jurgis exclaimed. "I can earn money!"

"Yes," she answered—"but we thought you were in jail. How could we know when you would return? They will not work for nothing."

Marija went on to tell how she had tried to find a midwife, and how they had demanded ten, fifteen, even twenty-five dollars, and that in cash. "And I had only a quarter," she said. "I have spent every cent of my money—all that I had in the bank; and I owe the doctor who has been coming to see me, and he has stopped because he thinks I don't mean to pay him. And we owe Aniele for two weeks' rent, and she is nearly starving, and is afraid of being turned out. We have been borrowing and begging to keep alive, and there is nothing more we can do—"

"And the children?" cried Jurgis.

"The children have not been home for three days, the weather has been so bad. They could not know what is happening—it came suddenly, two months before we expected it."

Jurgis was standing by the table, and he caught himself with his hand; his head sank and his arms shook—it looked as if he were going to collapse. Then suddenly Aniele got up and came hobbling toward him, fumbling in her skirt pocket. She drew out a dirty rag, in one corner of which she had something tied.

"Here, Jurgis!" she said, "I have some money. Palauk! See!"

She unwrapped it and counted it out—thirty-four cents. "You go, now," she said, "and try and get somebody yourself. And maybe the rest can help—give him some money, you; he will pay you back some day, and it will do him good to have something to think about, even if he doesn't succeed. When he comes back, maybe it will be over."

And so the other women turned out the contents of their pocketbooks; most of them had only pennies and nickels, but they gave him all. Mrs. Olszewski, who lived next door, and had a husband who was a skilled cattle butcher, but a drinking man, gave nearly half a dollar, enough to raise the whole sum to a dollar and a quarter. Then Jurgis thrust it into his pocket, still holding it tightly in his fist, and started away at a run.

## Chapter 19

"Madame Haupt Hebamme", ran a sign, swinging from a second-story window over a saloon on the avenue; at a side door was another sign, with a hand pointing up a dingy flight of stairs. Jurgis went up them, three at a time.

Madame Haupt was frying pork and onions, and had her door half open to let out the smoke. When he tried to knock upon it, it swung open the rest of the way, and he had a glimpse of her, with a black bottle turned up to her lips. Then he knocked louder, and she started and put it away. She was a Dutchwoman, enormously fat—when she walked she rolled like a small boat on the ocean, and the dishes in the cupboard jostled each other. She wore a filthy blue wrapper, and her teeth were black.

"Vot is it?" she said, when she saw Jurgis.

He had run like mad all the way and was so out of breath he could hardly speak. His hair was flying and his eyes wild—he looked like a man that had risen from the tomb. "My wife!" he panted. "Come quickly!" Madame Haupt set the frying pan to one side and wiped her hands on her wrapper.

"You vant me to come for a case?" she inquired.

"Yes," gasped Jurgis.

"I haf yust come back from a case," she said. "I haf had no time to eat my dinner. Still—if it is so bad—"

"Yes—it is!" cried he.

"Vell, den, perhaps—vot you pay?"

"I—I—how much do you want?" Jurgis stammered.

"Tventy-five dollars." His face fell. "I can't pay that," he said.

The woman was watching him narrowly. "How much do you pay?" she demanded.

"Must I pay now—right away?"

"Yes; all my customers do."

"I—I haven't much money," Jurgis began in an agony of dread. "I've been in—in trouble—and my money is gone. But I'll pay you—every cent—just as soon as I can; I can work—"

"Vot is your work?"

"I have no place now. I must get one. But I—"

"How much haf you got now?"

He could hardly bring himself to reply. When he said "A dollar and a quarter," the woman laughed in his face.

"I vould not put on my hat for a dollar and a quarter," she said.

"It's all I've got," he pleaded, his voice breaking. "I must get some one—my wife will die. I can't help it—I—"

Madame Haupt had put back her pork and onions on the stove. She turned to him and answered, out of the steam and noise: "Git me ten dollars cash, und so you can pay me the rest next mont'."

"I can't do it—I haven't got it!" Jurgis protested. "I tell you I have only a dollar and a quarter."

The woman turned to her work. "I don't believe you," she said. "Dot is all to try to sheat me. Vot is de reason a big man like you has got only a dollar und a quarter?"

"I've just been in jail," Jurgis cried—he was ready to get down upon his knees to the woman—"and I had no money before, and my family has almost starved."

"Vere is your friends, dot ought to help you?"

"They are all poor," he answered. "They gave me this. I have done everything I can—"

"Haven't you got notting you can sell?"

"I have nothing, I tell you—I have nothing," he cried, frantically.

"Can't you borrow it, den? Don't your store people trust you?" Then, as he shook his head, she went on: "Listen to me—if you git me you vill be glad of it. I vill save your wife und baby for you, and it vill not seem like mooch to you in de end. If you loose dem now how you tink you feel den? Und here is a lady dot knows her business—I could send you to people in dis block, und dey vould tell you—"

Madame Haupt was pointing her cooking-fork at Jurgis persuasively; but her words were more than he could bear. He flung up his hands with a gesture of despair and turned and started away. "It's no use," he exclaimed—but suddenly he heard the woman's voice behind him again—

"I vill make it five dollars for you."

She followed behind him, arguing with him. "You vill be foolish not to take such an offer," she said. "You von't find nobody go out on a rainy day like dis for less. Vy, I haf never took a case in my life so sheap as dot. I couldn't pay mine room rent—"

Jurgis interrupted her with an oath of rage. "If I haven't got it," he shouted, "how can I pay it? Damn it, I would pay you if I could, but I tell you I haven't got it. I haven't got it! Do you hear me I haven't got it!"

He turned and started away again. He was halfway down the stairs before Madame Haupt could shout to him: "Vait! I vill go mit you! Come back!"

He went back into the room again.

"It is not goot to tink of anybody suffering," she said, in a melancholy voice. "I might as vell go mit you for noffing as vot you offer me, but I vill try to help you. How far is it?"

"Three or four blocks from here."

"Tree or four! Und so I shall get soaked! Gott in Himmel, it ought to be vorth more! Vun dollar und a quarter, und a day like dis!—But you understand now—you vill pay me de rest of twenty-five dollars soon?"

"As soon as I can."

"Some time dis mont'?"

"Yes, within a month," said poor Jurgis. "Anything! Hurry up!"

"Vere is de dollar und a quarter?" persisted Madame Haupt, relentlessly.

Jurgis put the money on the table and the woman counted it and stowed it away. Then she wiped her greasy hands again and proceeded to get ready, complaining all the time; she was so fat that it was painful for her to move, and she grunted and gasped at every step. She took off her wrapper without even taking the trouble to turn her back to Jurgis, and put on her corsets and dress. Then there was a black bonnet which had to be adjusted carefully, and an umbrella which was mislaid, and a bag full of necessaries which had to be collected from here and there—the man being nearly crazy with anxiety in the meantime. When they were on the street he kept about four paces ahead of her, turning now and then, as if he could hurry her on by the force of his desire. But Madame Haupt could only go so far at a step, and it took all her attention to get the needed breath for that.

They came at last to the house, and to the group of frightened women in the kitchen. It was not over yet, Jurgis learned—he heard Ona crying still; and meantime Madame Haupt removed her bonnet and laid it on the mantelpiece, and got out of her bag, first an old dress and then a saucer of goose grease, which she proceeded to rub upon her hands. The more cases this goose grease is used in, the better luck it brings to the midwife, and so she keeps it upon her kitchen mantelpiece or stowed away in a cupboard with her dirty clothes, for months, and sometimes even for years.

Then they escorted her to the ladder, and Jurgis heard her give an exclamation of dismay. "Gott in Himmel, vot for haf you brought me to a place like dis? I could not climb up dot ladder. I could not git troo a trap door! I vill not try it—vy, I might kill myself already. Vot sort of a place is dot for a woman to bear a child in—up in a garret, mit only a ladder to it? You ought to be ashamed of yourselves!" Jurgis stood in the doorway and listened to her scolding, half drowning out the horrible moans and screams of Ona.

At last Aniele succeeded in pacifying her, and she essayed the ascent; then, however, she had to be stopped while the old woman cautioned her about the floor of the garret. They had no real floor—they had laid old boards in one part to make a place for the family to live; it was all right and safe there, but the other part of the garret had only the joists of the floor, and the lath and plaster of the ceiling below, and if one stepped on this there would be a catastrophe. As it was half dark up above, perhaps one of the others had best go up first with a candle. Then there were more outcries and threatening, until at last

Jurgis had a vision of a pair of elephantine legs disappearing through the trap door, and felt the house shake as Madame Haupt started to walk. Then suddenly Aniele came to him and took him by the arm.

"Now," she said, "you go away. Do as I tell you—you have done all you can, and you are only in the way. Go away and stay away."

"But where shall I go?" Jurgis asked, helplessly.

"I don't know where," she answered. "Go on the street, if there is no other place—only go! And stay all night!"

In the end she and Marija pushed him out of the door and shut it behind him. It was just about sundown, and it was turning cold—the rain had changed to snow, and the slush was freezing. Jurgis shivered in his thin clothing, and put his hands into his pockets and started away. He had not eaten since morning, and he felt weak and ill; with a sudden throb of hope he recollected he was only a few blocks from the saloon where he had been wont to eat his dinner. They might have mercy on him there, or he might meet a friend. He set out for the place as fast as he could walk.

"Hello, Jack," said the saloon keeper, when he entered—they call all foreigners and unskilled men "Jack" in Packingtown. "Where've you been?"

Jurgis went straight to the bar. "I've been in jail," he said, "and I've just got out. I walked home all the way, and I've not a cent, and had nothing to eat since this morning. And I've lost my home, and my wife's ill, and I'm done up."

The saloon-keeper gazed at him, with his haggard white face and his blue trembling lips. Then he pushed a big bottle toward him. "Fill her up!" he said.

Jurgis could hardly hold the bottle, his hands shook so.

"Don't be afraid," said the saloon-keeper, "fill her up!"

So Jurgis drank a large glass of whisky, and then turned to the lunch counter, in obedience to the other's suggestion. He ate all he dared, stuffing it in as fast as he could; and then, after trying to speak his gratitude, he went and sat down by the big red stove in the middle of the room.

It was too good to last, however—like all things in this hard world. His soaked clothing began to steam, and the horrible stench of fertilizer to fill the room. In an hour or so the packing houses would be closing and the men coming in from their work; and they would not come into a place that smelt of Jurgis. Also it was Saturday night, and in a couple of hours would come a violin and a cornet, and in the rear part of the saloon the families of the neighborhood would dance and feast upon wienerwurst and lager, until two or three o'clock in the morning. The saloon-keeper coughed once or twice, and then remarked, "Say, Jack, I'm afraid you'll have to quit."

He was used to the sight of human wrecks, this saloon-keeper; he "fired" dozens of them every night, just as haggard and cold and forlorn as this one. But they were all men who had given up and been counted out, while Jurgis was still in the fight, and had reminders of decency about him. As he got up meekly, the other reflected that he had always been a steady man, and might soon be a good customer again. "You've been up against it, I see," he said. "Come this way."

In the rear of the saloon were the cellar stairs. There was a door above and another below, both safely padlocked, making the stairs an admirable place to stow away a customer who might still chance to have money, or a political light whom it was not advisable to kick out of doors.

So Jurgis spent the night. The whisky had only half warmed him, and he could not sleep, exhausted as he was; he would nod forward, and then start up, shivering with the cold, and begin to remember again. Hour after hour passed, until he could only persuade himself that it was not morning by the sounds of music and laughter and singing that were to be heard from the room. When at last these ceased, he expected that he would be turned out into the street; as this did not happen, he fell to wondering whether the man had forgotten him.

In the end, when the silence and suspense were no longer to be borne, he got up and hammered on the door; and the proprietor came, yawning and rubbing his eyes. He was keeping open all night, and dozing between customers.

"I want to go home," Jurgis said. "I'm worried about my wife—I can't wait any longer."

"Why the hell didn't you say so before?" said the man. "I thought you didn't have any home to go to." Jurgis went outside. It was four o'clock in the morning, and as black as night. There were three or four inches of fresh snow on the ground, and the flakes were falling thick and fast. He turned toward Aniele's and started at a run.

There was a light burning in the kitchen window and the blinds were drawn. The door was unlocked and Jurgis rushed in.

Aniele, Marija, and the rest of the women were huddled about the stove, exactly as before; with them were several newcomers, Jurgis noticed—also he noticed that the house was silent.

"Well?" he said.

No one answered him, they sat staring at him with their pale faces. He cried again: "Well?"

And then, by the light of the smoky lamp, he saw Marija who sat nearest him, shaking her head slowly. "Not yet," she said.

And Jurgis gave a cry of dismay. "Not yet?"

Again Marija's head shook. The poor fellow stood dumfounded. "I don't hear her," he gasped.

"She's been quiet a long time," replied the other.

There was another pause—broken suddenly by a voice from the attic: "Hello, there!"

Several of the women ran into the next room, while Marija sprang toward Jurgis. "Wait here!" she cried, and the two stood, pale and trembling, listening. In a few moments it became clear that Madame Haupt was engaged in descending the ladder, scolding and exhorting again, while the ladder creaked in protest. In a moment or two she reached the ground, angry and breathless, and they heard her coming into the room. Jurgis gave one glance at her, and then turned white and reeled. She had her jacket off, like one of the workers on the killing beds. Her hands and arms were smeared with blood, and blood was splashed upon her clothing and her face.

She stood breathing hard, and gazing about her; no one made a sound. "I haf done my best," she began suddenly. "I can do noffing more—dere is no use to try."

Again there was silence.

"It ain't my fault," she said. "You had ought to haf had a doctor, und not vaited so long—it vas too late already ven I come." Once more there was deathlike stillness. Marija was clutching Jurgis with all the power of her one well arm.

Then suddenly Madame Haupt turned to Aniele. "You haf not got something to drink, hey?" she queried. "Some brandy?"

Aniclc shook her head.

"Herr Gott!" exclaimed Madame Haupt. "Such people! Perhaps you vill give me someting to eat den—I haf had noffing since yesterday morning, und I haf vorked myself near to death here. If I could haf known it vas like dis, I vould never haf come for such money as you gif me." At this moment she chanced to look round, and saw Jurgis: She shook her finger at him. "You understand me," she said, "you pays me dot money yust de same! It is not my fault dat you send for me so late I can't help your vife. It is not my fault if der baby comes mit one arm first, so dot I can't save it. I haf tried all night, und in dot place vere it is not fit for dogs to be born, und mit notting to eat only vot I brings in mine own pockets."

Here Madame Haupt paused for a moment to get her breath; and Marija, seeing the beads of sweat on Jurgis's forehead, and feeling the quivering of his frame, broke out in a low voice: "How is Ona?"

"How is she?" echoed Madame Haupt. "How do you tink she can be ven you leave her to kill herself so? I told dem dot ven they send for de priest. She is young, und she might haf got over it, und been vell und strong, if she had been treated right. She fight hard, dot girl—she is not yet quite dead."

And Jurgis gave a frantic scream. "Dead!"

"She vill die, of course," said thc other angrily. "Der baby is dead now."

The garret was lighted by a candle stuck upon a board; it had almost burned itself out, and was sputtering and smoking as Jurgis rushed up the ladder. He could make out dimly in one corner a pallet of rags and old blankets, spread upon the floor; at the foot of it was a crucifix, and near it a priest muttering a prayer. In a far corner crouched Elzbieta, moaning and wailing. Upon the pallet lay Ona.

She was covered with a blanket, but he could see her shoulders and one arm lying bare; she was so shrunken he would scarcely have known her—she was all but a skeleton, and as white as a piece of chalk. Her eyelids were closed, and she lay still as death. He staggered toward her and fell upon his knees with a cry of anguish: "Ona! Ona!"

She did not stir. He caught her hand in his, and began to clasp it frantically, calling: "Look at me! Answer me! It is Jurgis come back—don't you hear me?"

There was the faintest quivering of the eyelids, and he called again in frenzy: "Ona! Ona!"

Then suddenly her eyes opened one instant. One instant she looked at him—there was a flash of recognition between them, he saw her afar off, as through a dim vista, standing forlorn. He stretched out his arms to her, he called her in wild despair; a fearful yearning surged up in him, hunger for her that was agony, desire that was a new being born within him, tearing his heartstrings, torturing him. But it was all in vain—she faded from him, she slipped back and was gone. And a wail of anguish burst from him, great sobs shook all his frame, and hot tears ran down his cheeks and fell upon her. He clutched her hands, he shook her, he caught her in his arms and pressed her to him but she lay cold and still—she was gone—she was gone!

The word rang through him like the sound of a bell, echoing in the far depths of him, making forgotten chords to vibrate, old shadowy fears to stir—fears of the dark, fears of the void, fears of annihilation. She was dead! She was dead! He would never see her again, never hear her again! An icy horror of loneliness seized him; he saw himself standing apart and watching all the world fade away from him—a world of shadows, of fickle dreams. He was like a little child, in his fright and grief; he called and called, and got no answer, and his cries of despair echoed through the house, making the women downstairs draw nearer to each other in fear. He was inconsolable, beside himself—the priest came and laid his hand upon his shoulder and whispered to him, but he heard not a sound. He was gone away himself, stumbling through the shadows, and groping after the soul that had fled.

So he lay. The gray dawn came up and crept into the attic. The priest left, the women left, and he was alone with the still, white figure—quieter now, but moaning and shuddering, wrestling with the grisly fiend. Now and then he would raise himself and stare at the white mask before him, then hide his eyes because he could not bear it. Dead! dead! And she was only a girl, she was barely eighteen! Her life had hardly begun—and here she lay murdered—mangled, tortured to death!

It was morning when he rose up and came down into the kitchen—haggard and ashen gray, reeling and dazed. More of the neighbors had come in, and they stared at him in silence as he sank down upon a chair by the table and buried his face in his arms.

A few minutes later the front door opened; a blast of cold and snow rushed in, and behind it little Kotrina, breathless from running, and blue with the cold. "I'm home again!" she exclaimed. "I could hardly—"

And then, seeing Jurgis, she stopped with an exclamation. Looking from one to another she saw that something had happened, and she asked, in a lower voice: "What's the matter?"

Before anyone could reply, Jurgis started up; he went toward her, walking unsteadily. "Where have you been?" he demanded.

"Selling papers with the boys," she said. "The snow—"

"Have you any money?" he demanded.

"Yes."

"How much?"

"Nearly three dollars, Jurgis."

"Give it to me."

Kotrina, frightened by his manner, glanced at the others. "Give it to me!" he commanded again, and she put her hand into her pocket and pulled out a lump of coins tied in a bit of rag. Jurgis took it without a word, and went out of the door and down the street.

Three doors away was a saloon. "Whisky," he said, as he entered, and as the man pushed him some, he tore at the rag with his teeth and pulled out half a dollar. "How much is the bottle?" he said. "I want to get drunk."

# Chapter 20

But a big man cannot stay drunk very long on three dollars. That was Sunday morning, and Monday night Jurgis came home, sober and sick, realizing that he had spent every cent the family owned, and had not bought a single instant's forgetfulness with it.

Ona was not yet buried; but the police had been notified, and on the morrow they would put the body in a pine coffin and take it to the potter's field. Elzbieta was out begging now, a few pennies from each of the neighbors, to get enough to pay for a mass for her; and the children were upstairs starving to death, while he, good-for-nothing rascal, had been spending their money on drink. So spoke Aniele, scornfully, and when he started toward the fire she added the information that her kitchen was no longer for him to fill with his phosphate stinks. She had crowded all her boarders into one room on Ona's account, but now he could go up in the garret where he belonged—and not there much longer, either, if he did not pay her some rent.

Jurgis went without a word, and, stepping over half a dozen sleeping boarders in the next room, ascended the ladder. It was dark up above; they could not afford any light; also it was nearly as cold as outdoors. In a corner, as far away from the corpse as possible, sat Marija, holding little Antanas in her one good arm and trying to soothe him to sleep. In another corner crouched poor little Juozapas, wailing because he had had nothing to eat all day. Marija said not a word to Jurgis; he crept in like a whipped cur, and went and sat down by the body.

Perhaps he ought to have meditated upon the hunger of the children, and upon his own baseness; but he thought only of Ona, he gave himself up again to the luxury of grief. He shed no tears, being ashamed to make a sound; he sat motionless and shuddering with his anguish. He had never dreamed how much he loved Ona, until now that she was gone; until now that he sat here, knowing that on the morrow they would take her away, and that he would never lay eyes upon her again—never all the days of his life. His old love, which had been starved to death, beaten to death, awoke in him again; the floodgates of memory were lifted—he saw all their life together, saw her as he had seen her in Lithuania, the first day at the fair, beautiful as the flowers, singing like a bird. He saw her as he had married her, with all her tenderness, with her heart of wonder; the very words she had spoken seemed to ring now in his ears, the tears she had shed to be wet upon his cheek. The long, cruel battle with misery and hunger had hardened and embittered him, but it had not changed her—she had been the same hungry soul to the end, stretching out her arms to him, pleading with him, begging him for love and tenderness. And she had suffered—so cruelly she had suffered, such agonies, such infamies—ah, God, the memory of them was not to be borne. What a monster of wickedness, of heartlessness, he had been! Every angry word that he had ever spoken came back to him and cut him like a knife; every selfish act that he had done—with what torments he paid for them now! And such devotion and awe as welled up in his soul—now that it could never be spoken, now that it was too late, too late! His bosom-was choking with it, bursting with it; he crouched here in the darkness beside her, stretching out his arms to her—and she was gone forever, she was dead! He could have screamed aloud with the horror and despair of it; a sweat of agony beaded his forehead, yet he dared not make a sound—he scarcely dared to breathe, because of his shame and loathing of himself.

Late at night came Elzbieta, having gotten the money for a mass, and paid for it in advance, lest she should be tempted too sorely at home. She brought also a bit of stale rye bread that some one had given her, and with that they quieted the children and got them to sleep. Then she came over to Jurgis and sat down beside him.

She said not a word of reproach—she and Marija had chosen that course before; she would only plead with him, here by the corpse of his dead wife. Already Elzbieta had choked down her tears, grief being crowded out of her soul by fear. She had to bury one of her children—but then she had done it three times before, and each time risen up and gone back to take up the battle for the rest. Elzbieta was one of the primitive creatures: like the angleworm, which goes on living though cut in half; like a hen, which, deprived of her chickens one by one, will mother the last that is left her. She did this because it was her nature—she asked no questions about the justice of it, nor the worth-whileness of life in which destruction and death ran riot.

And this old common-sense view she labored to impress upon Jurgis, pleading with him with tears in her eyes. Ona was dead, but the others were left and they must be saved. She did not ask for her own children. She and Marija could care for them somehow, but there was Antanas, his own son. Ona had given Antanas to him—the little fellow was the only remembrance of her that he had; he must treasure it and protect it, he must show himself a man. He knew what Ona would have had him do, what she would ask of him at this moment, if she could speak to him. It was a terrible thing that she should have died as she had; but the life had been too hard for her, and she had to go. It was terrible that they were not able to bury her, that he could not even have a day to mourn her—but so it was. Their fate was pressing; they had not a cent, and the children would perish—some money must be had. Could he not be a man for Ona's sake, and pull himself together? In a little while they would be out of danger—now that they had given up the house they could live more cheaply, and with all the children working they could get along, if only he would not go to pieces. So Elzbieta went on, with feverish intensity. It was a struggle for life with her; she was not afraid that Jurgis would go on drinking, for he had no money for that, but she was wild with dread at the thought that he might desert them, might take to the road, as Jonas had done.

But with Ona's dead body beneath his eyes, Jurgis could not well think of treason to his child. Yes, he said, he would try, for the sake of Antanas. He would give the little fellow his chance—would get to work at once, yes, tomorrow, without even waiting for Ona to be buried. They might trust him, he would keep his word, come what might.

And so he was out before daylight the next morning, headache, heartache, and all. He went straight to Graham's fertilizer mill, to see if he could get back his job. But the boss shook his head when he saw him—no, his place had been filled long ago, and there was no room for him.

"Do you think there will be?" Jurgis asked. "I may have to wait."

"No," said the other, "it will not be worth your while to wait—there will be nothing for you here."

Jurgis stood gazing at him in perplexity. "What is the matter?" he asked. "Didn't I do my work?"

The other met his look with one of cold indifference, and answered, "There will be nothing for you here, I said."

Jurgis had his suspicions as to the dreadful meaning of that incident, and he went away with a sinking at the heart. He went and took his stand with the mob of hungry wretches who were standing about in the snow before the time station. Here he stayed, breakfastless, for two hours, until the throng was driven away by the clubs of the police. There was no work for him that day.

Jurgis had made a good many acquaintances in his long services at the yards—there were saloonkeepers who would trust him for a drink and a sandwich, and members of his old union who would lend him a dime at a pinch. It was not a question of life and death for him, therefore; he might hunt all day, and come again on the morrow, and try hanging on thus for weeks, like hundreds and thousands of others. Meantime, Teta Elzbieta would go and beg, over in the Hyde Park district, and the children would bring home enough to pacify Aniele, and keep them all alive.

It was at the end of a week of this sort of waiting, roaming about in the bitter winds or loafing in saloons, that Jurgis stumbled on a chance in one of the cellars of Jones's big packing plant. He saw a foreman passing the open doorway, and hailed him for a job.

"Push a truck?" inquired the man, and Jurgis answered, "Yes, sir!" before the words were well out of his mouth.

"What's your name?" demanded the other.

"Jurgis Rudkus."

"Worked in the yards before?"

"Yes."

"Whereabouts?"

"Two places—Brown's killing beds and Durham's fertilizer mill."

"Why did you leave there?"

"The first time I had an accident, and the last time I was sent up for a month."

"I see. Well, I'll give you a trial. Come early tomorrow and ask for Mr. Thomas."

So Jurgis rushed home with the wild tidings that he had a job—that the terrible siege was over. The remnants of the family had quite a celebration that night; and in the morning Jurgis was at the place half an hour before the time of opening. The foreman came in shortly afterward, and when he saw Jurgis he frowned.

"Oh," he said, "I promised you a job, didn't I?"

"Yes, sir," said Jurgis.

"Well, I'm sorry, but I made a mistake. I can't use you."

Jurgis stared, dumfounded. "What's the matter?" he gasped.

"Nothing," said the man, "only I can't use you."

There was the same cold, hostile stare that he had had from the boss of the fertilizer mill. He knew that there was no use in saying a word, and he turned and went away.

Out in the saloons the men could tell him all about the meaning of it; they gazed at him with pitying eyes—poor devil, he was blacklisted! What had he done? they asked—knocked down his boss? Good heavens, then he might have known! Why, he stood as much chance of getting a job in Packingtown as of being chosen mayor of Chicago. Why had he wasted his time hunting? They had him on a secret list in every office, big and little, in the place. They had his name by this time in St. Louis and New York, in Omaha and Boston, in Kansas City and St. Joseph. He was condemned and sentenced, without trial and without appeal; he could never work for the packers again—he could not even clean cattle pens or drive a truck in any place where they controlled. He might try it, if he chose, as hundreds had tried it, and found out for themselves. He would never be told anything about it; he would never get any more satisfaction than he had gotten just now; but he would always find when the time came that he was not needed. It would not do for him to give any other name, either—they had company "spotters" for just that purpose, and he wouldn't keep a job in Packingtown three days. It was worth a fortune to the packers to keep their blacklist effective, as a warning to the men and a means of keeping down union agitation and political discontent.

Jurgis went home, carrying these new tidings to the family council. It was a most cruel thing; here in this district was his home, such as it was, the place he was used to and the friends he knew—and now every possibility of employment in it was closed to him. There was nothing in Packingtown but packing houses; and so it was the same thing as evicting him from his home.

He and the two women spent all day and half the night discussing it. It would be convenient, downtown, to the children's place of work; but then Marija was on the road to recovery, and had hopes of getting a job in the yards; and though she did not see her old-time lover once a month, because of the misery of their state, yet she could not make up her mind to go away and give him up forever. Then, too, Elzbieta had heard something about a chance to scrub floors in Durham's offices and was waiting every day for word. In the end it was decided that Jurgis should go downtown to strike out for himself, and they would decide after he got a job. As there was no one from whom he could borrow there, and he dared not beg for fear of being arrested, it was arranged that every day he should meet one of the children and be given fifteen cents of their earnings, upon which he could keep going. Then all day he was to pace the streets with hundreds and thousands of other homeless wretches inquiring at stores, warehouses, and factories for a chance; and at night he was to crawl into some doorway or underneath a truck, and hide there until midnight, when he might get into one of the station houses, and spread a newspaper upon the floor, and lie down in the midst of a throng of "bums" and beggars, reeking with alcohol and tobacco, and filthy with vermin and disease.

So for two weeks more Jurgis fought with the demon of despair. Once he got a chance to load a truck for half a day, and again he carried an old woman's valise and was given a quarter. This let him into a lodging-house on several nights when he might otherwise have frozen to death; and it also gave him a chance now and then to buy a newspaper in the morning and hunt up jobs while his rivals were watching and waiting for a paper to be thrown away. This, however, was really not the advantage it seemed, for the newspaper advertisements were a cause of much loss of precious time and of many weary journeys. A full half of these were "fakes," put in by the endless variety of establishments which preyed upon the helpless ignorance of the unemployed. If Jurgis lost only his time, it was because he had nothing else to lose; whenever a smooth-tongued agent would tell him of the wonderful positions he had on hand, he could only shake his head sorrowfully and say that he had not the necessary dollar to deposit; when it was explained to him what "big money" he and all his family could make by coloring photographs, he could only promise to come in again when he had two dollars to invest in the outfit.

In the end Jurgis got a chance through an accidental meeting with an old-time acquaintance of his union days. He met this man on his way to work in the giant factories of the Harvester Trust; and his friend told him to come along and he would speak a good word for him to his boss, whom he knew well. So Jurgis trudged four or five miles, and passed through a waiting throng of unemployed at the gate under the escort of his friend. His knees nearly gave way beneath him when the foreman, after looking him over and questioning him, told him that he could find an opening for him.

How much this accident meant to Jurgis he realized only by stages; for he found that the harvester works were the sort of place to which philanthropists and reformers pointed with pride. It had some thought for its employees; its workshops were big and roomy, it provided a restaurant where the workmen could buy good food at cost, it had even a reading room, and decent places where its girl-hands could rest; also the work was free from many of the elements of filth and repulsiveness that prevailed at the stockyards. Day after day Jurgis discovered these things—things never expected nor dreamed of by him—until this new place came to seem a kind of a heaven to him.

It was an enormous establishment, covering a hundred and sixty acres of ground, employing five thousand people, and turning out over three hundred thousand machines every year—a good part of all the harvesting and mowing machines used in the country. Jurgis saw very little of it, of course—it was all specialized work, the same as at the stockyards; each one of the hundreds of parts of a mowing machine was made separately, and sometimes handled by hundreds of men. Where Jurgis worked there was a machine which cut and stamped a certain piece of steel about two square inches in size; the pieces came tumbling out upon a tray, and all that human hands had to do was to pile them in regular rows, and change the trays at intervals. This was done by a single boy, who stood with eyes and thought centered upon it, and fingers flying so fast that the sounds of the bits of steel striking upon each other was like the music of an express train as one hears it in a sleeping car at night. This was "piece-work," of course; and besides it was made certain that the boy did not idle, by setting the machine to match the highest possible speed of human hands. Thirty thousand of these pieces he handled every day, nine or ten million every year—how many in a lifetime it rested with the gods to say. Near by him men sat bending over whirling grindstones, putting the finishing touches to the steel knives of the reaper; picking them out of a basket with the right hand, pressing first one side and then the other against the stone and finally dropping them with the left hand into another basket. One of these men told Jurgis that he had sharpened three thousand pieces of steel a day for thirteen years. In the next room were wonderful machines that ate up long steel rods by slow stages, cutting them off, seizing the pieces, stamping heads upon them, grinding them and polishing them, threading them, and finally dropping them into a basket, all ready to bolt the harvesters together. From yet another machine came tens of thousands of steel burs to fit upon these bolts. In other places all these various parts were dipped into troughs of paint and hung up to dry, and then slid along on trolleys to a room where men streaked them with red and yellow, so that they might look cheerful in the harvest fields.

Jurgis's friend worked upstairs in the casting rooms, and his task was to make the molds of a certain part. He shoveled black sand into an iron receptacle and pounded it tight and set it aside to harden; then it would be taken out, and molten iron poured into it. This man, too, was paid by the mold—or rather for perfect castings, nearly half his work going for naught. You might see him, along with dozens of others, toiling like one possessed by a whole community of demons; his arms working like the driving rods of an engine, his long, black hair flying wild, his eyes starting out, the sweat rolling in rivers down his face. When he had shoveled the mold full of sand, and reached for the pounder to pound it with, it was after the manner of a canoeist running rapids and seizing a pole at sight of a submerged rock. All day long this man would toil thus, his whole being centered upon the purpose of making twenty-three instead of twenty-two and a half cents an hour; and then his product would be reckoned up by the census taker, and jubilant captains of industry would boast of it in their banquet halls, telling how our workers are nearly twice as efficient as those of any other country. If we are the greatest nation the sun ever shone upon, it would seem to be mainly because we have been able to goad our wage-earners to this pitch of frenzy; though there are a few other things that are great among us including our drink-bill, which is a billion and a quarter of dollars a year, and doubling itself every decade.

There was a machine which stamped out the iron plates, and then another which, with a mighty thud, mashed them to the shape of the sitting-down portion of the American farmer. Then they were piled upon a truck, and it was Jurgis's task to wheel them to the room where the machines were "assembled." This was child's play for him, and he got a dollar and seventy-five cents a day for it; on Saturday he paid Aniele the seventy-five cents a week he owed her for the use of her garret, and also redeemed his overcoat, which Elzbieta had put in pawn when he was in jail.

This last was a great blessing. A man cannot go about in midwinter in Chicago with no overcoat and not pay for it, and Jurgis had to walk or ride five or six miles back and forth to his work. It so happened that half of this was in one direction and half in another, necessitating a change of cars; the law required that transfers be given at all intersecting points, but the railway corporation had gotten round this by arranging a pretense at separate ownership. So whenever he wished to ride, he had to pay ten cents each way, or over ten per cent of his income to this power, which had gotten its franchises long ago by buying up the city council, in the face of popular clamor amounting almost to a rebellion. Tired as he felt at night, and dark and bitter cold as it was in the morning, Jurgis generally chose to walk; at the hours other workmen were traveling, the streetcar monopoly saw fit to put on so few cars that there would be men hanging to every foot of the backs of them and often crouching upon the snow-covered roof. Of course the doors could never be closed, and so the cars were as cold as outdoors; Jurgis, like many others, found it better to spend his fare for a drink and a free lunch, to give him strength to walk.

These, however, were all slight matters to a man who had escaped from Durham's fertilizer mill. Jurgis began to pick up heart again and to make plans. He had lost his house but then the awful load of the rent and interest was off his shoulders, and when Marija was well again they could start over and save. In the shop where he worked was a man, a Lithuanian like himself, whom the others spoke of in admiring whispers, because of the mighty feats he was performing. All day he sat at a machine turning bolts; and then in the evening he went to the public school to study English and learn to read. In addition, because he had a family of eight children to support and his earnings were not enough, on Saturdays and Sundays he served as a watchman; he was required to press two buttons at opposite ends of a building every five minutes, and as the walk only took him two minutes, he had three minutes to study between each trip. Jurgis felt jealous of this fellow; for that was the sort of thing he himself had dreamed of, two or three years ago. He might do it even yet, if he had a fair chance—he might attract attention and become a skilled man or a boss, as some had done in this place. Suppose that Marija could get a job in the big mill where they made binder twine—then they would move into this neighborhood, and he would really have a chance. With a hope like that, there was some use in living; to find a place where you were treated like a human being—by God! he would show them how he could appreciate it. He laughed to himself as he thought how he would hang on to this job!

And then one afternoon, the ninth of his work in the place, when he went to get his overcoat he saw a group of men crowded before a placard on the door, and when he went over and asked what it was, they told him that beginning with the morrow his department of the harvester works would be closed until further notice!

# Chapter 21

That was the way they did it! There was not half an hour's warning—the works were closed! It had happened that way before, said the men, and it would happen that way forever. They had made all the harvesting machines that the world needed, and now they had to wait till some wore out! It was nobody's fault—that was the way of it; and thousands of men and women were turned out in the dead of winter, to live upon their savings if they had any, and otherwise to die. So many tens of thousands already in the city, homeless and begging for work, and now several thousand more added to them!

Jurgis walked home-with his pittance of pay in his pocket, heartbroken, overwhelmed. One more bandage had been torn from his eyes, one more pitfall was revealed to him! Of what help was kindness and decency on the part of employers—when they could not keep a job for him, when there were more harvesting machines made than the world was able to buy! What a hellish mockery it was, anyway, that a man should slave to make harvesting machines for the country, only to be turned out to starve for doing his duty too well!

It took him two days to get over this heart-sickening disappointment. He did not drink anything, because Elzbieta got his money for safekeeping, and knew him too well to be in the least frightened by his angry demands. He stayed up in the garret however, and sulked—what was the use of a man's hunting a job when it was taken from him before he had time to learn the work? But then their money was going again, and little Antanas was hungry, and crying with the bitter cold of the garret. Also Madame Haupt, the midwife, was after him for some money. So he went out once more.

For another ten days he roamed the streets and alleys of the huge city, sick and hungry, begging for any work. He tried in stores and offices, in restaurants and hotels, along the docks and in the railroad yards, in warehouses and mills and factories where they made products that went to every corner of the world. There were often one or two chances—but there were always a hundred men for every chance, and his turn would not come. At night he crept into sheds and cellars and doorways—until there came a spell of belated winter weather, with a raging gale, and the thermometer five degrees below zero at sundown and falling all night. Then Jurgis fought like a wild beast to get into the big Harrison Street police station, and slept down in a corridor, crowded with two other men upon a single step.

He had to fight often in these days to fight for a place near the factory gates, and now and again with gangs on the street. He found, for instance, that the business of carrying satchels for railroad passengers was a pre-empted one—whenever he essayed it, eight or ten men and boys would fall upon him and force him to run for his life. They always had the policeman "squared," and so there was no use in expecting protection.

That Jurgis did not starve to death was due solely to the pittance the children brought him. And even this was never certain. For one thing the cold was almost more than the children could bear; and then they, too, were in perpetual peril from rivals who plundered and beat them. The law was against them, too—little Vilimas, who was really eleven, but did not look to be eight, was stopped on the streets by a severe old lady in spectacles, who told him that he was too young to be working and that if he did not stop selling papers she would send a truant officer after him. Also one night a strange man caught little Kotrina by the arm and tried to persuade her into a dark cellar-way, an experience which filled her with such terror that she was hardly to be kept at work.

At last, on a Sunday, as there was no use looking for work, Jurgis went home by stealing rides on the cars. He found that they had been waiting for him for three days—there was a chance of a job for him.

It was quite a story. Little Juozapas, who was near crazy with hunger these days, had gone out on the street to beg for himself. Juozapas had only one leg, having been run over by a wagon when a little child, but he had got himself a broomstick, which he put under his arm for a crutch. He had fallen in with some other children and found the way to Mike Scully's dump, which lay three or four blocks away. To this place there came every day many hundreds of wagon-loads of garbage and trash from the lake front, where the rich people lived; and in the heaps the children raked for food—there were hunks of bread and potato peelings and apple cores and meat bones, all of it half frozen and quite unspoiled. Little Juozapas gorged himself, and came home with a newspaper full, which he was feeding to Antanas when his mother came in. Elzbieta was horrified, for she did not believe that the food out of the dumps was fit to eat. The next day, however, when no harm came of it and Juozapas began to cry with hunger, she gave in and said that he might go again. And that afternoon he came home with a story of how while he had been digging away with a stick, a lady upon the street had called him. A real fine lady, the little boy explained, a beautiful lady; and she wanted to know all about him, and whether he got the garbage for chickens, and why he walked with a broomstick, and why Ona had died, and how Jurgis had come to go to jail, and what was the matter with Marija, and everything. In the end she had asked where he lived, and said that she was coming to see him, and bring him a new crutch to walk with. She had on a hat with a bird upon it, Juozapas added, and a long fur snake around her neck.

She really came, the very next morning, and climbed the ladder to the garret, and stood and stared about her, turning pale at the sight of the blood stains on the floor where Ona had died. She was a "settlement worker," she explained to Elzbieta—she lived around on Ashland Avenue. Elzbieta knew the place, over a feed store; somebody had wanted her to go there, but she had not cared to, for she thought that it must have something to do with religion, and the priest did not like her to have anything to do with strange religions. They were rich people who came to live there to find out about the poor people; but what good they expected it would do them to know, one could not imagine. So spoke Elzbieta, naively, and the young lady laughed and was rather at a loss for an answer—she stood and gazed about her, and thought of a cynical remark that had been made to her, that she was standing upon the brink of the pit of hell and throwing in snowballs to lower the temperature.

Elzbieta was glad to have somebody to listen, and she told all their woes—what had happened to Ona, and the jail, and the loss of their home, and Marija's accident, and how Ona had died, and how Jurgis could get no work. As she listened the pretty young lady's eyes filled with tears, and in the midst of it she burst into weeping and hid her face on Elzbieta's shoulder, quite regardless of the fact that the woman had on a dirty old wrapper and that the garret was full of fleas. Poor Elzbieta was ashamed of herself for having told so woeful a tale, and the other had to beg and plead with her to get her to go on. The end of it was that the young lady sent them a basket of things to eat, and left a letter that Jurgis was to take to a gentleman who was superintendent in one of the mills of the great steelworks in South Chicago. "He will get Jurgis something to do," the young lady had said, and added, smiling through her tears—"If he doesn't, he will never marry me."

The steel-works were fifteen miles away, and as usual it was so contrived that one had to pay two fares to get there. Far and wide the sky was flaring with the red glare that leaped from rows of towering chimneys—for it was pitch dark when Jurgis arrived. The vast works, a city in themselves, were surrounded by a stockade; and already a full hundred men were waiting at the gate where new hands were taken on. Soon after daybreak whistles began to blow, and then suddenly thousands of men appeared, streaming from saloons and boardinghouses across the way, leaping from trolley cars that passed—it seemed as if they rose out of the ground, in the dim gray light. A river of them poured in through the gate—and then gradually ebbed away again, until there were only a few late ones running, and the watchman pacing up and down, and the hungry strangers stamping and shivering.

Jurgis presented his precious letter. The gatekeeper was surly, and put him through a catechism, but he insisted that he knew nothing, and as he had taken the precaution to seal his letter, there was nothing for the gatekeeper to do but send it to the person to whom it was addressed. A messenger came back to say that Jurgis should wait, and so he came inside of the gate, perhaps not sorry enough that there were others less fortunate watching him with greedy eyes. The great mills were getting under way—one could hear a vast stirring, a rolling and rumbling and hammering. Little by little the scene grew plain: towering, black buildings here and there, long rows of shops and sheds, little railways branching everywhere, bare gray cinders underfoot and oceans of billowing black smoke above. On one side of the grounds ran a railroad with a dozen tracks, and on the other side lay the lake, where steamers came to load.

Jurgis had time enough to stare and speculate, for it was two hours before he was summoned. He went into the office building, where a company timekeeper interviewed him. The superintendent was busy, he said, but he (the timekeeper) would try to find Jurgis a job. He had never worked in a steel mill before? But he was ready for anything? Well, then, they would go and see.

So they began a tour, among sights that made Jurgis stare amazed. He wondered if ever he could get used to working in a place like this, where the air shook with deafening thunder, and whistles shrieked warnings on all sides of him at once; where miniature steam engines came rushing upon him, and sizzling, quivering, white-hot masses of metal sped past him, and explosions of fire and flaming sparks dazzled him and scorched his face. The men in these mills were all black with soot, and hollow-eyed and gaunt; they worked with fierce intensity, rushing here and there, and never lifting their eyes from their tasks. Jurgis clung to his guide like a scared child to its nurse, and while the latter hailed one foreman after another to ask if they could use another unskilled man, he stared about him and marveled.

He was taken to the Bessemer furnace, where they made billets of steel—a dome-like building, the size of a big theater. Jurgis stood where the balcony of the theater would have been, and opposite, by the stage, he saw three giant caldrons, big enough for all the devils of hell to brew their broth in, full of something white and blinding, bubbling and splashing, roaring as if volcanoes were blowing through it—one had to shout to be heard in the place. Liquid fire would leap from these caldrons and scatter like bombs below—and men were working there, seeming careless, so that Jurgis caught his breath with fright. Then a whistle would toot, and across the curtain of the theater would come a little engine with a carload of something to be dumped into one of the receptacles; and then another whistle would toot, down by the stage, and another train would back up—and suddenly, without an instant's warning, one of the giant kettles began to tilt and topple, flinging out a jet of hissing, roaring flame. Jurgis shrank back appalled, for he thought it was an accident; there fell a pillar of white flame, dazzling as the sun, swishing like a huge tree falling in the forest. A torrent of sparks swept all the way across the building, overwhelming everything, hiding it from sight; and then Jurgis looked through the fingers of his hands, and saw pouring out of the caldron a cascade of living, leaping fire, white with a whiteness not of earth, scorching the eyeballs. Incandescent rainbows shone above it, blue, red, and golden lights played about it; but the stream itself was white, ineffable. Out of regions of wonder it streamed, the very river of life; and the soul leaped up at the sight of it, fled back upon it, swift and resistless, back into far-off lands, where beauty and terror dwell. Then the great caldron tilted back again, empty, and Jurgis saw to his relief that no one was hurt, and turned and followed his guide out into the sunlight.

They went through the blast furnaces, through rolling mills where bars of steel were tossed about and chopped like bits of cheese. All around and above giant machine arms were flying, giant wheels were turning, great hammers crashing; traveling cranes creaked and groaned overhead, reaching down iron hands and seizing iron prey—it was like standing in the center of the earth, where the machinery of time was revolving.

By and by they came to the place where steel rails were made; and Jurgis heard a toot behind him, and jumped out of the way of a car with a white-hot ingot upon it, the size of a man's body. There was a sudden crash and the car came to a halt, and the ingot toppled out upon a moving platform, where steel fingers and arms seized hold of it, punching it and prodding it into place, and hurrying it into the grip of huge rollers. Then it came out upon the other side, and there were more crashings and clatterings, and over it was flopped, like a pancake on a gridiron, and seized again and rushed back at you through another squeezer. So amid deafening uproar it clattered to and fro, growing thinner and flatter and longer. The ingot seemed almost a living thing; it did not want to run this mad course, but it was in the grip of fate, it was tumbled on, screeching and clanking and shivering in protest. By and by it was long and thin, a great red snake escaped from purgatory; and then, as it slid through the rollers, you would have sworn that it was alive—it writhed and squirmed, and wriggles and shudders passed out through its tail, all but flinging it off by their violence. There was no rest for it until it was cold and black—and then it needed only to be cut and straightened to be ready for a railroad.

It was at the end of this rail's progress that Jurgis got his chance. They had to be moved by men with crowbars, and the boss here could use another man. So he took off his coat and set to work on the spot.

It took him two hours to get to this place every day and cost him a dollar and twenty cents a week. As this was out of the question, he wrapped his bedding in a bundle and took it with him, and one of his fellow workingmen introduced him to a Polish lodging-house, where he might have the privilege of sleeping upon the floor for ten cents a night. He got his meals at free-lunch counters, and every Saturday night he went home—bedding and all—and took the greater part of his money to the family. Elzbieta was sorry for this arrangement, for she feared that it would get him into the habit of living without them, and once a week was not very often for him to see his baby; but there was no other way of arranging it. There was no chance for a woman at the steelworks, and Marija was now ready for work again, and lured on from day to day by the hope of finding it at the yards.

In a week Jurgis got over his sense of helplessness and bewilderment in the rail mill. He learned to find his way about and to take all the miracles and terrors for granted, to work without hearing the rumbling and crashing. From blind fear he went to the other extreme; he became reckless and indifferent, like all the rest of the men, who took but little thought of themselves in the ardor of their work. It was wonderful, when one came to think of it, that these men should have taken an interest in the work they did—they had no share in it—they were paid by the hour, and paid no more for being interested. Also they knew that if they were hurt they would be flung aside and forgotten—and still they would hurry to their task by dangerous short cuts, would use methods that were quicker and more effective in spite of the fact that they were also risky. His fourth day at his work Jurgis saw a man stumble while running in front of a car, and have his foot mashed off, and before he had been there three weeks he was witness of a yet more dreadful accident. There was a row of brick furnaces, shining white through every crack with the molten steel inside. Some of these were bulging dangerously, yet men worked before them, wearing blue glasses when they opened and shut the doors. One morning as Jurgis was passing, a furnace blew out, spraying two men with a shower of liquid fire. As they lay screaming and rolling upon the ground in agony, Jurgis rushed to help them, and as a result he lost a good part of the skin from the inside of one of his hands. The company doctor bandaged it up, but he got no other thanks from any one, and was laid up for eight working days without any pay.

Most fortunately, at this juncture, Elzbieta got the long-awaited chance to go at five o'clock in the morning and help scrub the office floors of one of the packers. Jurgis came home and covered himself with blankets to keep warm, and divided his time between sleeping and playing with little Antanas. Juozapas was away raking in the dump a good part of the time, and Elzbieta and Marija were hunting for more work.

Antanas was now over a year and a half old, and was a perfect talking machine. He learned so fast that every week when Jurgis came home it seemed to him as if he had a new child. He would sit down and listen and stare at him, and give vent to delighted exclamations—"Palauk! Muma! Tu mano szirdele!" The little fellow was now really the one delight that Jurgis had in the world—his one hope, his one victory. Thank God, Antanas was a boy! And he was as tough as a pine knot, and with the appetite of a wolf. Nothing had hurt him, and nothing could hurt him; he had come through all the suffering and deprivation unscathed—only shriller-voiced and more determined in his grip upon life. He was a terrible child to manage, was Antanas, but his father did not mind that—he would watch him and smile to himself with satisfaction. The more of a fighter he was the better—he would need to fight before he got through.

Jurgis had got the habit of buying the Sunday paper whenever he had the money; a most wonderful paper could be had for only five cents, a whole armful, with all the news of the world set forth in big headlines, that Jurgis could spell out slowly, with the children to help him at the long words. There was battle and murder and sudden death—it was marvelous how they ever heard about so many entertaining and thrilling happenings; the stories must be all true, for surely no man could have made such things up, and besides, there were pictures of them all, as real as life. One of these papers was as good as a circus, and nearly as good as a spree—certainly a most wonderful treat for a workingman, who was tired out and stupefied, and had never had any education, and whose work was one dull, sordid grind, day after day, and year after year, with never a sight of a green field nor an hour's entertainment, nor anything but liquor to stimulate his imagination. Among other things, these papers had pages full of comical pictures, and these were the main joy in life to little Antanas. He treasured them up, and would drag them out and make his father tell him about them; there were all sorts of animals among them, and Antanas could tell the names of all of them, lying upon the floor for hours and pointing them out with his chubby little fingers. Whenever the story was plain enough for Jurgis to make out, Antanas would have it repeated to him, and then he would remember it, prattling funny little sentences and mixing it up with other stories in an irresistible fashion. Also his quaint pronunciation of words was such a delight—and the phrases he would pick up and remember, the most outlandish and impossible things! The first time that the little rascal burst out with "God damn," his father nearly rolled off the chair with glee; but in the end he was sorry for this, for Antanas was soon "God-damning" everything and everybody.

And then, when he was able to use his hands, Jurgis took his bedding again and went back to his task of shifting rails. It was now April, and the snow had given place to cold rains, and the unpaved street in front of Aniele's house was turned into a canal. Jurgis would have to wade through it to get home, and if it was late he might easily get stuck to his waist in the mire. But he did not mind this much—it was a promise that summer was coming. Marija had now gotten a place as beef-trimmer in one of the smaller packing plants; and he told himself that he had learned his lesson now, and would meet with no more accidents—so that at last there was prospect of an end to their long agony. They could save money again, and when another winter came they would have a comfortable place; and the children would be off the streets and in school again, and they might set to work to nurse back into life their habits of decency and kindness. So once more Jurgis began to make plans and dream dreams.

And then one Saturday night he jumped off the car and started home, with the sun shining low under the edge of a bank of clouds that had been pouring floods of water into the mud-soaked street. There was a rainbow in the sky, and another in his breast—for he had thirty-six hours' rest before him, and a chance to see his family. Then suddenly he came in sight of the house, and noticed that there was a crowd before the door. He ran up the steps and pushed his way in, and saw Aniele's kitchen crowded with excited women. It reminded him so vividly of the time when he had come home from jail and found Ona dying, that his heart almost stood still. "What's the matter?" he cried.

A dead silence had fallen in the room, and he saw that every one was staring at him. "What's the matter?" he exclaimed again.

And then, up in the garret, he heard sounds of wailing, in Marija's voice. He started for the ladder—and Aniele seized him by the arm. "No, no!" she exclaimed. "Don't go up there!"

"What is it?" he shouted.

And the old woman answered him weakly: "It's Antanas. He's dead. He was drowned out in the street!"

# Chapter 22

Jurgis took the news in a peculiar way. He turned deadly pale, but he caught himself, and for half a minute stood in the middle of the room, clenching his hands tightly and setting his teeth. Then he pushed Aniele aside and strode into the next room and climbed the ladder.

In the corner was a blanket, with a form half showing beneath it; and beside it lay Elzbieta, whether crying or in a faint, Jurgis could not tell. Marija was pacing the room, screaming and wringing her hands. He clenched his hands tighter yet, and his voice was hard as he spoke.

"How did it happen?" he asked.

Marija scarcely heard him in her agony. He repeated the question, louder and yet more harshly. "He fell off the sidewalk!" she wailed. The sidewalk in front of the house was a platform made of half-rotten boards, about five feet above the level of the sunken street.

"How did he come to be there?" he demanded.

"He went—he went out to play," Marija sobbed, her voice choking her. "We couldn't make him stay in. He must have got caught in the mud!"

"Are you sure that he is dead?" he demanded.

"Ai! ai!" she wailed. "Yes; we had the doctor."

Then Jurgis stood a few seconds, wavering. He did not shed a tear. He took one glance more at the blanket with the little form beneath it, and then turned suddenly to the ladder and climbed down again. A silence fell once more in the room as he entered. He went straight to the door, passed out, and started down the street.

When his wife had died, Jurgis made for the nearest saloon, but he did not do that now, though he had his week's wages in his pocket. He walked and walked, seeing nothing, splashing through mud and water. Later on he sat down upon a step and hid his face in his hands and for half an hour or so he did not move. Now and then he would whisper to himself: "Dead! Dead!"

Finally, he got up and walked on again. It was about sunset, and he went on and on until it was dark, when he was stopped by a railroad crossing. The gates were down, and a long train of freight cars was thundering by. He stood and watched it; and all at once a wild impulse seized him, a thought that had been lurking within him, unspoken, unrecognized, leaped into sudden life. He started down the track, and when he was past the gate-keeper's shanty he sprang forward and swung himself on to one of the cars.

By and by the train stopped again, and Jurgis sprang down and ran under the car, and hid himself upon the truck. Here he sat, and when the train started again, he fought a battle with his soul. He gripped his hands and set his teeth together—he had not wept, and he would not—not a tear! It was past and over, and he was done with it—he would fling it off his shoulders, be free of it, the whole business, that night. It should go like a black, hateful nightmare, and in the morning he would be a new man. And every time that a thought of it assailed him—a tender memory, a trace of a tear—he rose up, cursing with rage, and pounded it down.

He was fighting for his life; he gnashed his teeth together in his desperation. He had been a fool, a fool! He had wasted his life, he had wrecked himself, with his accursed weakness; and now he was done with it—he would tear it out of him, root and branch! There should be no more tears and no more tenderness; he had had enough of them—they had sold him into slavery! Now he was going to be free, to tear off his shackles, to rise up and fight. He was glad that the end had come—it had to come some time, and it was just as well now. This was no world for women and children, and the sooner they got out of it the better for them. Whatever Antanas might suffer where he was, he could suffer no more than he would have had he stayed upon earth. And meantime his father had thought the last thought about him that he meant to; he was going to think of himself, he was going to fight for himself, against the world that had baffled him and tortured him!

So he went on, tearing up all the flowers from the garden of his soul, and setting his heel upon them. The train thundered deafeningly, and a storm of dust blew in his face; but though it stopped now and then through the night, he clung where he was—he would cling there until he was driven off, for every mile that he got from Packingtown meant another load from his mind.

Whenever the cars stopped a warm breeze blew upon him, a breeze laden with the perfume of fresh fields, of honeysuckle and clover. He snuffed it, and it made his heart beat wildly—he was out in the country again! He was going to live in the country! When the dawn came he was peering out with hungry eyes, getting glimpses of meadows and woods and rivers. At last he could stand it no longer, and when the train stopped again he crawled out. Upon the top of the car was a brakeman, who shook his fist and swore; Jurgis waved his hand derisively, and started across the country.

Only think that he had been a countryman all his life; and for three long years he had never seen a country sight nor heard a country sound! Excepting for that one walk when he left jail, when he was too much worried to notice anything, and for a few times that he had rested in the city parks in the winter time when he was out of work, he had literally never seen a tree! And now he felt like a bird lifted up and borne away upon a gale; he stopped and stared at each new sight of wonder—at a herd of cows, and a meadow full of daisies, at hedgerows set thick with June roses, at little birds singing in the trees.

Then he came to a farm-house, and after getting himself a stick for protection, he approached it. The farmer was greasing a wagon in front of the barn, and Jurgis went to him. "I would like to get some breakfast, please," he said.

"Do you want to work?" said the farmer.

"No," said Jurgis. "I don't."

"Then you can't get anything here," snapped the other.

"I meant to pay for it," said Jurgis.

"Oh," said the farmer; and then added sarcastically, "We don't serve breakfast after 7 A.M."

"I am very hungry," said Jurgis gravely; "I would like to buy some food."

"Ask the woman," said the farmer, nodding over his shoulder. The "woman" was more tractable, and for a dime Jurgis secured two thick sandwiches and a piece of pie and two apples. He walked off eating the pie, as the least convenient thing to carry. In a few minutes he came to a stream, and he climbed a fence and walked down the bank, along a woodland path. By and by he found a comfortable spot, and there he devoured his meal, slaking his thirst at the stream. Then he lay for hours, just gazing and drinking in joy; until at last he felt sleepy, and lay down in the shade of a bush.

When he awoke the sun was shining hot in his face. He sat up and stretched his arms, and then gazed at the water sliding by. There was a deep pool, sheltered and silent, below him, and a sudden wonderful idea rushed upon him. He might have a bath! The water was free, and he might get into it—all the way into it! It would be the first time that he had been all the way into the water since he left Lithuania!

When Jurgis had first come to the stockyards he had been as clean as any workingman could well be. But later on, what with sickness and cold and hunger and discouragement, and the filthiness of his work, and the vermin in his home, he had given up washing in winter, and in summer only as much of him as would go into a basin. He had had a shower bath in jail, but nothing since—and now he would have a swim!

The water was warm, and he splashed about like a very boy in his glee. Afterward he sat down in the water near the bank, and proceeded to scrub himself—soberly and methodically, scouring every inch of him with sand. While he was doing it he would do it thoroughly, and see how it felt to be clean. He even scrubbed his head with sand, and combed what the men called "crumbs" out of his long, black hair, holding his head under water as long as he could, to see if he could not kill them all. Then, seeing that the sun was still hot, he took his clothes from the bank and proceeded to wash them, piece by piece; as the dirt and grease went floating off downstream he grunted with satisfaction and soused the clothes again, venturing even to dream that he might get rid of the fertilizer.

He hung them all up, and while they were drying he lay down in the sun and had another long sleep. They were hot and stiff as boards on top, and a little damp on the underside, when he awakened; but being hungry, he put them on and set out again. He had no knife, but with some labor he broke himself a good stout club, and, armed with this, he marched down the road again.

Before long he came to a big farmhouse, and turned up the lane that led to it. It was just supper-time, and the farmer was washing his hands at the kitchen door. "Please, sir," said Jurgis, "can I have something to eat? I can pay." To which the farmer responded promptly, "We don't feed tramps here. Get out!"

Jurgis went without a word; but as he passed round the barn he came to a freshly ploughed and harrowed field, in which the farmer had set out some young peach trees; and as he walked he jerked up a row of them by the roots, more than a hundred trees in all, before he reached the end of the field. That was his answer, and it showed his mood; from now on he was fighting, and the man who hit him would get all that he gave, every time.

Beyond the orchard Jurgis struck through a patch of woods, and then a field of winter grain, and came at last to another road. Before long he saw another farmhouse, and, as it was beginning to cloud over a little, he asked here for shelter as well as food. Seeing the farmer eying him dubiously, he added, "I'll be glad to sleep in the barn."

"Well, I dunno," said the other. "Do you smoke?"

"Sometimes," said Jurgis, "but I'll do it out of doors." When the man had assented, he inquired, "How much will it cost me? I haven't very much money."

"I reckon about twenty cents for supper," replied the farmer. "I won't charge ye for the barn."

So Jurgis went in, and sat down at the table with the farmer's wife and half a dozen children. It was a bountiful meal—there were baked beans and mashed potatoes and asparagus chopped and stewed, and a dish of strawberries, and great, thick slices of bread, and a pitcher of milk. Jurgis had not had such a feast since his wedding day, and he made a mighty effort to put in his twenty cents' worth.

They were all of them too hungry to talk; but afterward they sat upon the steps and smoked, and the farmer questioned his guest. When Jurgis had explained that he was a workingman from Chicago, and that he did not know just whither he was bound, the other said, "Why don't you stay here and work for me?"

"I'm not looking for work just now," Jurgis answered.

"I'll pay ye good," said the other, eying his big form—"a dollar a day and board ye. Help's terrible scarce round here."

"Is that winter as well as summer?" Jurgis demanded quickly.

"N—no," said the farmer; "I couldn't keep ye after November—I ain't got a big enough place for that."

"I see," said the other, "that's what I thought. When you get through working your horses this fall, will you turn them out in the snow?" (Jurgis was beginning to think for himself nowadays.)

"It ain't quite the same," the farmer answered, seeing the point. "There ought to be work a strong fellow like you can find to do, in the cities, or some place, in the winter time."

"Yes," said Jurgis, "that's what they all think; and so they crowd into the cities, and when they have to beg or steal to live, then people ask 'em why they don't go into the country, where help is scarce." The farmer meditated awhile.

"How about when your money's gone?" he inquired, finally. "You'll have to, then, won't you?"

"Wait till she's gone," said Jurgis; "then I'll see."

He had a long sleep in the barn and then a big breakfast of coffee and bread and oatmeal and stewed cherries, for which the man charged him only fifteen cents, perhaps having been influenced by his arguments. Then Jurgis bade farewell, and went on his way.

Such was the beginning of his life as a tramp. It was seldom he got as fair treatment as from this last farmer, and so as time went on he learned to shun the houses and to prefer sleeping in the fields. When it rained he would find a deserted building, if he could, and if not, he would wait until after dark and then, with his stick ready, begin a stealthy approach upon a barn. Generally he could get in before the dog got scent of him, and then he would hide in the hay and be safe until morning; if not, and the dog attacked him, he would rise up and make a retreat in battle order. Jurgis was not the mighty man he had once been, but his arms were still good, and there were few farm dogs he needed to hit more than once.

Before long there came raspberries, and then blackberries, to help him save his money; and there were apples in the orchards and potatoes in the ground—he learned to note the places and fill his pockets after dark. Twice he even managed to capture a chicken, and had a feast, once in a deserted barn and the other time in a lonely spot alongside of a stream. When all of these things failed him he used his money carefully, but without worry—for he saw that he could earn more whenever he chose. Half an hour's chopping wood in his lively fashion was enough to bring him a meal, and when the farmer had seen him working he would sometimes try to bribe him to stay.

But Jurgis was not staying. He was a free man now, a buccaneer. The old wanderlust had got into his blood, the joy of the unbound life, the joy of seeking, of hoping without limit. There were mishaps and discomforts—but at least there was always something new; and only think what it meant to a man who for years had been penned up in one place, seeing nothing but one dreary prospect of shanties and factories, to be suddenly set loose beneath the open sky, to behold new landscapes, new places, and new people every hour! To a man whose whole life had consisted of doing one certain thing all day, until he was so exhausted that he could only lie down and sleep until the next day—and to be now his own master, working as he pleased and when he pleased, and facing a new adventure every hour!

Then, too, his health came back to him, all his lost youthful vigor, his joy and power that he had mourned and forgotten! It came with a sudden rush, bewildering him, startling him; it was as if his dead childhood had come back to him, laughing and calling! What with plenty to eat and fresh air and exercise that was taken as it pleased him, he would waken from his sleep and start off not knowing what to do with his energy, stretching his arms, laughing, singing old songs of home that came back to him. Now and then, of course, he could not help but think of little Antanas, whom he should never see again, whose little voice he should never hear; and then he would have to battle with himself. Sometimes at night he would waken dreaming of Ona, and stretch out his arms to her, and wet the ground with his tears. But in the morning he would get up and shake himself, and stride away again to battle with the world.

He never asked where he was nor where he was going; the country was big enough, he knew, and there was no danger of his coming to the end of it. And of course he could always have company for the asking—everywhere he went there were men living just as he lived, and whom he was welcome to join. He was a stranger at the business, but they were not clannish, and they taught him all their tricks—what towns and villages it was best to keep away from, and how to read the secret signs upon the fences, and when to beg and when to steal, and just how to do both. They laughed at his ideas of paying for anything with money or with work—for they got all they wanted without either. Now and then Jurgis camped out with a gang of them in some woodland haunt, and foraged with them in the neighborhood at night. And then among them some one would "take a shine" to him, and they would go off together and travel for a week, exchanging reminiscences.

Of these professional tramps a great many had, of course, been shiftless and vicious all their lives. But the vast majority of them had been workingmen, had fought the long fight as Jurgis had, and found that it was a losing fight, and given up. Later on he encountered yet another sort of men, those from whose ranks the tramps were recruited, men who were homeless and wandering, but still seeking work—seeking it in the harvest fields. Of these there was an army, the huge surplus labor army of society; called into being under the stern system of nature, to do the casual work of the world, the tasks which were transient and irregular, and yet which had to be done. They did not know that they were such, of course; they only knew that they sought the job, and that the job was fleeting. In the early summer they would be in Texas, and as the crops were ready they would follow north with the season, ending with the fall in Manitoba. Then they would seek out the big lumber camps, where there was winter work; or failing in this, would drift to the cities, and live upon what they had managed to save, with the help of such transient work as was there the loading and unloading of steamships and drays, the digging of ditches and the shoveling of snow. If there were more of them on hand than chanced to be needed, the weaker ones died off of cold and hunger, again according to the stern system of nature.

It was in the latter part of July, when Jurgis was in Missouri, that he came upon the harvest work. Here were crops that men had worked for three or four months to prepare, and of which they would lose nearly all unless they could find others to help them for a week or two. So all over the land there was a cry for labor—agencies were set up and all the cities were drained of men, even college boys were brought by the carload, and hordes of frantic farmers would hold up trains and carry off wagon-loads of men by main force. Not that they did not pay them well—any man could get two dollars a day and his board, and the best men could get two dollars and a half or three.

The harvest-fever was in the very air, and no man with any spirit in him could be in that region and not catch it. Jurgis joined a gang and worked from dawn till dark, eighteen hours a day, for two weeks without a break. Then he had a sum of money that would have been a fortune to him in the old days of misery—but what could he do with it now? To be sure he might have put it in a bank, and, if he were fortunate, get it back again when he wanted it. But Jurgis was now a homeless man, wandering over a continent; and what did he know about banking and drafts and letters of credit? If he carried the money about with him, he would surely be robbed in the end; and so what was there for him to do but enjoy it while he could? On a Saturday night he drifted into a town with his fellows; and because it was raining, and there was no other place provided for him, he went to a saloon. And there were some who treated him and whom he had to treat, and there was laughter and singing and good cheer; and then out of the rear part of the saloon a girl's face, red-cheeked and merry, smiled at Jurgis, and his heart thumped suddenly in his throat. He nodded to her, and she came and sat by him, and they had more drink, and then he went upstairs into a room with her, and the wild beast rose up within him and screamed, as it has screamed in the Jungle from the dawn of time. And then because of his memories and his shame, he was glad when others joined them, men and women; and they had more drink and spent the night in wild rioting and debauchery. In the van of the surplus-labor army, there followed another, an army of women, they also struggling for life under the stern system of nature. Because there were rich men who sought pleasure, there had been ease and plenty for them so long as they were young and beautiful; and later on, when they were crowded out by others younger and more beautiful, they went out to follow upon the trail of the workingmen. Sometimes they came of themselves, and the saloon-keepers shared with them; or sometimes they were handled by agencies, the same as the labor army. They were in the towns in harvest time, near the lumber camps in the winter, in the cities when the men came there; if a regiment were encamped, or a railroad or canal being made, or a great exposition getting ready, the crowd of women were on hand, living in shanties or saloons or tenement rooms, sometimes eight or ten of them together.

In the morning Jurgis had not a cent, and he went out upon the road again. He was sick and disgusted, but after the new plan of his life, he crushed his feelings down. He had made a fool of himself, but he could not help it now—all he could do was to see that it did not happen again. So he tramped on until exercise and fresh air banished his headache, and his strength and joy returned. This happened to him every time, for Jurgis was still a creature of impulse, and his pleasures had not yet become business. It would be a long time before he could be like the majority of these men of the road, who roamed until the hunger for drink and for women mastered them, and then went to work with a purpose in mind, and stopped when they had the price of a spree.

On the contrary, try as he would, Jurgis could not help being made miserable by his conscience. It was the ghost that would not down. It would come upon him in the most unexpected places—sometimes it fairly drove him to drink.

One night he was caught by a thunderstorm, and he sought shelter in a little house just outside of a town. It was a working-man's home, and the owner was a Slav like himself, a new emigrant from White Russia; he bade Jurgis welcome in his home language, and told him to come to the kitchen-fire and dry himself. He had no bed for him, but there was straw in the garret, and he could make out. The man's wife was cooking the supper, and their children were playing about on the floor. Jurgis sat and exchanged thoughts with him about the old country, and the places where they had been and the work they had done. Then they ate, and afterward sat and smoked and talked more about America, and how they found it. In the middle of a sentence, however, Jurgis stopped, seeing that the woman had brought a big basin of water and was proceeding to undress her youngest baby. The rest had crawled into the closet where they slept, but the baby was to have a bath, the workingman explained. The nights had begun to be chilly, and his mother, ignorant as to the climate in America, had sewed him up for the winter; then it had turned warm again, and some kind of a rash had broken out on the child. The doctor had said she must bathe him every night, and she, foolish woman, believed him.

Jurgis scarcely heard the explanation; he was watching the baby. He was about a year old, and a sturdy little fellow, with soft fat legs, and a round ball of a stomach, and eyes as black as coals. His pimples did not seem to bother him much, and he was wild with glee over the bath, kicking and squirming and chuckling with delight, pulling at his mother's face and then at his own little toes. When she put him into the basin he sat in the midst of it and grinned, splashing the water over himself and squealing like a little pig. He spoke in Russian, of which Jurgis knew some; he spoke it with the quaintest of baby accents—and every word of it brought back to Jurgis some word of his own dead little one, and stabbed him like a knife. He sat perfectly motionless, silent, but gripping his hands tightly, while a storm gathered in his bosom and a flood heaped itself up behind his eyes. And in the end he could bear it no more, but buried his face in his hands and burst into tears, to the alarm and amazement of his hosts. Between the shame of this and his woe Jurgis could not stand it, and got up and rushed out into the rain.

He went on and on down the road, finally coming to a black woods, where he hid and wept as if his heart would break. Ah, what agony was that, what despair, when the tomb of memory was rent open and the ghosts of his old life came forth to scourge him! What terror to see what he had been and now could never be—to see Ona and his child and his own dead self stretching out their arms to him, calling to him across a bottomless abyss—and to know that they were gone from him forever, and he writhing and suffocating in the mire of his own vileness!

# Chapter 23

Early in the fall Jurgis set out for Chicago again. All the joy went out of tramping as soon as a man could not keep warm in the hay; and, like many thousands of others, he deluded himself with the hope that by coming early he could avoid the rush. He brought fifteen dollars with him, hidden away in one of his shoes, a sum which had been saved from the saloon-keepers, not so much by his conscience, as by the fear which filled him at the thought of being out of work in the city in the winter time.

He traveled upon the railroad with several other men, hiding in freight cars at night, and liable to be thrown off at any time, regardless of the speed of the train. When he reached the city he left the rest, for he had money and they did not, and he meant to save himself in this fight. He would bring to it all the skill that practice had brought him, and he would stand, whoever fell. On fair nights he would sleep in the park or on a truck or an empty barrel or box, and when it was rainy or cold he would stow himself upon a shelf in a ten-cent lodging-house, or pay three cents for the privileges of a "squatter" in a tenement hallway. He would eat at free lunches, five cents a meal, and never a cent more—so he might keep alive for two months and more, and in that time he would surely find a job. He would have to bid farewell to his summer cleanliness, of course, for he would come out of the first night's lodging with his clothes alive with vermin. There was no place in the city where he could wash even his face, unless he went down to the lake front—and there it would soon be all ice.

First he went to the steel mill and the harvester works, and found that his places there had been filled long ago. He was careful to keep away from the stockyards—he was a single man now, he told himself, and he meant to stay one, to have his wages for his own when he got a job. He began the long, weary round of factories and warehouses, tramping all day, from one end of the city to the other, finding everywhere from ten to a hundred men ahead of him. He watched the newspapers, too—but no longer was he to be taken in by smooth-spoken agents. He had been told of all those tricks while "on the road."

In the end it was through a newspaper that he got a job, after nearly a month of seeking. It was a call for a hundred laborers, and though he thought it was a "fake," he went because the place was near by. He found a line of men a block long, but as a wagon chanced to come out of an alley and break the line, he saw his chance and sprang to seize a place. Men threatened him and tried to throw him out, but he cursed and made a disturbance to attract a policeman, upon which they subsided, knowing that if the latter interfered it would be to "fire" them all.

An hour or two later he entered a room and confronted a big Irishman behind a desk.

"Ever worked in Chicago before?" the man inquired; and whether it was a good angel that put it into Jurgis's mind, or an intuition of his sharpened wits, he was moved to answer, "No, sir."

"Where do you come from?"

"Kansas City, sir."

"Any references?"

"No, sir. I'm just an unskilled man. I've got good arms."

"I want men for hard work—it's all underground, digging tunnels for telephones. Maybe it won't suit you."

"I'm willing, sir—anything for me. What's the pay?"

"Fifteen cents an hour."

"I'm willing, sir."

"All right; go back there and give your name."

So within half an hour he was at work, far underneath the streets of the city. The tunnel was a peculiar one for telephone wires; it was about eight feet high, and with a level floor nearly as wide. It had innumerable branches—a perfect spider web beneath the city; Jurgis walked over half a mile with his gang to the place where they were to work. Stranger yet, the tunnel was lighted by electricity, and upon it was laid a double-tracked, narrow-gauge railroad!

But Jurgis was not there to ask questions, and he did not give the matter a thought. It was nearly a year afterward that he finally learned the meaning of this whole affair. The City Council had passed a quiet and innocent little bill allowing a company to construct telephone conduits under the city streets; and upon the strength of this, a great corporation had proceeded to tunnel all Chicago with a system of railway freight-subways. In the city there was a combination of employers, representing hundreds of millions of capital, and formed for the purpose of crushing the labor unions. The chief union which troubled it was the teamsters'; and when these freight tunnels were completed, connecting all the big factories and stores with the railroad depots, they would have the teamsters' union by the throat. Now and then there were rumors and murmurs in the Board of Aldermen, and once there was a committee to investigate—but each time another small fortune was paid over, and the rumors died away; until at last the city woke up with a start to find the work completed. There was a tremendous scandal, of course; it was found that the city records had been falsified and other crimes committed, and some of Chicago's big capitalists got into jail—figuratively speaking. The aldermen declared that they had had no idea of it all, in spite of the fact that the main entrance to the work had been in the rear of the saloon of one of them.

It was in a newly opened cut that Jurgis worked, and so he knew that he had an all-winter job. He was so rejoiced that he treated himself to a spree that night, and with the balance of his money he hired himself a place in a tenement room, where he slept upon a big homemade straw mattress along with four other workingmen. This was one dollar a week, and for four more he got his food in a boardinghouse near his work. This would leave him four dollars extra each week, an unthinkable sum for him. At the outset he had to pay for his digging tools, and also to buy a pair of heavy boots, since his shoes were falling to pieces, and a flannel shirt, since the one he had worn all summer was in shreds. He spent a week meditating whether or not he should also buy an overcoat. There was one belonging to a Hebrew collar button peddler, who had died in the room next to him, and which the landlady was holding for her rent; in the end, however, Jurgis decided to do without it, as he was to be underground by day and in bed at night.

This was an unfortunate decision, however, for it drove him more quickly than ever into the saloons. From now on Jurgis worked from seven o'clock until half-past five, with half an hour for dinner; which meant that he never saw the sunlight on weekdays. In the evenings there was no place for him to go except a barroom; no place where there was light and warmth, where he could hear a little music or sit with a companion and talk. He had now no home to go to; he had no affection left in his life—only the pitiful mockery of it in the camaraderie of vice. On Sundays the churches were open—but where was there a church in which an ill-smelling workingman, with vermin crawling upon his neck, could sit without seeing people edge away and look annoyed? He had, of course, his corner in a close though unheated room, with a window opening upon a blank wall two feet away; and also he had the bare streets, with the winter gales sweeping through them; besides this he had only the saloons—and, of course, he had to drink to stay in them. If he drank now and then he was free to make himself at home, to gamble with dice or a pack of greasy cards, to play at a dingy pool table for money, or to look at a beer-stained pink "sporting paper," with pictures of murderers and half-naked women. It was for such pleasures as these that he spent his money; and such was his life during the six weeks and a half that he toiled for the merchants of Chicago, to enable them to break the grip of their teamsters' union.

In a work thus carried out, not much thought was given to the welfare of the laborers. On an average, the tunneling cost a life a day and several manglings; it was seldom, however, that more than a dozen or two men heard of any one accident. The work was all done by the new boring machinery, with as little blasting as possible; but there would be falling rocks and crushed supports, and premature explosions— and in addition all the dangers of railroading. So it was that one night, as Jurgis was on his way out with his gang, an engine and a loaded car dashed round one of the innumerable right-angle branches and struck him upon the shoulder, hurling him against the concrete wall and knocking him senseless.

When he opened his eyes again it was to the clanging of the bell of an ambulance. He was lying in it, covered by a blanket, and it was threading its way slowly through the holiday-shopping crowds. They took him to the county hospital, where a young surgeon set his arm; then he was washed and laid upon a bed in a ward with a score or two more of maimed and mangled men.

Jurgis spent his Christmas in this hospital, and it was the pleasantest Christmas he had had in America. Every year there were scandals and investigations in this institution, the newspapers charging that doctors were allowed to try fantastic experiments upon the patients; but Jurgis knew nothing of this—his only complaint was that they used to feed him upon tinned meat, which no man who had ever worked in Packingtown would feed to his dog. Jurgis had often wondered just who ate the canned corned beef and "roast beef" of the stockyards; now he began to understand—that it was what you might call "graft meat," put up to be sold to public officials and contractors, and eaten by soldiers and sailors, prisoners and inmates of institutions, "shantymen" and gangs of railroad laborers.

Jurgis was ready to leave the hospital at the end of two weeks. This did not mean that his arm was strong and that he was able to go back to work, but simply that he could get along without further attention, and that his place was needed for some one worse off than he. That he was utterly helpless, and had no means of keeping himself alive in the meantime, was something which did not concern the hospital authorities, nor any one else in the city.

As it chanced, he had been hurt on a Monday, and had just paid for his last week's board and his room rent, and spent nearly all the balance of his Saturday's pay. He had less than seventy-five cents in his pockets, and a dollar and a half due him for the day's work he had done before he was hurt. He might possibly have sued the company, and got some damages for his injuries, but he did not know this, and it was not the company's business to tell him. He went and got his pay and his tools, which he left in a pawnshop for fifty cents. Then he went to his landlady, who had rented his place and had no other for him; and then to his boardinghouse keeper, who looked him over and questioned him. As he must certainly be helpless for a couple of months, and had boarded there only six weeks, she decided very quickly that it would not be worth the risk to keep him on trust.

So Jurgis went out into the streets, in a most dreadful plight. It was bitterly cold, and a heavy snow was falling, beating into his face. He had no overcoat, and no place to go, and two dollars and sixty-five cents in his pocket, with the certainty that he could not earn another cent for months. The snow meant no chance to him now; he must walk along and see others shoveling, vigorous and active—and he with his left arm bound to his side! He could not hope to tide himself over by odd jobs of loading trucks; he could not even sell newspapers or carry satchels, because he was now at the mercy of any rival. Words could not paint the terror that came over him as he realized all this. He was like a wounded animal in the forest; he was forced to compete with his enemies upon unequal terms. There would be no consideration for him because of his weakness—it was no one's business to help him in such distress, to make the fight the least bit easier for him. Even if he took to begging, he would be at a disadvantage, for reasons which he was to discover in good time.

In the beginning he could not think of anything except getting out of the awful cold. He went into one of the saloons he had been wont to frequent and bought a drink, and then stood by the fire shivering and waiting to be ordered out. According to an unwritten law, the buying a drink included the privilege of loafing for just so long; then one had to buy another drink or move on. That Jurgis was an old customer entitled him to a somewhat longer stop; but then he had been away two weeks, and was evidently "on the bum." He might plead and tell his "hard luck story," but that would not help him much; a saloon-keeper who was to be moved by such means would soon have his place jammed to the doors with "hoboes" on a day like this.

So Jurgis went out into another place, and paid another nickel. He was so hungry this time that he could not resist the hot beef stew, an indulgence which cut short his stay by a considerable time. When he was again told to move on, he made his way to a "tough" place in the "Levee" district, where now and then he had gone with a certain rat-eyed Bohemian workingman of his acquaintance, seeking a woman. It was Jurgis's vain hope that here the proprietor would let him remain as a "sitter." In low-class places, in the dead of winter, saloon-keepers would often allow one or two forlorn-looking bums who came in covered with snow or soaked with rain to sit by the fire and look miserable to attract custom. A workingman would come in, feeling cheerful after his day's work was over, and it would trouble him to have to take his glass with such a sight under his nose; and so he would call out: "Hello, Bub, what's the matter? You look as if you'd been up against it!" And then the other would begin to pour out some tale of misery, and the man would say, "Come have a glass, and maybe that'll brace you up." And so they would drink together, and if the tramp was sufficiently wretched-looking, or good enough at the "gab," they might have two; and if they were to discover that they were from the same country, or had lived in the same city or worked at the same trade, they might sit down at a table and spend an hour or two in talk—and before they got through the saloon-keeper would have taken in a dollar. All of this might seem diabolical, but the saloon-keeper was in no wise to blame for it. He was in the same plight as the manufacturer who has to adulterate and misrepresent his product. If he does not, some one else will; and the saloon-keeper, unless he is also an alderman, is apt to be in debt to the big brewers, and on the verge of being sold out.

The market for "sitters" was glutted that afternoon, however, and there was no place for Jurgis. In all he had to spend six nickels in keeping a shelter over him that frightful day, and then it was just dark, and the station houses would not open until midnight! At the last place, however, there was a bartender who knew him and liked him, and let him doze at one of the tables until the boss came back; and also, as he was going out, the man gave him a tip—on the next block there was a religious revival of some sort, with preaching and singing, and hundreds of hoboes would go there for the shelter and warmth.

Jurgis went straightway, and saw a sign hung out, saying that the door would open at seven-thirty; then he walked, or half ran, a block, and hid awhile in a doorway and then ran again, and so on until the hour. At the end he was all but frozen, and fought his way in with the rest of the throng (at the risk of having his arm broken again), and got close to the big stove.

By eight o'clock the place was so crowded that the speakers ought to have been flattered; the aisles were filled halfway up, and at the door men were packed tight enough to walk upon. There were three elderly gentlemen in black upon the platform, and a young lady who played the piano in front. First they sang a hymn, and then one of the three, a tall, smooth-shaven man, very thin, and wearing black spectacles, began an address. Jurgis heard smatterings of it, for the reason that terror kept him awake—he knew that he snored abominably, and to have been put out just then would have been like a sentence of death to him.

The evangelist was preaching "sin and redemption," the infinite grace of God and His pardon for human frailty. He was very much in earnest, and he meant well, but Jurgis, as he listened, found his soul filled with hatred. What did he know about sin and suffering—with his smooth, black coat and his neatly starched collar, his body warm, and his belly full, and money in his pocket—and lecturing men who were struggling for their lives, men at the death grapple with the demon powers of hunger and cold!—This, of course, was unfair; but Jurgis felt that these men were out of touch with the life they discussed, that they were unfitted to solve its problems; nay, they themselves were part of the problem—they were part of the order established that was crushing men down and beating them! They were of the triumphant and insolent possessors; they had a hall, and a fire, and food and clothing and money, and so they might preach to hungry men, and the hungry men must be humble and listen! They were trying to save their souls—and who but a fool could fail to see that all that was the matter with their souls was that they had not been able to get a decent existence for their bodies?

At eleven the meeting closed, and the desolate audience filed out into the snow, muttering curses upon the few traitors who had got repentance and gone up on the platform. It was yet an hour before the station house would open, and Jurgis had no overcoat—and was weak from a long illness. During that hour he nearly perished. He was obliged to run hard to keep his blood moving at all—and then he came back to the station house and found a crowd blocking the street before the door! This was in the month of January, 1904, when the country was on the verge of "hard times," and the newspapers were reporting the shutting down of factories every day—it was estimated that a million and a half men were thrown out of work before the spring. So all the hiding places of the city were crowded, and before that station house door men fought and tore each other like savage beasts. When at last the place was jammed and they shut the doors, half the crowd was still outside; and Jurgis, with his helpless arm, was among them. There was no choice then but to go to a lodging-house and spend another dime. It really broke his heart to do this, at half-past twelve o'clock, after he had wasted the night at the meeting and on the street. He would be turned out of the lodging-house promptly at seven—they had the shelves which served as bunks so contrived that they could be dropped, and any man who was slow about obeying orders could be tumbled to the floor.

This was one day, and the cold spell lasted for fourteen of them. At the end of six days every cent of Jurgis' money was gone; and then he went out on the streets to beg for his life.

He would begin as soon as the business of the city was moving. He would sally forth from a saloon, and, after making sure there was no policeman in sight, would approach every likely-looking person who passed him, telling his woeful story and pleading for a nickel or a dime. Then when he got one, he would dart round the corner and return to his base to get warm; and his victim, seeing him do this, would go away, vowing that he would never give a cent to a beggar again. The victim never paused to ask where else Jurgis could have gone under the circumstances—where he, the victim, would have gone. At the saloon Jurgis could not only get more food and better food than he could buy in any restaurant for the same money, but a drink in the bargain to warm him up. Also he could find a comfortable seat by a fire, and could chat with a companion until he was as warm as toast. At the saloon, too, he felt at home. Part of the saloon-keeper's business was to offer a home and refreshments to beggars in exchange for the proceeds of their foragings; and was there any one else in the whole city who would do this—would the victim have done it himself?

Poor Jurgis might have been expected to make a successful beggar. He was just out of the hospital, and desperately sick-looking, and with a helpless arm; also he had no overcoat, and shivered pitifully. But, alas, it was again the case of the honest merchant, who finds that the genuine and unadulterated article is driven to the wall by the artistic counterfeit. Jurgis, as a beggar, was simply a blundering amateur in competition with organized and scientific professionalism. He was just out of the hospital—but the story was worn threadbare, and how could he prove it? He had his arm in a sling—and it was a device a regular beggar's little boy would have scorned. He was pale and shivering—but they were made up with cosmetics, and had studied the art of chattering their teeth. As to his being without an overcoat, among them you would meet men you could swear had on nothing but a ragged linen duster and a pair of cotton trousers—so cleverly had they concealed the several suits of all-wool underwear beneath. Many of these professional mendicants had comfortable homes, and families, and thousands of dollars in the bank; some of them had retired upon their earnings, and gone into the business of fitting out and doctoring others, or working children at the trade. There were some who had both their arms bound tightly to their sides, and padded stumps in their sleeves, and a sick child hired to carry a cup for them. There were some who had no legs, and pushed themselves upon a wheeled platform—some who had been favored with blindness, and were led by pretty little dogs. Some less fortunate had mutilated themselves or burned themselves, or had brought horrible sores upon themselves with chemicals; you might suddenly encounter upon the street a man holding out to you a finger rotting and discolored with gangrene—or one with livid scarlet wounds half escaped from their filthy bandages. These desperate ones were the dregs of the city's cesspools, wretches who hid at night in the rain-soaked cellars of old ramshackle tenements, in "stale-beer dives" and opium joints, with abandoned women in the last stages of the harlot's progress—women who had been kept by Chinamen and turned away at last to die. Every day the police net would drag hundreds of them off the streets, and in the detention hospital you might see them, herded together in a miniature inferno, with hideous, beastly faces, bloated and leprous with disease, laughing, shouting, screaming in all stages of drunkenness, barking like dogs, gibbering like apes, raving and tearing themselves in delirium.

# Chapter 24

In the face of all his handicaps, Jurgis was obliged to make the price of a lodging, and of a drink every hour or two, under penalty of freezing to death. Day after day he roamed about in the arctic cold, his soul filled full of bitterness and despair. He saw the world of civilization then more plainly than ever he had seen it before; a world in which nothing counted but brutal might, an order devised by those who possessed it for the subjugation of those who did not. He was one of the latter; and all outdoors, all life, was to him one colossal prison, which he paced like a pent-up tiger, trying one bar after another, and finding them all beyond his power. He had lost in the fierce battle of greed, and so was doomed to be exterminated; and all society was busied to see that he did not escape the sentence. Everywhere that he turned were prison bars, and hostile eyes following him; the well-fed, sleek policemen, from whose glances he shrank, and who seemed to grip their clubs more tightly when they saw him; the saloon-keepers, who never ceased to watch him while he was in their places, who were jealous of every moment he lingered after he had paid his money; the hurrying throngs upon the streets, who were deaf to his entreaties, oblivious of his very existence—and savage and contemptuous when he forced himself upon them. They had their own affairs, and there was no place for him among them. There was no place for him anywhere—every direction he turned his gaze, this fact was forced upon him: Everything was built to express it to him: the residences, with their heavy walls and bolted doors, and basement windows barred with iron; the great warehouses filled with the products of the whole world, and guarded by iron shutters and heavy gates; the banks with their unthinkable billions of wealth, all buried in safes and vaults of steel.

And then one day there befell Jurgis the one adventure of his life. It was late at night, and he had failed to get the price of a lodging. Snow was falling, and he had been out so long that he was covered with it, and was chilled to the bone. He was working among the theater crowds, flitting here and there, taking large chances with the police, in his desperation half hoping to be arrested. When he saw a blue-coat start toward him, however, his heart failed him, and he dashed down a side street and fled a couple of blocks. When he stopped again he saw a man coming toward him, and placed himself in his path.

"Please, sir," he began, in the usual formula, "will you give me the price of a lodging? I've had a broken arm, and I can't work, and I've not a cent in my pocket. I'm an honest working-man, sir, and I never begged before! It's not my fault, sir—"

Jurgis usually went on until he was interrupted, but this man did not interrupt, and so at last he came to a breathless stop. The other had halted, and Jurgis suddenly noticed that he stood a little unsteadily. "Whuzzat you say?" he queried suddenly, in a thick voice.

Jurgis began again, speaking more slowly and distinctly; before he was half through the other put out his hand and rested it upon his shoulder. "Poor ole chappie!" he said. "Been up—hic—up—against it, hey?"

Then he lurched toward Jurgis, and the hand upon his shoulder became an arm about his neck. "Up against it myself, ole sport," he said. "She's a hard ole world."

They were close to a lamppost, and Jurgis got a glimpse of the other. He was a young fellow—not much over eighteen, with a handsome boyish face. He wore a silk hat and a rich soft overcoat with a fur collar; and he smiled at Jurgis with benignant sympathy. "I'm hard up, too, my goo' fren'," he said. "I've got cruel parents, or I'd set you up. Whuzzamatter whizyer?"

"I've been in the hospital."

"Hospital!" exclaimed the young fellow, still smiling sweetly, "thass too bad! Same's my Aunt Polly—hic—my Aunt Polly's in the hospital, too—ole auntie's been havin' twins! Whuzzamatter whiz you?"

"I've got a broken arm—" Jurgis began.

"So," said the other, sympathetically. "That ain't so bad—you get over that. I wish somebody'd break my arm, ole chappie—damfidon't! Then they'd treat me better—hic—hole me up, ole sport! Whuzzit you wamme do?"

"I'm hungry, sir," said Jurgis.

"Hungry! Why don't you hassome supper?"

"I've got no money, sir."

"No money! Ho, ho—less be chums, ole boy—jess like me! No money, either—a'most busted! Why don't you go home, then, same's me?"

"I haven't any home," said Jurgis.

"No home! Stranger in the city, hey? Goo' God, thass bad! Better come home wiz me—yes, by Harry, thass the trick, you'll come home an' hassome supper—hic—wiz me! Awful lonesome—nobody home! Guv'ner gone abroad—Bubby on's honeymoon—Polly havin' twins—every damn soul gone away! Nuff—hic—nuff to drive a feller to drink, I say! Only ole Ham standin' by, passin' plates—damfican eat like that, no sir! The club for me every time, my boy, I say. But then they won't lemme sleep there—guv'ner's orders, by Harry—home every night, sir! Ever hear anythin' like that? 'Every mornin' do?' I asked him. 'No, sir, every night, or no allowance at all, sir.' Thass my guv'ner—'nice as nails, by Harry! Tole ole Ham to watch me, too—servants spyin' on me—whuzyer think that, my fren'? A nice, quiet—hic—goodhearted young feller like me, an' his daddy can't go to Europe—hup!—an' leave him in peace! Ain't that a shame, sir? An' I gotter go home every evenin' an' miss all the fun, by Harry! Thass whuzzamatter now—thass why I'm here! Hadda come away an' leave Kitty—hic—left her cryin', too—whujja think of that, ole sport? 'Lemme go, Kittens,' says I—'come early an' often—I go where duty—hic—calls me. Farewell, farewell, my own true love—farewell, farewehell, my—own true—love!'"

This last was a song, and the young gentleman's voice rose mournful and wailing, while he swung upon Jurgis's neck. The latter was glancing about nervously, lest some one should approach. They were still alone, however.

"But I came all right, all right," continued the youngster, aggressively, "I can—hic—I can have my own way when I want it, by Harry—Freddie Jones is a hard man to handle when he gets goin'! 'No, sir,' says I, 'by thunder, and I don't need anybody goin' home with me, either—whujja take me for, hey? Think I'm drunk, dontcha, hey?—I know you! But I'm no more drunk than you are, Kittens,' says I to her. And then says she, 'Thass true, Freddie dear' (she's a smart one, is Kitty), 'but I'm stayin' in the flat, an' you're goin' out into the cold, cold night!' 'Put it in a pome, lovely Kitty,' says I. 'No jokin', Freddie, my boy,' says she. 'Lemme call a cab now, like a good dear'—but I can call my own cabs, dontcha fool yourself—and I know what I'm a-doin', you bet! Say, my fren', whatcha say—willye come home an' see me, an' hassome supper? Come 'long like a good feller—don't be haughty! You're up against it, same as me, an' you can unerstan' a feller; your heart's in the right place, by Harry—come 'long, ole chappie, an' we'll light up the house, an' have some fizz, an' we'll raise hell, we will—whoop-la! S'long's I'm inside the house I can do as I please—the guv'ner's own very orders, b'God! Hip! hip!"

They had started down the street, arm in arm, the young man pushing Jurgis along, half dazed. Jurgis was trying to think what to do—he knew he could not pass any crowded place with his new acquaintance without attracting attention and being stopped. It was only because of the falling snow that people who passed here did not notice anything wrong.

Suddenly, therefore, Jurgis stopped. "Is it very far?" he inquired.

"Not very," said the other, "Tired, are you, though? Well, we'll ride—whatcha say? Good! Call a cab!"

And then, gripping Jurgis tight with one hand, the young fellow began searching his pockets with the other. "You call, ole sport, an' I'll pay," he suggested. "How's that, hey?"

And he pulled out from somewhere a big roll of bills. It was more money than Jurgis had ever seen in his life before, and he stared at it with startled eyes.

"Looks like a lot, hey?" said Master Freddie, fumbling with it. "Fool you, though, ole chappie—they're all little ones! I'll be busted in one week more, sure thing—word of honor. An' not a cent more till the first—hic—guv'ner's orders—hic—not a cent, by Harry! Nuff to set a feller crazy, it is. I sent him a cable, this af'noon—thass one reason more why I'm goin' home. 'Hangin' on the verge of starvation,' I says—'for the honor of the family—hic—sen' me some bread. Hunger will compel me to join you—Freddie.' Thass what I wired him, by Harry, an' I mean it—I'll run away from school, b'God, if he don't sen' me some."

After this fashion the young gentleman continued to prattle on—and meantime Jurgis was trembling with excitement. He might grab that wad of bills and be out of sight in the darkness before the other could collect his wits. Should he do it? What better had he to hope for, if he waited longer? But Jurgis had never committed a crime in his life, and now he hesitated half a second too long. "Freddie" got one bill loose, and then stuffed the rest back into his trousers' pocket.

"Here, ole man," he said, "you take it." He held it out fluttering. They were in front of a saloon; and by the light of the window Jurgis saw that it was a hundred-dollar bill! "You take it," the other repeated. "Pay the cabbie an' keep the change—I've got—hic—no head for business! Guv'ner says so hisself, an' the guv'ner knows—the guv'ner's got a head for business, you bet! 'All right, guv'ner,' I told him, 'you run the show, and I'll take the tickets!' An' so he set Aunt Polly to watch me—hic—an' now Polly's off in the hospital havin' twins, an' me out raisin' Cain! Hello, there! Hey! Call him!"

A cab was driving by; and Jurgis sprang and called, and it swung round to the curb. Master Freddie clambered in with some difficulty, and Jurgis had started to follow, when the driver shouted: "Hi, there! Get out—you!"

Jurgis hesitated, and was half obeying; but his companion broke out: "Whuzzat? Whuzzamatter wiz you, hey?"

And the cabbie subsided, and Jurgis climbed in. Then Freddie gave a number on the Lake Shore Drive, and the carriage started away. The youngster leaned back and snuggled up to Jurgis, murmuring contentedly; in half a minute he was sound asleep, Jurgis sat shivering, speculating as to whether he might not still be able to get hold of the roll of bills. He was afraid to try to go through his companion's pockets, however; and besides the cabbie might be on the watch. He had the hundred safe, and he would have to be content with that.

At the end of half an hour or so the cab stopped. They were out on the waterfront, and from the east a freezing gale was blowing off the ice-bound lake. "Here we are," called the cabbie, and Jurgis awakened his companion.

Master Freddie sat up with a start.

"Hello!" he said. "Where are we? Whuzzis? Who are you, hey? Oh, yes, sure nuff! Mos' forgot you—hic—ole chappie! Home, are we? Lessee! Br-r-r—it's cold! Yes—come 'long—we're home—it ever so—hic—humble!"

Before them there loomed an enormous granite pile, set far back from the street, and occupying a whole block. By the light of the driveway lamps Jurgis could see that it had towers and huge gables, like a medieval castle. He thought that the young fellow must have made a mistake—it was inconceivable to him that any person could have a home like a hotel or the city hall. But he followed in silence, and they went up the long flight of steps, arm in arm.

"There's a button here, ole sport," said Master Freddie. "Hole my arm while I find her! Steady, now—oh, yes, here she is! Saved!"

A bell rang, and in a few seconds the door was opened. A man in blue livery stood holding it, and gazing before him, silent as a statue.

They stood for a moment blinking in the light. Then Jurgis felt his companion pulling, and he stepped in, and the blue automaton closed the door. Jurgis's heart was beating wildly; it was a bold thing for him to do—into what strange unearthly place he was venturing he had no idea. Aladdin entering his cave could not have been more excited.

The place where he stood was dimly lighted; but he could see a vast hall, with pillars fading into the darkness above, and a great staircase opening at the far end of it. The floor was of tesselated marble, smooth as glass, and from the walls strange shapes loomed out, woven into huge portieres in rich, harmonious colors, or gleaming from paintings, wonderful and mysterious-looking in the half-light, purple and red and golden, like sunset glimmers in a shadowy forest.

The man in livery had moved silently toward them; Master Freddie took off his hat and handed it to him, and then, letting go of Jurgis' arm, tried to get out of his overcoat. After two or three attempts he accomplished this, with the lackey's help, and meantime a second man had approached, a tall and portly personage, solemn as an executioner. He bore straight down upon Jurgis, who shrank away nervously; he seized him by the arm without a word, and started toward the door with him. Then suddenly came Master Freddie's voice, "Hamilton! My fren' will remain wiz me."

The man paused and half released Jurgis. "Come 'long ole chappie," said the other, and Jurgis started toward him.

"Master Frederick!" exclaimed the man.

"See that the cabbie—hic—is paid," was the other's response; and he linked his arm in Jurgis'. Jurgis was about to say, "I have the money for him," but he restrained himself. The stout man in uniform signaled to the other, who went out to the cab, while he followed Jurgis and his young master.

They went down the great hall, and then turned. Before them were two huge doors.

"Hamilton," said Master Freddie.

"Well, sir?" said the other.

"Whuzzamatter wizze dinin'-room doors?"

"Nothing is the matter, sir."

"Then why dontcha openum?"

The man rolled them back; another vista lost itself in the darkness. "Lights," commanded Master Freddie; and the butler pressed a button, and a flood of brilliant incandescence streamed from above, half-blinding Jurgis. He stared; and little by little he made out the great apartment, with a domed ceiling from which the light poured, and walls that were one enormous painting—nymphs and dryads dancing in a flower-strewn glade—Diana with her hounds and horses, dashing headlong through a mountain streamlet—a group of maidens bathing in a forest pool—all life-size, and so real that Jurgis thought that it was some work of enchantment, that he was in a dream palace. Then his eye passed to the long table in the center of the hall, a table black as ebony, and gleaming with wrought silver and gold. In the center of it was a huge carven bowl, with the glistening gleam of ferns and the red and purple of rare orchids, glowing from a light hidden somewhere in their midst.

"This's the dinin' room," observed Master Freddie. "How you like it, hey, ole sport?"

He always insisted on having an answer to his remarks, leaning over Jurgis and smiling into his face. Jurgis liked it.

"Rummy ole place to feed in all 'lone, though," was Freddie's comment—"rummy's hell! Whuzya think, hey?" Then another idea occurred to him and he went on, without waiting: "Maybe you never saw anythin—hic—like this 'fore? Hey, ole chappie?"

"No," said Jurgis.

"Come from country, maybe—hey?"

"Yes," said Jurgis.

"Aha! I thosso! Lossa folks from country never saw such a place. Guv'ner brings 'em—free show—hic—reg'lar circus! Go home tell folks about it. Ole man Jones's place—Jones the packer—beef-trust man. Made it all out of hogs, too, damn ole scoundrel. Now we see where our pennies go—rebates, an' private car lines—hic—by Harry! Bully place, though—worth seein'! Ever hear of Jones the packer, hey, ole chappie?"

Jurgis had started involuntarily; the other, whose sharp eyes missed nothing, demanded: "Whuzzamatter, hey? Heard of him?"

And Jurgis managed to stammer out: "I have worked for him in the yards."

"What!" cried Master Freddie, with a yell. "You! In the yards? Ho, ho! Why, say, thass good! Shake hands on it, ole man—by Harry! Guv'ner ought to be here—glad to see you. Great fren's with the men, guv'ner—labor an' capital, commun'ty 'f int'rests, an' all that—hic! Funny things happen in this world, don't they, ole man? Hamilton, lemme interduce you—fren' the family—ole fren' the guv'ner's—works in the yards. Come to spend the night wiz me, Hamilton—have a hot time. Me fren', Mr.—whuzya name, ole chappie? Tell us your name."

"Rudkus—Jurgis Rudkus."

"My fren', Mr. Rednose, Hamilton—shake han's."

The stately butler bowed his head, but made not a sound; and suddenly Master Freddie pointed an eager finger at him. "I know whuzzamatter wiz you, Hamilton—lay you a dollar I know! You think—hic—you think I'm drunk! Hey, now?"

And the butler again bowed his head. "Yes, sir," he said, at which Master Freddie hung tightly upon Jurgis's neck and went into a fit of laughter. "Hamilton, you damn ole scoundrel," he roared, "I'll 'scharge you for impudence, you see 'f I don't! Ho, ho, ho! I'm drunk! Ho, ho!"

The two waited until his fit had spent itself, to see what new whim would seize him. "Whatcha wanta do?" he queried suddenly. "Wanta see the place, ole chappie? Wamme play the guv'ner—show you roun'? State parlors—Looee Cans—Looee Sez—chairs cost three thousand apiece. Tea room Maryanntnet—picture of shepherds dancing—Ruysdael—twenty-three thousan'! Ballroom—balc'ny pillars—hic—imported—special ship—sixty-eight thousan'! Ceilin' painted in Rome—whuzzat feller's name, Hamilton—Mattatoni? Macaroni? Then this place—silver bowl—Benvenuto Cellini—rummy ole Dago! An' the organ—thirty thousan' dollars, sir—starter up, Hamilton, let Mr. Rednose hear it. No—never mind—clean forgot—says he's hungry, Hamilton—less have some supper. Only—hic—don't less have it here—come up to my place, ole sport—nice an' cosy. This way—steady now, don't slip on the floor. Hamilton, we'll have a cole spread, an' some fizz—don't leave out the fizz, by Harry. We'll have some of the eighteen-thirty Madeira. Hear me, sir?"

"Yes, sir," said the butler, "but, Master Frederick, your father left orders—

And Master Frederick drew himself up to a stately height. "My father's orders were left to me—hic—an' not to you," he said. Then, clasping Jurgis tightly by the neck, he staggered out of the room; on the way another idea occurred to him, and he asked: "Any—hic—cable message for me, Hamilton?"

"No, sir," said the butler.

"Guv'ner must be travelin'. An' how's the twins, Hamilton?"

"They are doing well, sir."

"Good!" said Master Freddie; and added fervently: "God bless 'em, the little lambs!"

They went up the great staircase, one step at a time; at the top of it there gleamed at them out of the shadows the figure of a nymph crouching by a fountain, a figure ravishingly beautiful, the flesh warm and glowing with the hues of life. Above was a huge court, with domed roof, the various apartments opening into it. The butler had paused below but a few minutes to give orders, and then followed them; now he pressed a button, and the hall blazed with light. He opened a door before them, and then pressed another button, as they staggered into the apartment.

It was fitted up as a study. In the center was a mahogany table, covered with books, and smokers' implements; the walls were decorated with college trophies and colors—flags, posters, photographs and knickknacks—tennis rackets, canoe paddles, golf clubs, and polo sticks. An enormous moose head, with horns six feet across, faced a buffalo head on the opposite wall, while bear and tiger skins covered the polished floor. There were lounging chairs and sofas, window seats covered with soft cushions of fantastic designs; there was one corner fitted in Persian fashion, with a huge canopy and a jeweled lamp beneath. Beyond, a door opened upon a bedroom, and beyond that was a swimming pool of the purest marble, that had cost about forty thousand dollars.

Master Freddie stood for a moment or two, gazing about him; then out of the next room a dog emerged, a monstrous bulldog, the most hideous object that Jurgis had ever laid eyes upon. He yawned, opening a mouth like a dragon's; and he came toward the young man, wagging his tail. "Hello, Dewey!" cried his master. "Been havin' a snooze, ole boy? Well, well—hello there, whuzzamatter?" (The dog was snarling at Jurgis.) "Why, Dewey—this' my fren', Mr. Rednose—ole fren' the guv'ner's! Mr. Rednose, Admiral Dewey; shake han's—hic. Ain't he a daisy, though—blue ribbon at the New York show—eighty-five hundred at a clip! How's that, hey?"

The speaker sank into one of the big armchairs, and Admiral Dewey crouched beneath it; he did not snarl again, but he never took his eyes off Jurgis. He was perfectly sober, was the Admiral.

The butler had closed the door, and he stood by it, watching Jurgis every second. Now there came footsteps outside, and, as he opened the door a man in livery entered, carrying a folding table, and behind him two men with covered trays. They stood like statues while the first spread the table and set out the contents of the trays upon it. There were cold pates, and thin slices of meat, tiny bread and butter sandwiches with the crust cut off, a bowl of sliced peaches and cream (in January), little fancy cakes, pink and green and yellow and white, and half a dozen ice-cold bottles of wine.

"Thass the stuff for you!" cried Master Freddie, exultantly, as he spied them. "Come 'long, ole chappie, move up."

And he seated himself at the table; the waiter pulled a cork, and he took the bottle and poured three glasses of its contents in succession down his throat. Then he gave a long-drawn sigh, and cried again to Jurgis to seat himself.

The butler held the chair at the opposite side of the table, and Jurgis thought it was to keep him out of it; but finally he understand that it was the other's intention to put it under him, and so he sat down, cautiously and mistrustingly. Master Freddie perceived that the attendants embarrassed him, and he remarked with a nod to them, "You may go."

They went, all save the butler.

"You may go too, Hamilton," he said.

"Master Frederick—" the man began.

"Go!" cried the youngster, angrily. "Damn you, don't you hear me?"

The man went out and closed the door; Jurgis, who was as sharp as he, observed that he took the key out of the lock, in order that he might peer through the keyhole.

Master Frederick turned to the table again. "Now," he said, "go for it."

Jurgis gazed at him doubtingly. "Eat!" cried the other. "Pile in, ole chappie!"

"Don't you want anything?" Jurgis asked.

"Ain't hungry," was the reply—"only thirsty. Kitty and me had some candy—you go on."

So Jurgis began, without further parley. He ate as with two shovels, his fork in one hand and his knife in the other; when he once got started his wolf-hunger got the better of him, and he did not stop for breath until he had cleared every plate. "Gee whiz!" said the other, who had been watching him in wonder.

Then he held Jurgis the bottle. "Lessee you drink now," he said; and Jurgis took the bottle and turned it up to his mouth, and a wonderfully unearthly liquid ecstasy poured down his throat, tickling every nerve of him, thrilling him with joy. He drank the very last drop of it, and then he gave vent to a long-drawn "Ah!"

"Good stuff, hey?" said Freddie, sympathetically; he had leaned back in the big chair, putting his arm behind his head and gazing at Jurgis.

And Jurgis gazed back at him. He was clad in spotless evening dress, was Freddie, and looked very handsome—he was a beautiful boy, with light golden hair and the head of an Antinous. He smiled at Jurgis confidingly, and then started talking again, with his blissful insouciance. This time he talked for ten minutes at a stretch, and in the course of the speech he told Jurgis all of his family history. His big brother Charlie was in love with the guileless maiden who played the part of "Little Bright-Eyes" in "The Kaliph of Kamskatka." He had been on the verge of marrying her once, only "the guv'ner" had sworn to disinherit him, and had presented him with a sum that would stagger the imagination, and that had staggered the virtue of "Little Bright-Eyes." Now Charlie had got leave from college, and had gone away in his automobile on the next best thing to a honeymoon. "The guv'ner" had made threats to disinherit another of his children also, sister Gwendolen, who had married an Italian marquis with a string of titles and a dueling record. They lived in his chateau, or rather had, until he had taken to firing the breakfast dishes at her; then she had cabled for help, and the old gentleman had gone over to find out what were his Grace's terms. So they had left Freddie all alone, and he with less than two thousand dollars in his pocket. Freddie was up in arms and meant serious business, as they would find in the end—if there was no other way of bringing them to terms he would have his "Kittens" wire that she was about to marry him, and see what happened then.

So the cheerful youngster rattled on, until he was tired out. He smiled his sweetest smile at Jurgis, and then he closed his eyes, sleepily. Then he opened them again, and smiled once more, and finally closed them and forgot to open them.

For several minutes Jurgis sat perfectly motionless, watching him, and reveling in the strange sensation of the champagne. Once he stirred, and the dog growled; after that he sat almost holding his breath—until after a while the door of the room opened softly, and the butler came in.

He walked toward Jurgis upon tiptoe, scowling at him; and Jurgis rose up, and retreated, scowling back. So until he was against the wall, and then the butler came close, and pointed toward the door. "Get out of here! " he whispered.

Jurgis hesitated, giving a glance at Freddie, who was snoring softly. "If you do, you son of a—" hissed the butler, "I'll mash in your face for you before you get out of here!"

And Jurgis wavered but an instant more. He saw "Admiral Dewey" coming up behind the man and growling softly, to back up his threats. Then he surrendered and started toward the door.

They went out without a sound, and down the great echoing staircase, and through the dark hall. At the front door he paused, and the butler strode close to him.

"Hold up your hands," he snarled. Jurgis took a step back, clinching his one well fist.

"What for?" he cried; and then understanding that the fellow proposed to search him, he answered, "I'll see you in hell first."

"Do you want to go to jail?" demanded the butler, menacingly. "I'll have the police—"

"Have 'em!" roared Jurgis, with fierce passion. "But you won't put your hands on me till you do! I haven't touched anything in your damned house, and I'll not have you touch me!"

So the butler, who was terrified lest his young master should waken, stepped suddenly to the door, and opened it. "Get out of here!" he said; and then as Jurgis passed through the opening, he gave him a ferocious kick that sent him down the great stone steps at a run, and landed him sprawling in the snow at the bottom.

# Chapter 25

Jurgis got up, wild with rage, but the door was shut and the great castle was dark and impregnable. Then the icy teeth of the blast bit into him, and he turned and went away at a run.

When he stopped again it was because he was coming to frequented streets and did not wish to attract attention. In spite of that last humiliation, his heart was thumping fast with triumph. He had come out ahead on that deal! He put his hand into his trousers' pocket every now and then, to make sure that the precious hundred-dollar bill was still there.

Yet he was in a plight—a curious and even dreadful plight, when he came to realize it. He had not a single cent but that one bill! And he had to find some shelter that night he had to change it!

Jurgis spent half an hour walking and debating the problem. There was no one he could go to for help—he had to manage it all alone. To get it changed in a lodging-house would be to take his life in his hands—he would almost certainly be robbed, and perhaps murdered, before morning. He might go to some hotel or railroad depot and ask to have it changed; but what would they think, seeing a "bum" like him with a hundred dollars? He would probably be arrested if he tried it; and what story could he tell? On the morrow Freddie Jones would discover his loss, and there would be a hunt for him, and he would lose his money. The only other plan he could think of was to try in a saloon. He might pay them to change it, if it could not be done otherwise.

He began peering into places as he walked; he passed several as being too crowded—then finally, chancing upon one where the bartender was all alone, he gripped his hands in sudden resolution and went in.

"Can you change me a hundred-dollar bill?" he demanded.

The bartender was a big, husky fellow, with the jaw of a prize fighter, and a three weeks' stubble of hair upon it. He stared at Jurgis. "What's that youse say?" he demanded.

"I said, could you change me a hundred-dollar bill?"

"Where'd youse get it?" he inquired incredulously.

"Never mind," said Jurgis; "I've got it, and I want it changed. I'll pay you if you'll do it."

The other stared at him hard. "Lemme see it," he said.

"Will you change it?" Jurgis demanded, gripping it tightly in his pocket.

"How the hell can I know if it's good or not?" retorted the bartender. "Whatcher take me for, hey?"

Then Jurgis slowly and warily approached him; he took out the bill, and fumbled it for a moment, while the man stared at him with hostile eyes across the counter. Then finally he handed it over.

The other took it, and began to examine it; he smoothed it between his fingers, and held it up to the light; he turned it over, and upside down, and edgeways. It was new and rather stiff, and that made him dubious. Jurgis was watching him like a cat all the time.

"Humph," he said, finally, and gazed at the stranger, sizing him up—a ragged, ill-smelling tramp, with no overcoat and one arm in a sling—and a hundred-dollar bill! "Want to buy anything?" he demanded.

"Yes," said Jurgis, "I'll take a glass of beer."

"All right," said the other, "I'll change it." And he put the bill in his pocket, and poured Jurgis out a glass of beer, and set it on the counter. Then he turned to the cash register, and punched up five cents, and began to pull money out of the drawer. Finally, he faced Jurgis, counting it out—two dimes, a quarter, and fifty cents. "There," he said.

For a second Jurgis waited, expecting to see him turn again. "My ninety-nine dollars," he said.

"What ninety-nine dollars?" demanded the bartender.

"My change!" he cried—"the rest of my hundred!"

"Go on," said the bartender, "you're nutty!"

And Jurgis stared at him with wild eyes. For an instant horror reigned in him—black, paralyzing, awful horror, clutching him at the heart; and then came rage, in surging, blinding floods—he screamed aloud, and seized the glass and hurled it at the other's head. The man ducked, and it missed him by half an inch; he rose again and faced Jurgis, who was vaulting over the bar with his one well arm, and dealt him a smashing blow in the face, hurling him backward upon the floor. Then, as Jurgis scrambled to his feet again and started round the counter after him, he shouted at the top of his voice, "Help! help!"

Jurgis seized a bottle off the counter as he ran; and as the bartender made a leap he hurled the missile at him with all his force. It just grazed his head, and shivered into a thousand pieces against the post of the door. Then Jurgis started back, rushing at the man again in the middle of the room. This time, in his blind frenzy, he came without a bottle, and that was all the bartender wanted—he met him halfway and floored him with a sledgehammer drive between the eyes. An instant later the screen doors flew open, and two men rushed in—just as Jurgis was getting to his feet again, foaming at the mouth with rage, and trying to tear his broken arm out of its bandages.

"Look out!" shouted the bartender. "He's got a knife!" Then, seeing that the two were disposed to join the fray, he made another rush at Jurgis, and knocked aside his feeble defense and sent him tumbling again; and the three flung themselves upon him, rolling and kicking about the place.

A second later a policeman dashed in, and the bartender yelled once more—"Look out for his knife!" Jurgis had fought himself half to his knees, when the policeman made a leap at him, and cracked him across the face with his club. Though the blow staggered him, the wild-beast frenzy still blazed in him, and he got to his feet, lunging into the air. Then again the club descended, full upon his head, and he dropped like a log to the floor.

The policeman crouched over him, clutching his stick, waiting for him to try to rise again; and meantime the barkeeper got up, and put his hand to his head. "Christ!" he said, "I thought I was done for that time. Did he cut me?"

"Don't see anything, Jake," said the policeman. "What's the matter with him?"

"Just crazy drunk," said the other. "A lame duck, too—but he 'most got me under the bar. Youse had better call the wagon, Billy."

"No," said the officer. "He's got no more fight in him, I guess—and he's only got a block to go." He twisted his hand in Jurgis's collar and jerked at him. "Git up here, you!" he commanded.

But Jurgis did not move, and the bartender went behind the bar, and after stowing the hundred-dollar bill away in a safe hiding place, came and poured a glass of water over Jurgis. Then, as the latter began to moan feebly, the policeman got him to his feet and dragged him out of the place. The station house was just around the corner, and so in a few minutes Jurgis was in a cell.

He spent half the night lying unconscious, and the balance moaning in torment, with a blinding headache and a racking thirst. Now and then he cried aloud for a drink of water, but there was no one to hear him. There were others in that same station house with split heads and a fever; there were hundreds of them in the great city, and tens of thousands of them in the great land, and there was no one to hear any of them.

In the morning Jurgis was given a cup of water and a piece of bread, and then hustled into a patrol wagon and driven to the nearest police court. He sat in the pen with a score of others until his turn came.

The bartender—who proved to be a well-known bruiser—was called to the stand. He took the oath and told his story. The prisoner had come into his saloon after midnight, fighting drunk, and had ordered a glass of beer and tendered a dollar bill in payment. He had been given ninety-five cents' change, and had demanded ninety-nine dollars more, and before the plaintiff could even answer had hurled the glass at him and then attacked him with a bottle of bitters, and nearly wrecked the place.

Then the prisoner was sworn—a forlorn object, haggard and unshorn, with an arm done up in a filthy bandage, a cheek and head cut, and bloody, and one eye purplish black and entirely closed. "What have you to say for yourself?" queried the magistrate.

"Your Honor," said Jurgis, "I went into his place and asked the man if he could change me a hundred-dollar bill. And he said he would if I bought a drink. I gave him the bill and then he wouldn't give me the change."

The magistrate was staring at him in perplexity. "You gave him a hundred-dollar bill!" he exclaimed.

"Yes, your Honor," said Jurgis.

"Where did you get it?"

"A man gave it to me, your Honor."

"A man? What man, and what for?"

"A young man I met upon the street, your Honor. I had been begging."

There was a titter in the courtroom; the officer who was holding Jurgis put up his hand to hide a smile, and the magistrate smiled without trying to hide it. "It's true, your Honor!" cried Jurgis, passionately.

"You had been drinking as well as begging last night, had you not?" inquired the magistrate. "No, your Honor—" protested Jurgis. "I—"

"You had not had anything to drink?"

"Why, yes, your Honor, I had—"

"What did you have?"

"I had a bottle of something—I don't know what it was—something that burned—"

There was again a laugh round the courtroom, stopping suddenly as the magistrate looked up and frowned. "Have you ever been arrested before?" he asked abruptly.

The question took Jurgis aback. "I—I—" he stammered.

"Tell me the truth, now!" commanded the other, sternly.

"Yes, your Honor," said Jurgis.

"How often?"

"Only once, your Honor."

"What for?"

"For knocking down my boss, your Honor. I was working in the stockyards, and he—"

"I see," said his Honor; "I guess that will do. You ought to stop drinking if you can't control yourself. Ten days and costs. Next case."

Jurgis gave vent to a cry of dismay, cut off suddenly by the policeman, who seized him by the collar. He was jerked out of the way, into a room with the convicted prisoners, where he sat and wept like a child in his impotent rage. It seemed monstrous to him that policemen and judges should esteem his word as nothing in comparison with the bartender's—poor Jurgis could not know that the owner of the saloon paid five dollars each week to the policeman alone for Sunday privileges and general favors—nor that the pugilist bartender was one of the most trusted henchmen of the Democratic leader of the district, and had helped only a few months before to hustle out a record-breaking vote as a testimonial to the magistrate, who had been made the target of odious kid-gloved reformers.

Jurgis was driven out to the Bridewell for the second time. In his tumbling around he had hurt his arm again, and so could not work, but had to be attended by the physician. Also his head and his eye had to be tied up—and so he was a pretty-looking object when, the second day after his arrival, he went out into the exercise court and encountered—Jack Duane!

The young fellow was so glad to see Jurgis that he almost hugged him. "By God, if it isn't 'the Stinker'!" he cried. "And what is it—have you been through a sausage machine?"

"No," said Jurgis, "but I've been in a railroad wreck and a fight." And then, while some of the other prisoners gathered round he told his wild story; most of them were incredulous, but Duane knew that Jurgis could never have made up such a yarn as that.

"Hard luck, old man," he said, when they were alone; "but maybe it's taught you a lesson."

"I've learned some things since I saw you last," said Jurgis mournfully. Then he explained how he had spent the last summer, "hoboing it," as the phrase was. "And you?" he asked finally. "Have you been here ever since?"

"Lord, no!" said the other. "I only came in the day before yesterday. It's the second time they've sent me up on a trumped-up charge—I've had hard luck and can't pay them what they want. Why don't you quit Chicago with me, Jurgis?"

"I've no place to go," said Jurgis, sadly.

"Neither have I," replied the other, laughing lightly. "But we'll wait till we get out and see."

In the Bridewell Jurgis met few who had been there the last time, but he met scores of others, old and young, of exactly the same sort. It was like breakers upon a beach; there was new water, but the wave looked just the same. He strolled about and talked with them, and the biggest of them told tales of their prowess, while those who were weaker, or younger and inexperienced, gathered round and listened in admiring silence. The last time he was there, Jurgis had thought of little but his family; but now he was free to listen to these men, and to realize that he was one of them—that their point of view was his point of view, and that the way they kept themselves alive in the world was the way he meant to do it in the future.

And so, when he was turned out of prison again, without a penny in his pocket, he went straight to Jack Duane. He went full of humility and gratitude; for Duane was a gentleman, and a man with a profession—and it was remarkable that he should be willing to throw in his lot with a humble workingman, one who had even been a beggar and a tramp. Jurgis could not see what help he could be to him; but he did not understand that a man like himself—who could be trusted to stand by any one who was kind to him—was as rare among criminals as among any other class of men.

The address Jurgis had was a garret room in the Ghetto district, the home of a pretty little French girl, Duane's mistress, who sewed all day, and eked out her living by prostitution. He had gone elsewhere, she told Jurgis—he was afraid to stay there now, on account of the police. The new address was a cellar dive, whose proprietor said that he had never heard of Duane; but after he had put Jurgis through a catechism he showed him a back stairs which led to a "fence" in the rear of a pawnbroker's shop, and thence to a number of assignation rooms, in one of which Duane was hiding.

Duane was glad to see him; he was without a cent of money, he said, and had been waiting for Jurgis to help him get some. He explained his plan—in fact he spent the day in laying bare to his friend the criminal world of the city, and in showing him how he might earn himself a living in it. That winter he would have a hard time, on account of his arm, and because of an unwonted fit of activity of the police; but so long as he was unknown to them he would be safe if he were careful. Here at "Papa" Hanson's (so they called the old man who kept the dive) he might rest at ease, for "Papa" Hanson was "square"—would stand by him so long as he paid, and gave him an hour's notice if there were to be a police raid. Also Rosensteg, the pawnbroker, would buy anything he had for a third of its value, and guarantee to keep it hidden for a year.

There was an oil stove in the little cupboard of a room, and they had some supper; and then about eleven o'clock at night they sallied forth together, by a rear entrance to the place, Duane armed with a slingshot. They came to a residence district, and he sprang up a lamppost and blew out the light, and then the two dodged into the shelter of an area step and hid in silence.

Pretty soon a man came by, a workingman—and they let him go. Then after a long interval came the heavy tread of a policeman, and they held their breath till he was gone. Though half-frozen, they waited a full quarter of an hour after that—and then again came footsteps, walking briskly. Duane nudged Jurgis, and the instant the man had passed they rose up. Duane stole out as silently as a shadow, and a second later Jurgis heard a thud and a stifled cry. He was only a couple of feet behind, and he leaped to stop the man's mouth, while Duane held him fast by the arms, as they had agreed. But the man was limp and showed a tendency to fall, and so Jurgis had only to hold him by the collar, while the other, with swift fingers, went through his pockets—ripping open, first his overcoat, and then his coat, and then his vest, searching inside and outside, and transferring the contents into his own pockets. At last, after feeling of the man's fingers and in his necktie, Duane whispered, "That's all!" and they dragged him to the area and dropped him in. Then Jurgis went one way and his friend the other, walking briskly.

The latter arrived first, and Jurgis found him examining the "swag." There was a gold watch, for one thing, with a chain and locket; there was a silver pencil, and a matchbox, and a handful of small change, and finally a card-case. This last Duane opened feverishly—there were letters and checks, and two theater-tickets, and at last, in the back part, a wad of bills. He counted them—

there was a twenty, five tens, four fives, and three ones. Duane drew a long breath. "That lets us out!" he said.

After further examination, they burned the card-case and its contents, all but the bills, and likewise the picture of a little girl in the locket. Then Duane took the watch and trinkets downstairs, and came back with sixteen dollars. "The old scoundrel said the case was filled," he said. "It's a lie, but he knows I want the money."

They divided up the spoils, and Jurgis got as his share fifty-five dollars and some change. He protested that it was too much, but the other had agreed to divide even. That was a good haul, he said, better than average.

When they got up in the morning, Jurgis was sent out to buy a paper; one of the pleasures of committing a crime was the reading about it afterward. "I had a pal that always did it," Duane remarked, laughing—"until one day he read that he had left three thousand dollars in a lower inside pocket of his party's vest!"

There was a half-column account of the robbery—it was evident that a gang was operating in the neighborhood, said the paper, for it was the third within a week, and the police were apparently powerless. The victim was an insurance agent, and he had lost a hundred and ten dollars that did not belong to him. He had chanced to have his name marked on his shirt, otherwise he would not have been identified yet. His assailant had hit him too hard, and he was suffering from concussion of the brain; and also he had been half-frozen when found, and would lose three fingers on his right hand. The enterprising newspaper reporter had taken all this information to his family, and told how they had received it.

Since it was Jurgis's first experience, these details naturally caused him some worriment; but the other laughed coolly—it was the way of the game, and there was no helping it. Before long Jurgis would think no more of it than they did in the yards of knocking out a bullock. "It's a case of us or the other fellow, and I say the other fellow, every time," he observed.

"Still," said Jurgis, reflectively, "he never did us any harm."

"He was doing it to somebody as hard as he could, you can be sure of that," said his friend.

Duane had already explained to Jurgis that if a man of their trade were known he would have to work all the time to satisfy the demands of the police. Therefore it would be better for Jurgis to stay in hiding and never be seen in public with his pal. But Jurgis soon got very tired of staying in hiding. In a couple of weeks he was feeling strong and beginning to use his arm, and then he could not stand it any longer. Duane, who had done a job of some sort by himself, and made a truce with the powers, brought over Marie, his little French girl, to share with him; but even that did not avail for long, and in the end he had to give up arguing, and take Jurgis out and introduce him to the saloons and "sporting houses" where the big crooks and "holdup men" hung out.

And so Jurgis got a glimpse of the high-class criminal world of Chicago. The city, which was owned by an oligarchy of business men, being nominally ruled by the people, a huge army of graft was necessary for the purpose of effecting the transfer of power. Twice a year, in the spring and fall elections, millions of dollars were furnished by the business men and expended by this army; meetings were held and clever speakers were hired, bands played and rockets sizzled, tons of documents and reservoirs of drinks were distributed, and tens of thousands of votes were bought for cash. And this army of graft had, of course, to be maintained the year round. The leaders and organizers were maintained by the business men directly—aldermen and legislators by means of bribes, party officials out of the campaign funds, lobbyists and corporation lawyers in the form of salaries, contractors by means of jobs, labor union leaders by subsidies, and newspaper proprietors and editors by advertisements. The rank and file, however, were either foisted upon the city, or else lived off the population directly. There was the police department, and the fire and water departments, and the whole balance of the civil list, from the meanest office boy to the head of a city department; and for the horde who could find no room in these, there was the world of vice and crime, there was license to seduce, to swindle and plunder and prey. The law forbade Sunday drinking; and this had delivered the saloon-keepers into the hands of the police, and made an alliance between them necessary. The law forbade prostitution; and this had brought the "madames" into the combination. It was the same with the gambling-house keeper and the poolroom man, and the same with any other man or woman who had a means of getting "graft," and was willing to pay over a share of it: the green-goods man and the highwayman, the pickpocket and the sneak thief, and the receiver of stolen goods, the seller of adulterated milk, of stale fruit and diseased meat, the proprietor of unsanitary tenements, the fake doctor and the usurer, the beggar and the "pushcart man," the prize fighter and the professional slugger, the race-track "tout," the procurer, the white-slave agent, and the expert seducer of young girls. All of these agencies of corruption were banded together, and leagued in blood brotherhood with the politician and the police; more often than not they were one and the same person,—the police captain would own the brothel he pretended to raid, the politician would open his headquarters in his saloon. "Hinkydink" or "Bathhouse John," or others of that ilk, were proprietors of the most notorious dives in Chicago, and also the "gray wolves" of the city council, who gave away the streets of the city to the business men; and those who patronized their places were the gamblers and prize fighters who set the law at defiance, and the burglars and holdup men who kept the whole city in terror. On election day all these powers of vice and crime were one power; they could tell within one per cent what the vote of their district would be, and they could change it at an hour's notice.

A month ago Jurgis had all but perished of starvation upon the streets; and now suddenly, as by the gift of a magic key, he had entered into a world where money and all the good things of life came freely. He was introduced by his friend to an Irishman named "Buck" Halloran, who was a political "worker" and on the inside of things. This man talked with Jurgis for a while, and then told him that he had a little plan by which a man who looked like a workingman might make some easy money; but it was a private affair, and had to be kept quiet. Jurgis expressed himself as agreeable, and the other took him that afternoon (it was Saturday) to a place where city laborers were being paid off. The paymaster sat in a little booth, with a pile of envelopes before him, and two policemen standing by. Jurgis went, according to directions, and gave the name of "Michael O'Flaherty," and received an envelope, which he took around the corner and delivered to Halloran, who was waiting for him in a saloon. Then he went again; and gave the name of "Johann Schmidt," and a third time, and give the name of "Serge Reminitsky." Halloran had quite a list of imaginary workingmen, and Jurgis got an envelope for each one. For this work he received five dollars, and was told that he might have it every week, so long as he kept quiet. As Jurgis was excellent at keeping quiet, he soon won the trust of "Buck" Halloran, and was introduced to others as a man who could be depended upon.

This acquaintance was useful to him in another way, also before long Jurgis made his discovery of the meaning of "pull," and just why his boss, Connor, and also the pugilist bartender, had been able to send him to jail. One night there was given a ball, the "benefit" of "One-eyed Larry," a lame man who played the violin in one of the big "high-class" houses of prostitution on Clark Street, and was a wag and a popular character on the "Levee." This ball was held in a big dance hall, and was one of the occasions when the city's powers of debauchery gave themselves up to madness. Jurgis attended and got half insane with drink, and began quarreling over a girl; his arm was pretty strong by then, and he set to work to clean out the place, and ended in a cell in the police station. The police station being crowded to the doors, and stinking with "bums," Jurgis did not relish staying there to sleep off his liquor, and sent for Halloran, who called up the district leader and had Jurgis bailed out by telephone at four o'clock in the morning. When he was arraigned that same morning, the district leader had already seen the clerk of the court and explained that Jurgis Rudkus was a decent fellow, who had been indiscreet; and so Jurgis was fined ten dollars and the fine was "suspended"—which meant that he did not have to pay for it, and never would have to pay it, unless somebody chose to bring it up against him in the future.

Among the people Jurgis lived with now money was valued according to an entirely different standard from that of the people of Packingtown; yet, strange as it may seem, he did a great deal less drinking than he had as a workingman. He had not the same provocations of exhaustion and hopelessness; he had now something to work for, to struggle for. He soon found that if he kept his wits about him, he would come upon new opportunities; and being naturally an active man, he not only kept sober himself, but helped to steady his friend, who was a good deal fonder of both wine and women than he.

One thing led to another. In the saloon where Jurgis met "Buck" Halloran he was sitting late one night with Duane, when a "country customer" (a buyer for an out-of-town merchant) came in, a little more than half "piped." There was no one else in the place but the bartender, and as the man went out again Jurgis and Duane followed him; he went round the corner, and in a dark place made by a combination of the elevated railroad and an unrented building, Jurgis leaped forward and shoved a revolver under his nose, while Duane, with his hat pulled over his eyes, went through the man's pockets with lightning fingers. They got his watch and his "wad," and were round the corner again and into the saloon before he could shout more than once. The bartender, to whom they had tipped the wink, had the cellar door open for them, and they vanished, making their way by a secret entrance to a brothel next door. From the roof of this there was access to three similar places beyond. By means of these passages the customers of any one place could be gotten out of the way, in case a falling out with the police chanced to lead to a raid; and also it was necessary to have a way of getting a girl out of reach in case of an emergency. Thousands of them came to Chicago answering advertisements for "servants" and "factory hands," and found themselves trapped by fake employment agencies, and locked up in a bawdy-house. It was generally enough to take all their clothes away from them; but sometimes they would have to be "doped" and kept prisoners for weeks; and meantime their parents might be telegraphing the police, and even coming on to see why nothing was done. Occasionally there was no way of satisfying them but to let them search the place to which the girl had been traced.

For his help in this little job, the bartender received twenty out of the hundred and thirty odd dollars that the pair secured; and naturally this put them on friendly terms with him, and a few days later he introduced them to a little "sheeny" named Goldberger, one of the "runners" of the "sporting house" where they had been hidden. After a few drinks Goldberger began, with some hesitation, to narrate how he had had a quarrel over his best girl with a professional "cardsharp," who had hit him in the jaw. The fellow was a stranger in Chicago, and if he was found some night with his head cracked there would be no one to care very much. Jurgis, who by this time would cheerfully have cracked the heads of all the gamblers in Chicago, inquired what would be coming to him; at which the Jew became still more confidential, and said that he had some tips on the New Orleans races, which he got direct from the police captain of the district, whom he had got out of a bad scrape, and who "stood in" with a big syndicate of horse owners. Duane took all this in at once, but Jurgis had to have the whole race-track situation explained to him before he realized the importance of such an opportunity.

There was the gigantic Racing Trust. It owned the legislatures in every state in which it did business; it even owned some of the big newspapers, and made public opinion—there was no power in the land that could oppose it unless, perhaps, it were the Poolroom Trust. It built magnificent racing parks all over the country, and by means of enormous purses it lured the people to come, and then it organized a gigantic shell game, whereby it plundered them of hundreds of millions of dollars every year. Horse racing had once been a sport, but nowadays it was a business; a horse could be "doped" and doctored, undertrained or overtrained; it could be made to fall at any moment—or its gait could be broken by lashing it with the whip, which all the spectators would take to be a desperate effort to keep it in the lead. There were scores of such tricks; and sometimes it was the owners who played them and made fortunes, sometimes it was the jockeys and trainers, sometimes it was outsiders, who bribed them—but most of the time it was the chiefs of the trust. Now for instance, they were having winter racing in New Orleans and a syndicate was laying out each day's program in advance, and its agents in all the Northern cities were "milking" the poolrooms. The word came by long-distance telephone in a cipher code, just a little while before each race; and any man who could get the secret had as good as a fortune. If Jurgis did not believe it, he could try it, said the little Jew—let them meet at a certain house on the morrow and make a test. Jurgis was willing, and so was Duane, and so they went to one of the high-class poolrooms where brokers and merchants gambled (with society women in a private room), and they put up ten dollars each upon a horse called "Black Beldame," a six to one shot, and won. For a secret like that they would have done a good many sluggings—but the next day Goldberger informed them that the offending gambler had got wind of what was coming to him, and had skipped the town.

There were ups and downs at the business; but there was always a living, inside of a jail, if not out of it. Early in April the city elections were due, and that meant prosperity for all the powers of graft. Jurgis, hanging round in dives and gambling houses and brothels, met with the heelers of both parties, and from their conversation he came to understand all the ins and outs of the game, and to hear of a number of ways in which he could make himself useful about election time. "Buck" Halloran was a "Democrat," and so Jurgis became a Democrat also; but he was not a bitter one—the Republicans were good fellows, too, and were to have a pile of money in this next campaign. At the last election the Republicans had paid four dollars a vote to the Democrats' three; and "Buck" Halloran sat one night playing cards with Jurgis and another man, who told how Halloran had been charged with the job voting a "bunch" of thirty-seven newly landed Italians, and how he, the narrator, had met the Republican worker who was after the very same gang, and how the three had effected a bargain, whereby the Italians were to vote half and half, for a glass of beer apiece, while the balance of the fund went to the conspirators!

Not long after this, Jurgis, wearying of the risks and vicissitudes of miscellaneous crime, was moved to give up the career for that of a politician. Just at this time there was a tremendous uproar being raised concerning the alliance between the criminals and the police. For the criminal graft was one in which the business men had no direct part—it was what is called a "side line," carried by the police. "Wide open" gambling and debauchery made the city pleasing to "trade," but burglaries and holdups did not. One night it chanced that while Jack Duane was drilling a safe in a clothing store he was caught red-handed by the night watchman, and turned over to a policeman, who chanced to know him well, and who took the responsibility of letting him make his escape. Such a howl from the newspapers followed this that Duane was slated for sacrifice, and barely got out of town in time. And just at that juncture it happened that Jurgis was introduced to a man named Harper whom he recognized as the night watchman at Brown's, who had been instrumental in making him an American citizen, the first year of his arrival at the yards. The other was interested in the coincidence, but did not remember Jurgis—he had handled too many "green ones" in his time, he said. He sat in a dance hall with Jurgis and Halloran until one or two in the morning, exchanging experiences. He had a long story to tell of his quarrel with the superintendent of his department, and how he was now a plain workingman, and a good union man as well. It was not until some months afterward that Jurgis understood that the quarrel with the superintendent had been prearranged, and that Harper was in reality drawing a salary of twenty dollars a week from the packers for an inside report of his union's secret proceedings. The yards were seething with agitation just then, said the man, speaking as a unionist. The people of Packingtown had borne about all that they would bear, and it looked as if a strike might begin any week.

After this talk the man made inquiries concerning Jurgis, and a couple of days later he came to him with an interesting proposition. He was not absolutely certain, he said, but he thought that he could get him a regular salary if he would come to Packingtown and do as he was told, and keep his mouth shut. Harper—"Bush" Harper, he was called—was a right-hand man of Mike Scully, the Democratic boss of the stockyards; and in the coming election there was a peculiar situation. There had come to Scully a proposition to nominate a certain rich brewer who lived upon a swell boulevard that skirted the district, and who coveted the big badge and the "honorable" of an alderman. The brewer was a Jew, and had no brains, but he was harmless, and would put up a rare campaign fund. Scully had accepted the offer, and then gone to the Republicans with a proposition. He was not sure that he could manage the "sheeny," and he did not mean to take any chances with his district; let the Republicans nominate a certain obscure but amiable friend of Scully's, who was now setting tenpins in the cellar of an Ashland Avenue saloon, and he, Scully, would elect him with the "sheeny's" money, and the Republicans might have the glory, which was more than they would get otherwise. In return for this the Republicans would agree to put up no candidate the following year, when Scully himself came up for reelection as the other alderman from the ward. To this the Republicans had assented at once; but the hell of it was—so Harper explained—that the Republicans were all of them fools—a man had to be a fool to be a Republican in the stockyards, where Scully was king. And they didn't know how to work, and of course it would not do for the Democratic workers, the noble redskins of the War Whoop League, to support the Republican openly. The difficulty would not have been so great except for another fact—there had been a curious development in stockyards politics in the last year or two, a new party having leaped into being. They were the Socialists; and it was a devil of a mess, said "Bush" Harper. The one image which the word "Socialist" brought to Jurgis was of poor little Tamoszius Kuszleika, who had called himself one, and would go out with a couple of other men and a soap-box, and shout himself hoarse on a street corner Saturday nights. Tamoszius had tried to explain to Jurgis what it was all about, but Jurgis, who was not of an imaginative turn, had never quite got it straight; at present he was content with his companion's explanation that the Socialists were the enemies of American institutions—could not be bought, and would not combine or make any sort of a "dicker." Mike Scully was very much worried over the opportunity which his last deal gave to them—the stockyards Democrats were furious at the idea of a rich capitalist for their candidate, and while they were changing they might possibly conclude that a Socialist firebrand was preferable to a Republican bum. And so right here was a chance for Jurgis to make himself a place in the world, explained "Bush" Harper; he had been a union man, and he was known in the yards as a workingman; he must have hundreds of acquaintances, and as he had never talked politics with them he might come out as a Republican now without exciting the least suspicion. There were barrels of money for the use of those who could deliver the goods; and Jurgis might count upon Mike Scully, who had never yet gone back on a friend. Just what could he do? Jurgis asked, in some perplexity, and the other explained in detail. To begin with, he would have to go to the yards and work, and he mightn't relish that; but he would have what he earned, as well as the rest that came to him. He would get active in the union again, and perhaps try to get an office, as he, Harper, had; he would tell all his friends the good points of Doyle, the Republican nominee, and the bad ones of the "sheeny"; and then Scully would furnish a meeting place, and he would start the "Young Men's Republican Association," or something of that sort, and have the rich brewer's best beer by the hogshead, and fireworks and speeches, just like the War Whoop League. Surely Jurgis must know hundreds of men who would like that sort of fun; and there would be the regular Republican leaders and workers to help him out, and they would deliver a big enough majority on election day.

When he had heard all this explanation to the end, Jurgis demanded: "But how can I get a job in Packingtown? I'm blacklisted."

At which "Bush" Harper laughed. "I'll attend to that all right," he said.

And the other replied, "It's a go, then; I'm your man." So Jurgis went out to the stockyards again, and was introduced to the political lord of the district, the boss of Chicago's mayor. It was Scully who owned the brick-yards and the dump and the ice pond—though Jurgis did not know it. It was Scully who was to blame for the unpaved street in which Jurgis's child had been drowned; it was Scully who had put into office the magistrate who had first sent Jurgis to jail; it was Scully who was principal stockholder in the company which had sold him the ramshackle tenement, and then robbed him of it. But Jurgis knew none of these things—any more than he knew that Scully was but a tool and puppet of the packers. To him Scully was a mighty power, the "biggest" man he had ever met.

He was a little, dried-up Irishman, whose hands shook. He had a brief talk with his visitor, watching him with his ratlike eyes, and making up his mind about him; and then he gave him a note to Mr. Harmon, one of the head managers of Durham's—

"The bearer, Jurgis Rudkus, is a particular friend of mine, and I would like you to find him a good place, for important reasons. He was once indiscreet, but you will perhaps be so good as to overlook that."

Mr. Harmon looked up inquiringly when he read this. "What does he mean by 'indiscreet'?" he asked.

"I was blacklisted, sir," said Jurgis.

At which the other frowned. "Blacklisted?" he said. "How do you mean?" And Jurgis turned red with embarrassment.

He had forgotten that a blacklist did not exist. "I—that is—I had difficulty in getting a place," he stammered.

"What was the matter?"

"I got into a quarrel with a foreman—not my own boss, sir—and struck him."

"I see," said the other, and meditated for a few moments. "What do you wish to do?" he asked.

"Anything, sir," said Jurgis—"only I had a broken arm this winter, and so I have to be careful."

"How would it suit you to be a night watchman?"

"That wouldn't do, sir. I have to be among the men at night."

"I see—politics. Well, would it suit you to trim hogs?"

"Yes, sir," said Jurgis.

And Mr. Harmon called a timekeeper and said, "Take this man to Pat Murphy and tell him to find room for him somehow."

And so Jurgis marched into the hog-killing room, a place where, in the days gone by, he had come begging for a job. Now he walked jauntily, and smiled to himself, seeing the frown that came to the boss's face as the timekeeper said, "Mr. Harmon says to put this man on." It would overcrowd his department and spoil the record he was trying to make—but he said not a word except "All right."

And so Jurgis became a workingman once more; and straightway he sought out his old friends, and joined the union, and began to "root" for "Scotty" Doyle. Doyle had done him a good turn once, he explained, and was really a bully chap; Doyle was a workingman himself, and would represent the workingmen—why did they want to vote for a millionaire "sheeny," and what the hell had Mike Scully ever done for them that they should back his candidates all the time? And meantime Scully had given Jurgis a note to the Republican leader of the ward, and he had gone there and met the crowd he was to work with. Already they had hired a big hall, with some of the brewer's money, and every night Jurgis brought in a dozen new members of the "Doyle Republican Association." Pretty soon they had a grand opening night; and there was a brass band, which marched through the streets, and fireworks and bombs and red lights in front of the hall; and there was an enormous crowd, with two overflow meetings—so that the pale and trembling candidate had to recite three times over the little speech which one of Scully's henchmen had written, and which he had been a month learning by heart. Best of all, the famous and eloquent Senator Spareshanks, presidential candidate, rode out in an automobile to discuss the sacred privileges of American citizenship, and protection and prosperity for the American workingman. His inspiriting address was quoted to the extent of half a column in all the morning newspapers, which also said that it could be stated upon excellent authority that the unexpected popularity developed by Doyle, the Republican candidate for alderman, was giving great anxiety to Mr. Scully, the chairman of the Democratic City Committee.

The chairman was still more worried when the monster torchlight procession came off, with the members of the Doyle Republican Association all in red capes and hats, and free beer for every voter in the ward—the best beer ever given away in a political campaign, as the whole electorate testified. During this parade, and at innumerable cart-tail meetings as well, Jurgis labored tirelessly. He did not make any speeches—there were lawyers and other experts for that—but he helped to manage things; distributing notices and posting placards and bringing out the crowds; and when the show was on he attended to the fireworks and the beer. Thus in the course of the campaign he handled many hundreds of dollars of the Hebrew brewer's money, administering it with naive and touching fidelity. Toward the end, however, he learned that he was regarded with hatred by the rest of the "boys," because he compelled them either to make a poorer showing than he or to do without their share of the pie. After that Jurgis did his best to please them, and to make up for the time he had lost before he discovered the extra bungholes of the campaign barrel.

He pleased Mike Scully, also. On election morning he was out at four o'clock, "getting out the vote"; he had a two-horse carriage to ride in, and he went from house to house for his friends, and escorted them in triumph to the polls. He voted half a dozen times himself, and voted some of his friends as often; he brought bunch after bunch of the newest foreigners—Lithuanians, Poles, Bohemians, Slovaks—and when he had put them through the mill he turned them over to another man to take to the next polling place. When Jurgis first set out, the captain of the precinct gave him a hundred dollars, and three times in the course of the day he came for another hundred, and not more than twenty-five out of each lot got stuck in his own pocket. The balance all went for actual votes, and on a day of Democratic landslides they elected "Scotty" Doyle, the ex-tenpin setter, by nearly a thousand plurality—and beginning at five o'clock in the afternoon, and ending at three the next morning, Jurgis treated himself to a most unholy and horrible "jag." Nearly every one else in Packingtown did the same, however, for there was universal exultation over this triumph of popular government, this crushing defeat of an arrogant plutocrat by the power of the common people.

# Chapter 26

After the elections Jurgis stayed on in Packingtown and kept his job. The agitation to break up the police protection of criminals was continuing, and it seemed to him best to "lay low" for the present. He had nearly three hundred dollars in the bank, and might have considered himself entitled to a vacation; but he had an easy job, and force of habit kept him at it. Besides, Mike Scully, whom he consulted, advised him that something might "turn up" before long.

Jurgis got himself a place in a boardinghouse with some congenial friends. He had already inquired of Aniele, and learned that Elzbieta and her family had gone downtown, and so he gave no further thought to them. He went with a new set, now, young unmarried fellows who were "sporty." Jurgis had long ago cast off his fertilizer clothing, and since going into politics he had donned a linen collar and a greasy red necktie. He had some reason for thinking of his dress, for he was making about eleven dollars a week, and two-thirds of it he might spend upon his pleasures without ever touching his savings.

Sometimes he would ride down-town with a party of friends to the cheap theaters and the music halls and other haunts with which they were familiar. Many of the saloons in Packingtown had pool tables, and some of them bowling alleys, by means of which he could spend his evenings in petty gambling. Also, there were cards and dice. One time Jurgis got into a game on a Saturday night and won prodigiously, and because he was a man of spirit he stayed in with the rest and the game continued until late Sunday afternoon, and by that time he was "out" over twenty dollars. On Saturday nights, also, a number of balls were generally given in Packingtown; each man would bring his "girl" with him, paying half a dollar for a ticket, and several dollars additional for drinks in the course of the festivities, which continued until three or four o'clock in the morning, unless broken up by fighting. During all this time the same man and woman would dance together, half-stupefied with sensuality and drink.

Before long Jurgis discovered what Scully had meant by something "turning up." In May the agreement between the packers and the unions expired, and a new agreement had to be signed. Negotiations were going on, and the yards were full of talk of a strike. The old scale had dealt with the wages of the skilled men only; and of the members of the Meat Workers' Union about two-thirds were unskilled men. In Chicago these latter were receiving, for the most part, eighteen and a half cents an hour, and the unions wished to make this the general wage for the next year. It was not nearly so large a wage as it seemed—in the course of the negotiations the union officers examined time checks to the amount of ten thousand dollars, and they found that the highest wages paid had been fourteen dollars a week, and the lowest two dollars and five cents, and the average of the whole, six dollars and sixty-five cents. And six dollars and sixty-five cents was hardly too much for a man to keep a family on, considering the fact that the price of dressed meat had increased nearly fifty per cent in the last five years, while the price of "beef on the hoof" had decreased as much, it would have seemed that the packers ought to be able to pay it; but the packers were unwilling to pay it—they rejected the union demand, and to show what their purpose was, a week or two after the agreement expired they put down the wages of about a thousand men to sixteen and a half cents, and it was said that old man Jones had vowed he would put them to fifteen before he got through. There were a million and a half of men in the country looking for work, a hundred thousand of them right in Chicago; and were the packers to let the union stewards march into their places and bind them to a contract that would lose them several thousand dollars a day for a year? Not much!

All this was in June; and before long the question was submitted to a referendum in the unions, and the decision was for a strike. It was the same in all the packing house cities; and suddenly the newspapers and public woke up to face the gruesome spectacle of a meat famine. All sorts of pleas for a reconsideration were made, but the packers were obdurate; and all the while they were reducing wages, and heading off shipments of cattle, and rushing in wagon-loads of mattresses and cots. So the men boiled over, and one night telegrams went out from the union headquarters to all the big packing centers—to St. Paul, South Omaha, Sioux City, St. Joseph, Kansas City, East St. Louis, and New York—and the next day at noon between fifty and sixty thousand men drew off their working clothes and marched out of the factories, and the great "Beef Strike" was on.

Jurgis went to his dinner, and afterward he walked over to see Mike Scully, who lived in a fine house, upon a street which had been decently paved and lighted for his especial benefit. Scully had gone into semi-retirement, and looked nervous and worried. "What do you want?" he demanded, when he saw Jurgis.

"I came to see if maybe you could get me a place during the strike," the other replied.

And Scully knit his brows and eyed him narrowly. In that morning's papers Jurgis had read a fierce denunciation of the packers by Scully, who had declared that if they did not treat their people better the city authorities would end the matter by tearing down their plants. Now, therefore, Jurgis was not a little taken aback when the other demanded suddenly, "See here, Rudkus, why don't you stick by your job?"

Jurgis started. "Work as a scab?" he cried.

"Why not?" demanded Scully. "What's that to you?"

"But—but—" stammered Jurgis. He had somehow taken it for granted that he should go out with his union. "The packers need good men, and need them bad," continued the other, "and they'll treat a man right that stands by them. Why don't you take your chance and fix yourself?"

"But," said Jurgis, "how could I ever be of any use to you—in politics?"

"You couldn't be it anyhow," said Scully, abruptly.

"Why not?" asked Jurgis.

"Hell, man!" cried the other. "Don't you know you're a Republican? And do you think I'm always going to elect Republicans? My brewer has found out already how we served him, and there is the deuce to pay."

Jurgis looked dumfounded. He had never thought of that aspect of it before. "I could be a Democrat," he said.

"Yes," responded the other, "but not right away; a man can't change his politics every day. And besides, I don't need you—there'd be nothing for you to do. And it's a long time to election day, anyhow; and what are you going to do meantime?"

"I thought I could count on you," began Jurgis.

"Yes," responded Scully, "so you could—I never yet went back on a friend. But is it fair to leave the job I got you and come to me for another? I have had a hundred fellows after me today, and what can I do? I've put seventeen men on the city payroll to clean streets this one week, and do you think I can keep that up forever? It wouldn't do for me to tell other men what I tell you, but you've been on the inside, and you ought to have sense enough to see for yourself. What have you to gain by a strike?"

"I hadn't thought," said Jurgis.

"Exactly," said Scully, "but you'd better. Take my word for it, the strike will be over in a few days, and the men will be beaten; and meantime what you can get out of it will belong to you. Do you see?"

And Jurgis saw. He went back to the yards, and into the workroom. The men had left a long line of hogs in various stages of preparation, and the foreman was directing the feeble efforts of a score or two of clerks and stenographers and office boys to finish up the job and get them into the chilling rooms. Jurgis went straight up to him and announced, "I have come back to work, Mr. Murphy."

The boss's face lighted up. "Good man!" he cried. "Come ahead!"

"Just a moment," said Jurgis, checking his enthusiasm. "I think I ought to get a little more wages."

"Yes," replied the other, "of course. What do you want?"

Jurgis had debated on the way. His nerve almost failed him now, but he clenched his hands. "I think I ought to have' three dollars a day," he said.

"All right," said the other, promptly; and before the day was out our friend discovered that the clerks and stenographers and office boys were getting five dollars a day, and then he could have kicked himself!

So Jurgis became one of the new "American heroes," a man whose virtues merited comparison with those of the martyrs of Lexington and Valley Forge. The resemblance was not complete, of course, for Jurgis was generously paid and comfortably clad, and was provided with a spring cot and a mattress and three substantial meals a day; also he was perfectly at ease, and safe from all peril of life and limb, save only in the case that a desire for beer should lead him to venture outside of the stockyards gates. And even in the exercise of this privilege he was not left unprotected; a good part of the inadequate police force of Chicago was suddenly diverted from its work of hunting criminals, and rushed out to serve him. The police, and the strikers also, were determined that there should be no violence; but there was another party interested which was minded to the contrary—and that was the press. On the first day of his life as a strikebreaker Jurgis quit work early, and in a spirit of bravado he challenged three men of his acquaintance to go outside and get a drink. They accepted, and went through the big Halsted Street gate, where several policemen were watching, and also some union pickets, scanning sharply those who passed in and out. Jurgis and his companions went south on Halsted Street; past the hotel, and then suddenly half a dozen men started across the street toward them and proceeded to argue with them concerning the error of their ways. As the arguments were not taken in the proper spirit, they went on to threats; and suddenly one of them jerked off the hat of one of the four and flung it over the fence. The man started after it, and then, as a cry of "Scab!" was raised and a dozen people came running out of saloons and doorways, a second man's heart failed him and he followed. Jurgis and the fourth stayed long enough to give themselves the satisfaction of a quick exchange of blows, and then they, too, took to their heels and fled back of the hotel and into the yards again. Meantime, of course, policemen were coming on a run, and as a crowd gathered other police got excited and sent in a riot call. Jurgis knew nothing of this, but went back to "Packers' Avenue," and in front of the "Central Time Station" he saw one of his companions, breathless and wild with excitement, narrating to an ever growing throng how the four had been attacked and surrounded by a howling mob, and had been nearly torn to pieces. While he stood listening, smiling cynically, several dapper young men stood by with notebooks in their hands, and it was not more than two hours later that Jurgis saw newsboys running about with armfuls of newspapers, printed in red and black letters six inches high:

VIOLENCE IN THE YARDS! STRIKEBREAKERS SURROUNDED BY FRENZIED MOB!

If he had been able to buy all of the newspapers of the United States the next morning, he might have discovered that his beer-hunting exploit was being perused by some two score millions of people, and had served as a text for editorials in half the staid and solemn business-men's newspapers in the land.

Jurgis was to see more of this as time passed. For the present, his work being over, he was free to ride into the city, by a railroad direct from the yards, or else to spend the night in a room where cots had been laid in rows. He chose the latter, but to his regret, for all night long gangs of strikebreakers kept arriving. As very few of the better class of workingmen could be got for such work, these specimens of the new American hero contained an assortment of the criminals and thugs of the city, besides Negroes and the lowest foreigners—Greeks, Roumanians, Sicilians, and Slovaks. They had been attracted more by the prospect of disorder than by the big wages; and they made the night hideous with singing and carousing, and only went to sleep when the time came for them to get up to work.

In the morning before Jurgis had finished his breakfast, "Pat" Murphy ordered him to one of the superintendents, who questioned him as to his experience in the work of the killing room. His heart began to thump with excitement, for he divined instantly that his hour had come—that he was to be a boss!

Some of the foremen were union members, and many who were not had gone out with the men. It was in the killing department that the packers had been left most in the lurch, and precisely here that they could least afford it; the smoking and canning and salting of meat might wait, and all the by-products might be wasted—but fresh meats must be had, or the restaurants and hotels and brownstone houses would feel the pinch, and then "public opinion" would take a startling turn.

An opportunity such as this would not come twice to a man; and Jurgis seized it. Yes, he knew the work, the whole of it, and he could teach it to others. But if he took the job and gave satisfaction he would expect to keep it—they would not turn him off at the end of the strike? To which the superintendent replied that he might safely trust Durham's for that—they proposed to teach these unions a lesson, and most of all those foremen who had gone back on them. Jurgis would receive five dollars a day during the strike, and twenty-five a week after it was settled.

So our friend got a pair of "slaughter pen" boots and "jeans," and flung himself at his task. It was a weird sight, there on the killing beds—a throng of stupid black Negroes, and foreigners who could not understand a word that was said to them, mixed with pale-faced, hollow-chested bookkeepers and clerks, half-fainting for the tropical heat and the sickening stench of fresh blood—and all struggling to dress a dozen or two cattle in the same place where, twenty-four hours ago, the old killing gang had been speeding, with their marvelous precision, turning out four hundred carcasses every hour!

The Negroes and the "toughs" from the Levee did not want to work, and every few minutes some of them would feel obliged to retire and recuperate. In a couple of days Durham and Company had electric fans up to cool off the rooms for them, and even couches for them to rest on; and meantime they could go out and find a shady corner and take a "snooze," and as there was no place for any one in particular, and no system, it might be hours before their boss discovered them. As for the poor office employees, they did their best, moved to it by terror; thirty of them had been "fired" in a bunch that first morning for refusing to serve, besides a number of women clerks and typewriters who had declined to act as waitresses.

It was such a force as this that Jurgis had to organize. He did his best, flying here and there, placing them in rows and showing them the tricks; he had never given an order in his life before, but he had taken enough of them to know, and he soon fell into the spirit of it, and roared and stormed like any old stager. He had not the most tractable pupils, however. "See hyar, boss," a big black "buck" would begin, "ef you doan' like de way Ah does dis job, you kin get somebody else to do it." Then a crowd would gather and listen, muttering threats. After the first meal nearly all the steel knives had been missing, and now every Negro had one, ground to a fine point, hidden in his boots.

There was no bringing order out of such a chaos, Jurgis soon discovered; and he fell in with the spirit of the thing—there was no reason why he should wear himself out with shouting. If hides and guts were slashed and rendered useless there was no way of tracing it to any one; and if a man lay off and forgot to come back there was nothing to be gained by seeking him, for all the rest would quit in the meantime. Everything went, during the strike, and the packers paid. Before long Jurgis found that the custom of resting had suggested to some alert minds the possibility of registering at more than one place and earning more than one five dollars a day. When he caught a man at this he "fired" him, but it chanced to be in a quiet corner, and the man tendered him a ten-dollar bill and a wink, and he took them. Of course, before long this custom spread, and Jurgis was soon making quite a good income from it.

In the face of handicaps such as these the packers counted themselves lucky if they could kill off the cattle that had been crippled in transit and the hogs that had developed disease. Frequently, in the course of a two or three days' trip, in hot weather and without water, some hog would develop cholera, and die; and the rest would attack him before he had ceased kicking, and when the car was opened there would be nothing of him left but the bones. If all the hogs in this carload were not killed at once, they would soon be down with the dread disease, and there would be nothing to do but make them into lard. It was the same with cattle that were gored and dying, or were limping with broken bones stuck through their flesh—they must be killed, even if brokers and buyers and superintendents had to take off their coats and help drive and cut and skin them. And meantime, agents of the packers were gathering gangs of Negroes in the country districts of the far South, promising them five dollars a day and board, and being careful not to mention there was a strike; already carloads of them were on the way, with special rates from the railroads, and all traffic ordered out of the way. Many towns and cities were taking advantage of the chance to clear out their jails and workhouses—in Detroit the magistrates would release every man who agreed to leave town within twenty-four hours, and agents of the packers were in the courtrooms to ship them right. And meantime trainloads of supplies were coming in for their accommodation, including beer and whisky, so that they might not be tempted to go outside. They hired thirty young girls in Cincinnati to "pack fruit," and when they arrived put them at work canning corned beef, and put cots for them to sleep in a public hallway, through which the men passed. As the gangs came in day and night, under the escort of squads of police, they stowed away in unused workrooms and storerooms, and in the car sheds, crowded so closely together that the cots touched. In some places they would use the same room for eating and sleeping, and at night the men would put their cots upon the tables, to keep away from the swarms of rats.

But with all their best efforts, the packers were demoralized. Ninety per cent of the men had walked out; and they faced the task of completely remaking their labor force—and with the price of meat up thirty per cent, and the public clamoring for a settlement. They made an offer to submit the whole question at issue to arbitration; and at the end of ten days the unions accepted it, and the strike was called off. It was agreed that all the men were to be re-employed within forty-five days, and that there was to be "no discrimination against union men."

This was an anxious time for Jurgis. If the men were taken back "without discrimination," he would lose his present place. He sought out the superintendent, who smiled grimly and bade him "wait and see." Durham's strikebreakers were few of them leaving.

Whether or not the "settlement" was simply a trick of the packers to gain time, or whether they really expected to break the strike and cripple the unions by the plan, cannot be said; but that night there went out from the office of Durham and Company a telegram to all the big packing centers, "Employ no union leaders." And in the morning, when the twenty thousand men thronged into the yards, with their dinner pails and working clothes, Jurgis stood near the door of the hog-trimming room, where he had worked before the strike, and saw a throng of eager men, with a score or two of policemen watching them; and he saw a superintendent come out and walk down the line, and pick out man after man that pleased him; and one after another came, and there were some men up near the head of the line who were never picked—they being the union stewards and delegates, and the men Jurgis had heard making speeches at the meetings. Each time, of course, there were louder murmurings and angrier looks. Over where the cattle butchers were waiting, Jurgis heard shouts and saw a crowd, and he hurried there. One big butcher, who was president of the Packing Trades Council, had been passed over five times, and the men were wild with rage; they had appointed a committee of three to go in and see the superintendent, and the committee had made three attempts, and each time the police had clubbed them back from the door. Then there were yells and hoots, continuing until at last the superintendent came to the door. "We all go back or none of us do!" cried a hundred voices. And the other shook his fist at them, and shouted, "You went out of here like cattle, and like cattle you'll come back!"

Then suddenly the big butcher president leaped upon a pile of stones and yelled: "It's off, boys. We'll all of us quit again!" And so the cattle butchers declared a new strike on the spot; and gathering their members from the other plants, where the same trick had been played, they marched down Packers' Avenue, which was thronged with a dense mass of workers, cheering wildly. Men who had already got to work on the killing beds dropped their tools and joined them; some galloped here and there on horseback, shouting the tidings, and within half an hour the whole of Packingtown was on strike again, and beside itself with fury.

There was quite a different tone in Packingtown after this—the place was a seething caldron of passion, and the "scab" who ventured into it fared badly. There were one or two of these incidents each day, the newspapers detailing them, and always blaming them upon the unions. Yet ten years before, when there were no unions in Packingtown, there was a strike, and national troops had to be called, and there were pitched battles fought at night, by the light of blazing freight trains. Packingtown was always a center of violence; in "Whisky Point," where there were a hundred saloons and one glue factory, there was always fighting, and always more of it in hot weather. Any one who had taken the trouble to consult the station house blotter would have found that there was less violence that summer than ever before—and this while twenty thousand men were out of work, and with nothing to do all day but brood upon bitter wrongs. There was no one to picture the battle the union leaders were fighting—to hold this huge army in rank, to keep it from straggling and pillaging, to cheer and encourage and guide a hundred thousand people, of a dozen different tongues, through six long weeks of hunger and disappointment and despair.

Meantime the packers had set themselves definitely to the task of making a new labor force. A thousand or two of strikebreakers were brought in every night, and distributed among the various plants. Some of them were experienced workers,—butchers, salesmen, and managers from the packers' branch stores, and a few union men who had deserted from other cities; but the vast majority were "green" Negroes from the cotton districts of the far South, and they were herded into the packing plants like sheep. There was a law forbidding the use of buildings as lodginghouses unless they were licensed for the purpose, and provided with proper windows, stairways, and fire escapes; but here, in a "paint room," reached only by an enclosed "chute," a room without a single window and only one door, a hundred men were crowded upon mattresses on the floor. Up on the third story of the "hog house" of Jones's was a storeroom, without a window, into which they crowded seven hundred men, sleeping upon the bare springs of cots, and with a second shift to use them by day. And when the clamor of the public led to an investigation into these conditions, and the mayor of the city was forced to order the enforcement of the law, the packers got a judge to issue an injunction forbidding him to do it!

Just at this time the mayor was boasting that he had put an end to gambling and prize fighting in the city; but here a swarm of professional gamblers had leagued themselves with the police to fleece the strikebreakers; and any night, in the big open space in front of Brown's, one might see brawny Negroes stripped to the waist and pounding each other for money, while a howling throng of three or four thousand surged about, men and women, young white girls from the country rubbing elbows with big buck Negroes with daggers in their boots, while rows of woolly heads peered down from every window of the surrounding factories. The ancestors of these black people had been savages in Africa; and since then they had been chattel slaves, or had been held down by a community ruled by the traditions of slavery. Now for the first time they were free—free to gratify every passion, free to wreck themselves. They were wanted to break a strike, and when it was broken they would be shipped away, and their present masters would never see them again; and so whisky and women were brought in by the carload and sold to them, and hell was let loose in the yards. Every night there were stabbings and shootings; it was said that the packers had blank permits, which enabled them to ship dead bodies from the city without troubling the authorities. They lodged men and women on the same floor; and with the night there began a saturnalia of debauchery—scenes such as never before had been witnessed in America. And as the women were the dregs from the brothels of Chicago, and the men were for the most part ignorant country Negroes, the nameless diseases of vice were soon rife; and this where food was being handled which was sent out to every corner of the civilized world.

The "Union Stockyards" were never a pleasant place; but now they were not only a collection of slaughterhouses, but also the camping place of an army of fifteen or twenty thousand human beasts. All day long the blazing midsummer sun beat down upon that square mile of abominations: upon tens of thousands of cattle crowded into pens whose wooden floors stank and steamed contagion; upon bare, blistering, cinder-strewn railroad tracks, and huge blocks of dingy meat factories, whose labyrinthine passages defied a breath of fresh air to penetrate them; and there were not merely rivers of hot blood, and car-loads of moist flesh, and rendering vats and soap caldrons, glue factories and fertilizer tanks, that smelt like the craters of hell—there were also tons of garbage festering in the sun, and the greasy laundry of the workers hung out to dry, and dining rooms littered with food and black with flies, and toilet rooms that were open sewers.

And then at night, when this throng poured out into the streets to play—fighting, gambling, drinking and carousing, cursing and screaming, laughing and singing, playing banjoes and dancing! They were worked in the yards all the seven days of the week, and they had their prize fights and crap games on Sunday nights as well; but then around the corner one might see a bonfire blazing, and an old, gray-headed Negress, lean and witchlike, her hair flying wild and her eyes blazing, yelling and chanting of the fires of perdition and the blood of the "Lamb," while men and women lay down upon the ground and moaned and screamed in convulsions of terror and remorse.

Such were the stockyards during the strike; while the unions watched in sullen despair, and the country clamored like a greedy child for its food, and the packers went grimly on their way. Each day they added new workers, and could be more stern with the old ones—could put them on piecework, and dismiss them if they did not keep up the pace. Jurgis was now one of their agents in this process; and he could feel the change day by day, like the slow starting up of a huge machine. He had gotten used to being a master of men; and because of the stifling heat and the stench, and the fact that he was a "scab" and knew it and despised himself. He was drinking, and developing a villainous temper, and he stormed and cursed and raged at his men, and drove them until they were ready to drop with exhaustion.

Then one day late in August, a superintendent ran into the place and shouted to Jurgis and his gang to drop their work and come. They followed him outside, to where, in the midst of a dense throng, they saw several two-horse trucks waiting, and three patrol-wagon loads of police. Jurgis and his men sprang upon one of the trucks, and the driver yelled to the crowd, and they went thundering away at a gallop. Some steers had just escaped from the yards, and the strikers had got hold of them, and there would be the chance of a scrap!

They went out at the Ashland Avenue gate, and over in the direction of the "dump." There was a yell as soon as they were sighted, men and women rushing out of houses and saloons as they galloped by. There were eight or ten policemen on the truck, however, and there was no disturbance until they came to a place where the street was blocked with a dense throng. Those on the flying truck yelled a warning and the crowd scattered pell-mell, disclosing one of the steers lying in its blood. There were a good many cattle butchers about just then, with nothing much to do, and hungry children at home; and so some one had knocked out the steer—and as a first-class man can kill and dress one in a couple of minutes, there were a good many steaks and roasts already missing. This called for punishment, of course; and the police proceeded to administer it by leaping from the truck and cracking at every head they saw. There were yells of rage and pain, and the terrified people fled into houses and stores, or scattered helter-skelter down the street. Jurgis and his gang joined in the sport, every man singling out his victim, and striving to bring him to bay and punch him. If he fled into a house his pursuer would smash in the flimsy door and follow him up the stairs, hitting every one who came within reach, and finally dragging his squealing quarry from under a bed or a pile of old clothes in a closet.

Jurgis and two policemen chased some men into a bar-room. One of them took shelter behind the bar, where a policeman cornered him and proceeded to whack him over the back and shoulders, until he lay down and gave a chance at his head. The others leaped a fence in the rear, balking the second policeman, who was fat; and as he came back, furious and cursing, a big Polish woman, the owner of the saloon, rushed in screaming, and received a poke in the stomach that doubled her up on the floor. Meantime Jurgis, who was of a practical temper, was helping himself at the bar; and the first policeman, who had laid out his man, joined him, handing out several more bottles, and filling his pockets besides, and then, as he started to leave, cleaning off all the balance with a sweep of his club. The din of the glass crashing to the floor brought the fat Polish woman to her feet again, but another policeman came up behind her and put his knee into her back and his hands over her eyes—and then called to his companion, who went back and broke open the cash drawer and filled his pockets with the contents. Then the three went outside, and the man who was holding the woman gave her a shove and dashed out himself. The gang having already got the carcass on to the truck, the party set out at a trot, followed by screams and curses, and a shower of bricks and stones from unseen enemies. These bricks and stones would figure in the accounts of the "riot" which would be sent out to a few thousand newspapers within an hour or two; but the episode of the cash drawer would never be mentioned again, save only in the heartbreaking legends of Packingtown.

It was late in the afternoon when they got back, and they dressed out the remainder of the steer, and a couple of others that had been killed, and then knocked off for the day. Jurgis went downtown to supper, with three friends who had been on the other trucks, and they exchanged reminiscences on the way. Afterward they drifted into a roulette parlor, and Jurgis, who was never lucky at gambling, dropped about fifteen dollars. To console himself he had to drink a good deal, and he went back to Packingtown about two o'clock in the morning, very much the worse for his excursion, and, it must be confessed, entirely deserving the calamity that was in store for him.

As he was going to the place where he slept, he met a painted-cheeked woman in a greasy "kimono," and she put her arm about his waist to steady him; they turned into a dark room they were passing—but scarcely had they taken two steps before suddenly a door swung open, and a man entered, carrying a lantern. "Who's there?" he called sharply. And Jurgis started to mutter some reply; but at the same instant the man raised his light, which flashed in his face, so that it was possible to recognize him. Jurgis stood stricken dumb, and his heart gave a leap like a mad thing. The man was Connor!

Connor, the boss of the loading gang! The man who had seduced his wife—who had sent him to prison, and wrecked his home, ruined his life! He stood there, staring, with the light shining full upon him.

Jurgis had often thought of Connor since coming back to Packingtown, but it had been as of something far off, that no longer concerned him. Now, however, when he saw him, alive and in the flesh, the same thing happened to him that had happened before—a flood of rage boiled up in him, a blind frenzy seized him. And he flung himself at the man, and smote him between the eyes—and then, as he fell, seized him by the throat and began to pound his head upon the stones.

The woman began screaming, and people came rushing in. The lantern had been upset and extinguished, and it was so dark they could not see a thing;

but they could hear Jurgis panting, and hear the thumping of his victim's skull, and they rushed there and tried to pull him off. Precisely as before, Jurgis came away with a piece of his enemy's flesh between his teeth; and, as before, he went on fighting with those who had interfered with him, until a policeman had come and beaten him into insensibility.

And so Jurgis spent the balance of the night in the stockyards station house. This time, however, he had money in his pocket, and when he came to his senses he could get something to drink, and also a messenger to take word of his plight to "Bush" Harper. Harper did not appear, however, until after the prisoner, feeling very weak and ill, had been hailed into court and remanded at five hundred dollars' bail to await the result of his victim's injuries. Jurgis was wild about this, because a different magistrate had chanced to be on the bench, and he had stated that he had never been arrested before, and also that he had been attacked first—and if only someone had been there to speak a good word for him, he could have been let off at once.

But Harper explained that he had been downtown, and had not got the message. "What's happened to you?" he asked.

"I've been doing a fellow up," said Jurgis, "and I've got to get five hundred dollars' bail."

"I can arrange that all right," said the other—"though it may cost you a few dollars, of course. But what was the trouble?"

"It was a man that did me a mean trick once," answered Jurgis.

"Who is he?"

"He's a foreman in Brown's or used to be. His name's Connor."

And the other gave a start. "Connor!" he cried. "Not Phil Connor!"

"Yes," said Jurgis, "that's the fellow. Why?"

"Good God!" exclaimed the other, "then you're in for it, old man! I can't help you!"

"Not help me! Why not?"

"Why, he's one of Scully's biggest men—he's a member of the War-Whoop League, and they talked of sending him to the legislature! Phil Connor! Great heavens!"

Jurgis sat dumb with dismay.

"Why, he can send you to Joliet, if he wants to!" declared the other.

"Can't I have Scully get me off before he finds out about it?" asked Jurgis, at length.

"But Scully's out of town," the other answered. "I don't even know where he is—he's run away to dodge the strike."

That was a pretty mess, indeed. Poor Jurgis sat half-dazed. His pull had run up against a bigger pull, and he was down and out! "But what am I going to do?" he asked, weakly.

"How should I know?" said the other. "I shouldn't even dare to get bail for you—why, I might ruin myself for life!"

Again there was silence. "Can't you do it for me," Jurgis asked, "and pretend that you didn't know who I'd hit?"

"But what good would that do you when you came to stand trial?" asked Harper. Then he sat buried in thought for a minute or two. "There's nothing—unless it's this," he said. "I could have your bail reduced; and then if you had the money you could pay it and skip."

"How much will it be?" Jurgis asked, after he had had this explained more in detail.

"I don't know," said the other. "How much do you own?"

"I've got about three hundred dollars," was the answer.

"Well," was Harper's reply, "I'm not sure, but I'll try and get you off for that. I'll take the risk for friendship's sake—for I'd hate to see you sent to state's prison for a year or two."

And so finally Jurgis ripped out his bankbook—which was sewed up in his trousers—and signed an order, which "Bush" Harper wrote, for all the money to be paid out. Then the latter went and got it, and hurried to the court, and explained to the magistrate that Jurgis was a decent fellow and a friend of Scully's, who had been attacked by a strike-breaker. So the bail was reduced to three hundred dollars, and Harper went on it himself; he did not tell this to Jurgis, however—nor did he tell him that when the time for trial came it would be an easy matter for him to avoid the forfeiting of the bail, and pocket the three hundred dollars as his reward for the risk of offending Mike Scully! All that he told Jurgis was that he was now free, and that the best thing he could do was to clear out as quickly as possible; and so Jurgis overwhelmed with gratitude and relief, took the dollar and fourteen cents that was left him out of all his bank account, and put it with the two dollars and quarter that was left from his last night's celebration, and boarded a streetcar and got off at the other end of Chicago.

# Chapter 27

Poor Jurgis was now an outcast and a tramp once more. He was crippled—he was as literally crippled as any wild animal which has lost its claws, or been torn out of its shell. He had been shorn, at one cut, of all those mysterious weapons whereby he had been able to make a living easily and to escape the consequences of his actions. He could no longer command a job when he wanted it; he could no longer steal with impunity—he must take his chances with the common herd. Nay worse, he dared not mingle with the herd—he must hide himself, for he was one marked out for destruction. His old companions would betray him, for the sake of the influence they would gain thereby; and he would be made to suffer, not merely for the offense he had committed, but for others which would be laid at his door, just as had been done for some poor devil on the occasion of that assault upon the "country customer" by him and Duane.

And also he labored under another handicap now. He had acquired new standards of living, which were not easily to be altered. When he had been out of work before, he had been content if he could sleep in a doorway or under a truck out of the rain, and if he could get fifteen cents a day for saloon lunches. But now he desired all sorts of other things, and suffered because he had to do without them. He must have a drink now and then, a drink for its own sake, and apart from the food that came with it. The craving for it was strong enough to master every other consideration—he would have it, though it were his last nickel and he had to starve the balance of the day in consequence.

Jurgis became once more a besieger of factory gates. But never since he had been in Chicago had he stood less chance of getting a job than just then. For one thing, there was the economic crisis, the million or two of men who had been out of work in the spring and summer, and were not yet all back, by any means. And then there was the strike, with seventy thousand men and women all over the country idle for a couple of months—twenty thousand in Chicago, and many of them now seeking work throughout the city. It did not remedy matters that a few days later the strike was given up and about half the strikers went back to work; for every one taken on, there was a "scab" who gave up and fled. The ten or fifteen thousand "green" Negroes, foreigners, and criminals were now being turned loose to shift for themselves. Everywhere Jurgis went he kept meeting them, and he was in an agony of fear lest some one of them should know that he was "wanted." He would have left Chicago, only by the time he had realized his danger he was almost penniless; and it would be better to go to jail than to be caught out in the country in the winter time.

At the end of about ten days Jurgis had only a few pennies left; and he had not yet found a job—not even a day's work at anything, not a chance to carry a satchel. Once again, as when he had come out of the hospital, he was bound hand and foot, and facing the grisly phantom of starvation. Raw, naked terror possessed him, a maddening passion that would never leave him, and that wore him down more quickly than the actual want of food. He was going to die of hunger! The fiend reached out its scaly arms for him—it touched him, its breath came into his face; and he would cry out for the awfulness of it, he would wake up in the night, shuddering, and bathed in perspiration, and start up and flee. He would walk, begging for work, until he was exhausted; he could not remain still—he would wander on, gaunt and haggard, gazing about him with restless eyes. Everywhere he went, from one end of the vast city to the other, there were hundreds of others like him; everywhere was the sight of plenty and the merciless hand of authority waving them away. There is one kind of prison where the man is behind bars, and everything that he desires is outside; and there is another kind where the things are behind the bars, and the man is outside.

When he was down to his last quarter, Jurgis learned that before the bakeshops closed at night they sold out what was left at half price, and after that he would go and get two loaves of stale bread for a nickel, and break them up and stuff his pockets with them, munching a bit from time to time. He would not spend a penny save for this; and, after two or three days more, he even became sparing of the bread, and would stop and peer into the ash barrels as he walked along the streets, and now and then rake out a bit of something, shake it free from dust, and count himself just so many minutes further from the end.

So for several days he had been going about, ravenous all the time, and growing weaker and weaker, and then one morning he had a hideous experience, that almost broke his heart. He was passing down a street lined with warehouses, and a boss offered him a job, and then, after he had started to work, turned him off because he was not strong enough. And he stood by and saw another man put into his place, and then picked up his coat, and walked off, doing all that he could to keep from breaking down and crying like a baby. He was lost! He was doomed! There was no hope for him! But then, with a sudden rush, his fear gave place to rage. He fell to cursing. He would come back there after dark, and he would show that scoundrel whether he was good for anything or not!

He was still muttering this when suddenly, at the corner, he came upon a green-grocery, with a tray full of cabbages in front of it. Jurgis, after one swift glance about him, stooped and seized the biggest of them, and darted round the corner with it. There was a hue and cry, and a score of men and boys started in chase of him; but he came to an alley, and then to another branching off from it and leading him into another street, where he fell into a walk, and slipped his cabbage under his coat and went off unsuspected in the crowd. When he had gotten a safe distance away he sat down and devoured half the cabbage raw, stowing the balance away in his pockets till the next day.

Just about this time one of the Chicago newspapers, which made much of the "common people," opened a "free-soup kitchen" for the benefit of the unemployed. Some people said that they did this for the sake of the advertising it gave them, and some others said that their motive was a fear lest all their readers should be starved off; but whatever the reason, the soup was thick and hot, and there was a bowl for every man, all night long. When Jurgis heard of this, from a fellow "hobo," he vowed that he would have half a dozen bowls before morning; but, as it proved, he was lucky to get one, for there was a line of men two blocks long before the stand, and there was just as long a line when the place was finally closed up.

This depot was within the danger line for Jurgis—in the "Levee" district, where he was known; but he went there, all the same, for he was desperate, and beginning to think of even the Bridewell as a place of refuge. So far the weather had been fair, and he had slept out every night in a vacant lot; but now there fell suddenly a shadow of the advancing winter, a chill wind from the north and a driving storm of rain. That day Jurgis bought two drinks for the sake of the shelter, and at night he spent his last two pennies in a "stale-beer dive." This was a place kept by a Negro, who went out and drew off the old dregs of beer that lay in barrels set outside of the saloons; and after he had doctored it with chemicals to make it "fizz," he sold it for two cents a can, the purchase of a can including the privilege of sleeping the night through upon the floor, with a mass of degraded outcasts, men and women.

All these horrors afflicted Jurgis all the more cruelly, because he was always contrasting them with the opportunities he had lost. For instance, just now it was election time again—within five or six weeks the voters of the country would select a President; and he heard the wretches with whom he associated discussing it, and saw the streets of the city decorated with placards and banners—and what words could describe the pangs of grief and despair that shot through him?

For instance, there was a night during this cold spell. He had begged all day, for his very life, and found not a soul to heed him, until toward evening he saw an old lady getting off a streetcar and helped her down with her umbrellas and bundles and then told her his "hard-luck story," and after answering all her suspicious questions satisfactorily, was taken to a restaurant and saw a quarter paid down for a meal. And so he had soup and bread, and boiled beef and potatoes and beans, and pie and coffee, and came out with his skin stuffed tight as a football. And then, through the rain and the darkness, far down the street he saw red lights flaring and heard the thumping of a bass drum; and his heart gave a leap, and he made for the place on the run—knowing without the asking that it meant a political meeting.

The campaign had so far been characterized by what the newspapers termed "apathy." For some reason the people refused to get excited over the struggle, and it was almost impossible to get them to come to meetings, or to make any noise when they did come. Those which had been held in Chicago so far had proven most dismal failures, and tonight, the speaker being no less a personage than a candidate for the vice-presidency of the nation, the political managers had been trembling with anxiety. But a merciful providence had sent this storm of cold rain—and now all it was necessary to do was to set off a few fireworks, and thump awhile on a drum, and all the homeless wretches from a mile around would pour in and fill the hall! And then on the morrow the newspapers would have a chance to report the tremendous ovation, and to add that it had been no "silk-stocking" audience, either, proving clearly that the high tariff sentiments of the distinguished candidate were pleasing to the wage-earners of the nation.

So Jurgis found himself in a large hall, elaborately decorated with flags and bunting; and after the chairman had made his little speech, and the orator of the evening rose up, amid an uproar from the band—only fancy the emotions of Jurgis upon making the discovery that the personage was none other than the famous and eloquent Senator Spareshanks, who had addressed the "Doyle Republican Association" at the stockyards, and helped to elect Mike Scully's tenpin setter to the Chicago Board of Aldermen!

In truth, the sight of the senator almost brought the tears into Jurgis's eyes. What agony it was to him to look back upon those golden hours, when he, too, had a place beneath the shadow of the plum tree! When he, too, had been of the elect, through whom the country is governed—when he had had a bung in the campaign barrel for his own! And this was another election in which the Republicans had all the money; and but for that one hideous accident he might have had a share of it, instead of being where he was!

The eloquent senator was explaining the system of protection; an ingenious device whereby the workingman permitted the manufacturer to charge him higher prices, in order that he might receive higher wages; thus taking his money out of his pocket with one hand, and putting a part of it back with the other. To the senator this unique arrangement had somehow become identified with the higher verities of the universe. It was because of it that Columbia was the gem of the ocean; and all her future triumphs, her power and good repute among the nations, depended upon the zeal and fidelity with which each citizen held up the hands of those who were toiling to maintain it. The name of this heroic company was "the Grand Old Party"—

And here the band began to play, and Jurgis sat up with a violent start. Singular as it may seem, Jurgis was making a desperate effort to understand what the senator was saying—to comprehend the extent of American prosperity, the enormous expansion of American commerce, and the Republic's future in the Pacific and in South America, and wherever else the oppressed were groaning. The reason for it was that he wanted to keep awake. He knew that if he allowed himself to fall asleep he would begin to snore loudly; and so he must listen—he must be interested! But he had eaten such a big dinner, and he was so exhausted, and the hall was so warm, and his seat was so comfortable! The senator's gaunt form began to grow dim and hazy, to tower before him and dance about, with figures of exports and imports. Once his neighbor gave him a savage poke in the ribs, and he sat up with a start and tried to look innocent; but then he was at it again, and men began to stare at him with annoyance, and to call out in vexation. Finally one of them called a policeman, who came and grabbed Jurgis by the collar, and jerked him to his feet, bewildered and terrified. Some of the audience turned to see the commotion, and Senator Spareshanks faltered in his speech; but a voice shouted cheerily: "We're just firing a bum! Go ahead, old sport!" And so the crowd roared, and the senator smiled genially, and went on; and in a few seconds poor Jurgis found himself landed out in the rain, with a kick and a string of curses.

He got into the shelter of a doorway and took stock of himself. He was not hurt, and he was not arrested—more than he had any right to expect. He swore at himself and his luck for a while, and then turned his thoughts to practical matters. He had no money, and no place to sleep; he must begin begging again.

He went out, hunching his shoulders together and shivering at the touch of the icy rain. Coming down the street toward him was a lady, well dressed, and protected by an umbrella; and he turned and walked beside her. "Please, ma'am," he began, "could you lend me the price of a night's lodging? I'm a poor working-man—"

Then, suddenly, he stopped short. By the light of a street lamp he had caught sight of the lady's face. He knew her.

It was Alena Jasaityte, who had been the belle of his wedding feast! Alena Jasaityte, who had looked so beautiful, and danced with such a queenly air, with Juozas Raczius, the teamster! Jurgis had only seen her once or twice afterward, for Juozas had thrown her over for another girl, and Alena had gone away from Packingtown, no one knew where. And now he met her here!

She was as much surprised as he was. "Jurgis Rudkus!" she gasped. "And what in the world is the matter with you?"

"I—I've had hard luck," he stammered. "I'm out of work, and I've no home and no money. And you, Alena—are you married?"

"No," she answered, "I'm not married, but I've got a good place."

They stood staring at each other for a few moments longer. Finally Alena spoke again. "Jurgis," she said, "I'd help you if I could, upon my word I would, but it happens that I've come out without my purse, and I honestly haven't a penny with me: I can do something better for you, though—I can tell you how to get help. I can tell you where Marija is."

Jurgis gave a start. "Marija!" he exclaimed.

"Yes," said Alena; "and she'll help you. She's got a place, and she's doing well; she'll be glad to see you."

It was not much more than a year since Jurgis had left Packingtown, feeling like one escaped from jail; and it had been from Marija and Elzbieta that he was escaping. But now, at the mere mention of them, his whole being cried out with joy. He wanted to see them; he wanted to go home! They would help him—they would be kind to him. In a flash he had thought over the situation.

He had a good excuse for running away—his grief at the death of his son; and also he had a good excuse for not returning—the fact that they had left Packingtown. "All right," he said, "I'll go."

So she gave him a number on Clark Street, adding, "There's no need to give you my address, because Marija knows it." And Jurgis set out, without further ado. He found a large brownstone house of aristocratic appearance, and rang the basement bell. A young colored girl came to the door, opening it about an inch, and gazing at him suspiciously.

"What do you want?" she demanded.

"Does Marija Berczynskas live here?" he inquired.

"I dunno," said the girl. "What you want wid her?"

"I want to see her," said he; "she's a relative of mine."

The girl hesitated a moment. Then she opened the door and said, "Come in." Jurgis came and stood in the hall, and she continued: "I'll go see. What's yo' name?"

"Tell her it's Jurgis," he answered, and the girl went upstairs. She came back at the end of a minute or two, and replied, "Dey ain't no sich person here."

Jurgis's heart went down into his boots. "I was told this was where she lived!" he cried. But the girl only shook her head. "De lady says dey ain't no sich person here," she said.

And he stood for a moment, hesitating, helpless with dismay. Then he turned to go to the door. At the same instant, however, there came a knock upon it, and the girl went to open it. Jurgis heard the shuffling of feet, and then heard her give a cry; and the next moment she sprang back, and past him, her eyes shining white with terror, and bounded up the stairway, screaming at the top of her lungs: "Police! Police! We're pinched!"

Jurgis stood for a second, bewildered. Then, seeing blue-coated forms rushing upon him, he sprang after the Negress. Her cries had been the signal for a wild uproar above; the house was full of people, and as he entered the hallway he saw them rushing hither and thither, crying and screaming with alarm. There were men and women, the latter clad for the most part in wrappers, the former in all stages of dishabille. At one side Jurgis caught a glimpse of a big apartment with plush-covered chairs, and tables covered with trays and glasses. There were playing cards scattered all over the floor—one of the tables had been upset, and bottles of wine were rolling about, their contents running out upon the carpet. There was a young girl who had fainted, and two men who were supporting her; and there were a dozen others crowding toward the front door.

Suddenly, however, there came a series of resounding blows upon it, causing the crowd to give back. At the same instant a stout woman, with painted cheeks and diamonds in her ears, came running down the stairs, panting breathlessly: "To the rear! Quick!"

She led the way to a back staircase, Jurgis following; in the kitchen she pressed a spring, and a cupboard gave way and opened, disclosing a dark passageway. "Go in!" she cried to the crowd, which now amounted to twenty or thirty, and they began to pass through. Scarcely had the last one disappeared, however, before there were cries from in front, and then the panic-stricken throng poured out again, exclaiming: "They're there too! We're trapped!"

"Upstairs!" cried the woman, and there was another rush of the mob, women and men cursing and screaming and fighting to be first. One flight, two, three—and then there was a ladder to the roof, with a crowd packed at the foot of it, and one man at the top, straining and struggling to lift the trap door. It was not to be stirred, however, and when the woman shouted up to unhook it, he answered: "It's already unhooked. There's somebody sitting on it!"

And a moment later came a voice from downstairs: "You might as well quit, you people. We mean business, this time."

So the crowd subsided; and a few moments later several policemen came up, staring here and there, and leering at their victims. Of the latter the men were for the most part frightened and sheepish-looking. The women took it as a joke, as if they were used to it—though if they had been pale, one could not have told, for the paint on their cheeks. One black-eyed young girl perched herself upon the top of the balustrade, and began to kick with her slippered foot at the helmets of the policemen, until one of them caught her by the ankle and pulled her down. On the floor below four or five other girls sat upon trunks in the hall, making fun of the procession which filed by them. They were noisy and hilarious, and had evidently been drinking; one of them, who wore a bright red kimono, shouted and screamed in a voice that drowned out all the other sounds in the hall—and Jurgis took a glance at her, and then gave a start, and a cry, "Marija!"

She heard him, and glanced around; then she shrank back and half sprang to her feet in amazement. "Jurgis!" she gasped.

For a second or two they stood staring at each other. "How did you come here?" Marija exclaimed.

"I came to see you," he answered.

"When?"

"Just now."

"But how did you know—who told you I was here?"

"Alena Jasaityte. I met her on the street."

Again there was a silence, while they gazed at each other. The rest of the crowd was watching them, and so Marija got up and came closer to him. "And you?" Jurgis asked. "You live here?"

"Yes," said Marija, "I live here." Then suddenly came a hail from below: "Get your clothes on now, girls, and come along. You'd best begin, or you'll be sorry—it's raining outside."

"Br-r-r!" shivered some one, and the women got up and entered the various doors which lined the hallway.

"Come," said Marija, and took Jurgis into her room, which was a tiny place about eight by six, with a cot and a chair and a dressing stand and some dresses hanging behind the door. There were clothes scattered about on the floor, and hopeless confusion everywhere—boxes of rouge and bottles of perfume mixed with hats and soiled dishes on the dresser, and a pair of slippers and a clock and a whisky bottle on a chair.

Marija had nothing on but a kimono and a pair of stockings; yet she proceeded to dress before Jurgis, and without even taking the trouble to close the door. He had by this time divined what sort of a place he was in; and he had seen a great deal of the world since he had left home, and was not easy to shock—and yet it gave him a painful start that Marija should do this. They had always been decent people at home, and it seemed to him that the memory of old times ought to have ruled her. But then he laughed at himself for a fool. What was he, to be pretending to decency!

"How long have you been living here?" he asked.

"Nearly a year," she answered.

"Why did you come?"

"I had to live," she said; "and I couldn't see the children starve."

He paused for a moment, watching her. "You were out of work?" he asked, finally.

"I got sick," she replied, "and after that I had no money. And then Stanislovas died—"

"Stanislovas dead!"

"Yes," said Marija, "I forgot. You didn't know about it."

"How did he die?"

"Rats killed him," she answered.

Jurgis gave a gasp. "Rats killed him!"

"Yes," said the other; she was bending over, lacing her shoes as she spoke. "He was working in an oil factory—at least he was hired by the men to get their beer. He used to carry cans on a long pole; and he'd drink a little out of each can, and one day he drank too much, and fell asleep in a corner, and got locked up in the place all night. When they found him the rats had killed him and eaten him nearly all up."

Jurgis sat, frozen with horror. Marija went on lacing up her shoes. There was a long silence.

Suddenly a big policeman came to the door. "Hurry up, there," he said.

"As quick as I can," said Marija, and she stood up and began putting on her corsets with feverish haste.

"Are the rest of the people alive?" asked Jurgis, finally.

"Yes," she said.

"Where are they?"

"They live not far from here. They're all right now."

"They are working?" he inquired.

"Elzbieta is," said Marija, "when she can. I take care of them most of the time—I'm making plenty of money now."

Jurgis was silent for a moment. "Do they know you live here—how you live?" he asked.

"Elzbieta knows," answered Marija. "I couldn't lie to her. And maybe the children have found out by this time. It's nothing to be ashamed of—we can't help it."

"And Tamoszius?" he asked. "Does he know?"

Marija shrugged her shoulders. "How do I know?" she said. "I haven't seen him for over a year. He got blood poisoning and lost one finger, and couldn't play the violin any more; and then he went away."

Marija was standing in front of the glass fastening her dress. Jurgis sat staring at her. He could hardly believe that she was the same woman he had known in the old days; she was so quiet—so hard! It struck fear to his heart to watch her.

Then suddenly she gave a glance at him. "You look as if you had been having a rough time of it yourself," she said.

"I have," he answered. "I haven't a cent in my pockets, and nothing to do."

"Where have you been?"

"All over. I've been hoboing it. Then I went back to the yards—just before the strike." He paused for a moment, hesitating. "I asked for you," he added. "I found you had gone away, no one knew where. Perhaps you think I did you a dirty trick running away as I did, Marija—"

"No," she answered, "I don't blame you. We never have—any of us. You did your best—the job was too much for us." She paused a moment, then added: "We were too ignorant—that was the trouble. We didn't stand any chance. If I'd known what I know now we'd have won out."

"You'd have come here?" said Jurgis.

"Yes," she answered; "but that's not what I meant. I meant you—how differently you would have behaved—about Ona."

Jurgis was silent; he had never thought of that aspect of it.

"When people are starving," the other continued, "and they have anything with a price, they ought to sell it, I say. I guess you realize it now when it's too late. Ona could have taken care of us all, in the beginning." Marija spoke without emotion, as one who had come to regard things from the business point of view.

"I—yes, I guess so," Jurgis answered hesitatingly. He did not add that he had paid three hundred dollars, and a foreman's job, for the satisfaction of knocking down "Phil" Connor a second time.

The policeman came to the door again just then. “Come on, now,” he said. “Lively!”

“All right,” said Marija, reaching for her hat, which was big enough to be a drum major’s, and full of ostrich feathers. She went out into the hall and Jurgis followed, the policeman remaining to look under the bed and behind the door.

“What’s going to come of this?” Jurgis asked, as they started down the steps.

“The raid, you mean? Oh, nothing—it happens to us every now and then. The madame’s having some sort of time with the police; I don’t know what it is, but maybe they’ll come to terms before morning. Anyhow, they won’t do anything to you. They always let the men off.”

“Maybe so,” he responded, “but not me—I’m afraid I’m in for it.”

“How do you mean?”

“I’m wanted by the police,” he said, lowering his voice, though of course their conversation was in Lithuanian. “They’ll send me up for a year or two, I’m afraid.”

“Hell!” said Marija. “That’s too bad. I’ll see if I can’t get you off.”

Downstairs, where the greater part of the prisoners were now massed, she sought out the stout personage with the diamond earrings, and had a few whispered words with her. The latter then approached the police sergeant who was in charge of the raid. “Billy,” she said, pointing to Jurgis, “there’s a fellow who came in to see his sister. He’d just got in the door when you knocked. You aren’t taking hoboes, are you?”

The sergeant laughed as he looked at Jurgis. “Sorry,” he said, “but the orders are every one but the servants.”

So Jurgis slunk in among the rest of the men, who kept dodging behind each other like sheep that have smelled a wolf. There were old men and young men, college boys and gray-beards old enough to be their grandfathers; some of them wore evening dress—there was no one among them save Jurgis who showed any signs of poverty.

When the roundup was completed, the doors were opened and the party marched out. Three patrol wagons were drawn up at the curb, and the whole neighborhood had turned out to see the sport; there was much chaffing, and a universal craning of necks. The women stared about them with defiant eyes, or laughed and joked, while the men kept their heads bowed, and their hats pulled over their faces. They were crowded into the patrol wagons as if into streetcars, and then off they went amid a din of cheers. At the station house Jurgis gave a Polish name and was put into a cell with half a dozen others; and while these sat and talked in whispers, he lay down in a corner and gave himself up to his thoughts.

Jurgis had looked into the deepest reaches of the social pit, and grown used to the sights in them. Yet when he had thought of all humanity as vile and hideous, he had somehow always excepted his own family that he had loved; and now this sudden horrible discovery—Marija a whore, and Elzbieta and the children living off her shame! Jurgis might argue with himself all he chose, that he had done worse, and was a fool for caring—but still he could not get over the shock of that sudden unveiling, he could not help being sunk in grief because of it. The depths of him were troubled and shaken, memories were stirred in him that had been sleeping so long he had counted them dead. Memories of the old life—his old hopes and his old yearnings, his old dreams of decency and independence! He saw Ona again, he heard her gentle voice pleading with him. He saw little Antanas, whom he had meant to make a man. He saw his trembling old father, who had blessed them all with his wonderful love. He lived again through that day of horror when he had discovered Ona's shame—God, how he had suffered, what a madman he had been! How dreadful it had all seemed to him; and now, today, he had sat and listened, and half agreed when Marija told him he had been a fool! Yes—told him that he ought to have sold his wife's honor and lived by it!—And then there was Stanislovas and his awful fate—that brief story which Marija had narrated so calmly, with such dull indifference! The poor little fellow, with his frostbitten fingers and his terror of the snow—his wailing voice rang in Jurgis's ears, as he lay there in the darkness, until the sweat started on his forehead. Now and then he would quiver with a sudden spasm of horror, at the picture of little Stanislovas shut up in the deserted building and fighting for his life with the rats!

All these emotions had become strangers to the soul of Jurgis; it was so long since they had troubled him that he had ceased to think they might ever trouble him again. Helpless, trapped, as he was, what good did they do him—why should he ever have allowed them to torment him? It had been the task of his recent life to fight them down, to crush them out of him; never in his life would he have suffered from them again, save that they had caught him unawares, and overwhelmed him before he could protect himself. He heard the old voices of his soul, he saw its old ghosts beckoning to him, stretching out their arms to him! But they were far-off and shadowy, and the gulf between them was black and bottomless; they would fade away into the mists of the past once more. Their voices would die, and never again would he hear them—and so the last faint spark of manhood in his soul would flicker out.

# Chapter 28

After breakfast Jurgis was driven to the court, which was crowded with the prisoners and those who had come out of curiosity or in the hope of recognizing one of the men and getting a case for blackmail. The men were called up first, and reprimanded in a bunch, and then dismissed; but, Jurgis, to his terror, was called separately, as being a suspicious-looking case. It was in this very same court that he had been tried, that time when his sentence had been "suspended"; it was the same judge, and the same clerk. The latter now stared at Jurgis, as if he half thought that he knew him; but the judge had no suspicions—just then his thoughts were upon a telephone message he was expecting from a friend of the police captain of the district, telling what disposition he should make of the case of "Polly" Simpson, as the "madame" of the house was known. Meantime, he listened to the story of how Jurgis had been looking for his sister, and advised him dryly to keep his sister in a better place; then he let him go, and proceeded to fine each of the girls five dollars, which fines were paid in a bunch from a wad of bills which Madame Polly extracted from her stocking.

Jurgis waited outside and walked home with Marija. The police had left the house, and already there were a few visitors; by evening the place would be running again, exactly as if nothing had happened. Meantime, Marija took Jurgis upstairs to her room, and they sat and talked. By daylight, Jurgis was able to observe that the color on her cheeks was not the old natural one of abounding health; her complexion was in reality a parchment yellow, and there were black rings under her eyes.

"Have you been sick?" he asked.

"Sick?" she said. "Hell!" (Marija had learned to scatter her conversation with as many oaths as a longshoreman or a mule driver.) "How can I ever be anything but sick, at this life?"

She fell silent for a moment, staring ahead of her gloomily. "It's morphine," she said, at last. "I seem to take more of it every day."

"What's that for?" he asked.

"It's the way of it; I don't know why. If it isn't that, it's drink. If the girls didn't booze they couldn't stand it any time at all. And the madame always gives them dope when they first come, and they learn to like it; or else they take it for headaches and such things, and get the habit that way. I've got it, I know; I've tried to quit, but I never will while I'm here."

"How long are you going to stay?" he asked.

"I don't know," she said. "Always, I guess. What else could I do?"

"Don't you save any money?"

"Save!" said Marija. "Good Lord, no! I get enough, I suppose, but it all goes. I get a half share, two dollars and a half for each customer, and sometimes I make twenty-five or thirty dollars a night, and you'd think I ought to save something out of that! But then I am charged for my room and my meals—and such prices as you never heard of; and then for extras, and drinks—for everything I get, and some I don't. My laundry bill is nearly twenty dollars each week alone—think of that! Yet what can I do? I either have to stand it or quit, and it would be the same anywhere else. It's all I can do to save the fifteen dollars I give Elzbieta each week, so the children can go to school."

Marija sat brooding in silence for a while; then, seeing that Jurgis was interested, she went on: "That's the way they keep the girls—they let them run up debts, so they can't get away. A young girl comes from abroad, and she doesn't know a word of English, and she gets into a place like this, and when she wants to go the madame shows her that she is a couple of hundred dollars in debt, and takes all her clothes away, and threatens to have her arrested if she doesn't stay and do as she's told. So she stays, and the longer she stays, the more in debt she gets. Often, too, they are girls that didn't know what they were coming to, that had hired out for housework. Did you notice that little French girl with the yellow hair, that stood next to me in the court?"

Jurgis answered in the affirmative.

"Well, she came to America about a year ago. She was a store clerk, and she hired herself to a man to be sent here to work in a factory. There were six of them, all together, and they were brought to a house just down the street from here, and this girl was put into a room alone, and they gave her some dope in her food, and when she came to she found that she had been ruined. She cried, and screamed, and tore her hair, but she had nothing but a wrapper, and couldn't get away, and they kept her half insensible with drugs all the time, until she gave up. She never got outside of that place for ten months, and then they sent her away, because she didn't suit. I guess they'll put her out of here, too—she's getting to have crazy fits, from drinking absinthe. Only one of the girls that came out with her got away, and she jumped out of a second-story window one night. There was a great fuss about that—maybe you heard of it."

"I did," said Jurgis, "I heard of it afterward." (It had happened in the place where he and Duane had taken refuge from their "country customer." The girl had become insane, fortunately for the police.)

"There's lots of money in it," said Marija—"they get as much as forty dollars a head for girls, and they bring them from all over. There are seventeen in this place, and nine different countries among them. In some places you might find even more. We have half a dozen French girls—I suppose it's because the madame speaks the language. French girls are bad, too, the worst of all, except for the Japanese. There's a place next door that's full of Japanese women, but I wouldn't live in the same house with one of them."

Marija paused for a moment or two, and then she added: "Most of the women here are pretty decent—you'd be surprised. I used to think they did it because they liked to; but fancy a woman selling herself to every kind of man that comes, old or young, black or white—and doing it because she likes to!"

"Some of them say they do," said Jurgis.

"I know," said she; "they say anything. They're in, and they know they can't get out. But they didn't like it when they began—you'd find out—it's always misery! There's a little Jewish girl here who used to run errands for a milliner, and got sick and lost her place; and she was four days on the streets without a mouthful of food, and then she went to a place just around the corner and offered herself, and they made her give up her clothes before they would give her a bite to eat!"

Marija sat for a minute or two, brooding somberly. "Tell me about yourself, Jurgis," she said, suddenly. "Where have you been?"

So he told her the long story of his adventures since his flight from home; his life as a tramp, and his work in the freight tunnels, and the accident; and then of Jack Duane, and of his political career in the stockyards, and his downfall and subsequent failures. Marija listened with sympathy; it was easy to believe the tale of his late starvation, for his face showed it all. "You found me just in the nick of time," she said. "I'll stand by you—I'll help you till you can get some work."

"I don't like to let you—" he began.

"Why not? Because I'm here?"

"No, not that," he said. "But I went off and left you—"

"Nonsense!" said Marija. "Don't think about it. I don't blame you."

"You must be hungry," she said, after a minute or two. "You stay here to lunch—I'll have something up in the room."

She pressed a button, and a colored woman came to the door and took her order. "It's nice to have somebody to wait on you," she observed, with a laugh, as she lay back on the bed.

As the prison breakfast had not been liberal, Jurgis had a good appetite, and they had a little feast together, talking meanwhile of Elzbieta and the children and old times. Shortly before they were through, there came another colored girl, with the message that the "madame" wanted Marija—"Lithuanian Mary," as they called her here.

"That means you have to go," she said to Jurgis.

So he got up, and she gave him the new address of the family, a tenement over in the Ghetto district. "You go there," she said. "They'll be glad to see you."

But Jurgis stood hesitating.

"I—I don't like to," he said. "Honest, Marija, why don't you just give me a little money and let me look for work first?"

"How do you need money?" was her reply. "All you want is something to eat and a place to sleep, isn't it?"

"Yes," he said; "but then I don't like to go there after I left them—and while I have nothing to do, and while you—you—"

"Go on!" said Marija, giving him a push. "What are you talking?—I won't give you money," she added, as she followed him to the door, "because you'll drink it up, and do yourself harm. Here's a quarter for you now, and go along, and they'll be so glad to have you back, you won't have time to feel ashamed. Good-by!"

So Jurgis went out, and walked down the street to think it over. He decided that he would first try to get work, and so he put in the rest of the day wandering here and there among factories and warehouses without success. Then, when it was nearly dark, he concluded to go home, and set out; but he came to a restaurant, and went in and spent his quarter for a meal; and when he came out he changed his mind—the night was pleasant, and he would sleep somewhere outside, and put in the morrow hunting, and so have one more chance of a job. So he started away again, when suddenly he chanced to look about him, and found that he was walking down the same street and past the same hall where he had listened to the political speech the night before. There was no red fire and no band now, but there was a sign out, announcing a meeting, and a stream of people pouring in through the entrance. In a flash Jurgis had decided that he would chance it once more, and sit down and rest while making up his mind what to do. There was no one taking tickets, so it must be a free show again.

He entered. There were no decorations in the hall this time; but there was quite a crowd upon the platform, and almost every seat in the place was filled. He took one of the last, far in the rear, and straightway forgot all about his surroundings. Would Elzbieta think that he had come to sponge off her, or would she understand that he meant to get to work again and do his share? Would she be decent to him, or would she scold him? If only he could get some sort of a job before he went—if that last boss had only been willing to try him!

—Then suddenly Jurgis looked up. A tremendous roar had burst from the throats of the crowd, which by this time had packed the hall to the very doors. Men and women were standing up, waving handkerchiefs, shouting, yelling. Evidently the speaker had arrived, thought Jurgis; what fools they were making of themselves! What were they expecting to get out of it anyhow—what had they to do with elections, with governing the country? Jurgis had been behind the scenes in politics.

He went back to his thoughts, but with one further fact to reckon with—that he was caught here. The hall was now filled to the doors; and after the meeting it would be too late for him to go home, so he would have to make the best of it outside. Perhaps it would be better to go home in the morning, anyway, for the children would be at school, and he and Elzbieta could have a quiet explanation. She always had been a reasonable person; and he really did mean to do right. He would manage to persuade her of it—and besides, Marija was willing, and Marija was furnishing the money. If Elzbieta were ugly, he would tell her that in so many words.

So Jurgis went on meditating; until finally, when he had been an hour or two in the hall, there began to prepare itself a repetition of the dismal catastrophe of the night before. Speaking had been going on all the time, and the audience was clapping its hands and shouting, thrilling with excitement; and little by little the sounds were beginning to blur in Jurgis's ears, and his thoughts were beginning to run together, and his head to wobble and nod. He caught himself many times, as usual, and made desperate resolutions; but the hall was hot and close, and his long walk and is dinner were too much for him—in the end his head sank forward and he went off again.

And then again someone nudged him, and he sat up with his old terrified start! He had been snoring again, of course! And now what? He fixed his eyes ahead of him, with painful intensity, staring at the platform as if nothing else ever had interested him, or ever could interest him, all his life. He imagined the angry exclamations, the hostile glances; he imagined the policeman striding toward him—reaching for his neck. Or was he to have one more chance? Were they going to let him alone this time? He sat trembling; waiting—

And then suddenly came a voice in his ear, a woman's voice, gentle and sweet, "If you would try to listen, comrade, perhaps you would be interested."

Jurgis was more startled by that than he would have been by the touch of a policeman. He still kept his eyes fixed ahead, and did not stir; but his heart gave a great leap. Comrade! Who was it that called him "comrade"?

He waited long, long; and at last, when he was sure that he was no longer watched, he stole a glance out of the corner of his eyes at the woman who sat beside him. She was young and beautiful; she wore fine clothes, and was what is called a "lady." And she called him "comrade"!

He turned a little, carefully, so that he could see her better; then he began to watch her, fascinated. She had apparently forgotten all about him, and was looking toward the platform. A man was speaking there—Jurgis heard his voice vaguely; but all his thoughts were for this woman's face. A feeling of alarm stole over him as he stared at her. It made his flesh creep. What was the matter with her, what could be going on, to affect any one like that? She sat as one turned to stone, her hands clenched tightly in her lap, so tightly that he could see the cords standing out in her wrists. There was a look of excitement upon her face, of tense effort, as of one struggling mightily, or witnessing a struggle. There was a faint quivering of her nostrils; and now and then she would moisten her lips with feverish haste. Her bosom rose and fell as she breathed, and her excitement seemed to mount higher and higher, and then to sink away again, like a boat tossing upon ocean surges. What was it? What was the matter? It must be something that the man was saying, up there on the platform. What sort of a man was he? And what sort of thing was this, anyhow?—So all at once it occurred to Jurgis to look at the speaker.

It was like coming suddenly upon some wild sight of nature—a mountain forest lashed by a tempest, a ship tossed about upon a stormy sea. Jurgis had an unpleasant sensation, a sense of confusion, of disorder, of wild and meaningless uproar. The man was tall and gaunt, as haggard as his auditor himself; a thin black beard covered half of his face, and one could see only two black hollows where the eyes were. He was speaking rapidly, in great excitement; he used many gestures—as he spoke he moved here and there upon the stage, reaching with his long arms as if to seize each person in his audience. His voice was deep, like an organ; it was some time, however, before Jurgis thought of the voice—he was too much occupied with his eyes to think of what the man was saying. But suddenly it seemed as if the speaker had begun pointing straight at him, as if he had singled him out particularly for his remarks; and so Jurgis became suddenly aware of his voice, trembling, vibrant with emotion, with pain and longing, with a burden of things unutterable, not to be compassed by words. To hear it was to be suddenly arrested, to be gripped, transfixed.

"You listen to these things," the man was saying, "and you say, 'Yes, they are true, but they have been that way always.' Or you say, 'Maybe it will come, but not in my time—it will not help me.' And so you return to your daily round of toil, you go back to be ground up for profits in the world-wide mill of economic might! To toil long hours for another's advantage; to live in mean and squalid homes, to work in dangerous and unhealthful places; to wrestle with the specters of hunger and privation, to take your chances of accident, disease, and death. And each day the struggle becomes fiercer, the pace more cruel; each day you have to toil a little harder, and feel the iron hand of circumstance close upon you a little tighter. Months pass, years maybe—and then you come again; and again I am here to plead with you, to know if want and misery have yet done their work with you, if injustice and oppression have yet opened your eyes! I shall still be waiting—there is nothing else that I can do. There is no wilderness where I can hide from these things, there is no haven where I can escape them; though I travel to the ends of the earth, I find the same accursed system—I find that all the fair and noble impulses of humanity, the dreams of poets and the agonies of martyrs, are shackled and bound in the service of organized and predatory Greed! And therefore I cannot rest, I cannot be silent; therefore I cast aside comfort and happiness, health and good repute—and go out into the world and cry out the pain of my spirit! Therefore I am not to be silenced by poverty and sickness, not by hatred and obloquy, by threats and ridicule—not by prison and persecution, if they should come—not by any power that is upon the earth or above the earth, that was, or is, or ever can be created. If I fail tonight, I can only try tomorrow; knowing that the fault must be mine—that if once the vision of my soul were spoken upon earth, if once the anguish of its defeat were uttered in human speech, it would break the stoutest barriers of prejudice, it would shake the most sluggish soul to action! It would abash the most cynical, it would terrify the most selfish; and the voice of mockery would be silenced, and fraud and falsehood would slink back into their dens, and the truth would stand forth alone! For I speak with the voice of the millions who are voiceless! Of them that are oppressed and have no comforter! Of the disinherited of life, for whom there is no respite and no deliverance, to whom the world is a prison, a dungeon of torture, a tomb! With the voice of the little child who toils tonight in a Southern cotton mill, staggering with exhaustion, numb with agony, and knowing no hope but the grave! Of the mother who sews by candlelight in her tenement garret, weary and weeping, smitten with the mortal hunger of her babes! Of the man who lies upon a bed of rags, wrestling in his last sickness and leaving his loved ones to perish! Of the young girl who, somewhere at this moment, is walking the streets of this horrible city, beaten and starving, and making her choice between the brothel and the lake! With the voice of those, whoever and wherever they may be, who are caught beneath the wheels of the Juggernaut of Greed! With the voice of humanity, calling for deliverance! Of the everlasting soul of Man, arising from the dust; breaking its way out of its prison—rending the bands of oppression and ignorance—groping its way to the light!"

The speaker paused. There was an instant of silence, while men caught their breaths, and then like a single sound there came a cry from a thousand people. Through it all Jurgis sat still, motionless and rigid, his eyes fixed upon the speaker; he was trembling, smitten with wonder.

Suddenly the man raised his hands, and silence fell, and he began again.

"I plead with you," he said, "whoever you may be, provided that you care about the truth; but most of all I plead with working-man, with those to whom the evils I portray are not mere matters of sentiment, to be dallied and toyed with, and then perhaps put aside and forgotten—to whom they are the grim and relentless realities of the daily grind, the chains upon their limbs, the lash upon their backs, the iron in their souls. To you, working-men! To you, the toilers, who have made this land, and have no voice in its councils! To you, whose lot it is to sow that others may reap, to labor and obey, and ask no more than the wages of a beast of burden, the food and shelter to keep you alive from day to day. It is to you that I come with my message of salvation, it is to you that I appeal. I know how much it is to ask of you—I know, for I have been in your place, I have lived your life, and there is no man before me here tonight who knows it better. I have known what it is to be a street-waif, a bootblack, living upon a crust of bread and sleeping in cellar stairways and under empty wagons. I have known what it is to dare and to aspire, to dream mighty dreams and to see them perish—to see all the fair flowers of my spirit trampled into the mire by the wild-beast powers of my life. I know what is the price that a working-man pays for knowledge—I have paid for it with food and sleep, with agony of body and mind, with health, almost with life itself; and so, when I come to you with a story of hope and freedom, with the vision of a new earth to be created, of a new labor to be dared, I am not surprised that I find you sordid and material, sluggish and incredulous. That I do not despair is because I know also the forces that are driving behind you—because I know the raging lash of poverty, the sting of contempt and mastership, 'the insolence of office and the spurns.' Because I feel sure that in the crowd that has come to me tonight, no matter how many may be dull and heedless, no matter how many may have come out of idle curiosity, or in order to ridicule—there will be some one man whom pain and suffering have made desperate, whom some chance vision of wrong and horror has startled and shocked into attention. And to him my words will come like a sudden flash of lightning to one who travels in darkness—revealing the way before him, the perils and the obstacles—solving all problems, making all difficulties clear! The scales will fall from his eyes, the shackles will be torn from his limbs—he will leap up with a cry of thankfulness, he will stride forth a free man at last! A man delivered from his self-created slavery! A man who will never more be trapped—whom no blandishments will cajole, whom no threats will frighten; who from tonight on will move forward, and not backward, who will study and understand, who will gird on his sword and take his place in the army of his comrades and brothers. Who will carry the good tidings to others, as I have carried them to him—priceless gift of liberty and light that is neither mine nor his, but is the heritage of the soul of man! Working-men, working-men—comrades! open your eyes and look about you! You have lived so long in the toil and heat that your senses are dulled, your souls are numbed; but realize once in your lives this world in which you dwell—tear off the rags of its customs and conventions—behold it as it is, in all its hideous nakedness! Realize it, realize it! Realize that out upon the plains of Manchuria tonight two hostile armies are facing each other—that now, while we are seated here, a million human beings may be hurled at each other's throats, striving with the fury of maniacs to tear each other to pieces! And this in the twentieth century, nineteen hundred years since the Prince of Peace was born on earth! Nineteen hundred years that his words have been preached as divine, and here two armies of men are rending and tearing each other like the wild beasts of the forest! Philosophers have reasoned, prophets have denounced, poets have wept and pleaded—and still this hideous Monster roams at large! We have schools and colleges, newspapers and books; we have searched the heavens and the earth, we have weighed and probed and reasoned—and all to equip men to destroy each other! We call it War, and pass it by—but do not put me off with platitudes and conventions—come with me, come with me—realize it! See the bodies of men pierced by bullets, blown into pieces by bursting shells! Hear the crunching of the bayonet, plunged into human flesh; hear the groans and shrieks of agony, see the faces of men crazed by pain, turned into fiends by fury and hate! Put your hand upon that piece of flesh—it is hot and quivering—just now it was a part of a man! This blood is still steaming—it was driven by a human heart! Almighty God! and this goes on—it is systematic, organized, premeditated! And we know it, and read of it, and take it for granted; our papers tell of it, and the presses are not stopped—our churches know of it, and do not close their doors—the people behold it, and do not rise up in horror and revolution!

"Or perhaps Manchuria is too far away for you—come home with me then, come here to Chicago. Here in this city to-night ten thousand women are shut up in foul pens, and driven by hunger to sell their bodies to live. And we know it, we make it a jest! And these women are made in the image of your mothers, they may be your sisters, your daughters; the child whom you left at home tonight, whose laughing eyes will greet you in the morning—that fate may be waiting for her! To-night in Chicago there are ten thousand men, homeless and wretched, willing to work and begging for a chance, yet starving, and fronting in terror the awful winter cold! Tonight in Chicago there are a hundred thousand children wearing out their strength and blasting their lives in the effort to earn their bread! There are a hundred thousand mothers who are living in misery and squalor, struggling to earn enough to feed their little ones! There are a hundred thousand old people, cast off and helpless, waiting for death to take them from their torments! There are a million people, men and women and children, who share the curse of the wage-slave; who toil every hour they can stand and see, for just enough to keep them alive; who are condemned till the end of their days to monotony and weariness, to hunger and misery, to heat and cold, to dirt and disease, to ignorance and drunkenness and vice! And then turn over the page with me, and gaze upon the other side of the picture. There are a thousand—ten thousand, maybe—who are the masters of these slaves, who own their toil. They do nothing to earn what they receive, they do not even have to ask for it—it comes to them of itself, their only care is to dispose of it. They live in palaces, they riot in luxury and extravagance—such as no words can describe, as makes the imagination reel and stagger, makes the soul grow sick and faint. They spend hundreds of dollars for a pair of shoes, a handkerchief, a garter; they spend millions for horses and automobiles and yachts, for palaces and banquets, for little shiny stones with which to deck their bodies. Their life is a contest among themselves for supremacy in ostentation and recklessness, in the destroying of useful and necessary things, in the wasting of the labor and the lives of their fellow creatures, the toil and anguish of the nations, the sweat and tears and blood of the human race! It is all theirs—it comes to them; just as all the springs pour into streamlets, and the streamlets into rivers, and the rivers into the oceans—so, automatically and inevitably, all the wealth of society comes to them. The farmer tills the soil, the miner digs in the earth, the weaver tends the loom, the mason carves the stone; the clever man invents, the shrewd man directs, the wise man studies, the inspired man sings—and all the result, the products of the labor of brain and muscle, are gathered into one stupendous stream and poured into their laps! The whole of society is in their grip, the whole labor of the world lies at their mercy—and like fierce wolves they rend and destroy, like ravening vultures they devour and tear! The whole power of mankind belongs to them, forever and beyond recall—do what it can, strive as it will, humanity lives for them and dies for them! They own not merely the labor of society, they have bought the governments; and everywhere they use their raped and stolen power to intrench themselves in their privileges, to dig wider and deeper the channels through which the river of profits flows to them!—And you, workingmen, workingmen! You have been brought up to it, you plod on like beasts of burden, thinking only of the day and its pain—yet is there a man among you who can believe that such a system will continue forever—is there a man here in this audience tonight so hardened and debased that he dare rise up before me and say that he believes it can continue forever; that the product of the labor of society, the means of existence of the human race, will always belong to idlers and parasites, to be spent for the gratification of vanity and lust—to be spent for any purpose whatever, to be at the disposal of any individual will whatever—that somehow, somewhere, the labor of humanity will not belong to humanity, to be used for the purposes of humanity, to be controlled by the will of humanity? And if this is ever to be, how is it to be—what power is there that will bring it about? Will it be the task of your masters, do you think—will they write the charter of your liberties? Will they forge you the sword of your deliverance, will they marshal you the army and lead it to the fray? Will their wealth be spent for the purpose—will they build colleges and churches to teach you, will they print papers to herald your progress, and organize political parties to guide and carry on the struggle? Can you not see that the task is your task—yours to dream, yours to resolve, yours to execute? That if ever it is carried out, it will be in the face of every obstacle that wealth and mastership can oppose—in the face of ridicule and slander, of hatred and persecution, of the bludgeon and the jail? That it will be by the power of your naked bosoms, opposed to the rage of oppression! By the grim and bitter teaching of blind and merciless affliction! By the painful gropings of the untutored mind, by the feeble stammerings of the uncultured voice! By the sad and lonely hunger of the spirit; by seeking and striving and yearning, by heartache and despairing, by agony and sweat of blood! It will be by money paid for with hunger, by knowledge stolen from sleep, by thoughts communicated under the shadow of the gallows! It will be a movement beginning in the far-off past, a thing obscure and unhonored, a thing easy to ridicule, easy to despise; a thing unlovely, wearing the aspect of vengeance and hate—but to you, the working-man, the wage-slave, calling with a voice insistent, imperious—with a voice that you cannot escape, wherever upon the earth you may be! With the voice of all your wrongs, with the voice of all your desires; with the voice of your duty and your hope—of everything in the world that is worth while to you! The voice of the poor, demanding that poverty shall cease! The voice of the oppressed, pronouncing the doom of oppression! The voice of power, wrought out of suffering—of resolution, crushed out of weakness—of joy and courage, born in the bottomless pit of anguish and despair! The voice of Labor, despised and outraged; a mighty giant, lying prostrate—mountainous, colossal, but blinded, bound, and ignorant of his strength. And now a dream of resistance haunts him, hope battling with fear; until suddenly he stirs, and a fetter snaps—and a thrill shoots through him, to the farthest ends of his huge body, and in a flash the dream becomes an act! He starts, he lifts himself; and the bands are shattered, the burdens roll off him—he rises—towering, gigantic; he springs to his feet, he shouts in his newborn exultation—"

And the speaker's voice broke suddenly, with the stress of his feelings; he stood with his arms stretched out above him, and the power of his vision seemed to lift him from the floor. The audience came to its feet with a yell; men waved their arms, laughing aloud in their excitement. And Jurgis was with them, he was shouting to tear his throat; shouting because he could not help it, because the stress of his feeling was more than he could bear. It was not merely the man's words, the torrent of his eloquence. It was his presence, it was his voice: a voice with strange intonations that rang through the chambers of the soul like the clanging of a bell—that gripped the listener like a mighty hand about his body, that shook him and startled him with sudden fright, with a sense of things not of earth, of mysteries never spoken before, of presences of awe and terror! There was an unfolding of vistas before him, a breaking of the ground beneath him, an upheaving, a stirring, a trembling; he felt himself suddenly a mere man no longer—there were powers within him undreamed of, there were demon forces contending, age-long wonders struggling to be born; and he sat oppressed with pain and joy, while a tingling stole down into his finger tips, and his breath came hard and fast. The sentences of this man were to Jurgis like the crashing of thunder in his soul; a flood of emotions surged up in him—all his old hopes and longings, his old griefs and rages and despairs. All that he had ever felt in his whole life seemed to come back to him at once, and with one new emotion, hardly to be described. That he should have suffered such oppressions and such horrors was bad enough; but that he should have been crushed and beaten by them, that he should have submitted, and forgotten, and lived in peace—ah, truly that was a thing not to be put into words, a thing not to be borne by a human creature, a thing of terror and madness! "What," asks the prophet, "is the murder of them that kill the body, to the murder of them that kill the soul?" And Jurgis was a man whose soul had been murdered, who had ceased to hope and to struggle—who had made terms with degradation and despair; and now, suddenly, in one awful convulsion, the black and hideous fact was made plain to him! There was a falling in of all the pillars of his soul, the sky seemed to split above him—he stood there, with his clenched hands upraised, his eyes bloodshot, and the veins standing out purple in his face, roaring in the voice of a wild beast, frantic, incoherent, maniacal. And when he could shout no more he still stood there, gasping, and whispering hoarsely to himself: "By God! By God! By God!"

# Chapter 29

The man had gone back to a seat upon the platform, and Jurgis realized that his speech was over. The applause continued for several minutes; and then some one started a song, and the crowd took it up, and the place shook with it. Jurgis had never heard it, and he could not make out the words, but the wild and wonderful spirit of it seized upon him—it was the "Marseillaise!" As stanza after stanza of it thundered forth, he sat with his hands clasped, trembling in every nerve. He had never been so stirred in his life—it was a miracle that had been wrought in him. He could not think at all, he was stunned; yet he knew that in the mighty upheaval that had taken place in his soul, a new man had been born. He had been torn out of the jaws of destruction, he had been delivered from the thraldom of despair; the whole world had been changed for him—he was free, he was free! Even if he were to suffer as he had before, even if he were to beg and starve, nothing would be the same to him; he would understand it, and bear it. He would no longer be the sport of circumstances, he would be a man, with a will and a purpose; he would have something to fight for, something to die for, if need be! Here were men who would show him and help him; and he would have friends and allies, he would dwell in the sight of justice, and walk arm in arm with power.

The audience subsided again, and Jurgis sat back. The chairman of the meeting came forward and began to speak. His voice sounded thin and futile after the other's, and to Jurgis it seemed a profanation. Why should any one else speak, after that miraculous man—why should they not all sit in silence? The chairman was explaining that a collection would now be taken up to defray the expenses of the meeting, and for the benefit of the campaign fund of the party. Jurgis heard; but he had not a penny to give, and so his thoughts went elsewhere again.

He kept his eyes fixed on the orator, who sat in an armchair, his head leaning on his hand and his attitude indicating exhaustion. But suddenly he stood up again, and Jurgis heard the chairman of the meeting saying that the speaker would now answer any questions which the audience might care to put to him. The man came forward, and some one—a woman—arose and asked about some opinion the speaker had expressed concerning Tolstoy. Jurgis had never heard of Tolstoy, and did not care anything about him. Why should any one want to ask such questions, after an address like that? The thing was not to talk, but to do; the thing was to get bold of others and rouse them, to organize them and prepare for the fight! But still the discussion went on, in ordinary conversational tones, and it brought Jurgis back to the everyday world. A few minutes ago he had felt like seizing the hand of the beautiful lady by his side, and kissing it; he had felt like flinging his arms about the neck of the man on the other side of him. And now he began to realize again that he was a "hobo," that he was ragged and dirty, and smelled bad, and had no place to sleep that night!

And so, at last, when the meeting broke up, and the audience started to leave, poor Jurgis was in an agony of uncertainty. He had not thought of leaving—he had thought that the vision must last forever, that he had found comrades and brothers. But now he would go out, and the thing would fade away, and he would never be able to find it again! He sat in his seat, frightened and wondering; but others in the same row wanted to get out, and so he had to stand up and move along. As he was swept down the aisle he looked from one person to another, wistfully; they were all excitedly discussing the address—but there was nobody who offered to discuss it with him. He was near enough to the door to feel the night air, when desperation seized him. He knew nothing at all about that speech he had heard, not even the name of the orator; and he was to go away—no, no, it was preposterous, he must speak to some one; he must find that man himself and tell him. He would not despise him, tramp as he was!

So he stepped into an empty row of seats and watched, and when the crowd had thinned out, he started toward the platform. The speaker was gone; but there was a stage door that stood open, with people passing in and out, and no one on guard. Jurgis summoned up his courage and went in, and down a hallway, and to the door of a room where many people were crowded. No one paid any attention to him, and he pushed in, and in a corner he saw the man he sought. The orator sat in a chair, with his shoulders sunk together and his eyes half closed; his face was ghastly pale, almost greenish in hue, and one arm lay limp at his side. A big man with spectacles on stood near him, and kept pushing back the crowd, saying, "Stand away a little, please; can't you see the comrade is worn out?"

So Jurgis stood watching, while five or ten minutes passed. Now and then the man would look up, and address a word or two to those who were near him; and, at last, on one of these occasions, his glance rested on Jurgis. There seemed to be a slight hint of inquiry about it, and a sudden impulse seized the other. He stepped forward.

"I wanted to thank you, sir!" he began, in breathless haste. "I could not go away without telling you how much—how glad I am I heard you. I—I didn't know anything about it all—"

The big man with the spectacles, who had moved away, came back at this moment. "The comrade is too tired to talk to any one—" he began; but the other held up his hand.

"Wait," he said. "He has something to say to me." And then he looked into Jurgis's face. "You want to know more about Socialism?" he asked.

Jurgis started. "I—I—" he stammered. "Is it Socialism? I didn't know. I want to know about what you spoke of—I want to help. I have been through all that."

"Where do you live?" asked the other.

"I have no home," said Jurgis, "I am out of work."

"You are a foreigner, are you not?"

"Lithuanian, sir."

The man thought for a moment, and then turned to his friend. "Who is there, Walters?" he asked. "There is Ostrinski—but he is a Pole—"

"Ostrinski speaks Lithuanian," said the other. "All right, then; would you mind seeing if he has gone yet?"

The other started away, and the speaker looked at Jurgis again. He had deep, black eyes, and a face full of gentleness and pain. "You must excuse me, comrade," he said. "I am just tired out—I have spoken every day for the last month. I will introduce you to some one who will be able to help you as well as I could—"

The messenger had had to go no further than the door, he came back, followed by a man whom he introduced to Jurgis as "Comrade Ostrinski." Comrade Ostrinski was a little man, scarcely up to Jurgis's shoulder, wizened and wrinkled, very ugly, and slightly lame. He had on a long-tailed black coat, worn green at the seams and the buttonholes; his eyes must have been weak, for he wore green spectacles that gave him a grotesque appearance. But his handclasp was hearty, and he spoke in Lithuanian, which warmed Jurgis to him.

"You want to know about Socialism?" he said. "Surely. Let us go out and take a stroll, where we can be quiet and talk some."

And so Jurgis bade farewell to the master wizard, and went out. Ostrinski asked where he lived, offering to walk in that direction; and so he had to explain once more that he was without a home. At the other's request he told his story; how he had come to America, and what had happened to him in the stockyards, and how his family had been broken up, and how he had become a wanderer. So much the little man heard, and then he pressed Jurgis's arm tightly. "You have been through the mill, comrade!" he said. "We will make a fighter out of you!"

Then Ostrinski in turn explained his circumstances. He would have asked Jurgis to his home—but he had only two rooms, and had no bed to offer. He would have given up his own bed, but his wife was ill. Later on, when he understood that otherwise Jurgis would have to sleep in a hallway, he offered him his kitchen floor, a chance which the other was only too glad to accept. "Perhaps tomorrow we can do better," said Ostrinski. "We try not to let a comrade starve."

Ostrinski's home was in the Ghetto district, where he had two rooms in the basement of a tenement. There was a baby crying as they entered, and he closed the door leading into the bedroom. He had three young children, he explained, and a baby had just come. He drew up two chairs near the kitchen stove, adding that Jurgis must excuse the disorder of the place, since at such a time one's domestic arrangements were upset. Half of the kitchen was given up to a workbench, which was piled with clothing, and Ostrinski explained that he was a "pants finisher." He brought great bundles of clothing here to his home, where he and his wife worked on them. He made a living at it, but it was getting harder all the time, because his eyes were failing. What would come when they gave out he could not tell; there had been no saving anything—a man could barely keep alive by twelve or fourteen hours' work a day. The finishing of pants did not take much skill, and anybody could learn it, and so the pay was forever getting less. That was the competitive wage system; and if Jurgis wanted to understand what Socialism was, it was there he had best begin. The workers were dependent upon a job to exist from day to day, and so they bid against each other, and no man could get more than the lowest man would consent to work for. And thus the mass of the people were always in a life-and-death struggle with poverty. That was "competition," so far as it concerned the wage-earner, the man who had only his labor to sell; to those on top, the exploiters, it appeared very differently, of course—there were few of them, and they could combine and dominate, and their power would be unbreakable. And so all over the world two classes were forming, with an unbridged chasm between them—the capitalist class, with its enormous fortunes, and the proletariat, bound into slavery by unseen chains. The latter were a thousand to one in numbers, but they were ignorant and helpless, and they would remain at the mercy of their exploiters until they were organized—until they had become "class-conscious." It was a slow and weary process, but it would go on—it was like the movement of a glacier, once it was started it could never be stopped. Every Socialist did his share, and lived upon the vision of the "good time coming,"—when the working class should go to the polls and seize the powers of government, and put an end to private property in the means of production. No matter how poor a man was, or how much he suffered, he could never be really unhappy while he knew of that future; even if he did not live to see it himself, his children would, and, to a Socialist, the victory of his class was his victory. Also he had always the progress to encourage him; here in Chicago, for instance, the movement was growing by leaps and bounds. Chicago was the industrial center of the country, and nowhere else were the unions so strong; but their organizations did the workers little good, for the employers were organized, also; and so the strikes generally failed, and as fast as the unions were broken up the men were coming over to the Socialists.

Ostrinski explained the organization of the party, the machinery by which the proletariat was educating itself. There were "locals" in every big city and town, and they were being organized rapidly in the smaller places; a local had anywhere from six to a thousand members, and there were fourteen hundred of them in all, with a total of about twenty-five thousand members, who paid dues to support the organization. "Local Cook County," as the city organization was called, had eighty branch locals, and it alone was spending several thousand dollars in the campaign. It published a weekly in English, and one each in Bohemian and German; also there was a monthly published in Chicago, and a cooperative publishing house, that issued a million and a half of Socialist books and pamphlets every year. All this was the growth of the last few years—there had been almost nothing of it when Ostrinski first came to Chicago.

Ostrinski was a Pole, about fifty years of age. He had lived in Silesia, a member of a despised and persecuted race, and had taken part in the proletarian movement in the early seventies, when Bismarck, having conquered France, had turned his policy of blood and iron upon the "International." Ostrinski himself had twice been in jail, but he had been young then, and had not cared. He had had more of his share of the fight, though, for just when Socialism had broken all its barriers and become the great political force of the empire, he had come to America, and begun all over again. In America every one had laughed at the mere idea of Socialism then—in America all men were free. As if political liberty made wage slavery any the more tolerable! said Ostrinski.

The little tailor sat tilted back in his stiff kitchen chair, with his feet stretched out upon the empty stove, and speaking in low whispers, so as not to waken those in the next room. To Jurgis he seemed a scarcely less wonderful person than the speaker at the meeting; he was poor, the lowest of the low, hunger-driven and miserable—and yet how much he knew, how much he had dared and achieved, what a hero he had been! There were others like him, too—thousands like him, and all of them workingmen! That all this wonderful machinery of progress had been created by his fellows—Jurgis could not believe it, it seemed too good to be true.

That was always the way, said Ostrinski; when a man was first converted to Socialism he was like a crazy person—he could not understand how others could fail to see it, and he expected to convert all the world the first week. After a while he would realize how hard a task it was; and then it would be fortunate that other new hands kept coming, to save him from settling down into a rut. Just now Jurgis would have plenty of chance to vent his excitement, for a presidential campaign was on, and everybody was talking politics. Ostrinski would take him to the next meeting of the branch local, and introduce him, and he might join the party. The dues were five cents a week, but any one who could not afford this might be excused from paying. The Socialist party was a really democratic political organization—it was controlled absolutely by its own membership, and had no bosses. All of these things Ostrinski explained, as also the principles of the party. You might say that there was really but one Socialist principle—that of "no compromise," which was the essence of the proletarian movement all over the world. When a Socialist was elected to office he voted with old party legislators for any measure that was likely to be of help to the working class, but he never forgot that these concessions, whatever they might be, were trifles compared with the great purpose—the organizing of the working class for the revolution. So far, the rule in America had been that one

Socialist made another Socialist once every two years; and if they should maintain the same rate they would carry the country in 1912—though not all of them expected to succeed as quickly as that.

The Socialists were organized in every civilized nation; it was an international political party, said Ostrinski, the greatest the world had ever known. It numbered thirty million of adherents, and it cast eight million votes. It had started its first newspaper in Japan, and elected its first deputy in Argentina; in France it named members of cabinets, and in Italy and Australia it held the balance of power and turned out ministries. In Germany, where its vote was more than a third of the total vote of the empire, all other parties and powers had united to fight it. It would not do, Ostrinski explained, for the proletariat of one nation to achieve the victory, for that nation would be crushed by the military power of the others; and so the Socialist movement was a world movement, an organization of all mankind to establish liberty and fraternity. It was the new religion of humanity—or you might say it was the fulfillment of the old religion, since it implied but the literal application of all the teachings of Christ.

Until long after midnight Jurgis sat lost in the conversation of his new acquaintance. It was a most wonderful experience to him—an almost supernatural experience. It was like encountering an inhabitant of the fourth dimension of space, a being who was free from all one's own limitations. For four years, now, Jurgis had been wondering and blundering in the depths of a wilderness; and here, suddenly, a hand reached down and seized him, and lifted him out of it, and set him upon a mountain-top, from which he could survey it all—could see the paths from which he had wandered, the morasses into which he had stumbled, the hiding places of the beasts of prey that had fallen upon him. There were his Packingtown experiences, for instance—what was there about Packingtown that Ostrinski could not explain! To Jurgis the packers had been equivalent to fate; Ostrinski showed him that they were the Beef Trust. They were a gigantic combination of capital, which had crushed all opposition, and overthrown the laws of the land, and was preying upon the people. Jurgis recollected how, when he had first come to Packingtown, he had stood and watched the hog-killing, and thought how cruel and savage it was, and come away congratulating himself that he was not a hog; now his new acquaintance showed him that a hog was just what he had been—one of the packers' hogs. What they wanted from a hog was all the profits that could be got out of him; and that was what they wanted from the workingman, and also that was what they wanted from the public. What the hog thought of it, and what he suffered, were not considered; and no more was it with labor, and no more with the purchaser of meat. That was true everywhere in the world, but it was especially true in Packingtown; there seemed to be something about the work of slaughtering that tended to ruthlessness and ferocity—it was literally the fact that in the methods of the packers a hundred human lives did not balance a penny of profit. When Jurgis had made himself familiar with the Socialist literature, as he would very quickly, he would get glimpses of the Beef Trust from all sorts of aspects, and he would find it everywhere the same; it was the incarnation of blind and insensate Greed. It was a monster devouring with a thousand mouths, trampling with a thousand hoofs; it was the Great Butcher—it was the spirit of Capitalism made flesh. Upon the ocean of commerce it sailed as a pirate ship; it had hoisted the black flag and declared war upon civilization. Bribery and corruption were its everyday methods. In Chicago the city government was simply one of its branch offices; it stole billions of gallons of city water openly, it dictated to the courts the sentences of disorderly strikers, it forbade the mayor to enforce the building laws against it. In the national capital it had power to prevent inspection of its product, and to falsify government reports; it violated the rebate laws, and when an investigation was threatened it burned its books and sent its criminal agents out of the country. In the commercial world it was a Juggernaut car; it wiped out thousands of businesses every year, it drove men to madness and suicide. It had forced the price of cattle so low as to destroy the stock-raising industry, an occupation upon which whole states existed; it had ruined thousands of butchers who had refused to handle its products. It divided the country into districts, and fixed the price of meat in all of them; and it owned all the refrigerator cars, and levied an enormous tribute upon all poultry and eggs and fruit and vegetables. With the millions of dollars a week that poured in upon it, it was reaching out for the control of other interests, railroads and trolley lines, gas and electric light franchises—it already owned the leather and the grain business of the country. The people were tremendously stirred up over its encroachments, but nobody had any remedy to suggest; it was the task of Socialists to teach and organize them, and prepare them for the time when they were to seize the huge machine called the Beef Trust, and use it to produce food for human beings and not to heap up fortunes for a band of pirates. It was long after midnight when Jurgis lay down upon the floor of Ostrinski's kitchen; and yet it was an hour before he could get to sleep, for the glory of that joyful vision of the people of Packingtown marching in and taking possession of the Union Stockyards!

# Chapter 30

Jurgis had breakfast with Ostrinski and his family, and then he went home to Elzbieta. He was no longer shy about it—when he went in, instead of saying all the things he had been planning to say, he started to tell Elzbieta about the revolution! At first she thought he was out of his mind, and it was hours before she could really feel certain that he was himself. When, however, she had satisfied herself that he was sane upon all subjects except politics, she troubled herself no further about it. Jurgis was destined to find that Elzbieta's armor was absolutely impervious to Socialism. Her soul had been baked hard in the fire of adversity, and there was no altering it now; life to her was the hunt for daily bread, and ideas existed for her only as they bore upon that. All that interested her in regard to this new frenzy which had seized hold of her son-in-law was whether or not it had a tendency to make him sober and industrious; and when she found he intended to look for work and to contribute his share to the family fund, she gave him full rein to convince her of anything. A wonderfully wise little woman was Elzbieta; she could think as quickly as a hunted rabbit, and in half an hour she had chosen her life-attitude to the Socialist movement. She agreed in everything with Jurgis, except the need of his paying his dues; and she would even go to a meeting with him now and then, and sit and plan her next day's dinner amid the storm.

For a week after he became a convert Jurgis continued to wander about all day, looking for work; until at last he met with a strange fortune. He was passing one of Chicago's innumerable small hotels, and after some hesitation he concluded to go in. A man he took for the proprietor was standing in the lobby, and he went up to him and tackled him for a job.

"What can you do?" the man asked.

"Anything, sir," said Jurgis, and added quickly: "I've been out of work for a long time, sir. I'm an honest man, and I'm strong and willing—"

The other was eying him narrowly. "Do you drink?" he asked.

"No, sir," said Jurgis.

"Well, I've been employing a man as a porter, and he drinks. I've discharged him seven times now, and I've about made up my mind that's enough. Would you be a porter?"

"Yes, sir."

"It's hard work. You'll have to clean floors and wash spittoons and fill lamps and handle trunks—"

"I'm willing, sir."

"All right. I'll pay you thirty a month and board, and you can begin now, if you feel like it. You can put on the other fellow's rig."

And so Jurgis fell to work, and toiled like a Trojan till night. Then he went and told Elzbieta, and also, late as it was, he paid a visit to Ostrinski to let him know of his good fortune. Here he received a great surprise, for when he was describing the location of the hotel Ostrinski interrupted suddenly, "Not Hinds's!"

"Yes," said Jurgis, "that's the name."

To which the other replied, "Then you've got the best boss in Chicago—he's a state organizer of our party, and one of our best-known speakers!"

So the next morning Jurgis went to his employer and told him; and the man seized him by the hand and shook it. "By Jove!" he cried, "that lets me out. I didn't sleep all last night because I had discharged a good Socialist!"

So, after that, Jurgis was known to his "boss" as "Comrade Jurgis," and in return he was expected to call him "Comrade Hinds." "Tommy" Hinds, as he was known to his intimates, was a squat little man, with broad shoulders and a florid face, decorated with gray side whiskers. He was the kindest-hearted man that ever lived, and the liveliest—inexhaustible in his enthusiasm, and talking Socialism all day and all night. He was a great fellow to jolly along a crowd, and would keep a meeting in an uproar; when once he got really waked up, the torrent of his eloquence could be compared with nothing save Niagara.

Tommy Hinds had begun life as a blacksmith's helper, and had run away to join the Union army, where he had made his first acquaintance with "graft," in the shape of rotten muskets and shoddy blankets. To a musket that broke in a crisis he always attributed the death of his only brother, and upon worthless blankets he blamed all the agonies of his own old age. Whenever it rained, the rheumatism would get into his joints, and then he would screw up his face and mutter: "Capitalism, my boy, capitalism! 'Ecrasez l'infame!'" He had one unfailing remedy for all the evils of this world, and he preached it to every one; no matter whether the person's trouble was failure in business, or dyspepsia, or a quarrelsome mother-in-law, a twinkle would come into his eyes and he would say, "You know what to do about it—vote the Socialist ticket!"

Tommy Hinds had set out upon the trail of the Octopus as soon as the war was over. He had gone into business, and found himself in competition with the fortunes of those who had been stealing while he had been fighting. The city government was in their hands and the railroads were in league with them, and honest business was driven to the wall; and so Hinds had put all his savings into Chicago real estate, and set out singlehanded to dam the river of graft. He had been a reform member of the city council, he had been a Greenbacker, a Labor Unionist, a Populist, a Bryanite—and after thirty years of fighting, the year 1896 had served to convince him that the power of concentrated wealth could never be controlled, but could only be destroyed. He had published a pamphlet about it, and set out to organize a party of his own, when a stray Socialist leaflet had revealed to him that others had been ahead of him. Now for eight years he had been fighting for the party, anywhere, everywhere—whether it was a G.A.R. reunion, or a hotel-keepers' convention, or an Afro-American business-men's banquet, or a Bible society picnic, Tommy Hinds would manage to get himself invited to explain the relations of Socialism to the subject in hand. After that he would start off upon a tour of his own, ending at some place between New York and Oregon; and when he came back from there, he would go out to organize new locals for the state committee; and finally he would come home to rest—and talk Socialism in Chicago. Hinds's hotel was a very hot-bed of the propaganda; all the employees were party men, and if they were not when they came, they were quite certain to be before they went away. The proprietor would get into a discussion with some one in the lobby, and as the conversation grew animated, others would gather about to listen, until finally every one in the place would be crowded into a group, and a regular debate would be under way. This went on every night—when Tommy Hinds was not there to do it, his clerk did it; and when his clerk was away campaigning, the assistant attended to it, while Mrs. Hinds sat behind the desk and did the work. The clerk was an old crony of the proprietor's, an awkward, rawboned giant of a man, with a lean, sallow face, a broad mouth, and whiskers under his chin, the very type and body of a prairie farmer. He had been that all his life—he had fought the railroads in Kansas for fifty years, a Granger, a Farmers' Alliance man, a "middle-of-the-road" Populist. Finally, Tommy Hinds had revealed to him the wonderful idea of using the trusts instead of destroying them, and he had sold his farm and come to Chicago.

That was Amos Struver; and then there was Harry Adams, the assistant clerk, a pale, scholarly-looking man, who came from Massachusetts, of Pilgrim stock. Adams had been a cotton operative in Fall River, and the continued depression in the industry had worn him and his family out, and he had emigrated to South Carolina. In Massachusetts the percentage of white illiteracy is eight-tenths of one per cent, while in South Carolina it is thirteen and six-tenths per cent; also in South Carolina there is a property qualification for voters—and for these and other reasons child labor is the rule, and so the cotton mills were driving those of Massachusetts out of the business. Adams did not know this, he only knew that the Southern mills were running; but when he got there he found that if he was to live, all his family would have to work, and from six o'clock at night to six o'clock in the morning. So he had set to work to organize the mill hands, after the fashion in Massachusetts, and had been discharged; but he had gotten other work, and stuck at it, and at last there had been a strike for shorter hours, and Harry Adams had attempted to address a street meeting, which was the end of him. In the states of the far South the labor of convicts is leased to contractors, and when there are not convicts enough they have to be supplied. Harry Adams was sent up by a judge who was a cousin of the mill owner with whose business he had interfered; and though the life had nearly killed him, he had been wise enough not to murmur, and at the end of his term he and his family had left the state of South Carolina—hell's back yard, as he called it. He had no money for carfare, but it was harvest-time, and they walked one day and worked the next; and so Adams got at last to Chicago, and joined the Socialist party. He was a studious man, reserved, and nothing of an orator; but he always had a pile of books under his desk in the hotel, and articles from his pen were beginning to attract attention in the party press.

Contrary to what one would have expected, all this radicalism did not hurt the hotel business; the radicals flocked to it, and the commercial travelers all found it diverting. Of late, also, the hotel had become a favorite stopping place for Western cattlemen. Now that the Beef Trust had adopted the trick of raising prices to induce enormous shipments of cattle, and then dropping them again and scooping in all they needed, a stock raiser was very apt to find himself in Chicago without money enough to pay his freight bill; and so he had to go to a cheap hotel, and it was no drawback to him if there was an agitator talking in the lobby. These Western fellows were just "meat" for Tommy Hinds—he would get a dozen of them around him and paint little pictures of "the System." Of course, it was not a week before he had heard Jurgis's story, and after that he would not have let his new porter go for the world. "See here," he would say, in the middle of an argument, "I've got a fellow right here in my place who's worked there and seen every bit of it!" And then Jurgis would drop his work, whatever it was, and come, and the other would say, "Comrade Jurgis, just tell these gentlemen what you saw on the killing-beds." At first this request caused poor Jurgis the most acute agony, and it was like pulling teeth to get him to talk; but gradually he found out what was wanted, and in the end he learned to stand up and speak his piece with enthusiasm. His employer would sit by and encourage him with exclamations and shakes of the head; when Jurgis would give the formula for "potted ham," or tell about the condemned hogs that were dropped into the "destructors" at the top and immediately taken out again at the bottom, to be shipped into another state and made into lard, Tommy Hinds would bang his knee and cry, "Do you think a man could make up a thing like that out of his head?"

And then the hotel-keeper would go on to show how the Socialists had the only real remedy for such evils, how they alone "meant business" with the Beef Trust. And when, in answer to this, the victim would say that the whole country was getting stirred up, that the newspapers were full of denunciations of it, and the government taking action against it, Tommy Hinds had a knock-out blow all ready. "Yes," he would say, "all that is true—but what do you suppose is the reason for it? Are you foolish enough to believe that it's done for the public? There are other trusts in the country just as illegal and extortionate as the Beef Trust: there is the Coal Trust, that freezes the poor in winter—there is the Steel Trust, that doubles the price of every nail in your shoes—there is the Oil Trust, that keeps you from reading at night—and why do you suppose it is that all the fury of the press and the government is directed against the

Beef Trust?" And when to this the victim would reply that there was clamor enough over the Oil Trust, the other would continue: "Ten years ago Henry D. Lloyd told all the truth about the Standard Oil Company in his Wealth versus Commonwealth; and the book was allowed to die, and you hardly ever hear of it. And now, at last, two magazines have the courage to tackle 'Standard Oil' again, and what happens? The newspapers ridicule the authors, the churches defend the criminals, and the government—does nothing. And now, why is it all so different with the Beef Trust?"

Here the other would generally admit that he was "stuck"; and Tommy Hinds would explain to him, and it was fun to see his eyes open. "If you were a Socialist," the hotel-keeper would say, "you would understand that the power which really governs the United States today is the Railroad Trust. It is the Railroad Trust that runs your state government, wherever you live, and that runs the United States Senate. And all of the trusts that I have named are railroad trusts—save only the Beef Trust! The Beef Trust has defied the railroads—it is plundering them day by day through the Private Car; and so the public is roused to fury, and the papers clamor for action, and the government goes on the war-path! And you poor common people watch and applaud the job, and think it's all done for you, and never dream that it is really the grand climax of the century-long battle of commercial competition—the final death grapple between the chiefs of the Beef Trust and 'Standard Oil,' for the prize of the mastery and ownership of the United States of America!"

Such was the new home in which Jurgis lived and worked, and in which his education was completed. Perhaps you would imagine that he did not do much work there, but that would be a great mistake. He would have cut off one hand for Tommy Hinds; and to keep Hinds's hotel a thing of beauty was his joy in life. That he had a score of Socialist arguments chasing through his brain in the meantime did not interfere with this; on the contrary, Jurgis scrubbed the spittoons and polished the banisters all the more vehemently because at the same time he was wrestling inwardly with an imaginary recalcitrant. It would be pleasant to record that he swore off drinking immediately, and all the rest of his bad habits with it; but that would hardly be exact. These revolutionists were not angels; they were men, and men who had come up from the social pit, and with the mire of it smeared over them. Some of them drank, and some of them swore, and some of them ate pie with their knives; there was only one difference between them and all the rest of the populace—that they were men with a hope, with a cause to fight for and suffer for. There came times to Jurgis when the vision seemed far-off and pale, and a glass of beer loomed large in comparison; but if the glass led to another glass, and to too many glasses, he had something to spur him to remorse and resolution on the morrow. It was so evidently a wicked thing to spend one's pennies for drink, when the working class was wandering in darkness, and waiting to be delivered; the price of a glass of beer would buy fifty copies of a leaflet, and one could hand these out to the unregenerate, and then get drunk upon the thought of the good that was being accomplished. That was the way the movement had been made, and it was the only way it would progress; it availed nothing to know of it, without fighting for it—it was a thing for all, not for a few! A corollary of this proposition of course was, that any one who refused to receive the new gospel was personally responsible for keeping Jurgis from his heart's desire; and this, alas, made him uncomfortable as an acquaintance. He met some neighbors with whom Elzbieta had made friends in her neighborhood, and he set out to make Socialists of them by wholesale, and several times he all but got into a fight.

It was all so painfully obvious to Jurgis! It was so incomprehensible how a man could fail to see it! Here were all the opportunities of the country, the land, and the buildings upon the land, the railroads, the mines, the factories, and the stores, all in the hands of a few private individuals, called capitalists, for whom the people were obliged to work for wages. The whole balance of what the people produced went to heap up the fortunes of these capitalists, to heap, and heap again, and yet again—and that in spite of the fact that they, and every one about them, lived in unthinkable luxury! And was it not plain that if the people cut off the share of those who merely "owned," the share of those who worked would be much greater? That was as plain as two and two makes four; and it was the whole of it, absolutely the whole of it; and yet there were people who could not see it, who would argue about everything else in the world. They would tell you that governments could not manage things as economically as private individuals; they would repeat and repeat that, and think they were saying something! They could not see that "economical" management by masters meant simply that they, the people, were worked harder and ground closer and paid less! They were wage-earners and servants, at the mercy of exploiters whose one thought was to get as much out of them as possible; and they were taking an interest in the process, were anxious lest it should not be done thoroughly enough! Was it not honestly a trial to listen to an argument such as that?

And yet there were things even worse. You would begin talking to some poor devil who had worked in one shop for the last thirty years, and had never been able to save a penny; who left home every morning at six o'clock, to go and tend a machine, and come back at night too tired to take his clothes off; who had never had a week's vacation in his life, had never traveled, never had an adventure, never learned anything, never hoped anything—and when you started to tell him about Socialism he would sniff and say, "I'm not interested in that—I'm an individualist!" And then he would go on to tell you that Socialism was "paternalism," and that if it ever had its way the world would stop progressing. It was enough to make a mule laugh, to hear arguments like that; and yet it was no laughing matter, as you found out—for how many millions of such poor deluded wretches there were, whose lives had been so stunted by capitalism that they no longer knew what freedom was! And they really thought that it was "individualism" for tens of thousands of them to herd together and obey the orders of a steel magnate, and produce hundreds of millions of dollars of wealth for him, and then let him give them libraries; while for them to take the industry, and run it to suit themselves, and build their own libraries—that would have been "Paternalism"!

Sometimes the agony of such things as this was almost more than Jurgis could bear; yet there was no way of escape from it, there was nothing to do but to dig away at the base of this mountain of ignorance and prejudice. You must keep at the poor fellow; you must hold your temper, and argue with him, and watch for your chance to stick an idea or two into his head. And the rest of the time you must sharpen up your weapons—you must think out new replies to his objections, and provide yourself with new facts to prove to him the folly of his ways.

So Jurgis acquired the reading habit. He would carry in his pocket a tract or a pamphlet which some one had loaned him, and whenever he had an idle moment during the day he would plod through a paragraph, and then think about it while he worked. Also he read the newspapers, and asked questions about them. One of the other porters at Hinds's was a sharp little Irishman, who knew everything that Jurgis wanted to know; and while they were busy he would explain to him the geography of America, and its history, its constitution and its laws; also he gave him an idea of the business system of the country, the great railroads and corporations, and who owned them, and the labor unions, and the big strikes, and the men who had led them. Then at night, when he could get off, Jurgis would attend the Socialist meetings. During the campaign one was not dependent upon the street corner affairs, where the weather and the quality of the orator were equally uncertain; there were hall meetings every night, and one could hear speakers of national prominence. These discussed the political situation from every point of view, and all that troubled Jurgis was the impossibility of carrying off but a small part of the treasures they offered him.

There was a man who was known in the party as the "Little Giant." The Lord had used up so much material in the making of his head that there had not been enough to complete his legs; but he got about on the platform, and when he shook his raven whiskers the pillars of capitalism rocked. He had written a veritable encyclopedia upon the subject, a book that was nearly as big as himself—And then there was a young author, who came from California, and had been a salmon fisher, an oyster-pirate, a longshoreman, a sailor; who had tramped the country and been sent to jail, had lived in the Whitechapel slums, and been to the Klondike in search of gold. All these things he pictured in his books, and because he was a man of genius he forced the world to hear him. Now he was famous, but wherever he went he still preached the gospel of the poor. And then there was one who was known at the "millionaire Socialist." He had made a fortune in business, and spent nearly all of it in building up a magazine, which the post office department had tried to suppress, and had driven to Canada. He was a quiet-mannered man, whom you would have taken for anything in the world but a Socialist agitator. His speech was simple and informal—he could not understand why any one should get excited about these things. It was a process of economic evolution, he said, and he exhibited its laws and methods. Life was a struggle for existence, and the strong overcame the weak, and in turn were overcome by the strongest. Those who lost in the struggle were generally exterminated; but now and then they had been known to save themselves by combination—which was a new and higher kind of strength. It was so that the gregarious animals had overcome the predaceous; it was so, in human history, that the people had mastered the kings. The workers were simply the citizens of industry, and the Socialist movement was the expression of their will to survive. The inevitability of the revolution depended upon this fact, that they had no choice but to unite or be exterminated; this fact, grim and inexorable, depended upon no human will, it was the law of the economic process, of which the editor showed the details with the most marvelous precision.

And later on came the evening of the great meeting of the campaign, when Jurgis heard the two standard-bearers of his party. Ten years before there had been in Chicago a strike of a hundred and fifty thousand railroad employees, and thugs had been hired by the railroads to commit violence, and the President of the United States had sent in troops to break the strike, by flinging the officers of the union into jail without trial. The president of the union came out of his cell a ruined man; but also he came out a Socialist; and now for just ten years he had been traveling up and down the country, standing face to face with the people, and pleading with them for justice. He was a man of electric presence, tall and gaunt, with a face worn thin by struggle and suffering. The fury of outraged manhood gleamed in it—and the tears of suffering little children pleaded in his voice. When he spoke he paced the stage, lithe and eager, like a panther. He leaned over, reaching out for his audience; he pointed into their souls with an insistent finger. His voice was husky from much speaking, but the great auditorium was as still as death, and every one heard him.

And then, as Jurgis came out from this meeting, some one handed him a paper which he carried home with him and read; and so he became acquainted with the "Appeal to Reason." About twelve years previously a Colorado real-estate speculator had made up his mind that it was wrong to gamble in the necessities of life of human beings: and so he had retired and begun the publication of a Socialist weekly. There had come a time when he had to set his own type, but he had held on and won out, and now his publication was an institution. It used a carload of paper every week, and the mail trains would be hours loading up at the depot of the little Kansas town. It was a four-page weekly, which sold for less than half a cent a copy; its regular subscription list was a quarter of a million, and it went to every crossroads post office in America.

The "Appeal" was a "propaganda" paper. It had a manner all its own—it was full of ginger and spice, of Western slang and hustle: It collected news of the doings of the "plutes," and served it up for the benefit of the "American working-mule." It would have columns of the deadly parallel—the million dollars' worth of diamonds, or the fancy pet-poodle establishment of a society dame, beside the fate of Mrs. Murphy of San Francisco, who had starved to death on the streets, or of John Robinson, just out of the hospital, who had hanged himself in New York because he could not find work. It collected the stories of graft and misery from the daily press, and made a little pungent paragraphs out of them. "Three banks of Bungtown, South Dakota, failed, and more savings of the workers swallowed up!" "The mayor of Sandy Creek, Oklahoma, has skipped with a hundred thousand dollars. That's the kind of rulers the old partyites give you!" "The president of the Florida Flying Machine Company is in jail for bigamy. He was a prominent opponent of Socialism, which he said would break up the home!" The "Appeal" had what it called its "Army," about thirty thousand of the faithful, who did things for it; and it was always exhorting the "Army" to keep its dander up, and occasionally encouraging it with a prize competition, for anything from a gold watch to a private yacht or an eighty-acre farm. Its office helpers were all known to the "Army" by quaint titles—"Inky Ike," "the Bald-headed Man," "the Redheaded Girl," "the Bulldog," "the Office Goat," and "the One Hoss."

But sometimes, again, the "Appeal" would be desperately serious. It sent a correspondent to Colorado, and printed pages describing the overthrow of American institutions in that state. In a certain city of the country it had over forty of its "Army" in the headquarters of the Telegraph Trust, and no message of importance to Socialists ever went through that a copy of it did not go to the "Appeal." It would print great broadsides during the campaign; one copy that came to Jurgis was a manifesto addressed to striking workingmen, of which nearly a million copies had been distributed in the industrial centers, wherever the employers' associations had been carrying out their "open shop" program. "You have lost the strike!" it was headed. "And now what are you going to do about it?" It was what is called an "incendiary" appeal—it was written by a man into whose soul the iron had entered. When this edition appeared, twenty thousand copies were sent to the stockyards district; and they were taken out and stowed away in the rear of a little cigar store, and every evening, and on Sundays, the members of the Packingtown locals would get armfuls and distribute them on the streets and in the houses. The people of Packingtown had lost their strike, if ever a people had, and so they read these papers gladly, and twenty thousand were hardly enough to go round. Jurgis had resolved not to go near his old home again, but when he heard of this it was too much for him, and every night for a week he would get on the car and ride out to the stockyards, and help to undo his work of the previous year, when he had sent Mike Scully's ten-pin setter to the city Board of Aldermen.

It was quite marvelous to see what a difference twelve months had made in Packingtown—the eyes of the people were getting opened! The Socialists were literally sweeping everything before them that election, and Scully and the Cook County machine were at their wits' end for an "issue." At the very close of the campaign they bethought themselves of the fact that the strike had been broken by Negroes, and so they sent for a South Carolina fire-eater, the "pitchfork senator," as he was called, a man who took off his coat when he talked to workingmen, and damned and swore like a Hessian. This meeting they advertised extensively, and the Socialists advertised it too—with the result that about a thousand of them were on hand that evening. The "pitchfork senator" stood their fusillade of questions for about an hour, and then went home in disgust, and the balance of the meeting was a strictly party affair. Jurgis, who had insisted upon coming, had the time of his life that night; he danced about and waved his arms in his excitement—and at the very climax he broke loose from his friends, and got out into the aisle, and proceeded to make a speech himself! The senator had been denying that the Democratic party was corrupt; it was always the Republicans who bought the votes, he said—and here was Jurgis shouting furiously, "It's a lie! It's a lie!" After which he went on to tell them how he knew it—that he knew it because he had bought them himself! And he would have told the "pitchfork senator" all his experiences, had not Harry Adams and a friend grabbed him about the neck and shoved him into a seat.

# Chapter 31

One of the first things that Jurgis had done after he got a job was to go and see Marija. She came down into the basement of the house to meet him, and he stood by the door with his hat in his hand, saying, "I've got work now, and so you can leave here."

But Marija only shook her head. There was nothing else for her to do, she said, and nobody to employ her. She could not keep her past a secret—girls had tried it, and they were always found out. There were thousands of men who came to this place, and sooner or later she would meet one of them. "And besides," Marija added, "I can't do anything. I'm no good—I take dope. What could you do with me?"

"Can't you stop?" Jurgis cried.

"No," she answered, "I'll never stop. What's the use of talking about it—I'll stay here till I die, I guess. It's all I'm fit for." And that was all that he could get her to say—there was no use trying. When he told her he would not let Elzbieta take her money, she answered indifferently: "Then it'll be wasted here—that's all." Her eyelids looked heavy and her face was red and swollen; he saw that he was annoying her, that she only wanted him to go away. So he went, disappointed and sad.

Poor Jurgis was not very happy in his home-life. Elzbieta was sick a good deal now, and the boys were wild and unruly, and very much the worse for their life upon the streets. But he stuck by the family nevertheless, for they reminded him of his old happiness; and when things went wrong he could solace himself with a plunge into the Socialist movement. Since his life had been caught up into the current of this great stream, things which had before been the whole of life to him came to seem of relatively slight importance; his interests were elsewhere, in the world of ideas. His outward life was commonplace and uninteresting; he was just a hotel-porter, and expected to remain one while he lived; but meantime, in the realm of thought, his life was a perpetual adventure. There was so much to know—so many wonders to be discovered! Never in all his life did Jurgis forget the day before election, when there came a telephone message from a friend of Harry Adams, asking him to bring Jurgis to see him that night; and Jurgis went, and met one of the minds of the movement.

The invitation was from a man named Fisher, a Chicago millionaire who had given up his life to settlement work, and had a little home in the heart of the city's slums. He did not belong to the party, but he was in sympathy with it;

and he said that he was to have as his guest that night the editor of a big Eastern magazine, who wrote against Socialism, but really did not know what it was. The millionaire suggested that Adams bring Jurgis along, and then start up the subject of "pure food," in which the editor was interested.

Young Fisher's home was a little two-story brick house, dingy and weather-beaten outside, but attractive within. The room that Jurgis saw was half lined with books, and upon the walls were many pictures, dimly visible in the soft, yellow light; it was a cold, rainy night, so a log fire was crackling in the open hearth. Seven or eight people were gathered about it when Adams and his friend arrived, and Jurgis saw to his dismay that three of them were ladies. He had never talked to people of this sort before, and he fell into an agony of embarrassment. He stood in the doorway clutching his hat tightly in his hands, and made a deep bow to each of the persons as he was introduced; then, when he was asked to have a seat, he took a chair in a dark corner, and sat down upon the edge of it, and wiped the perspiration off his forehead with his sleeve. He was terrified lest they should expect him to talk.

There was the host himself, a tall, athletic young man, clad in evening dress, as also was the editor, a dyspeptic-looking gentleman named Maynard. There was the former's frail young wife, and also an elderly lady, who taught kindergarten in the settlement, and a young college student, a beautiful girl with an intense and earnest face. She only spoke once or twice while Jurgis was there—the rest of the time she sat by the table in the center of the room, resting her chin in her hands and drinking in the conversation. There were two other men, whom young Fisher had introduced to Jurgis as Mr. Lucas and Mr. Schliemann; he heard them address Adams as "Comrade," and so he knew that they were Socialists.

The one called Lucas was a mild and meek-looking little gentleman of clerical aspect; he had been an itinerant evangelist, it transpired, and had seen the light and become a prophet of the new dispensation. He traveled all over the country, living like the apostles of old, upon hospitality, and preaching upon street-corners when there was no hall. The other man had been in the midst of a discussion with the editor when Adams and Jurgis came in; and at the suggestion of the host they resumed it after the interruption. Jurgis was soon sitting spellbound, thinking that here was surely the strangest man that had ever lived in the world.

Nicholas Schliemann was a Swede, a tall, gaunt person, with hairy hands and bristling yellow beard; he was a university man, and had been a professor of philosophy—until, as he said, he had found that he was selling his character as well as his time. Instead he had come to America, where he lived in a garret room in this slum district, and made volcanic energy take the place of fire. He studied the composition of food-stuffs, and knew exactly how many proteids and carbohydrates his body needed; and by scientific chewing he said that he tripled the value of all he ate, so that it cost him eleven cents a day. About the first of July he would leave Chicago for his vacation, on foot; and when he struck the harvest fields he would set to work for two dollars and a half a day, and come home when he had another year's supply—a hundred and twenty-five dollars. That was the nearest approach to independence a man could make "under capitalism," he explained; he would never marry, for no sane man would allow himself to fall in love until after the revolution.

He sat in a big arm-chair, with his legs crossed, and his head so far in the shadow that one saw only two glowing lights, reflected from the fire on the hearth. He spoke simply, and utterly without emotion; with the manner of a teacher setting forth to a group of scholars an axiom in geometry, he would enunciate such propositions as made the hair of an ordinary person rise on end. And when the auditor had asserted his non-comprehension, he would proceed to elucidate by some new proposition, yet more appalling. To Jurgis the Herr Dr. Schliemann assumed the proportions of a thunderstorm or an earthquake. And yet, strange as it might seem, there was a subtle bond between them, and he could follow the argument nearly all the time. He was carried over the difficult places in spite of himself; and he went plunging away in mad career—a very Mazeppa-ride upon the wild horse Speculation.

Nicholas Schliemann was familiar with all the universe, and with man as a small part of it. He understood human institutions, and blew them about like soap bubbles. It was surprising that so much destructiveness could be contained in one human mind. Was it government? The purpose of government was the guarding of property-rights, the perpetuation of ancient force and modern fraud. Or was it marriage? Marriage and prostitution were two sides of one shield, the predatory man's exploitation of the sex-pleasure. The difference between them was a difference of class. If a woman had money she might dictate her own terms: equality, a life contract, and the legitimacy—that is, the property-rights—of her children. If she had no money, she was a proletarian, and sold herself for an existence. And then the subject became Religion, which was the Archfiend's deadliest weapon. Government oppressed the body of the wage-slave, but Religion oppressed his mind, and poisoned the stream of progress at its source. The working-man was to fix his hopes upon a future life, while his pockets were picked in this one; he was brought up to frugality, humility, obedience—in short to all the pseudo-virtues of capitalism. The destiny of civilization would be decided in one final death struggle between the Red International and the Black, between Socialism and the Roman Catholic Church; while here at home, "the stygian midnight of American evangelicalism—"

And here the ex-preacher entered the field, and there was a lively tussle. "Comrade" Lucas was not what is called an educated man; he knew only the Bible, but it was the Bible interpreted by real experience. And what was the use, he asked, of confusing Religion with men's perversions of it? That the church was in the hands of the merchants at the moment was obvious enough; but already there were signs of rebellion, and if Comrade Schliemann could come back a few years from now—

"Ah, yes," said the other, "of course, I have no doubt that in a hundred years the Vatican will be denying that it ever opposed Socialism, just as at present it denies that it ever tortured Galileo."

"I am not defending the Vatican," exclaimed Lucas, vehemently. "I am defending the word of God—which is one long cry of the human spirit for deliverance from the sway of oppression. Take the twenty-fourth chapter of the Book of Job, which I am accustomed to quote in my addresses as 'the Bible upon the Beef Trust'; or take the words of Isaiah—or of the Master himself! Not the elegant prince of our debauched and vicious art, not the jeweled idol of our society churches—but the Jesus of the awful reality, the man of sorrow and pain, the outcast, despised of the world, who had nowhere to lay his head—"

"I will grant you Jesus," interrupted the other.

"Well, then," cried Lucas, "and why should Jesus have nothing to do with his church—why should his words and his life be of no authority among those who profess to adore him? Here is a man who was the world's first revolutionist, the true founder of the Socialist movement; a man whose whole being was one flame of hatred for wealth, and all that wealth stands for,—for the pride of wealth, and the luxury of wealth, and the tyranny of wealth; who was himself a beggar and a tramp, a man of the people, an associate of saloon-keepers and women of the town; who again and again, in the most explicit language, denounced wealth and the holding of wealth: 'Lay not up for yourselves treasures on earth!'—'Sell that ye have and give alms!'—'Blessed are ye poor, for yours is the kingdom of Heaven!'—'Woe unto you that are rich, for ye have received your consolation!'—'Verily, I say unto you, that a rich man shall hardly enter into the kingdom of Heaven!' Who denounced in unmeasured terms the exploiters of his own time: 'Woe unto you, scribes and pharisees, hypocrites!'—'Woe unto you also, you lawyers!'—'Ye serpents, ye generation of vipers, how can ye escape the damnation of hell?' Who drove out the business men and brokers from the temple with a whip! Who was crucified—think of it—for an incendiary and a disturber of the social order! And this man they have made into the high priest of property and smug respectability, a divine sanction of all the horrors and abominations of modern commercial civilization! Jeweled images are made of him, sensual priests burn incense to him, and modern pirates of industry bring their dollars, wrung from the toil of helpless women and children, and build temples to him, and sit in cushioned seats and listen to his teachings expounded by doctors of dusty divinity—"

"Bravo!" cried Schliemann, laughing. But the other was in full career—he had talked this subject every day for five years, and had never yet let himself be stopped. "This Jesus of Nazareth!" he cried. "This class-conscious working-man! This union carpenter! This agitator, law-breaker, firebrand, anarchist! He, the sovereign lord and master of a world which grinds the bodies and souls of human beings into dollars—if he could come into the world this day and see the things that men have made in his name, would it not blast his soul with horror? Would he not go mad at the sight of it, he the Prince of Mercy and

Love! That dreadful night when he lay in the Garden of Gethsemane and writhed in agony until he sweat blood—do you think that he saw anything worse than he might see tonight upon the plains of Manchuria, where men march out with a jeweled image of him before them, to do wholesale murder for the benefit of foul monsters of sensuality and cruelty? Do you not know that if he were in St. Petersburg now, he would take the whip with which he drove out the bankers from his temple—"

Here the speaker paused an instant for breath. "No, comrade," said the other, dryly, "for he was a practical man. He would take pretty little imitation lemons, such as are now being shipped into Russia, handy for carrying in the pockets, and strong enough to blow a whole temple out of sight."

Lucas waited until the company had stopped laughing over this; then he began again: "But look at it from the point of view of practical politics, comrade. Here is an historical figure whom all men reverence and love, whom some regard as divine; and who was one of us—who lived our life, and taught our doctrine. And now shall we leave him in the hands of his enemies—shall we allow them to stifle and stultify his example? We have his words, which no one can deny; and shall we not quote them to the people, and prove to them what he was, and what he taught, and what he did? No, no, a thousand times no!—we shall use his authority to turn out the knaves and sluggards from his ministry, and we shall yet rouse the people to action!—"

Lucas halted again; and the other stretched out his hand to a paper on the table. "Here, comrade," he said, with a laugh, "here is a place for you to begin. A bishop whose wife has just been robbed of fifty thousand dollars' worth of diamonds! And a most unctuous and oily of bishops! An eminent and scholarly bishop! A philanthropist and friend of labor bishop—a Civic Federation decoy duck for the chloroforming of the wage-working-man!"

To this little passage of arms the rest of the company sat as spectators. But now Mr. Maynard, the editor, took occasion to remark, somewhat naively, that he had always understood that Socialists had a cut-and-dried program for the future of civilization; whereas here were two active members of the party, who, from what he could make out, were agreed about nothing at all. Would the two, for his enlightenment, try to ascertain just what they had in common, and why they belonged to the same party? This resulted, after much debating, in the formulating of two carefully worded propositions: First, that a Socialist believes in the common ownership and democratic management of the means of producing the necessities of life; and, second, that a Socialist believes that the means by which this is to be brought about is the class conscious political organization of the wage-earners. Thus far they were at one; but no farther. To Lucas, the religious zealot, the co-operative commonwealth was the New Jerusalem, the kingdom of Heaven, which is "within you." To the other, Socialism was simply a necessary step toward a far-distant goal, a step to be tolerated with impatience. Schliemann called himself a "philosophic anarchist"; and he explained that an anarchist was one who believed that the end of human existence was the free development of every personality, unrestricted by laws save those of its own being. Since the same kind of match would light every one's fire and the same-shaped loaf of bread would fill every one's stomach, it would be perfectly feasible to submit industry to the control of a majority vote. There was only one earth, and the quantity of material things was limited. Of intellectual and moral things, on the other hand, there was no limit, and one could have more without another's having less; hence "Communism in material production, anarchism in intellectual," was the formula of modern proletarian thought. As soon as the birth agony was over, and the wounds of society had been healed, there would be established a simple system whereby each man was credited with his labor and debited with his purchases; and after that the processes of production, exchange, and consumption would go on automatically, and without our being conscious of them, any more than a man is conscious of the beating of his heart. And then, explained Schliemann, society would break up into independent, self-governing communities of mutually congenial persons; examples of which at present were clubs, churches, and political parties. After the revolution, all the intellectual, artistic, and spiritual activities of men would be cared for by such "free associations"; romantic novelists would be supported by those who liked to read romantic novels, and impressionist painters would be supported by those who liked to look at impressionist pictures—and the same with preachers and scientists, editors and actors and musicians. If any one wanted to work or paint or pray, and could find no one to maintain him, he could support himself by working part of the time. That was the case at present, the only difference being that the competitive wage system compelled a man to work all the time to live, while, after the abolition of privilege and exploitation, any one would be able to support himself by an hour's work a day. Also the artist's audience of the present was a small minority of people, all debased and vulgarized by the effort it had cost them to win in the commercial battle, of the intellectual and artistic activities which would result when the whole of mankind was set free from the nightmare of competition, we could at present form no conception whatever.

And then the editor wanted to know upon what ground Dr. Schliemann asserted that it might be possible for a society to exist upon an hour's toil by each of its members. "Just what," answered the other, "would be the productive capacity of society if the present resources of science were utilized, we have no means of ascertaining; but we may be sure it would exceed anything that would sound reasonable to minds inured to the ferocious barbarities of capitalism. After the triumph of the international proletariat, war would of course be inconceivable; and who can figure the cost of war to humanity—not merely the value of the lives and the material that it destroys, not merely the cost of keeping millions of men in idleness, of arming and equipping them for battle and parade, but the drain upon the vital energies of society by the war attitude and the war terror, the brutality and ignorance, the drunkenness, prostitution, and crime it entails, the industrial impotence and the moral deadness? Do you think that it would be too much to say that two hours of the working time of every efficient member of a community goes to feed the red fiend of war?"

And then Schliemann went on to outline some of the wastes of competition: the losses of industrial warfare; the ceaseless worry and friction; the vices—such as drink, for instance, the use of which had nearly doubled in twenty years, as a consequence of the intensification of the economic struggle; the idle and unproductive members of the community, the frivolous rich and the pauperized poor; the law and the whole machinery of repression; the wastes of social ostentation, the milliners and tailors, the hairdressers, dancing masters, chefs and lackeys. "You understand," he said, "that in a society dominated by the fact of commercial competition, money is necessarily the test of prowess, and wastefulness the sole criterion of power. So we have, at the present moment, a society with, say, thirty per cent of the population occupied in producing useless articles, and one per cent occupied in destroying them. And this is not all; for the servants and panders of the parasites are also parasites, the milliners and the jewelers and the lackeys have also to be supported by the useful members of the community. And bear in mind also that this monstrous disease affects not merely the idlers and their menials, its poison penetrates the whole social body. Beneath the hundred thousand women of the elite are a million middle-class women, miserable because they are not of the elite, and trying to appear of it in public; and beneath them, in turn, are five million farmers' wives reading 'fashion papers' and trimming bonnets, and shop-girls and serving-maids selling themselves into brothels for cheap jewelry and imitation seal-skin robes. And then consider that, added to this competition in display, you have, like oil on the flames, a whole system of competition in selling! You have manufacturers contriving tens of thousands of catchpenny devices, storekeepers displaying them, and newspapers and magazines filled up with advertisements of them!"

"And don't forget the wastes of fraud," put in young Fisher.

"When one comes to the ultra-modern profession of advertising," responded Schliemann—"the science of persuading people to buy what they do not want—he is in the very center of the ghastly charnel house of capitalist destructiveness, and he scarcely knows which of a dozen horrors to point out first. But consider the waste in time and energy incidental to making ten thousand varieties of a thing for purposes of ostentation and snobbishness, where one variety would do for use! Consider all the waste incidental to the manufacture of cheap qualities of goods, of goods made to sell and deceive the ignorant; consider the wastes of adulteration,—the shoddy clothing, the cotton blankets, the unstable tenements, the ground-cork life-preservers, the adulterated milk, the aniline soda water, the potato-flour sausages—"

"And consider the moral aspects of the thing," put in the ex-preacher.

"Precisely," said Schliemann; "the low knavery and the ferocious cruelty incidental to them, the plotting and the lying and the bribing, the blustering and bragging, the screaming egotism, the hurrying and worrying. Of course, imitation and adulteration are the essence of competition—they are but another form of the phrase 'to buy in the cheapest market and sell in the dearest.' A government official has stated that the nation suffers a loss of a billion and a quarter dollars a year through adulterated foods; which means, of course, not only materials wasted that might have been useful outside of the human stomach, but doctors and nurses for people who would otherwise have been well, and undertakers for the whole human race ten or twenty years before the proper time. Then again, consider the waste of time and energy required to sell these things in a dozen stores, where one would do. There are a million or two of business firms in the country, and five or ten times as many clerks; and consider the handling and rehandling, the accounting and reaccounting, the planning and worrying, the balancing of petty profit and loss. Consider the whole machinery of the civil law made necessary by these processes; the libraries of ponderous tomes, the courts and juries to interpret them, the lawyers studying to circumvent them, the pettifogging and chicanery, the hatreds and lies! Consider the wastes incidental to the blind and haphazard production of commodities—the factories closed, the workers idle, the goods spoiling in storage; consider the activities of the stock manipulator, the paralyzing of whole industries, the overstimulation of others, for speculative purposes; the assignments and bank failures, the crises and panics, the deserted towns and the starving populations! Consider the energies wasted in the seeking of markets, the sterile trades, such as drummer, solicitor, bill-poster, advertising agent. Consider the wastes incidental to the crowding into cities, made necessary by competition and by monopoly railroad rates; consider the slums, the bad air, the disease and the waste of vital energies; consider the office buildings, the waste of time and material in the piling of story upon story, and the burrowing underground! Then take the whole business of insurance, the enormous mass of administrative and clerical labor it involves, and all utter waste—"

"I do not follow that," said the editor. "The Cooperative Commonwealth is a universal automatic insurance company and savings bank for all its members. Capital being the property of all, injury to it is shared by all and made up by all. The bank is the universal government credit-account, the ledger in which every individual's earnings and spendings are balanced. There is also a universal government bulletin, in which are listed and precisely described everything which the commonwealth has for sale. As no one makes any profit by the sale, there is no longer any stimulus to extravagance, and no misrepresentation; no cheating, no adulteration or imitation, no bribery or 'grafting.'"

"How is the price of an article determined?"

"The price is the labor it has cost to make and deliver it, and it is determined by the first principles of arithmetic. The million workers in the nation's wheat fields have worked a hundred days each, and the total product of the labor is a billion bushels, so the value of a bushel of wheat is the tenth part of a farm labor-day. If we employ an arbitrary symbol, and pay, say, five dollars a day for farm work, then the cost of a bushel of wheat is fifty cents."

"You say 'for farm work,'" said Mr. Maynard. "Then labor is not to be paid alike?"

"Manifestly not, since some work is easy and some hard, and we should have millions of rural mail carriers, and no coal miners. Of course the wages may be left the same, and the hours varied; one or the other will have to be varied continually, according as a greater or less number of workers is needed in any particular industry. That is precisely what is done at present, except that the transfer of the workers is accomplished blindly and imperfectly, by rumors and advertisements, instead of instantly and completely, by a universal government bulletin."

"How about those occupations in which time is difficult to calculate? What is the labor cost of a book?"

"Obviously it is the labor cost of the paper, printing, and binding of it—about a fifth of its present cost."

"And the author?"

"I have already said that the state could not control intellectual production. The state might say that it had taken a year to write the book, and the author might say it had taken thirty. Goethe said that every bon mot of his had cost a purse of gold. What I outline here is a national, or rather international, system for the providing of the material needs of men. Since a man has intellectual needs also, he will work longer, earn more, and provide for them to his own taste and in his own way. I live on the same earth as the majority, I wear the same kind of shoes and sleep in the same kind of bed; but I do not think the same kind of thoughts, and I do not wish to pay for such thinkers as the majority selects. I wish such things to be left to free effort, as at present. If people want to listen to a certain preacher, they get together and contribute what they please, and pay for a church and support the preacher, and then listen to him; I, who do not want to listen to him, stay away, and it costs me nothing. In the same way there are magazines about Egyptian coins, and Catholic saints, and flying machines, and athletic records, and I know nothing about any of them. On the other hand, if wage slavery were abolished, and I could earn some spare money without paying tribute to an exploiting capitalist, then there would be a magazine for the purpose of interpreting and popularizing the gospel of Friedrich Nietzsche, the prophet of Evolution, and also of Horace Fletcher, the inventor of the noble science of clean eating; and incidentally, perhaps, for the discouraging of long skirts, and the scientific breeding of men and women, and the establishing of divorce by mutual consent."

Dr. Schliemann paused for a moment. "That was a lecture," he said with a laugh, "and yet I am only begun!"

"What else is there?" asked Maynard.

"I have pointed out some of the negative wastes of competition," answered the other. "I have hardly mentioned the positive economies of co-operation. Allowing five to a family, there are fifteen million families in this country; and at least ten million of these live separately, the domestic drudge being either the wife or a wage slave. Now set aside the modern system of pneumatic house-cleaning, and the economies of co-operative cooking; and consider one single item, the washing of dishes. Surely it is moderate to say that the dish-washing for a family of five takes half an hour a day; with ten hours as a day's work, it takes, therefore, half a million able-bodied persons—mostly women to do the dish-washing of the country. And note that this is most filthy and deadening and brutalizing work; that it is a cause of anemia, nervousness, ugliness, and ill-temper; of prostitution, suicide, and insanity; of drunken husbands and degenerate children—for all of which things the community has naturally to pay. And now consider that in each of my little free communities there would be a machine which would wash and dry the dishes, and do it, not merely to the eye and the touch, but scientifically—sterilizing them—and do it at a saving of all the drudgery and nine-tenths of the time! All of these things you may find in the books of Mrs. Gilman; and then take Kropotkin's Fields, Factories, and Workshops, and read about the new science of agriculture, which has been built up in the last ten years; by which, with made soils and intensive culture, a gardener can raise ten or twelve crops in a season, and two hundred tons of vegetables upon a single acre; by which the population of the whole globe could be supported on the soil now cultivated in the United States alone! It is impossible to apply such methods now, owing to the ignorance and poverty of our scattered farming population; but imagine the problem of providing the food supply of our nation once taken in hand systematically and rationally, by scientists! All the poor and rocky land set apart for a national timber reserve, in which our children play, and our young men hunt, and our poets dwell! The most favorable climate and soil for each product selected; the exact requirements of the community known, and the acreage figured accordingly; the most improved machinery employed, under the direction of expert agricultural chemists! I was brought up on a farm, and I know the awful deadliness of farm work; and I like to picture it all as it will be after the revolution. To picture the great potato-planting machine, drawn by four horses, or an electric motor, ploughing the furrow, cutting and dropping and covering the potatoes, and planting a score of acres a day! To picture the great potato-digging machine, run by electricity, perhaps, and moving across a thousand-acre field, scooping up earth and potatoes, and dropping the latter into sacks! To every other kind of vegetable and fruit handled in the same way—apples and oranges picked by machinery, cows milked by electricity—things which are already done, as you may know. To picture the harvest fields of the future, to which millions of happy men and women come for a summer holiday, brought by special trains, the exactly needful number to each place! And to contrast all this with our present agonizing system of independent small farming,—a stunted, haggard, ignorant man, mated with a yellow, lean, and sad-eyed drudge, and toiling from four o'clock in the morning until nine at night, working the children as soon as they are able to walk, scratching the soil with its primitive tools, and shut out from all knowledge and hope, from all their benefits of science and invention, and all the joys of the spirit—held to a bare existence by competition in labor, and boasting of his freedom because he is too blind to see his chains!"

Dr. Schliemann paused a moment. "And then," he continued, "place beside this fact of an unlimited food supply, the newest discovery of physiologists, that most of the ills of the human system are due to overfeeding! And then again, it has been proven that meat is unnecessary as a food; and meat is obviously more difficult to produce than vegetable food, less pleasant to prepare and handle, and more likely to be unclean. But what of that, so long as it tickles the palate more strongly?"

"How would Socialism change that?" asked the girl-student, quickly. It was the first time she had spoken.

"So long as we have wage slavery," answered Schliemann, "it matters not in the least how debasing and repulsive a task may be, it is easy to find people to perform it. But just as soon as labor is set free, then the price of such work will begin to rise. So one by one the old, dingy, and unsanitary factories will come down—it will be cheaper to build new; and so the steamships will be provided with stoking machinery, and so the dangerous trades will be made safe, or substitutes will be found for their products. In exactly the same way, as the citizens of our Industrial Republic become refined, year by year the cost of slaughterhouse products will increase; until eventually those who want to eat meat will have to do their own killing—and how long do you think the custom would survive then?—To go on to another item—one of the necessary accompaniments of capitalism in a democracy is political corruption; and one of the consequences of civic administration by ignorant and vicious politicians, is that preventable diseases kill off half our population. And even if science were allowed to try, it could do little, because the majority of human beings are not yet human beings at all, but simply machines for the creating of wealth for others. They are penned up in filthy houses and left to rot and stew in misery, and the conditions of their life make them ill faster than all the doctors in the world could heal them; and so, of course, they remain as centers of contagion, poisoning the lives of all of us, and making happiness impossible for even the most selfish. For this reason I would seriously maintain that all the medical and surgical discoveries that science can make in the future will be of less importance than the application of the knowledge we already possess, when the disinherited of the earth have established their right to a human existence."

And here the Herr Doctor relapsed into silence again. Jurgis had noticed that the beautiful young girl who sat by the center-table was listening with something of the same look that he himself had worn, the time when he had first discovered Socialism. Jurgis would have liked to talk to her, he felt sure that she would have understood him. Later on in the evening, when the group broke up, he heard Mrs. Fisher say to her, in a low voice, "I wonder if Mr. Maynard will still write the same things about Socialism"; to which she answered, "I don't know—but if he does we shall know that he is a knave!"

And only a few hours after this came election day—when the long campaign was over, and the whole country seemed to stand still and hold its breath, awaiting the issue. Jurgis and the rest of the staff of Hinds's Hotel could hardly stop to finish their dinner, before they hurried off to the big hall which the party had hired for that evening.

But already there were people waiting, and already the telegraph instrument on the stage had begun clicking off the returns. When the final accounts were made up, the Socialist vote proved to be over four hundred thousand—an increase of something like three hundred and fifty per cent in four years. And that was doing well; but the party was dependent for its early returns upon messages from the locals, and naturally those locals which had been most successful were the ones which felt most like reporting; and so that night every one in the hall believed that the vote was going to be six, or seven, or even eight hundred thousand. Just such an incredible increase had actually been made in Chicago, and in the state; the vote of the city had been 6,700 in 1900, and now it was 47,000; that of Illinois had been 9,600, and now it was 69,000! So, as the evening waxed, and the crowd piled in, the meeting was a sight to be seen. Bulletins would be read, and the people would shout themselves hoarse—and then some one would make a speech, and there would be more shouting; and then a brief silence, and more bulletins. There would come messages from the secretaries of neighboring states, reporting their achievements; the vote of Indiana had gone from 2,300 to 12,000, of Wisconsin from 7,000 to 28,000; of Ohio from 4,800 to 36,000! There were telegrams to the national office from enthusiastic individuals in little towns which had made amazing and unprecedented increases in a single year: Benedict, Kansas, from 26 to 260; Henderson, Kentucky, from 19 to 111; Holland, Michigan, from 14 to 208; Cleo, Oklahoma, from 0 to 104; Martin's Ferry, Ohio, from 0 to 296—and many more of the same kind. There were literally hundreds of such towns; there would be reports from half a dozen of them in a single batch of telegrams. And the men who read the despatches off to the audience were old campaigners, who had been to the places and helped to make the vote, and could make appropriate comments: Quincy, Illinois, from 189 to 831—that was where the mayor had arrested a Socialist speaker! Crawford County, Kansas, from 285 to 1,975; that was the home of the "Appeal to Reason"! Battle Creek, Michigan, from 4,261 to 10,184; that was the answer of labor to the Citizens' Alliance Movement!

And then there were official returns from the various precincts and wards of the city itself! Whether it was a factory district or one of the "silk-stocking" wards seemed to make no particular difference in the increase; but one of the things which surprised the party leaders most was the tremendous vote that came rolling in from the stockyards. Packingtown comprised three wards of the city, and the vote in the spring of 1903 had been 500, and in the fall of the same year, 1,600. Now, only one year later, it was over 6,300—and the Democratic vote only 8,800! There were other wards in which the Democratic vote had been actually surpassed, and in two districts, members of the state legislature had been elected. Thus Chicago now led the country; it had set a new standard for the party, it had shown the workingmen the way!

—So spoke an orator upon the platform; and two thousand pairs of eyes were fixed upon him, and two thousand voices were cheering his every sentence. The orator had been the head of the city's relief bureau in the stockyards, until the sight of misery and corruption had made him sick. He was young, hungry-looking, full of fire; and as he swung his long arms and beat up the crowd, to Jurgis he seemed the very spirit of the revolution. "Organize! Organize! Organize!"—that was his cry. He was afraid of this tremendous vote, which his party had not expected, and which it had not earned. "These men are not Socialists!" he cried. "This election will pass, and the excitement will die, and people will forget about it; and if you forget about it, too, if you sink back and rest upon your oars, we shall lose this vote that we have polled to-day, and our enemies will laugh us to scorn! It rests with you to take your resolution—now, in the flush of victory, to find these men who have voted for us, and bring them to our meetings, and organize them and bind them to us! We shall not find all our campaigns as easy as this one. Everywhere in the country tonight the old party politicians are studying this vote, and setting their sails by it; and nowhere will they be quicker or more cunning than here in our own city. Fifty thousand Socialist votes in Chicago means a municipal-ownership Democracy in the spring! And then they will fool the voters once more, and all the powers of plunder and corruption will be swept into office again! But whatever they may do when they get in, there is one thing they will not do, and that will be the thing for which they were elected! They will not give the people of our city municipal ownership—they will not mean to do it, they will not try to do it; all that they will do is give our party in Chicago the greatest opportunity that has ever come to Socialism in America! We shall have the sham reformers self-stultified and self-convicted; we shall have the radical Democracy left without a lie with which to cover its nakedness! And then will begin the rush that will never be checked, the tide that will never turn till it has reached its flood—that will be irresistible, overwhelming—the rallying of the outraged workingmen of Chicago to our standard! And we shall organize them, we shall drill them, we shall marshal them for the victory! We shall bear down the opposition, we shall sweep if before us—and Chicago will be ours! Chicago will be ours! CHICAGO WILL BE OURS!"